TREACHERY
TIMES TWO

ALSO BY ROBERT McCAW

Koa Kāne Hawaiian Mysteries

Death of a Messenger

Off the Grid

Fire and Vengeance

TREACHERY TIMES TWO

A KOA KĀNE HAWAIIAN MYSTERY

ROBERT McCAW

OCEANVIEW ⌬ PUBLISHING
SARASOTA, FLORIDA

ISBN 978-1-60809-464-6

Published in the United States of America by Oceanview Publishing

Sarasota, Florida

www.oceanviewpub.com

10 9 8 7 6 5 4 3 2 1

PRINTED IN THE UNITED STATES OF AMERICA

To my wife, Calli, without whose encouragement, support, advice, and superb editing skills, I could not have written this book.

ACKNOWLEDGEMENTS

Among the many people who helped make this book possible are my dear friends in Hawai'i who generously shared their knowledge of the culture, history, and language of the Hawaiian people. To them I owe an enormous debt of gratitude.

Special thanks must also go to Makela Bruno-Kidani, who has tirelessly reviewed my use of the Hawaiian language, correcting my many mistakes. Where the Hawaiian words and phrases are accurate, she deserves the credit. Any errors are entirely of my doing.

This book would not have been launched without the amazing support of my agent, Mel Parker of Mel Parker Books, LLC. His faith in my work and his tireless efforts made the publication of this story possible. Many kudos as well to Fauzia Burke and Michelle Fitzgerald at FSB Associates who've introduced my books to so many readers. I would also be remiss if I failed to acknowledge Pat and Bob Gussin, owners of Oceanview Publishing, who have devoted their phenomenal energies to supporting and publishing my work and that of many other aspiring mystery and thriller writers.

TREACHERY TIMES TWO

CHAPTER ONE

PELE, MASQUERADING AS a glassy-haired old woman, wandered the lava trails around the massive smoking volcanic caldera called Kīlauea. Over millennia, her temper tantrums had created the Hawaiian Islands, including Kīlauea and the four other volcanoes that make up the Big Island of Hawai'i. Fiercely jealous of *Poli'ahu*, her sister deity, the snow goddess of Mauna Kea, and locked in eternal combat with *Kamapua'a*, the demigod of rain, *Pele's* exploits fueled the oral history of the islands.

Often called the stone-eating woman, she'd resided inside Halema'uma'u, the pit crater within Kīlauea's caldera on the Big Island's southeastern edge. Inside Halema'uma'u, *Pele's* red-hot lava often bubbled and smoked. Ancient Hawaiians left flowered *lei*s and other tributes to the fiery goddess while Western *haoles* gifted bottles of gin. She'd quaked and rumbled over the past millennia, but, whether driven by climate change or sheer perversity, *Pele's* sizzling rage had recently spiked to a 200-year high. In ancient times, she'd smothered an army of Hawaiian warriors, changing the course of Hawaiian history, and now she sought to teach present-day mortals renewed respect for her awesome powers.

Over the past month, thousands of earthquakes had rattled Hawai'i's Kīlauea caldera and the adjacent tiny village of Volcano,

shattering windows, cracking foundations, disrupting utility connections, and spreading concern among its residents. Some with
other places to go, had left, but most had lived for years with
Kīlauea's dangers and become inured to *Pele*'s antics.

The shaking opened fissures in the nearby Hawai'i Belt Road,
forcing motorists to slow to a crawl and, at times, closing the artery
altogether. Massive cracks surrounding Halema'uma'u and stretch-
ing across the remaining caldera floor warned of *Pele*'s continuing
anger and foretold calamities to come both near and far.

At the Jagger Volcano Observatory on the edge of the caldera, its
number two volcanologist stood looking out at the caldera. She was
observing the primordial landscape when a monster earthquake
rocked the building, making it vibrate beneath her feet. Glass shattered. Cracks darted across the concrete floor. Thunderous sounds
blasted her ears. She grabbed the edge of a massive worktable for
support. The seismometer on her computer screen began bouncing
off the chart before her computer suddenly stopped dead. She
scanned the scene through the windows, now empty holes devoid
of glass, overlooking the caldera and gasped.

Whole sections of the caldera floor had collapsed, plunging into
the abyss created by the withdrawal of magma from the chamber
beneath the volcano. Clouds of debris rose like thunderheads. In an
instant, the Halema'uma'u crater doubled in size and depth. The pit
that had been a small part of Kīlauea's five-square-mile caldera now
threatened to swallow it whole. Before the violent shaking could
tear the building apart around her, she ran for her life.

Unbeknownst to anyone near Kīlauea, *Pele*'s tentacles snaked
out from the crater into a small, neglected cemetery less than a
half-mile away on the outskirts of Volcano village. The ground
rolled and heaved, ancient rock walls crumbled, a giant tree crashed
to the ground, and headstones toppled. Cracks appeared across the

graveyard and expanded first by the foot and then by the yard. Subterranean forces propelled caskets upward. Boards splintered, and caskets broke open. Cadavers lay exposed. In destroying this sacred ground, *Pele* unearthed a man-made mystery.

* * *

On the other side of the Big Island, Hilo Chief Detective Koa Kāne stood in a different cemetery, the one behind the old white clapboard church on the edge of Kapaʻa. He didn't have to hunt for the gravestone he sought. He'd come often over the years and could have found his way blindfolded. After resolving each murder investigation, he always returned to Anthony Hazzard's tombstone. Penance for the man he'd killed thirty years earlier and solace for the guilt he'd suffered in the intervening years required it.

Hazzard's death had been on his mind of late, haunting his nightmares. It was like that for him when an investigation ended. Time buried many mistakes and healed many wounds, but not murder. It was a stain on his soul, one he'd carry to his deathbed.

Putting his hand on Hazzard's gravestone, Koa bowed his head and thought of the investigation just ended. He'd found justice for fourteen murdered schoolchildren and four of their teachers, just as he'd earlier solved the murders of an astronomer and a pair of loners living off the grid. Inadequate recompense for killing Hazzard, those successes did nothing to assuage his guilt. But they still empowered his empathy for murder victims and motivated him to pursue the most challenging cases. He stood for a long moment contemplating his life.

Turning away from the graveyard, the killer turned cop wondered what new crime would next command his attention and define his quest for atonement.

CHAPTER TWO

NĪELE JUMPED ON the bed and began licking Julia's face. She pushed the golden retriever away and sat up, sleepy-eyed. "Okay, okay, my girl, I know you need to go out." She threw off the sheet, walked to the window, and peered out, expecting another day of yellowish-gray vog, the volcanic smog caused by the continuing Kīlauea eruption. Instead, brisk trade winds had cleared away the foul air. Sunshine and blue sky ruled the day.

She dressed and slipped on her running shoes. Suddenly remembering yesterday's big earthquake, Julia did her usual check on the utility connections. With dozens of small quakes a day and frequent larger ones, the utility check had become a regular thing for Julia and most other Volcano Village residents. This morning all seemed to be in order. Turning to Nīele, she said, "You get a treat. We're going for a walk."

Nīele followed her to the kitchen, where Julia took the leash from its hook by the door. The dog jumped and whirled excitedly. Julia's words hadn't registered, but the leash was unambiguous. They walked through the neighborhood just south of Volcano village to the mile-long path through the forest where Julia let Nīele off her leash. The golden retriever scrambled through the trees, chasing a mongoose while Julia reveled in the rare clean air.

They passed through a stand of mature *'ōhi'a lehua* trees where bright red *'apapane* birds flitted through the forest canopy, feasting on the nectar from the tree's spiky red flowers. Julia paused beneath a huge *koa* tree, likely much older than her thirty-five years. Engrossed in the sounds and smells of the forest, Julia lost track of Nīele. When she finally called the dog, she didn't come. Julia called a second time, but still no Nīele.

Barking erupted ahead where the trail passed a small, abandoned graveyard, and she hurried toward the sound. A loud moaning growl, followed by a second and then a third sent chills down her spine. The barking intensified, and the growls turned into snarls. Julia began running. Out of breath, she emerged from the forest into a clearing beside the small rural graveyard. The scene terrified her.

The ground had ruptured, splitting the cemetery and causing stone walls to collapse. Headstones lay in a jumble. Violent subterranean forces had disinterred coffins. Wild boars, attracted by the smell of rotting flesh, had ripped open burial boxes and feasted on the remains. Bones and body parts lay strewn across the grass. Nīele, with her frantic barking, had interrupted this macabre picnic.

Three male wild hogs with long snouts, thick wiry hair, and small beady eyes glared at Nīele. Several more of the large tusked animals, oblivious to the commotion, continued to root through the graveyard. Julia feared for both herself and her dog. Originally brought to the islands by ancient Polynesians, pigs had inevitably escaped captivity and multiplied prodigiously. Herds of marauding boars devastated forests and even stripped previously lush patches bare. Weighing up to 400 pounds, they could charge at 30 miles an hour and often killed dogs or inflicted savage wounds on people. Neither she nor Nīele would stand a chance against this pack. Nīele might outrun them, but Julia, they could chase down.

One of the boars, more massive and closer than the others, sensed Julia's presence. Its head rose, its horn turned toward Julia, its large pointed ears pricked, and its beady black eyes focused on her. She stood fixated by the frightful animal's bright stare. The feral beast snarled. Julia had a premonition of death and knew she had to act.

Slowly backing away, she glanced to her left and then to her right while keeping the animals in her sight. She needed a tree—one she could climb high enough to escape the marauders. She spotted one with suitable branches off to her left and made a run for it. Sensing her fear, the big boar charged. Another followed. Reaching the tree, Julia grabbed a branch and then another until she had hauled herself ten feet above the ground. Growling and snarling, the boars circled beneath her. Panicked and gasping for breath, Julia used her cell phone to dial 911.

*   *   *

The 911 operator assigned Officer Johnnie Maru to respond to Julia's call. On an island with an irrepressible taste for *kālua* pork cooked in an *imu* or oven, Maru augmented his police salary by hunting pigs. Under normal circumstances, he'd have happily shot every boar in sight, but the hellish scene that greeted him when he neared the cemetery turned his stomach. Graveyards spooked him, and this one looked like something out of a horror movie. As much as he liked *kālua* pork, he wasn't sure he could eat hog meat after seeing the animals feasting on cadavers. If it weren't for the woman's panicked voice calling him from a tree pleading for help, he'd have tossed his breakfast.

When he moved toward the cemetery, one of the wild hogs challenged him. He drew his service Glock, but the giant boar just bellowed. Maru knew better than to wait for the animal to charge and shot the beast between the eyes. It died instantly, and the rest of the pack, stunned by the gunfire, scampered into the forest before the sound faded away.

Maru wanted nothing more than to return to his cruiser, but he couldn't leave the woman stranded in the woods. He took several deep breaths, held a wad of tissues over his nose, and skirted the cemetery. Julia's calls guided him to her, and he helped her down. After driving her back to her house, where Nīele cowered, he returned to the cemetery.

Maru, possessed of a dim wit, owned the longest minor disciplinary record in police department history. And now he had a new problem. He could already hear his colleagues back at HQ laughing about the dummy policeman who'd wandered into *Night of the Living Dead* and thought it was real.

After a half dozen deep breaths, he forced himself to examine the scene so he could describe it to the police dispatcher. Some titanic force had ripped up the graveyard, knocking over and breaking headstones. Coffins had been heaved out of the ground and ripped open. He started to dial the dispatcher.

Even Maru's fuzzy brain registered an oddity in the horrific scene. Something white fluttering in the breeze on the far side of the cemetery caught his eye. A piece of cloth maybe, but a clean white cloth in a disrupted graveyard. How did that get there? He approached and looked closer. More fabrics. Brightly colored. Moving still nearer, he saw the body, not a lifeless decomposing body from a broken casket, but the raw flesh of the recently deceased.

* * *

Chief Detective Koa Kāne arrived at the isolated Volcano cemetery ninety minutes after Julia's 911 call. The crime scene team was already there. Walking from his police SUV, he noted with approval that technicians had taped off the area surrounding the graveyard, created an entry path, and posted an officer to control access. He exchanged nods with Maru, and the gatekeeper entered his name on a log.

Georgina, the department's best crime scene tech, greeted him with a grim face. Short and slight of build, with a grandmotherly countenance, Georgina was known for her extraordinary tenacity and skill, along with a mischievous sense of humor.

"Bad?" he asked.

"Not if you like outdoor mortuaries," she responded, before giving him gloves and a face mask and leading him along a path between two stretches of yellow tape. She knelt next to a partially ravaged body lying facedown. A blue skirt with red trim, a bloodied white blouse, shoulder-length blond hair, and one high-heeled shoe on her left foot told Koa the victim was female. "*Haole*," Koa said, referring to a non-Hawaiian.

"Yeah," Georgina responded. "Definitely not Hawaiian."

"She hasn't been in this graveyard long," Georgina continued. "She wasn't formally buried, not without embalming and not in those clothes. I'm guessing whoever put her here wrapped her in that." She pointed to the tattered remnants of several black plastic garbage bags. "And dumped her, maybe in a shallow grave, maybe not. Hard to tell with the damned hogs rampaging through here."

"Cause of death?" Koa asked.

"Can't tell from the back. There's a shoulder wound. Looks like a bullet exit wound, but it wouldn't have been fatal, not without massive blood loss. We're waiting for Ronnie before we turn her over to check for other injuries." She referred to Ronnie Woo, the young Chinese police photographer, who pulled up in his police SUV while they talked. They stepped outside the tape and let Woo, who wore no mask and seemed oblivious to the carnage around him, record the gruesome scene with his Nikon.

Koa turned to Georgina. "We don't have an ME. Shizuo Hori is off-island." Koa referred to the aging obstetrician who doubled as the county's coroner.

"That's not a loss," Georgina responded. They'd both struggled for years under the weight of Shizuo's incompetence. Georgina pursed her lips. "I could ask Diaz. He might help us out."

Koa gave her a puzzled look. "Diaz?"

"Yeah. Professor Enrico Diaz. He teaches my forensic pathology class at UH Hilo. He's written textbooks and has a great reputation."

Koa considered her suggestion. He knew determining TOD would be challenging and required an expert. "Sure. Give him a call, but warn him the county doesn't pay much."

While Ronnie Woo took pictures and Georgina called her professor, Koa canvassed the cemetery. It lay about a hundred yards from the nearest street, surrounded by forest on three sides. Isolated, it oozed unattended seediness. Weeds and bushes grew inside the remains of a decrepit rock wall that encircled a couple dozen graves. Time and weather had damaged the headstones, making the dates hard to decipher, but one bore a 1930s date. Maybe a private family burial ground, but not one with flowers or other signs of a caring presence. Maybe abandoned. Not a bad place to conceal a body. If that had been the plan, he thought, *Pele* had foiled it.

An earthquake, most likely triggered by the collapse of the nearby Kīlauea caldera, had ripped three jagged, yard-wide cracks through the rows of markers, and the shaking had dislodged five caskets. Two had been torn open, either by the force of the quake or more likely by animals. Wild boars had attacked two of the partially decomposed corpses that had once been inside the disrupted burial boxes.

The newly deceased woman lay near one of the ravaged graves, and Koa agreed with Georgina that she'd most likely been buried atop one of the overturned caskets. Her body appeared mostly intact, except for the shoulder wound and a torn right leg, probably chewed by one of the hogs.

"Professor Enrico Diaz is on the way, and he'll forgo any payment. Shall we wait for him?"

Koa, impatient to determine the cause of death, rejected that suggestion. When Woo finished shooting pictures, Koa and Georgina, wearing evidence gloves, knelt and rolled the body onto its back. They didn't need an ME to determine the cause of death.

CHAPTER THREE

KOA GUESSED THE dead woman to be in her mid-thirties. A blond *haole*, she'd been pretty in life but no longer. The powder burns around one of the tiny, blood-soaked holes in her blouse left no doubt she'd been shot at point-blank range. One bullet had hit her shoulder, passed through her flesh, and left a nasty exit wound. The other bullet had entered the left side of her chest. That slug, still inside her body, had undoubtedly struck her heart. It was the kill shot, and Koa had little doubt that she'd died instantly. He judged the murder weapon to be small caliber, probably a .22.

"Jesus," Georgina exclaimed, "look at 'er hands."

Koa looked, and bile rose in his stomach. Someone had cut off the tips of the woman's thumbs and fingers, leaving bloody stumps. Koa had seen this kind of disfigurement in a drug cartel case. The savagery had made him angry then . . . and furious now. He vowed to himself, as he had back then, to identify the twisted monster who'd dared to kill and desecrate the body of another human being.

Swallowing his disgust, he said, "The killer didn't want us identifying this woman. The question is, why?"

Controlling his fury, Koa studied the body, taking in every detail. In his head, he called it listening to the victim . . . putting himself in her position . . . seeking to understand what she'd experienced in the minutes before she'd died ... and searching for the why of her death. The process often yielded clues and always fueled his empathy, empowering his drive to find justice.

Aside from the bullet wounds, damaged leg, and missing fingertips, she bore no other obvious wounds. Koa saw no indications that she'd struggled with her killer. Dressed in business attire, she wore little makeup and no jewelry. Her hair had been professionally cut and recently, too. Pushing up her lip with his gloved finger, he noted that her teeth were straight and even, most likely the result of orthodontia. He checked her arm. Although his cursory exam wasn't conclusive, he saw no indication of drug use. Overall, she appeared to have been healthy, well groomed, and of above-average economic status.

Nor did it appear to be a sex crime. He would need a medical examiner to be sure, but the gunshot wounds, the calculated nature of the disfigurement, the body's location in a graveyard, and her fully clothed condition made rape unlikely.

Few people had the stomach to disfigure the dead, and those who did usually had reasons. This killer had taken unusual precautions—not only hiding the body but also thwarting the most common means of identification. That suggested intelligence, organization, mental toughness, and discipline. His instincts told Koa this was no ordinary domestic fight gone nuclear. He was facing a hardened killer or killers with an agenda.

He focused on estimating the time of death. Her arms, neck, and face showed a greenish discoloration and appeared somewhat bloated, which he recognized as early putrefaction. Her eyes seemed to protrude, and her skin showed a faint web of green-black lines. That was the onset of marbling, another sign of putrefaction. She had been dead for more than twenty-four hours. Of that, Koa was sure, but environmental conditions affected the speed of decomposition. At this elevation, about 4000 feet, with the trade winds blowing, the average temperature would have been in the mid-50s or low 60s. It would have been cloudy roughly half the time with frequent rains. These conditions would slow decomposition, but he didn't know by how much.

He turned from the body to the plastic wrapping, consisting of several black plastic garbage bags taped together. When he lifted them, a high-heeled shoe, matching the one on the victim's left foot, tumbled out. Small clumps of damp earth clung to one side of the plastic. Her body had been wrapped and buried in wet soil. Burial in the cool, wet ground, like the mild temperatures, would have slowed decomposition. By how much, he wasn't sure. Without expert forensic analysis, he couldn't judge whether she'd been dead a few days, a week, or perhaps even longer.

Identification was always his priority. It would enable the police to retrace the victim's life. Only then could they discover where, when, and how she'd interacted with her killer or killers. Equally vital to Koa, a name and a personal history made the deceased real, deepened his empathy for them, and supercharged his hunt for the killer. He wanted to know the victim, her likes and dislikes, her life patterns, successes and disappointments, and strengths and foibles. Her life story would drive and sustain his resolve to ferret out her killer.

Although her desecrated fingers precluded easy identification, he still checked the woman's body for ID. No wallet, purse, phone, or personalized clothing, no identifying jewelry, no medical bracelet, and no visible tattoos. Nothing. Nor did they find her purse or ID anywhere else in the graveyard.

Johnnie Maru, who'd first responded to Julia's 911 call, approached with a tall, thin, balding man in his sixties. Georgina greeted her professor, and Koa moved outside the crime scene to introduce himself. Enrico Diaz had a long face, accentuated by his shiny bald head and bright blue, inquisitive eyes. He wore faded jeans, a lightweight blue jacket over a collared shirt, and hiking boots. Koa wondered if Georgina had warned him about the disrupted, muddy scene.

"Thank you for coming." Koa paused. "Forgive me if I'm abrupt, but I need to know your qualifications before allowing you into the crime scene."

"No offense taken. I'm a medical doctor with extensive experience in forensic pathology. I was the head ME in Seattle before the crushing workload drove me out and into academia."

An experienced ME was a gift from the gods. "You have access to a lab?" Koa asked, hopefully.

"Sure. We have a pathology lab at the school in Hilo."

"Okay. Let us walk you through the crime scene."

Koa and Georgina watched Diaz check the corpse's temperature and lividity and draw samples of her bodily fluids. He took close-up pictures of her discolored and marbled skin, collected several temperature readings from the ground, bagged examples of the earth, and cut a small square from the black plastic. Koa would have liked a step-by-step explanation, but waited until Diaz finished to ask, "What can you tell me about TOD?"

"Under normal circumstances, the discoloration and early marbling would suggest she's been dead between forty-eight and seventy-two hours, but it's been longer. Decomposition takes roughly twice as long when a body's been in water and eight times as long when the body's buried. Wrapped in plastic and buried in this cool muddy soil—" Diaz waved a hand to take in the cemetery— "I'd think she's been here for ten days to two weeks, but that's just a preliminary guess."

It was longer than Koa would have guessed, and he made a mental note to thank Georgina for lining up an experienced professional. "You can refine that guesstimate?" he asked.

"Yes, with some more data, a look at the blood chemistry, and an autopsy."

"What do you need from us?"

"Two things. I'm going to need authorization from the county to perform the autopsy. Second, I need weather data, day and night-time temperature, humidity, and rain amounts. Driving in, I noticed a weather station at one of the houses I passed. Getting localized data would be great."

"We'll see what we can do."

Diaz hesitated and then said, "You don't have an identification, do you?"

"No."

"You might try facial recognition software."

Koa shook his head. "The Seattle police must have had a bigger budget than Hawai'i County."

Diaz wasn't deterred. "One of my colleagues in the university IT department might be able to help. He's been experimenting with facial recognition technology for years and has some pretty sophisticated algorithms."

That, Koa thought, could be interesting. "Could it work even with the victim's facial bloating?"

"I can get a pretty good handle on the amount of bloating during the autopsy and build you a decent reproduction of her premortem face. It won't be perfect, but it might work."

"Your colleague could run the face against driver's license photos?"

"Yes, and social media platforms like Facebook, Twitter, Instagram, Snapchat, and other databases."

They might, Koa thought, just have a way to identify the deceased.

CHAPTER FOUR

AFTER YEARS OF trying, Koa had finally convinced the chief to fund an additional detective position. Koa had spent three months searching for the right person before Professor Kingman, a friend on the UH Criminal Justice faculty, recommended Makanui Kaʻuhane. "She was my student twice for different courses and wrote the best student thesis I've ever read. Better than many professional papers. But more than that, she's tough as flintstone, book smart like Einstein, and sensitive to vibes like a psychiatrist. You should talk to her," Kingman said. Then he added, "And she's proven her commitment to finding justice for crime victims. Proven it in spades."

Kingman's last remark caught Koa's attention. He was all about locking up criminals and securing justice for crime victims. He reviewed Makanui's resume and found her impressive. A native Hawaiian who could trace her ancestry back to the *aliʻi* who ruled Hawaiʻi before Western contact, she'd graduated with honors from UH's School of Criminal Justice before attending *Ke Kula Makaʻi*, the Honolulu police academy. After joining the Honolulu Police Department, she'd achieved an outstanding record, leading the HPD to send her to the Federal Law Enforcement Training Center in Glyno, Georgia. Makanui's stint at Glyno stood out in Koa's mind because few Hawaiʻi cops got that level of expert training.

Koa called a friend in the HPD to get the lowdown on Makanui. He got a glowing report. Makanui had been one of the department's best officers and had made detective after only four years on the force. After Glyno, the HPD had assigned her to its anti-terror unit, where she'd served a year before abruptly resigning. She'd been secretive about her reasons for leaving and her activities during the past nine months, so no one in the department knew why Makanui had left.

Koa invited Makanui to breakfast at Café Pesto on old Hilo's main drag. He chose the informal setting to put Makanui at ease and avoid the inevitable interruptions at police headquarters. As a Café Pesto regular, he prevailed upon the hosts to save them a window seat in the corner where they could talk privately. He arrived first and had no trouble recognizing her. Tall, trim, and athletic with short black hair and large bright black eyes, Makanui cut an imposing figure. To Koa's practiced eye, she also radiated "cop." He could never put his finger on exactly what triggered that impression—maybe a wariness in the eyes or a hardness around her mouth. Whatever the cause, he sensed she'd been on mean streets and knew how to handle herself in a tough situation.

"Thank you for coming," he said as they shook hands.

"Thanks for the opportunity," she responded. "I've read about some of your cases."

Over coffee, Koa probed her experience, skills, and judgment, peppering her with questions about her work with the HPD and her reaction to hypothetical situations. As she responded, reflecting on her professional history and experiences, she surpassed his highest expectations. Coupled with everything else he'd heard and read, he was confident that she had qualifications. Nevertheless, he couldn't risk hiring her without knowing why she'd resigned, what she'd been doing in the nine months since her resignation, and why she wanted to work on the Big Island rather than return to Honolulu.

As was his style, Koa decided on the direct approach. "I checked your record with the HPD and know they hold you in high regard. As you may know, I also talked to Professor Kingman, who speaks glowingly about you, but I have to be honest with you. You need to appreciate that before I can offer you a job, I need to know why you left the HPD and what you've been doing since then."

"I know, but I need your word that this stays between us. I think you'll understand why when you've heard what happened."

Koa agreed.

"Because of my Hawaiian heritage, most people think I grew up poor, but that's not how it was. My father had a successful business, which he sold before he retired. Then, he and my mother lived their dream, sailing their 53-foot open-ocean sailboat. They circumnavigated the globe, often together with other sailors in World ARC rallies, groups of open-ocean sailors who travel long distances.

"Eleven months ago, my parents were cruising in the Sulu Sea when Philippine pirates boarded their vessel about twenty-five miles west of Mindanao. They took my parents hostage, beat them badly, and nearly starved them to death during their captivity. After some difficult negotiations with the Abu Sayyaf terrorists behind the kidnapping, I assembled the $100,000 ransom and arranged their release."

Makanui sipped her coffee before continuing. "After I got my parents back to Hawai'i, I was determined to go after the people who'd kidnapped and abused them. I resigned from the HPD and hooked up with Anders, a Philippine anti-terror specialist I met at the Federal Law Enforcement Training Center. After gathering some intelligence to augment what I learned negotiating my parents' release, we hatched a plan to trap the pirates. We talked to

Professor Kingman, and he put us in touch with some solid people in the Philippine military. We bought a secondhand yacht and went sailing in the Sulu Sea."

"Where pirates kidnapped your parents?" Koa asked, working hard to keep the incredulity out of his voice.

"Yes. The Philippine government wasn't going to do the job, so I decided I'd take those terrorist kidnappers down."

"And you did it?" Koa asked, barely containing his astonishment.

"Yes. We sailed the same route my parents took. Nothing happened on the first trip, so we repeated the voyage."

Koa had a good idea where the story was going but still prompted. "And?"

"Pirates boarded our sailboat about three a.m. one night . . . three of them. A shootout ensued, and one guy died while we subdued the other two. We interrogated the bastards and learned the location of the pirate base before we turned them over to the Philippine military."

Makanui seemed to have reached the end of her story, and Koa asked, "And that was the end of it?"

"Well, not quite. I joined a medical group that went into the terrorist base camp after Philippine anti-terror soldiers raided it a week later. We found a bunch of dead Abu Sayyaf operatives and freed six more hostages."

"That's quite a story," Koa said with a touch of admiration in his voice. "Is there some reason you don't want to talk about it?"

"It's for my parents' safety and mine, too. Abu Sayyaf gets funding from Islamic jihadist groups, and there are Islamic radicals on the terrorist watch list in Honolulu. I think the risk of retaliation against either my parents or me is small, but still, the fewer people who know, the better."

"That's why you're not returning to the HPD?" Koa asked.

"That's right. If I went back, I'd be in the anti-terror unit, increasing the risk somebody might connect me to what happened in the Philippines."

"Are you in the clear with Philippine authorities?"

"So far as I know."

Koa cradled his coffee cup. "Pretty risky undertaking."

"I'd do it again under similar circumstances," Makanui responded.

"I've spent a lot of time on the ocean, mostly in small craft," Koa said, "but I have trouble imagining being out in the middle of a hostile sea, waiting for pirates to attack."

"The Sulu Sea is beautiful, especially at sunrise and sunset, and the days were peaceful. Nights were scary. Sometimes in the fog, we couldn't see ten feet and couldn't count on radar to pick up a pirate boat. We would be on full alert all night, every night. You know what I feared?"

"I can think of lots of things."

"When I was out there in the Sulu Sea, waiting for the kidnappers to come, I was afraid . . . afraid that the pirates wouldn't come . . . afraid that I'd never get a chance to catch the terrorists who caused my parents so much suffering. It made me think of all the people in the world who have no one to stand up for them, to right the wrongs inflicted on them. I can't help them all, but maybe I can even the score for some. That's what I want to do with my life."

Koa, who'd killed his father's nemesis and escaped punishment, felt like he'd found a kindred spirit in a woman who'd risked her life to take down the thugs who'd abducted her parents. Koa offered her the open detective position then and there. She accepted on the spot.

* * *

After four months with the department, she'd proven herself to be tough and savvy but also an engaging colleague. Among other surprises, Koa learned that she repeatedly competed in the Big Island Ironman triathlon, always finishing among the top ten women. He'd even introduced her to his seven-foot, two-inch fisherman buddy, Hook Hao.

Koa smiled at the memory. He'd arranged a meet and greet on the deck of the *Ka'upu*, the *Albatross*, Hook's commercial fishing trawler. Tall for a woman at five feet, eleven inches, Makanui had looked up into Hook's broad Hawaiian face and said, "I hear that you fish like 'Umi with the bones of Pae." She referred to a Hawaiian legend about magical fishhooks carved from the ankle bones of an old *kahuna* whose body 'Umi had stolen.

Hook roared with delight at the backhanded compliment, and the two proceeded to drink beer and swap sea stories, bonding like two old salts. The following day, Hook had taken her out on the *Ka'upu*, where she'd caught a 400-pound blue marlin. On an island that hosted more than a dozen annual fishing competitions, including the famous Hawaiian International Billfish Tournament, her catch was the talk of the police department and made the local newspaper, under the headline "Cop Catches Big Fish."

* * *

The police HQ conference room was under renovation, so Koa called his team together in one of the department's interrogation rooms. There were four of them and Koa—Makanui; Piki, the youngest detective on the force; and two female assistants, Haunani and Kalama. Both with black hair and round faces, they dressed alike and worked together so much that cops had trouble telling them apart and called them "the twins."

Koa would typically have included Sergeant Basa, who supported the detective bureau, but the brawny sergeant was away for three weeks of training with his National Guard unit.

Once they were all assembled in the cramped interrogation room, Haunani quipped, "Who's going to interrogate me?"

"Take all day to list your crimes," Kalama retorted, and everyone laughed.

"Not if I take the fifth," Haunani responded good-naturedly.

"Let me tell you what's happening," Koa began. "We are trying to ID the woman we just found in an old cemetery outside Volcano. Professor Diaz, our forensics expert, constructed an image of her premortem face, and his colleagues out at UH used facial recognition software to run that face against several different databases. They got several hundred possible hits."

"I thought facial recognition software was super accurate. How come we've got several hundred hits?" Piki asked. He looked too young to be a detective, was easily excited, and always in motion, like a hyperactive child. He had an unfortunate tendency to jump to conclusions, a flaw Koa overlooked because he attacked every project with incredible intensity. His hacker-level wizardry in digital research made him Koa's source for mining information from public and law enforcement databases.

"It's accurate enough," Koa responded, "but Professor Diaz didn't have much to go on. He had to reconstruct an image of the vic's face after she suffered substantial decomposition. As a result, we have a range of possibles for comparison."

Piki, jumping as usual to an unwarranted conclusion, groaned. "Tracking down hundreds of names is gonna be a ball buster."

"Maybe for you, but not for me," Kalama responded, again triggering laughter.

"It's not that bad," Koa said. "We've grouped the names. There are only twenty-seven locals with Hawai'i driver's licenses, and eighteen more with Hawai'i social media profiles, but no Hawai'i driver's licenses. We only get into the hundreds if our vic wasn't a local. Divvy up the list and get on the phones calling people in the first two groups. We're looking for someone who doesn't turn up." Koa paused. "If we have to check out hundreds, we'll turn the whole project over to Piki." That drew a groan from Piki and chuckles from everyone else.

The team members made their calls, and the results trickled in over the next day and a half. At first, they had eliminated all but twenty names; then, they were down to eight, and by the third report, they had accounted for all but three women.

Koa sent Piki to check out one of the names, while Koa and Makanui went looking for the last two. Cheryl Larson, the first of their missing women, had a driver's license address at a private residence in Leilani Gardens, a subdivision in the Puna district.

Koa shook his head. "This ain't gonna be fun." *Pele* had been erupting for the past several weeks from the prosaically named Fissure Number 8 in that Puna subdivision. The vent had spouted fountains of liquid rock shooting hundreds of feet in the air, building a volcanic cinder cone, and spreading thin, glassy particles of *Pele's* hair like strands of cotton candy. The heat from the eruption became so intense it created storm clouds glowing red in the night sky, which then produced localized torrents of rain. Gases long trapped in *Pele's* excreta bubbled and hissed into poisonous sulfur-dioxide clouds, often limiting vision to a few yards.

Cauldrons of molten rock had set houses alight, displaced thousands, damaged the Puna Geothermal Plant, burned forests, and cut highways isolating whole communities. *Pele's* volcanic excreta had sped for miles through braided channels before reaching the shoreline, where it filled idyllic bays, state parks, and treasured ponds, altering the ancient coastline and adding virgin land to the Big Island. Entering the ocean at temperatures over a thousand degrees, the lava boiled seawater, releasing towering plumes of deadly laze— steam laden with hydrochloric acid and fragments of glass. A more perfect representation of hell would tax the imagination.

As they made their way down Route 130 toward Leilani Gardens, Koa called one of the patrolmen assigned to watch over the community, who reported that Cheryl Larson's house, although close to the edge of a new lava flow, had survived. The cop added that the air stank and tephra covered the area, but he didn't know whether anybody still lived at Larson's address.

After a thirty-minute drive from police HQ in Hilo, they turned into Leilani Gardens, where they passed a police roadblock, and crunched slowly down a street covered with ash, tephra, and tiny strands of *Pele's* hair. Even with the windows closed and the AC recirculating, the foul smell of sulfur filled the vehicle. Makanui peered out at the wasteland. "I heard this area once produced half of the state's cut flowers. Now there's nothing."

"Yeah, and it smells like shit," Koa added. "Kapoho Bay's gone, too. Growing up, I used to swim there. The prettiest spot on the island. Now it's just a desolate lava delta."

More than an inch of ash covered the roadway, and it grew steadily thicker as they neared Cheryl Larson's place. The powdery gray stuff, mixed with *Pele's* hair and tephra, covered the trees and shrubs, robbing the scene of color. Finally, reaching the house, they found a depressing grisaille scene. The overpowering stench of sulfur, combined with the lack of tread marks in the ash-covered ground, told them no one had been home in days.

"She's not registered at either of the shelters," Makanui, who had been checking with her cell, said, "but we might find a former neighbor at one of them."

"Pāhoa or Keaʻau?" Koa asked, referring to the two main shelters set up for former residents from the areas *Pele* had rendered uninhabitable.

"Pāhoa's closer."

If Leilani Gardens represented the toll in property damage from *Pele*'s latest eruption, the Pāhoa shelter symbolized the human cost. The Red Cross, County Parks Department, and civil defense emergency management personnel had teamed up to house eighty people in the local gym and another 240 in tents and RVs on the adjacent athletic fields. Like any itinerant camp providing food and other necessities, it had attracted the homeless and others trying to survive on the fringes of society. Filled with people who'd lost their homes, and maybe their jobs, it was a uniformly grim place.

"God, I feel sorry for these poor souls," Makanui said.

"Yeah," Koa responded, "and most of them lacked property insurance because they lived in a high-risk area. The county should never have let them build in the lower east rift zone. That's been *Pele*'s playground time and again over the years."

The two officers split up and worked their way through the gym, asking about Cheryl Larson. With people lined up to use the bathrooms, tending to children, playing cards, or wandering off to gain a few moments of solitude, they couldn't be sure they'd touched base with everyone. No one with whom they did speak seemed to know Cheryl.

Outside they went from tent to camper until they found Mrs. Green, who'd lived down the street from Cheryl Larson in Leilani Gardens. The two women had been casual friends, and Mrs. Green knew that Cheryl, amidst a divorce proceeding, had changed her

cell number before the Puna eruption and had subsequently returned to the mainland to live with her family. Makanui called the
new phone number provided by Mrs. Green and verified that
Cheryl was not the lady in the cemetery.

Having struck out with Cheryl Larson, Koa and Makanui went
looking for Tiger Baldwin, the other woman on their list. On the
way back to Hilo, Koa asked, "Feel like telling me more about the
night the pirates attacked you and your friend in the Sulu Sea?"

"I was wondering when your curiosity would get the better of
you," Makanui said with a grin.

"Now, you know," he responded.

"It was late at night. We were under sail, blacked out except for a
single mast light. We left it on for the terrorist to see. The fog was
thick, limiting both sight and sound. Just the kind of night when
these raiders were most active. Anders, he was my companion, and I
were both armed and on high alert. I was on the bridge, and he was in
the cabin, but we both had video from cameras pointed fore and aft.

"We had no warning until suddenly something bumped the back
of the boat, and the video showed a man with an AK appear on
deck. We couldn't take him down without scaring the others away,
so we held our positions as though nothing had happened and
waited for them to make the next move. That's when they threw a
grappling hook over the stern to secure their boat, and then two
more bad guys boarded the yacht.

"One of them disappeared down the hatch into the cabin where
Anders surprised him and knocked him out cold. I tased one of his
buddies as he climbed to the bridge, and he collapsed like a bag of
shit. I exchanged gunfire with his partner. I had a vest, and he didn't."

"The vest saved you?"

"Yeah. And I've never been without one since then."

"They get mighty hot in this weather."

"Doesn't matter. Hot and alive beats cold and dead."

Arriving back in Hilo, they turned onto Kalaniana'ole Avenue. They passed Keaukaha Beach Park just beyond the Hilo breakwater before reaching the parking lot of an upscale two-story apartment building. A bit more than ten years old, the luxury property sat across the avenue from the ocean on a beautifully landscaped lot, amidst a riot of tropical flowers. Just as they pulled into a parking space, Koa's cell rang. He took Detective Piki's call, listened for a moment, said "got it," and hung up. Turning to Makanui, he said, "Piki found his missing woman. Let's hope this Baldwin lady is our vic. Otherwise, we'll have to work through the whole big list."

"Hope's not a strategy," Makanui said with a smile. "At least that's what they taught us in Glyno."

"No," Koa agreed, "but shoe leather is the oldest strategy in the book. Let's go see if this lady's home."

They entered the building, avoided the elevator as was Koa's habit, climbed the stairs to the second floor, and knocked on Baldwin's door. No answer. A second, harder knock produced no better results.

Makanui knocked at the neighboring apartment, and a thin, elderly woman in a wheelchair opened the door. Makanui introduced herself to Leilani Craig. Despite the warm weather, the frail woman wore a sweater buttoned to her neck. She had small, tired eyes behind her wire-rim glasses. She wore no makeup and had put up her yellow-gray hair in an ill-formed bun. She invited Makanui and Koa into her tidy living room, painted in bright but fading pastels. Leilani, like the room, exuded a tired but warm feeling.

Yes, she knew Tiger. "I've been missing her," Leilani said. "She's just the nicest person. Came by to see me every night. Brought me groceries." Leilani's hands fluttered in the air around her as she talked. "She picked up my medicine at the pharmacy. Helped me with my ceramics." She pointed to a display of a half-dozen ceramic cups, bowls, and vases, all in soft blue-gold tones, arrayed on a sideboard. "She was like a daughter, coming over all the time to check on me. But then she just up and left. Didn't even say goodbye."

"What do you mean just up and left?" Makanui asked.

"One night, she didn't come home, and then the movers came for her stuff."

"When did you last see her?"

"Let's see." Leilani paused, now picking at a scab on the back of her hand and struggling to recall. "Yes. Wednesday . . . a week ago last Wednesday. She brought me a chicken dinner, and we ate out on the balcony. She was just the nicest person."

Makanui did the math. Fourteen days ago. Consistent with the TOD of their victim. But something wasn't right. How could Tiger have moved the furniture out of her apartment unnoticed by this woman? "When did Tiger move out?"

"The movers came a day or two later. Over the weekend."

"And Tiger wasn't around?"

"I was out in the hall several times looking for her, but she wasn't here. Least I didn't see her. Thought it was kind of strange, but, you know, I didn't want to pry."

"Do you know what company moved the furniture?"

Leilani shook her head. "Come to think of it, they didn't have uniforms, just street clothes, and I never saw their truck."

When the two officers left Leilani's apartment, Koa turned to Makanui. "Something's off. Check out the other neighbors, while I talk to the resident manager."

They met in the lobby fifteen minutes later to compare notes. Makanui began first. "I talked to two other residents—same story. Nice lady. No one has seen her in the last couple of weeks or so. What'd you learn from the resident agent?"

"She gave notice a week ago Friday by a message left on voicemail. Didn't ask for a refund of her security deposit. Left no forwarding address. Movers had a work order and the keys to her apartment. The agent doesn't remember the company name on the form but did recall that the truck had no logo. And more bad news, the manager had Baldwin's apartment cleaned before putting it back on the market."

"Humm," Makanui said. "Looks like we may have found our vic, but we need some proof."

"Just what I was thinking," Koa responded.

They went back to the resident manager, who let them into Tiger Baldwin's former apartment. As expected, the place was empty. Not a stick of furniture remained, and a cleaning crew, an exceptionally thorough one, had been over the place.

Looking around, Koa doubted that they would find any DNA in the apartment, but he decided it was worth a try. "I'm going to ask Georgina to do her thing in here. It's a long shot, but if there's DNA, Georgina will find it."

"Which the lab in Honolulu will take two months to process," Makanui said, mournfully. "There's got to be a faster way."

"There might be a way," Koa responded. "I know from Professor Diaz that UH Hilo can sequence DNA. It might not be official, but it would give us a quick answer and something to go on."

"That would be great. Hope Georgina can work her magic." Makanui thought for a moment. "What about Tiger's wheels?"

"Check with DMV and have the dispatcher put out an APB."

CHAPTER FIVE

"WHAT'S NEXT?" MAKANUI asked when she and Koa returned to their SUV.

"X-CO," Koa responded

"X-CO? Never heard of it," Makanui responded.

"Neither have I," Koa said. "The resident manager showed me Baldwin's rental application. It listed X-CO as her employer. The address puts it in the warehouse area between the bay and the airport. It's not far."

Minutes later, they pulled into a parking lot in front of a concrete block building surrounded by a ten-foot chain-link fence topped by barbed wire. Outside the fence, a group of about thirty protestors carried signs, reading "Sovereignty for Hawai'i" and "End Military Oppression." A big Hawaiian man with bushy black hair stood on a soapbox screaming into a megaphone. "*Haoles* stole our kingdom. Restore Hawaiian sovereignty. Oppressors go home."

Koa recognized several of the protestors. "That's Ha'ilono and Nohea." He referred to two long-standing Hawaiian activists. "They led the big protest against the Thirty Meter Telescope on Mauna Kea. Got into a couple nasty scrapes with the police. Wonder what set them off this time?"

Taking in the signs, Makanui said, "Sounds anti-military."

"Yeah, looks that way," Koa responded. Spotting another familiar face in the crowd, Koa waved and headed toward the man, and the two exchanged *alohas*.

Koa had a long history with Makaiao, who was a distant relative on his mother's side of the family. Makaiao, fortyish and pure Hawaiian, had graduated from the University of Hawai'i at Mānoa with a degree in Hawaiian language and culture. One of the leading activists on the Big Island, he was also one of the smartest. A man who you could persuade with reason, but never one to be ignored. After several contentious episodes, he and Koa had come to share a cautious mutual respect. Makaiao had even helped the police a couple of times, but only when he found it in the interest of the sovereignty movement he so cherished.

The well-built man, wearing jeans, a Hawaiian shirt, and scuffed cowboy boots, stood nearly a head taller than Koa, who topped out at six-foot-two. Makaiao's thick hair, the ebony color of pāhoehoe lava, contrasted with teeth white as bleached whalebone. A jagged scar, the legacy of a knife fight, marred his right cheek. Unlike the typical Hawaiian activist who avoided the police, Makaiao was not afraid to be seen with Koa, who supposed Makaiao's extraordinary height contributed to the sense of self-confidence and security Makaiao's academic pedigree gave him.

"What's the deal here, brah?" Koa asked, adopting a touch of the local pidgin.

"Bad vibes, brah."

"What kine?" Koa asked.

Makaiao frowned, and his voice tensed with accusatory emotion. "This *haole* company comes here, steals our tax dollars, employs none of our people, and does zip for the community. Economic exploitation, just like 1893." The scar on his cheek moved as he talked, appearing to reaffirm his conviction.

Makaiao referred to the overthrow of the Hawaiian monarchy in 1893, but his complaint related to the modern practice of luring—some would say bribing—companies with tax incentives without ensuring that locals got jobs and other benefits. And native Hawaiians, lacking education and economic clout, often bore the brunt of such deals.

"An' that's not even the evil stuff, brah," Makaiao added.

That comment caught Koa's interest. "What evil stuff?"

"Computer voodoo. Secret shit. Trying to replace humans."

"Robots? Artificial intelligence?" Koa asked.

"Yeah, until it goes awry and kills us all." Makaiao's tone matched the disdain of his words.

Reflecting on the protest signs, Koa asked, "What's the military connection?"

"We seen 'em going up PTA." Makaiao waived one of his long arms toward the saddle between the mountains west of Hilo, pointing to the Army's Pōhakuloa Training Area. "Trynna make robot soldiers."

Although robot soldiers seemed far-fetched to Koa, he kept his skepticism to himself. Still, he didn't discount Makaiao's intel. If the man had seen X-CO employees up at Pōhakuloa, the company was most likely working with the Army. He slapped Makaiao on the back and turned away toward the X-CO facility. On the way, he and Makanui exchanged *alohas* with the other protestors. Only after they passed the last of them did Koa notice a guard with a German Shepherd on a leash patrolling inside the fence. "Looks like Fort Knox," Makanui said. "Wonder what they do in there."

Koa noticing several expensive BMWs, a Tesla, and a Mercedes parked near the fence, responded, "Whatever it is, it pays well. Check out the fancy wheels."

They proceeded to the gate, where Koa pressed an intercom button. A disembodied voice responded. Koa announced them as police officers and asked to speak to the manager. After an eight-minute wait in the blazing sun, an employee appeared and escorted them into a conference room off a small lobby, separated from the rest of the complex by a steel door equipped with what seemed to be a biometric reader. "Some kind of serious high-tech security," Makanui said once their escort left, closing the conference room door behind him.

"Yeah," Koa responded. "I get the feeling there's a tale to be told about our missing Tiger."

The two detectives sat alone at a rectangular conference table for a couple of minutes before a man entered. Projecting an air of authority, he introduced himself as R. Stamford Wingate, the managing director of X-CO. Wearing neatly tailored slacks, a white dress shirt, black wingtip oxfords, and a red tie, unusual business attire for the Big Island, he looked every inch a military officer with a square jaw, hawk-like black eyes, and close-cropped hair. "Are you here to clear out the damned protestors?" he asked.

"Afraid not," Koa responded.

"Then what can I do for you?" Wingate asked, his tone decidedly curt.

"We'd like to see one of your employees, a Ms. Tiger Baldwin," Koa responded.

"You're a bit late. She gave notice a month ago and quit a couple of weeks back."

Two weeks ago, Koa thought. Just about the time our unidentified victim took two bullets. "What did she do for X-CO?"

"She was a secretary."

A secretary with an upscale oceanside apartment. X-CO, Koa mused to himself, must pay well. "And just what is X-CO's business?"

"That's classified. What's your interest in Ms. Baldwin?"

"She may be missing," Koa responded, now letting a bit of his authority show. "We're trying to find her. Have you been in touch with her since she left?"

"No."

"She leave a forwarding address?" Koa asked.

"I don't think so."

Unsatisfied with Wingate's responses, Koa changed course. "Perhaps you could let us see her personnel file."

"That would be contrary to our company policy."

"Well," Koa hesitated, adding gravitas to his next words, "would a subpoena be more to your liking?"

Wingate seemed surprised but for just an instant. "She must be more than a missing person?"

The man was fishing for information, and, sensing something out of the ordinary, Koa responded, "Like I said, we're trying to locate her, and her personnel file should have useful information."

"Our lawyers would fight any subpoena," Wingate responded brusquely.

"Lot of expense to hide the personnel file of a former secretary," Koa responded evenly.

Wingate and Koa locked eyes for several seconds before the executive looked away. "Give me a few minutes. Let me see what I can do." Wingate turned and left the room.

Weird man and a strange company, Koa thought, while he and Makanui waited.

Ten minutes later, a young man entered the conference room and handed Koa a thin file. "Mr. Wingate told me to give this to you. It's a copy. You can keep it." He turned to leave.

"And your name is?" Koa asked.

The fellow stopped and rotated slowly back toward the two policemen. Wide-eyed, like he might not know the answer, he hesitated before saying, "Charlie, Charlie Haines." Then, before Koa could ask more questions, he fled.

"Not much *aloha* spirit in this concrete bunker," Makanui said as they left.

Back in his police SUV, Koa checked the file and found Tiger Baldwin's resignation letter, dated May 27. He read the text aloud: "Personal circumstances require me to return to the mainland. Friday, June 15, will be my last day at X-CO." After leafing quickly through the rest of the file, he added, "No forwarding address."

"Tiger Baldwin looks to be our vic, but we've got no way to be sure," Makanui said.

With more hope than conviction, Koa responded, "Let's see if Georgina can come up with DNA."

"From that apartment? Georgina's a genius, but she can't pull DNA out of thin air."

*   *   *

When he returned to police headquarters, Koa had a call from the chief, and, knowing that his boss didn't like waiting, hurried to the chief's office. Police Chief Lannua, dressed as always in a freshly ironed white shirt, was not in a cheerful mood.

"What were you doing out at X-CO?" Lannua asked without preface. The chief's unusual abruptness told Koa he'd stepped on a political land mine. After eight years in the senior detective's job, Koa usually knew where he needed to tread softly, but this time he must have missed something.

He and Lannua mostly worked well together, but the chief always protected the island's elite and people with money or political influence. His crankiness meant that X-CO had connections. "What's the story with X-CO?" Koa asked.

"It's a defense contractor into highly classified stuff with a real heavyweight board. Haven't you heard of Zhou Li?"

"The billionaire always in the news about electric cars, batteries, space exploration, and artificial intelligence?"

"Yeah, that's him. He's behind X-CO, and he has recruited a who's who of politicians and corporate big shots for the board."

The chief's words reminded Koa of a news story he'd seen. "He's the guy sponsoring the big artificial intelligence symposium here next week."

"Right. The governor and half the legislature will be attending. They're planning to use the event to entice more high-tech businesses to locate in Hilo. It's a big deal. You should have talked to me before threatening X-CO's managing director."

"Sorry, Chief. It was just a routine inquiry. We're trying to identify the dead woman recently found in a Volcano graveyard," Koa responded.

"I know about that. What's the connection to X-CO?"

Koa explained the results of the facial recognition search. "One of the possible matches was a former X-CO secretary."

"That's all you had, and you threatened X-CO with a subpoena?"

Someone, most likely Wingate, Koa mused, had called the chief, or maybe the mayor, to bitch about Koa's visit. Why, he wondered, would anyone care about a simple check on a former secretary? "That and an uncooperative executive," Koa said.

"Well," the chief began, "you stepped in it. Senator Chao, he's on the X-CO board, and his aide Kāwika Keahi called me to say the senator is hopping mad about the police harassing his company."

Koa had met Senator Chao only a few times but knew Kāwika Keahi like a brother. Both had grown up in Laupāhoehoe on the Big Island's Hāmākua coast, gone to the same elementary school, and later attended some of the same classes at the Kamehameha School for Hawaiians. Like many Hawaiian children, Keahi never knew his father, but his mother and Koa's mother had been best friends. She'd more or less adopted Keahi. Koa had gone to UH Mānoa on Oʻahu, while Keahi had gone to a backwater college. While Koa went into the military, Keahi had started as an unpaid intern and worked his way up through the ranks to become one of Senator Chao's principal aides. Chao had been in the US Senate for years, and as his senior aide, Keahi had connections with all of Hawaiʻi's leading officials and politicians. Just two months ago, Keahi's mother had passed away from cancer, and Koa, along with dozens of others, had attended her funeral, which had closed down Laupāhoehoe for three days.

The chief's statement surprised Koa. Why would Hawaiʻi's senior US Senator complain about his efforts to obtain a former secretary's personnel file? Not even his position on the X-CO board explained his involvement in such a mundane matter. Wingate must have complained to the senator or his aide, but why would Wingate care so much?

He took a deep breath and looked the chief in the eye. "Tiger Baldwin disappeared from her apartment without saying goodbye to her neighbor, collecting her security deposit, or leaving a forwarding address at roughly the same time someone murdered our victim. She listed her employer as X-CO, so I went to check. Wingate told me she gave notice about a month ago and then quit at just about the same time she left her apartment. That made Baldwin's notice significant evidence of her intentions. I didn't understand Wingate's objection and did what we frequently do with uncooperative witnesses. In the end, Wingate gave me the file, and I verified the content of her notice. It wasn't a big deal."

The stiffness drained from Lannua's posture, and he relaxed. "So, you're done with X-CO?"

"Looks that way," Koa said to satisfy his boss while preserving his ability to pursue the issue if necessary.

"Okay. I'll let the senator's aide know," the chief responded, turning back to the paperwork on his desk.

Koa left the chief's office more puzzled than when he arrived. X-CO's CEO had complained to Senator Chao or his aide, who'd protested to the mayor or the chief. Over a former secretary. It made no sense, and, like all attempts to influence his investigations, it annoyed Koa and made him suspicious. Despite what he'd said to the chief, he might have more questions for X-CO.

CHAPTER SIX

KOA SAT AT his desk engrossed in the graveyard autopsy report and forensics materials. Interrupted by a knock on his door, he looked up to see Makanui and his childhood friend Kāwika Keahi in the doorway with a young man behind them. "This fellow—" Makanui pointed to Keahi with a big grin—"claims to know you."

Koa jumped up from his desk to embrace Keahi. "*Aloha*, brah. What brings you to my door?"

"*Aloha*," Keahi returned the greeting. "I'm here to introduce a friend." He stepped aside and gestured the young man forward. "This is Bobby Hazzard. His grandfather ran one of the old sugar mills up on the Hāmākua coast. He's on the island researching his family history."

At the sight of the young man, Koa felt a shock as he'd only experienced in combat. His heart rate spiked, and for an instant, he wondered if he was having a heart attack. Dressed like a Ralph Lauren hiking ad, Bobby was a preppy reincarnation of his grandfather Anthony Hazzard—the man Koa had killed. Same tall, broad-shouldered, six-foot frame. Same big elongated face with widely spaced eyes and heavy eyebrows. Same unruly shock of jet-black hair. Same thick neck and beefy hands. Bobby wasn't yet as heavy as the old mill manager, but he'd get there in a few years. Koa couldn't help thinking that Anthony Hazzard's ghost had come back to haunt him.

Koa's mind flashed back to the day they pulled him out of class to tell him his father had died in an accident at the Hāmākua sugar mill. Only later did he find out that his father, caught between the giant rollers of a cane-crushing machine, had been crushed to death. Doubting that his dad—fully aware of the dangers posed by ill-maintained equipment in decaying mills—could have been so careless, Koa sought out his father's coworkers. From them, he heard that the gruesome incident had followed an acrimonious dispute with Anthony Hazzard, the mill manager. The deeper Koa dug back then, the more he became convinced that Hazzard had somehow orchestrated his father's murder.

Already blaming Hazzard for a long history of abuse his father had suffered at the mill, the near-certain knowledge that Hazzard caused his father's death had driven Koa beyond rational thought. His growing rage triggered the need for revenge. He used every free hour to spy on Hazzard, watching his movements and learning his routines. After a month of surveillance, he'd followed Hazzard to the man's remote hunting cabin in the Kohala Mountains and staked out the place, waiting for the right moment to strike. Daylight faded to twilight and then darkness. Koa waited until Hazzard had drunk himself into a near stupor. The big man had just returned to the cabin from the outhouse when Koa jumped him, securing him in a chokehold. Holding Hazzard in a headlock, Koa tightened his grip, nearly choking the man to death.

Some deep-seated moral instinct made Koa release Hazzard before the man died, only to have the mill manager shoot up to confront Koa. Bleary-eyed from alcohol, Hazzard still fought like a demon, and Koa took several blows before realizing he was outmatched and in mortal danger. Fighting for his life, he scanned his surroundings for a weapon and grabbed a fire iron from the stand beside the cabin's fireplace. Charging at Koa like a wounded bull, Hazzard swung his massive arms and balled fists. Koa raised the iron poker to defend himself, but Hazzard knocked him to his knees and was about to finish him off when Koa swung the poker. The metal shaft connected with Hazzard's head with a resounding thud, and the big man collapsed.

Stunned at his violence, Koa tried to revive the man. Lacking experience with CPR, he pushed and pulled at Hazzard's arms and legs, screamed in the man's ear, and threw water on his face, all to no avail. It took Koa some time to realize the poker had done its deadly work, and he'd killed the sugar baron.

Terrified that Hazzard's fellow sugar men would kill him or send him to prison for life, Koa became paralyzed with fear. He considered running away, giving himself up to the police, or burning the cabin to the ground. After sitting for hours, he came up with the idea of faking Hazzard's suicide. It might seem strange for the wealthy mill manager to take his own life, but Hawaiian sugar had fallen on hard times, mills were closing all around the island, and Koa had heard of at least one overseer who'd already taken his own life.

He'd arranged the suicide scene to account for the fatal head wound. After fashioning a noose and hanging the body from a rafter, he'd sawed through the rope and let Hazzard's body fall to the floor. He'd then placed the poker beneath the man's head, giving the appearance that Hazzard had fallen onto the fire iron. Finally, he'd left the cabin door open, knowing that wild pigs and other predators would ravage the place, confounding any investigation. Given the remoteness of the cabin, he'd also figured it would be days, or maybe even weeks, before anyone found the body.

For some time after Hazzard's death, Koa had been sure the police would come for him. Suffering from PTSD-like symptoms, he'd seen Hazzard's face in every man passing on the streets, in the clouds, and his dreams. He knew some in the sugar mill fraternity doubted that Hazzard had taken his own life, and Koa had worried they'd talk to the police. He remembered the raw fear he'd felt so long ago as if it had happened yesterday. It took years, but his initial panic had slowly dissipated, and he had come to believe his suicide ruse had succeeded. He'd felt safe.

Seeing Bobby Hazzard, his fear had come roaring back like a spike through his heart. Koa realized that both Keahi and Makanui were waiting for his response. Get a grip, he told himself. With enormous effort, Koa fought to appear dispassionate and maintain a neutral tone of voice. Stepping forward, he shook Bobby's hand. "*Aloha*. Nice to meet you, Mr. Hazzard. Welcome to the Big Island."

"Thank you, sir," the ghostly reincarnation of his nemesis responded with a smile.

Wondering why Keahi and Makanui had brought this stranger to his office, Koa asked, "What can we do for you?"

"Bobby's a friend of Senator Chao," Keahi announced. "He's here on the island learning about his heritage and checking up on the death of his grandfather some thirty years ago. The senator asked me to introduce him to you and hopes you can help him with his inquiries."

More bad news. The senior US Senator from Hawai'i and Chairman of the Senate Defense Appropriations Subcommittee, Howard Chao was, next to the governor, the most powerful politician in the state. His requests would motivate the chief to walk on hot lava in the service of Bobby Hazzard. No way Koa would be able to give the preppy kid short shrift.

Still putting his best face forward, Koa asked again, "What can we do for you?"

"I'm trying to learn everything I can about my grandfather, but I'm especially interested in his death here on the island in 1989. The police called it a suicide, and I thought I might be able to get access to their reports."

Koa focused on the words "called it a suicide" and wondered what Bobby Hazzard knew of the circumstances surrounding his grandfather's death. His rational mind told him that after thirty-plus years, there was no way that Bobby Hazzard could have suspicions, but the kid's words implied otherwise.

"I told Mr. Hazzard," Makanui explained, "that departmental policy generally prohibits the release of police reports to third parties for a lot of reasons, including possible compromise or embarrassment of witnesses."

"I understand that sensitivity," Bobby responded, "but my grandfather died over thirty years ago, and I doubt there were witnesses to his death, so I thought the department might make an exception."

Koa steeled himself. He needed to buy time to think and figure out how to counter the existential threat that stood before him after lying dormant for thirty years. He couldn't let on that he had the least concern about Bobby's request. He had to give the appearance of an uninvolved cop. Makanui had already pointed the way by citing departmental policy. "That it was suicide doesn't mean the police didn't talk to witnesses about your grandfather's activities or his state of mind," Koa explained.

Still, with Senator Chao and his aide in the picture, Koa needed to appear reasonable, even helpful. More to the point, he needed to know whether Bobby seriously doubted his grandfather's suicide, and if so, the basis for his doubts. If Bobby had evidence of anything other than suicide, Koa needed to understand its nature and probity. His mind raced for the best strategy. He couldn't just say no, and he didn't want to agree. He decided on mild curiosity. "You've come a long way. What do you hope to find?"

"I'm writing a family history, and I've done a lot of research on my grandfather in the family archives and with his relatives and mainland friends. He was a legend in our family. Separated from my grandmother, he became the adventurer who traveled to San Francisco, boarded a ship, and went off to paradise where he made a fortune. He sent money home and wrote elegant letters about his experiences on the sugar plantations. About the operations of the mill and the nature of the workers. About the people he met and his cabin in the mountains. About fishing and hunting and picnics at the beach under the palm trees. He was quite an artist and sent drawings of the cane cutters in the fields and the narrow-gauge sugar trains that carried the product to Hilo.

"When I was growing up, my father regaled us with stories about Grandpa. I imagined going to this magical place called Hawai'i and following in his footsteps. Grandpa was my hero. He bought my grandmother her place on Fifth Avenue, my parents' place, and set up trusts for my sister and me. I owe my legal education to him. We revered him. I didn't find out about his suicide until I was older, and it has always puzzled me. I'd like to understand better what happened."

Koa experienced a sinking feeling. It had never occurred to him that Hazzard had written letters that might someday surface. He had no idea the man had been an artist. With a foreboding sense, he wondered what Hazzard might have said about his state of mind or if he had ever mentioned Koa's father. Could there be anything in Hazzard's letters that might lead to a reopening of the investigation into Hazzard's death? It seemed unlikely, especially given the coroner's suicide ruling, but who knew? Maybe those letters would trigger the ultimate penalty he'd expected but escaped for all these years.

Determined to buy time, Koa said, "Let's take this one step at a time. Give us a couple of days to see if this thirty-year-old police file still exists. If we find it, then we can address the question of access. Does that work for you?"

"That would be great," Bobby responded.

"*Mahalo*, brah," Keahi added as he and Bobby turned to leave.

*   *   *

Koa waited until late at night after the records clerks had departed before visiting the police department archives. He had a key, so access presented no problem. Recent cases consisted mostly of computer files and were available online, but old, closed cases resided in cardboard containers or banker's boxes. He knew exactly where to look and, donning gloves to prevent leaving fingerprints, took down the cardboard case containing the investigatory files on Hazzard's death. It wasn't the first time he'd retrieved it. Shortly after becoming a detective, he'd studied everything in the case, reviewing each investigative and forensic step. He'd learned a great deal about how not to conduct a murder investigation.

He recalled those lessons while carrying the box of materials to a nearby conference room. He opened the container and removed the papers. For a potential murder investigation, the files were unusually thin. That alone reflected a limited inquiry. He read through the documents, refreshing his memory of them, paying careful attention to every word.

According to the first sketchy report, hikers had come upon the isolated cabin, found the door open, the interior ransacked by wild animals, and a decomposed body ravaged by feral pigs, rodents, and insects. The desecration and smell within the cabin had been horrific. Kaohi, an experienced police officer, long since retired, had been the lead investigating officer. He'd discovered a noose around the deceased's neck and a piece of rope with a frayed end hanging from a ceiling beam. The police had also found an overturned table, broken dishes, several empty whiskey bottles, and various iron fire tools scattered across the floor, including one beneath the dead man's head.

The advanced state of decomposition and scavenging by wild animals had left Kaohi and his partner with little untainted evidence of what had happened. The remote location, accessible only after a day-long hike, also hampered the police effort. Still, the investigation had been exceptionally cursory. Property records verified that Anthony Hazzard owned the cabin, and dental records confirmed his identity. In addition to Hazzard's prints, crime scene technicians found a single fingerprint belonging to an unidentified person but could never identify the owner. Kaohi had found no evidence of an intruder, but nothing in the files suggested that he or his partner had searched for such evidence. Nor did the reports indicate that the police technicians tried to match the ends of the frayed rope or determine why it had parted. Kaohi had not attempted to reconstruct how Hazzard might have fallen on the fire tools, and neither he nor his partner found a suicide note.

The coroner's report cataloged various injuries to Hazzard's body, most of which resulted from ravaging by animals, without any particular focus on his head injury. Decomposition prevented any test for the presence of alcohol. Still, based on the empty liquor bottles and interviews with coworkers who described Hazzard as a heavy drinker, the coroner presumed he'd been drunk. The coroner ruled the death a suicide by hanging without blood work or other tests for asphyxiation and never considered that Hazzard might have been dead before being hanged.

Kaohi and his partner had interviewed Hazzard's friends and coworkers, none of whom had any inkling that the sugar baron was depressed or suicidal, and all of whom expressed shock at his death. Alcohol often fueled suicides, but while colleagues described Hazzard as a heavy drinker, they universally remembered him as ebullient when drinking and unlikely to take his own life when under the influence.

Kaohi also discovered that Hazzard had purchased airline tickets for a long-planned vacation back to the mainland. According to his coworkers, Hazzard had looked forward to seeing his aging mother, adult son, and grandchildren. Kaohi had reasoned that people looking forward to family visits didn't usually kill themselves. And why, Kaohi asked, would a man contemplating hanging himself in the local forest buy expensive airline tickets for a trip to the mainland. The lack of a suicide note or any other logical explanation for suicide added to Kaohi's doubts. He had tried to keep the investigation open. Still, none of his superiors wanted an open unsolved case, and the coroner's report, cursory as it was, gave them ample justification to close the case.

Years ago, when Koa had first reviewed the file, he had feared that the unidentified fingerprint was his. He'd thought about destroying the fingerprint data, but it was listed in the index and mentioned in a print examiner's report, making it difficult to tamper with the files without detection.

He'd briefly entertained the notion of taking the fingerprint to an examiner, but as a police officer, his prints were in the system, and he wasn't about to incriminate himself. Instead, he began to study fingerprint comparison. He never became an expert, but he learned enough to conclude to his surprise and relief that the unidentified print found in Hazzard's cabin was not his. Someone else had been in the cabin, most likely before Hazzard's death. Maybe a long time before.

After reviewing the file yet again to be sure he hadn't missed anything, he considered the risk of letting Hazzard's grandson review the materials. Undeniably, the file revealed that the police and the coroner had done a shoddy job. That alone might encourage Bobby Hazzard to investigate further, but nothing in the records pointed to Koa.

Bobby Hazzard might, Koa supposed, learn that Koa's father had died in a sugar mill accident, but that was a matter of public record. The two deaths had been more than a month apart, and nothing appeared to connect them, let alone tie Koa to Hazzard's death.

Kaohi's name was the one thing that bothered Koa about turning over the file. Although long retired, the old cop was still around. Koa had met him at a party for retired cops. He'd taken care of himself and was in reasonably good mental and physical shape. If interrogated, he might remember something. In the end, Koa decided that the Kaohi risk was minuscule—certainly far less than the risk of secreting the file and starting a brouhaha over a records retention screwup with Senator Chao and his aide making inquiries.

Koa carefully reassembled the papers, replaced them in their cardboard case, and returned the container to its proper place in the records room. He'd have Makanui retrieve the materials, check to make any redactions required by police department regulations, and prepare it for Hazzard's grandson to review.

When he crawled into bed that evening, the nightmares that he'd suffered in the immediate wake of Hazzard's death returned with a vengeance to disrupt his sleep. Images, each with a terrifying twist, reared from his subconscious. Hazzard swinging at the end of the rope, not dead, but pointing an accusing finger at Koa. Hazzard struggling with him as he tried to saw through the hangman's rope. Hazzard's shadow swaying across the wall as he swung from the noose. Hazzard chasing him through the woods when he left the cabin. Hazzard laughing mercilessly outside Koa's prison cell. He woke in a panic, panting, his heart racing, and his nightclothes drenched.

His thrashing awakened Nālani, his girlfriend, and the love of his life. His agitation concerned her, but he reassured her that he was fine. Just a rare nightmare about the brutal engagement he survived in Mogadishu, where his best buddy had died in his arms from a sniper's bullet meant for Koa.

They'd met three years earlier at a fundraiser, and he'd been captivated by her smile. They'd dated and fallen madly in love. In many ways, they were an odd match. She so graceful and lithe; he ever the athlete. She smart and intuitive; he more coldly rational. Yet, none of their differences mattered. He'd taken her hiking, camping, canoeing, and fishing. She'd taught him about endangered species of birds, rare orchids, and the mysteries of Hawai'i Volcanoes National Park, where she worked as a ranger. They both loved Hawai'i and together shared the most thrilling, vibrant, and satisfying intimacy he'd ever experienced.

He'd always worried that his secret past would somehow infect his relationship with the woman who had come to mean more to him than he could ever have imagined. Over time, as their bond had grown and deepened, his worries had receded. Now his fears came back like an encroaching firestorm. He might lose his job, his honor, and his *ipo*, the lover of his dreams. He thought about getting up, but he felt an overpowering desire to be near Nālani. Sensing his need, she held him close, and he eventually drifted back to sleep.

CHAPTER SEVEN

SLIGHT OF STATURE, some would say tiny, with prematurely gray hair, thirty-five-year-old Georgina Pau thought of herself as the best crime scene tech on the Big Island police force, maybe even the best in the state. She prided herself on capturing every snippet of evidence at a crime scene, and as a result, her meticulous work had helped nail dozens of criminals.

In her present assignment, she sought DNA either to confirm that Tiger Baldwin's body had been in the Volcano cemetery or to rule out that possibility. Standing in the main room of Baldwin's former apartment, she knew the task would test her resourcefulness. There wasn't a stick of furniture anywhere, not even a trash bin. Worse, professionals had cleaned the apartment. They'd vacuumed and mopped the floors, washed the walls, wiped light switches, scrubbed the countertops, disinfected the bathroom, and even sanitized the doorknobs and cabinet pulls. She'd been cursed by the most thorough cleaning crew she'd ever seen.

She wasn't going to find DNA in the usual places—trash, cigarette butts, drinking glasses, bottles, bedding, clothing, or dirty laundry. Labs could recover DNA from some fingerprints, but that didn't look promising given the apartment's pristine state. Her visual inspection, occasionally aided by a magnifying glass, revealed no stray hairs or other sources of DNA. She found nothing in the kitchen drawers, cabinets, or closets. Nor in the bathroom medicine chest.

Retrieving her toolbox from her crime scene van, she disassembled the drain trap under the sink, looking for any stray hairs. She found none, and the faint smell of Drano indicated the futility of further efforts. She borrowed a stepladder from the complex maintenance man and, standing on the uppermost step, unfastened the cover on the bathroom ceiling exhaust fan. No stray hairs. She scraped a sample of grimy dust off the fan blades but doubted there'd be DNA to extract. She checked the shower drain, but again, no luck.

She stood in the middle of the apartment, looking around for any other possibilities. Nothing came to mind. Discouraged and nearly ready to give up, she heard a click and felt a current of cold air. Unlike many homes in Hawai'i, this one had air-conditioning, and it had just clicked on. A quick search led her to the air return vent in an alcove ceiling. Removing the vent cover, she extracted a rectangular air filter. Voila! Caught in the fiberglass mesh, she found three blond hairs, more than enough, she knew, for DNA analysis.

Following Koa's instructions, she sent an official sample to the state lab in Honolulu and hand-carried another to Professor Diaz at the Hilo branch of UH.

*   *   *

Later that day, Georgina slipped silently into Koa's office. Only when he sensed some disturbance in the atmosphere did he look up.

"You're a quiet one," he said, wondering how long she'd been standing there.

"The calm before the storm," she said, placing a two-page report on his desk.

"What's this?" he asked.

"A DNA comparison from Professor Diaz. We've identified your cemetery vic."

"You found DNA in *that* apartment?" Koa asked incredulously.

"In an air-conditioning filter."

"Nice work."

After Georgina left, it took Koa a few moments to appreciate that her efforts had indeed unleashed a storm of confusing facts. With the DNA confirmation that the victim was indeed Tiger Baldwin, Koa tried to place the known events in sequence. He peeled five Post-its from the pad on his desk, labeling them—*Tiger gives notice, Tiger quits job, Tiger disappears from her apartment, Tiger moves furniture, Tiger murdered.* It was the only sequence that fit the facts they had, but under what circumstances would Tiger have given nearly a month's notice to her employer and yet disappeared from her apartment without a goodbye to a neighbor with whom she had been close? Who left an apartment without requesting the return of a sizable security deposit? And who authorized movers to clear out their apartment without supervision?

Koa thought of another possible anomaly. Baldwin's resignation letter referred to her return to the mainland. He wondered if she'd made an air reservation. Picking up his phone, he called Makanui and asked her to check with the airlines.

He turned to Baldwin's X-CO personnel file. It contained a printout of an internet job application, acknowledgment of a TOP SECRET security clearance, medical insurance forms, payroll records, and her resignation letter, dated the previous month, bearing Tiger Baldwin's signature. Koa didn't find a job description, evaluations, emergency contact data, or forwarding address, and without those typical items, the file seemed conspicuously thin.

Koa's secret criminal history made him suspicious, often to the point of paranoia. His deep-seated fear of being deceived, the way he'd fooled the cops after killing Hazzard, drove him to question supposed facts that others took for granted. He went back through the personnel file, noting that X-CO had direct deposited Baldwin's paychecks into the First Hawaiian Bank's main Hilo branch.

Koa called Sam Napaka, a First Hawaiian VP, whom Koa knew from previous cases. They exchanged pleasantries before Koa asked, "Would I need a subpoena to see a customer signature card?"

He got the answer he feared. "Afraid so. It's technically customer financial information covered by bank privacy rules."

Koa, as usual, had a work-around. "If I showed you a signature, could you tell me if it's genuine?"

Napaka hesitated. "Yeah, I guess I could do that."

"Be there in ten," Koa said, ending the call.

Napaka was waiting for him when he entered the bank's main Hilo branch. Thin and balding, the banker wore khaki pants and a short-sleeve white business shirt. Koa had never seen him in anything else and wondered how many of the ensembles he had in his closet. He gave Napaka Tiger Baldwin's resignation letter. The banker disappeared into the back office, only to emerge, shaking his head. "The signatures do resemble each other, but they're subtle differences. You'll need a handwriting expert to be sure."

"Thanks, Sam. Do me one more favor." He handed Napaka the payroll records. "Do the direct deposits to Baldwin's account match these records?"

The banker looked dubious.

"Somebody murdered her," Koa said.

Napaka returned to the back office and did not waffle when he reappeared. "There's no match. Not even close."

Koa pressed his luck. "The deposits were larger?"

The banker nodded affirmatively. Somebody at X-CO, Koa realized, had tampered with Tiger Baldwin's personnel file. But why? Back in his office, that question nagged at Koa as he stared at the Post-its he'd used to create a sequence of events.

Koa answered his phone to hear Piki's uber-excited voice. "Hey, boss, we just got a missing person's report . . . a female . . . could be our graveyard vic."

Having just gotten Georgina's DNA match confirming that Tiger Baldwin was the victim, Koa almost dismissed Piki's call. He thought better and instead asked, "Who?"

"A woman named Tiger Baldwin reported missing by a professor at UH Hilo's Computer Science and Engineering Department."

"Was she taking a college course?" Koa asked.

"No idea. You want me to call the registrar?" Piki asked.

After a moment's hesitation, Koa said, "No. Let's you and I go check it out. Maybe even find someone who knew her."

Piki, serving as duty-detective, was otherwise engaged, so Koa asked Makanui to accompany him. Koa welcomed another road trip with Makanui because his curiosity about her Philippine exploits was again getting the best of him. Along the way to UH Hilo, he asked, "So, after you nailed the two pirates on your sailboat, how'd you get them to talk?"

"You ever been Tased?"

"Yeah. Once in a police training course," Koa responded.

"I'm betting you weren't eager for a second round."

"You've got that right. It's not as bad as getting shot, but it's mighty damn close," Koa responded, remembering one of the most physically painful experiences of his life.

"Anders, my partner, spoke Filipino and some dialects, so he did most of the interrogation. We separated the two terrorists so that we could check their stories against each other. One of them started talking after two Taser shots. Told us everything we wanted to know."

"And the other guy?" Koa asked.

"He was a slow learner."

"How slow?"

"Five times, we Tased him."

"And he survived?"

"Yeah. We had to clean him up, but he survived."

"Doesn't Amnesty International have something to say about Tasers and torture?"

"Hell of a lot safer than waterboarding."

"You and your friend had some guts to pull that off."

"Like a said, I'd do it again. Those animals got off easy after they starved my parents, day after day, for seven long months."

From Kāwili Street, they turned into the main UH Hilo campus and headed for the registrar's office. Inside, they met a young Hawaiian receptionist in shorts and sandals, wearing a black tee-shirt imprinted with the words "Education Is Important But Race Cars Are Importanter."

Makanui scowled at the tee-shirt. "Is that what the taxpayers subsidize you to learn?"

"It's a joke," the kid responded defensively.

Koa identified himself and asked if Tiger Baldwin was a student. Accessing the school's registration database, the kid responded, "There's no student by that name."

Puzzled, Koa asked, "Could she be an employee or faculty?"

After a second search, the kid said, "Okay, okay. I got her. She's an adjunct prof in the Computer Science and Engineering Department."

Koa exchanged looks with Makanui. Their "secretary" was a college professor. "Where's that department located?" Koa asked.

The kid pulled out a campus map and marked the way with a green felt-tipped pen. When they left the registrar's office, the sky had darkened, and Hilo's rain gods poured giant droplets on the town. The two officers ducked into one of the college's covered walkways, making it to the Computer Science and Engineering Department damp, but not drenched. Further inquiries led them to Professor Adriana Alfonso, the department chair, a bronze-skinned woman with a full heart-shaped face, framed by a headband that covered part of her thick gray shock of hair. Koa guessed her to be in her sixties, but she seemed spry and attractive. Posters of the Barcelona cathedral and the university there adorned her office walls. It was, Koa thought, probably where she had her roots or maybe attended school.

Koa motioned to Makanui, indicating that she should take the lead.

She identified herself and said, "Professor Alfonso, we understand that someone in this department reported a missing woman named Tiger Baldwin. Do you know anything about that?"

"That's right. I asked the registrar to call the police when she didn't show up for her scheduled lecture this morning and didn't answer her phone," Alfonso responded.

"Her lecture?" Makanui prompted.

"Yes. She is one of our guest lecturers. An expert in the architecture of artificial intelligence software. She's a brilliant educator and was supposed to lead a graduate seminar this morning."

Strange, Koa thought. His conversation with the banker Napaka had made him doubt the "secretary" line X-CO had fed him, and now it seemed that Baldwin had highly specialized tech skills.

"When did you last talk to her?" Makanui asked.

Alfonso turned to her computer for a moment before responding, "Monday, June 11. That's when we agreed on this morning's class."

"She talk about her work outside teaching?" Makanui asked.

"No. She never talked about her job."

"What did you talk about?"

Alfonso thought for a moment. "We talked about her project. She was running an experimental AI climate simulation on several university computers networked together. Cutting-edge stuff. Her grad students were excited about it."

"Her students?" Makanui asked. "Aren't they off for the summer?"

"Oh, no. I persuaded her to lead four seminars over the summer, two in June and two in July."

"So, she was planning on teaching later in July?"

"Yes. Of course."

"And she said nothing about returning to the mainland?" Makanui asked.

"No."

What the hell, Koa wondered, was going on. Why would Baldwin tell her employer she was resigning and returning to the mainland when she was committed to teaching summer classes at UH Hilo?

The answer seemed apparent—she wasn't a secretary, she'd never planned to return to the mainland, and she'd probably never written a resignation letter. X-CO's executives were covering up her death. The question was, why?

CHAPTER EIGHT

SUBDUED AND EXHAUSTED from another rough night, Koa downed two cups of strong black coffee, hugged Nālani, and headed for police headquarters. On the way, he contemplated how best to deal with Bobby Hazzard. In the ordinary course, he would ask Makanui to meet with the young man, let him review the file, and send him off in whatever direction he might choose. Unfortunately, Koa didn't know what Bobby Hazzard knew, could not predict his actions, and didn't want surprises. He needed to ferret out any evidence Bobby Hazzard had and determine what he'd learned while researching his grandfather's death.

Alternatively, Koa himself could meet with Bobby Hazzard, let him review the file, offer to help, and stay in touch. That might make Koa seem too interested, but Senator Chao's involvement gave Koa cover. Given the interest of the senator and his aide, the chief would expect Koa to be attentive to Bobby's needs. By letting him review, but not copy, the file, Koa might spur Bobby to ask questions that could shed light on his thinking. Koa decided to take that tack with a twist that might yield even more insight into Bobby Hazzard's thinking.

Koa met with Bobby later that morning in Koa's office. Once again, the kid dressed like the quintessential preppy, but this time

Tommy Bahama style in an *aloha* shirt. Koa had lots of experience with the islands' *aloha* ways and made polite inquiries about Bobby's background. "That's a nice letter of introduction you have from Senator Chao. How do you know the senator?"

"I worked as an unpaid summer intern in his DC office after my second year at Harvard law. It was only three weeks, but I got to be buddies with Kāwika Keahi, one of his senior aides. It was an awesome experience."

His inquiry, Koa thought, had paid off, but not in a positive way. He now knew he was dealing with a highly trained and undoubtedly smart young lawyer. "Must be a lot of competition for a position like that," Koa said.

Bobby grinned. "There is, but the senator and my father have been asshole buddies since they were together in B-school, and Dad supports the senator's campaigns."

More bad news, Koa thought. The kid's family had money. "You're in a law office?" Koa asked.

"Yeah, Wilkie, Wilkie & Jones. We're a small, but prestigious, New York firm doing mostly criminal work, but we're pretty well connected and get some big cases."

Christ, this kid must have experience in criminal cases. Could it get any worse? Koa wondered. "How long are you staying in the islands?"

"A couple of weeks."

At least, Koa thought, there was an end in sight—if he survived that long. Deciding he'd pushed the pleasantries far enough, he picked up the file from his desktop. "As you know," he began, "we don't usually release police files, but Detective Makanui has determined that there are no privacy or investigatory concerns. As you suggested, there were no witnesses to your grandfather's death. All of the people who provided the police with background on your grandfather have since passed away. The coroner concluded that your grandfather committed suicide, and the police closed the case more than thirty years ago. Given those factors, we are prepared to make an exception and let you review the file here at police headquarters, but not make a copy."

"I appreciate your help," Bobby responded enthusiastically.

Koa stood up. "Let me get you set up with a place where you can go through this stuff." They walked down a flight of stairs. "I'm afraid," Koa informed the young man, "that our conference rooms are all reserved or under renovation. I hope you don't mind if I put you in an interrogation room."

"No. Not at all," Hazzard responded.

After showing Anthony Hazzard's grandson into an interrogation room, giving him the file, and getting him a cup of coffee, Koa said, "Take as much time as you want with this. You can make notes, but no copies or verbatim quotes. Give me a call on my cell when you're finished." He handed over a card with his number and excused himself.

Slipping into the adjoining space and closing the door, Koa watched the young man through the interrogation room's one-way mirror for a couple of minutes before turning on the video recording system. He would, he thought, as he returned to his office, be able to study the kid's reactions to the file. He might not learn anything, but you never knew.

An hour and a half after Koa left Bobby Hazzard, the young man called. "I've finished with the file and have a few questions."

"I'll come down," Koa responded and headed downstairs for his third encounter with this unwelcome blast from his past. Before joining Hazzard, Koa turned off the recording system, ejected the CD, and pocketed it. He'd review it at the first opportunity.

When Koa entered the interrogation room, Bobby Hazzard was sitting at the table, staring off into space. The file lay closed on the table beside a small iPad Bobby had presumably used to scribble notes. Koa sat opposite the young man, who, after a moment, awoke from his reverie.

"It's pretty disappointing," Bobby said with a scowl.

"In what way?" Koa asked.

"You've read the file?"

"Yes," Koa acknowledged.

"Then, you must know. The police were incompetent," Bobby said with more than a touch of anger.

"In what way?" Koa asked.

"There's not the slightest hint of why," Bobby responded. "All the witnesses describe my grandfather as his regular self without a sign of depression. None of his friends or employees knew why Granddad, looking forward to visiting his family on the mainland, would have hanged himself. Nobody saw the slightest sign that he was depressed, let alone suicidal. Hell, he'd just bought a first-class ticket to fly back to New York."

Koa fixed on the words "first class." They reflected a fact that was not in the old police file. "You must have sources that were not available to the police back then."

"Not available," Hazzard said in a bitter tone, "because the police couldn't be bothered to come to New York to interview my father. He would have told the police that my grandfather traveled back to New York every year, bringing presents for his mother and spending time with my family. Grandpa was a patron of the Mount Sinai Children's Hospital and the Met. He put my father through university and business school and set up trusts for my sister and me.

"I was too young to have a clear memory of Granddad, but he was a legendary figure in my life growing up. My father and sister told great stories about Granddad's exploits at the Lincoln Center, Coney Island, Mohonk, and his place in Bar Harbor, Maine. And lots of other good times. Less than a month before he died, he'd booked a suite at the Carlyle Hotel in New York and purchased orchestra tickets to take my older sister to see Andrew Lloyd Webber's *Cats* at the Neil Simon Theater. Does that sound to you like a man contemplating suicide?"

Koa concealed his roiling emotions. Hazzard had beaten, cheated, and ultimately killed Koa's father. The man had forced his field hands to work under the murderous midday sun without water or breaks, docking their pay for the slightest infractions. Many of them collapsed from heatstroke, and some had never recovered. His refinery workers toiled in hazardous conditions around aging and ill-maintained equipment. Accidents, even fatal ones, were commonplace, and there was never any compensation. Koa had known Hazzard only as a ruthless and cruel sugar baron who'd tormented his workers and ultimately ordered Koa's father killed.

He'd never envisioned the man as having a son or grandchildren, let alone as a grandfatherly figure taking his grandchildren on family vacations or to a Broadway play. The thought triggered a wave of guilt before he forced this new picture from his mind. "No, those facts don't suggest suicide, but in my experience, most people have hidden demons which drive them to do strange things."

"You believe my grandfather committed suicide?" Hazzard asked.

Koa had been waiting for the question because it offered an opportunity to see if Hazzard's grandson had an alternative explanation for his grandfather's death. "That was long before my time as a police officer, so I don't have any special insight," Koa answered disingenuously. "What I do see is a coroner's report concluding that your grandfather committed suicide and a crime scene that doesn't suggest an alternative."

"The coroner's report is a joke," the young lawyer responded derisively.

Koa played dumb. "Why do you say that?"

"C'mon, Detective, if you read the report, you know there were no toxicology tests. Hell, the coroner didn't even check to see if my grandfather died of asphyxiation. Best forensic practices require such tests in virtually all hanging cases."

So, young Hazzard had read the relevant forensic literature or maybe talked to an expert. He was more sophisticated and better prepared than Koa would have guessed. Still, Koa had good rebuttal points. "Have you considered the lapse of a week or more after death and before hikers discovered the body? I think those same forensic texts say that most toxicology results have little value unless the specimens are collected shortly after death."

"I get it. You're just defending your department," Hazzard said with disgust.

Koa let a bit of impatience creep into his response. "I'm not defending anyone. I'm simply trying to help you understand what happened to your grandfather. I'll butt out if you'd prefer."

Silence enveloped the interrogation room for several moments before Hazzard said, "I'm sorry. I shouldn't have said that. I just don't understand what happened to my grandfather, and I'm letting my frustrations show."

"No apology needed." Koa paused. "Still, you haven't addressed the alternative. What do *you* think happened to your grandfather?"

"I don't know," Hazzard said wearily. "I just can't believe he hanged himself."

Koa knew suicides, especially by hanging, were difficult for the surviving relatives. Survivors always wondered if they'd done something to provoke the act or failed to take steps to prevent it. They frequently felt betrayed and angry at the deceased for the pain and guilt he or she had inflicted. He saw some of the latter in Bobby Hazzard. Still, Koa held his tongue. Instead, he said, "When the police investigate a possible suicide, they always look for alternatives. There's nothing in that file—" he pointed to the cardboard box on the table—"to suggest an alternative to suicide. As hard as it might be to accept the recorded cause of death, you need an alternative to support your doubts."

"I get it," Bobby Hazzard replied without enthusiasm.

"Think about what you've read and call me if you have more thoughts or questions," Koa said.

"Okay," Bobby said, and then paused as if just remembering something. "Do you think I should see the cabin where my grandfather died?"

Koa took his time, visualizing the old place. Seeing the remote cabin, likely now dilapidated, might make Bobby more willing to accept his grandfather's suicide. Getting there and back would be a two-day trek. That would get Bobby out of his hair for a while. "It's not a bad idea, but there might not be much to see after all these years."

CHAPTER NINE

THE ARTIFICIAL INTELLIGENCE Seminar was to be the single most important economic event of the year in Hilo. Zhou Li, the Chinese billionaire who headed X-CO and a raft of other businesses, had invited the world's leading AI scientists to a conference to be held at the University of Hawai'i performing arts center in Hilo. With his worldwide empire of defense, auto, battery, tunnel, and space companies, Zhou Li, the conference's keynote speaker, had attracted more than a hundred other CEOs and expert professionals from around the world.

Technology jobs represented a mere four percent of Hawai'i's economy, and the state ranked 44th nationwide in that sector. The state's tech jobs were mostly in the field of astronomy and associated with the thirteen telescopes atop Mauna Kea, the solar observatory on Mauna Loa, and the 'Imiloa Astronomy Center at UH Hilo. Hawai'i's governor and Hilo's mayor hoped to use the Artificial Intelligence Seminar to lure additional high-tech investment to the Big Island to diversify its heavy reliance on astronomy as the backbone of its technology industry.

Like many of Hawai'i's mainstream economic initiatives, this effort faced local political opposition and related security challenges. Protests by Hawai'i's native cultural, religious, and sovereignty

groups had already scuttled an inter-island ferry project. More recently, native protesters had stopped construction of the billion-
dollar Thirty Meter Telescope on the summit of Mauna Kea through
litigation and by blocking access to the proposed site. Although ancient Hawaiians had quarried and fashioned stone tools on a commercial scale atop Mauna Kea, the TMT's activist opponents
ignored that industrial legacy, preferring to exaggerate the mountain's religious significance in framing their protests. Even after the
Hawai'i Supreme Court finally cleared the TMT, tenacious protestors had prevailed, making it unlikely the groundbreaking optical
telescope would ever exist atop Mauna Kea.

Seeking a return to traditional environmental practices, Hawai'i's
native groups generally opposed most technical projects and even
sought closure of US military facilities in the islands. They had long
fought for the restoration of Kaho'olawe Island, where the Navy had
practiced bombing since WWII. Over the years, they engaged in
many disputes with the Army over the Pōhakuloa Training Area on
the Big Island. Given this history, Koa was not surprised that pickets
appeared regularly at the X-CO facility, and native leaders planned
to protest the AI Seminar.

Against this backdrop, Hawai'i Island Mayor Tenaka, an impressive man with a bodybuilder's physique who wielded authority like
the Army lieutenant colonel he'd once been, called a meeting of
seminar planners to discuss security arrangements for the AI event.
As usual, Ben Inaba, Tenaka's ever-present aide, took his place seated
to the right of the mayor in Tenaka's city hall conference room. The
state's senior US Senator Chao; Kāwika Keahi, the senator's principal aide; Lucia Bianche, the American representative of Zhou Li;
and X-CO CEO R. Samford Wingate rounded out the group.

Mayor Tenaka had invited Koa because of his personal and family
relationship with Makaiao. The mayor kept a close eye on the native

community and undoubtedly knew that native activists had been protesting outside X-CO. One of the mayor's sources might even have reported seeing Makaiao chatting with Koa during that protest. The county chief executive had witnessed Koa work with Makaiao to defuse other protests, including a recent demonstration over a native teenager's mishandled arrest. If things started to get out of hand at the AI Seminar, Tenaka would expect Koa to use his influence with the activist to restore calm.

Koa knew everyone at the table except Bianche. Well dressed in a neatly tailored gray linen pants suit, punctuated with a classic gold circle pin, the thirty-five-year-old brunette looked like a senior corporate executive. When they shook hands, Koa felt her firm, but not crushing, grip. She welcomed him with an *aloha* in a soft, friendly voice. "Nice to meet you, Detective Kāne. Senator Chao speaks highly of you."

"That's nice to know," Koa responded.

Before Tenaka could call the meeting to order, Wingate, who'd donned a suit coat over his white shirt and red power tie, launched into an impassioned speech. "The police need to lock up these damn protestors. Don't they realize that Hawai'i is part of America," Wingate caught his breath before continuing all too loudly. "They're intimidating my employees and disrupting our business."

Koa, who'd witnessed the peaceful demonstration outside X-CO's facilities, rolled his eyes. He'd seen no intimidation. Nor had he witnessed any disruption of X-CO's business. Like many *haoles*, Wingate had no understanding of Hawaiian history. He had no idea that after Kamehameha, the first, consolidated most of the islands into the Kingdom of Hawai'i in 1795, he and his successors ruled the kingdom for almost a hundred years until 1893. During that century-long period, the United States and the other major nations had recognized Hawai'i's sovereign independence.

Nor did Wingate know that from the mid-1800s, Western
sugar, pineapple, and other businesses pressured the Hawaiian
monarchy to advance their commercial interests to the detriment
of the island's native population. In 1887, *haole* businessmen went
so far as to threaten to assassinate the king, forcing him to adopt
the so-called Bayonet Constitution, requiring government office-
holders and voters to own property, thereby disenfranchising most
natives. Finally, in 1893, the Committee of Safety, a group of
Western businessmen, with the backing of US Marines from the
USS *Boston* in Honolulu harbor, staged a *coup d'état* against the
reigning monarch, Queen Lili'uokalani. Five years later, the US
annexed the islands.

Wingate was likewise unaware that Westerners had outlawed the
Hawaiian language in government and schools from 1896 to 1978.
Ignorant of, if not indifferent to, the island's history, Wingate
couldn't appreciate that the US extralegal expropriation and historical domination of Hawai'i energized and gave voice to its cultural,
religious, and sovereignty activists. While the rest of the US cele-
brated the Fourth of July, many Hawaiians, who chafed under their
perceived lack of independence, preferred to honor King Kamehameha Day.

Wingate also lacked any appreciation of the economic plight of
native Hawaiians, whom the *haole* Westerners had historically
pushed down the economic ladder. For decades, five mainland con-
glomerates had dominated the local economy. Sugar and pineapple
barons imported cheap foreign labor from China, Japan, Korea, the
Philippines, and elsewhere. They hired engineers from Portugal and
cowboys, called *paniolo*, from Mexico and Spain.

Oblivious to the reaction of his audience, Wingate plowed forward. "And we can't have protests around the university during the

seminar. We don't want protestors anywhere near the seminar. The police should haul them away and lock them up."

Koa had taken an instant disliking to Wingate during their first meeting at X-CO and now found the man's arrogant, lawless attitude distasteful. It also, he knew, offended the mayor, who worked hard to maintain a cordial, if often difficult, relationship with the island's activists. Facial expressions told Koa that Wingate's outburst also distressed Senator Chao and his aide Keahi. Native Hawaiians and those sympathetic to their cause represented a sizable portion of the senator's constituency. Indeed, Keahi spent a lot of time working with the native community.

The mayor nodded at Koa, who got the message. It fell to him to explain the law to Wingate. "There's not much we can do so long as the protests are peaceful," Koa explained. "And with the School of Hawaiian Studies here at UH Hilo, the protests are likely to be even larger."

"That's unacceptable!" Wingate raised his voice further. "Be creative. Arrest them for trespassing or disturbing the peace or something. It doesn't matter what. Lock 'em up for a few days."

"I'm sure you are aware, Mr. Wingate, that people have a right to assemble for peaceful protests," Koa said, spacing his words for emphasis, "and we're not going to violate their rights."

"What the hell do they want?" Wingate asked. "We're working with the Army, protecting their national security."

"What they want," Koa explained patiently, "is jobs, economic opportunity, a voice in government, and some respect. X-CO would do well to expand its efforts to employ local people and engage in community outreach."

"That's PC bullshit," Wingate said, turning to face Senator Chao. "Senator, perhaps you can talk some sense into these people."

For once, the senator had nothing to say. He, too, deferred to Koa, who smiled indulgently. "I doubt the senator wants to be on TV, confronting an important group of constituents."

"Then I'll talk to the military. We'll get the MPs down here," Wingate threatened.

Finally, Koa's friend Keahi came to Koa's aid. "The MPs have no jurisdiction in Hilo."

"Then maybe we should cancel the seminar," Wingate retorted.

"Calm down, Wingate," Lucia Bianche said in a soft, but not so friendly, voice.

Wingate clammed up like she'd slapped him across the face, and Koa instantly understood where the power lay within this X-CO contingent. Lucia Bianche might speak softly, but in the words of Teddy Roosevelt, Koa's second favorite president, she carried a big stick.

Bianche turned to Koa, her voice now cordial. "What do you suggest, Detective?"

"Several things," he began. "First, you need to cordon off an area for the protestors. Provide water and maybe even some snacks or plate lunches. Have a company representative explain what's going on. Perhaps provide a televised feed of part of the seminar.

"Second, it's essential to listen to the protestors. Invite their leaders to meet with company representatives. Be responsive to some of their concerns. Try to establish a dialogue.

"Third, it would be good for X-CO to engage in some form of public outreach. The observatories provide free public lectures and send experts to local schools to teach science to local students. Something like that. It won't stop the protests, but it helps dial back their intensity and lessen community support for the radicals.

"Fourth, we can have a small police presence, but it's going to be your responsibility to control access to the seminar sessions themselves. How does that sound?"

Before Bianche could respond, Koa's buddy Kāwika Keahi said, "Detective Kāne makes good points. You and Mr. Wingate should take them seriously."

Wingate scowled, and his expression said it was all nonsense, but Bianche set the tone. "Makes sense to me. I'll talk to our public relations guys. We'll see what we can do."

CHAPTER TEN

WHILE KOA WAS attending the seminar security meeting, Makanui's computer pinged with an incoming alert. The DMV had just recorded the sale of Tiger Baldwin's car to Kimo's used car lot. Makanui grabbed her keys and went to check it out.

Makanui found Kimo in the repair shop of Kimo's Preowned Autos just off the Māmalahoa Highway south of the Hilo airport. A big, overweight Hawaiian with thick forearms, bulging hands, and an oddly high-pitched voice, he greeted her with, "The pol-leece like buy da kine used cars?"

"Not today, I'm afraid," Makanui responded, "but I am here about a vehicle. I want to know about a green Honda CRV you bought recently."

Kimo reacted with alarm. "Somethin' wrog wit' da car?"

"Might be. Tell me about the woman who sold it."

With confusion in his voice, Kimo asked, "You talkin' 'bout da green 2018 Honda CRV I bought Monday of last week?"

"That's the car."

Makanui frowned as she realized that last Monday was almost certainly after Baldwin's death. She wanted to be sure she had it right and repeated, "Monday of last week. Are you sure?"

"Yeah, dat's the day, but I never saw no woman," Kimo insisted. "Bought it from a dude in a hurry to unload it. Got it for a sweet price."

"This dude have a name?" Makanui asked.

"Sure. Tiger something. The last name's on the bill of sale."

Makanui knew she was on to something. Vehicle title documents contained the owner's name and address, but no gender or other description of the owner. So, an unknown man could easily have impersonated Tiger Baldwin and peddled her car after her death.

"You pay cash?" Makanui asked.

"Dude wanted cash, but, hell, I don't keep that kinda bread lying around. Did two grand in cash and the rest by check."

"Made out to Tiger Baldwin?" Makanui asked.

"Yeah, man. Baldwin. That's what da title says. That's what da check says."

"You already cleaned the car for resale?" Makanui asked.

"Not yet."

"Sorry, Kimo," Makanui said, "but we're going to have to impound that car, and we need the paperwork."

"Shit, lady, I knew dat deal was too sweet to be true."

"It always is," Makanui said. "Now, what exactly did this dude look like?"

"I kin do bettah dan dat. Should have his mug on video."

In Kimo's cramped office at the back of the salesroom, Makanui watched while Kimo slowly rewound a security tape until he found an image of the man who'd sold Tiger Baldwin's car. He was clean-shaven with an athletic build, close-cropped hair, and an erect posture in his late thirties.

"We're going to need that tape, the paperwork for the sale of the car, and the keys. Leave it locked. I'll make arrangements for the folks from the police garage to come get it," Makanui explained to the unhappy used car salesman.

"I'm gonna get da car back, yeah? I mean, I paid good money for it," Kimo asked.

"Honestly, I'm not sure. It depends. If it's stolen, you might be out of luck. Talk to the county attorney. He'll make the call."

"Stolen?" Kimo protested. "How was I supposed to know dat?"

"You said the deal was too sweet to be true, didn't you?"

"Shit!" Kimo banged his fist on a desk as Makanui left.

Koa was back in the office when Makanui arrived. She gave him a reprise of her meeting with Kimo, and together they reviewed the video of the seller.

"He carries himself like a soldier," Makanui commented.

"Or an employee of a military contractor," Koa added.

* * *

Later that afternoon, Koa closed his office door and watched the video he'd made of Bobby Hazzard in the interrogation room reviewing the old police file. Koa didn't expect much but was curious to see how the young man reacted.

Bobby sat facing the camera with the file on the table in front of him. Although the police department hadn't installed top-of-the-line video equipment, the resolution was sharp enough for Koa to read the label on the file. Bobby first inventoried the papers, separating them into neat piles—the initial police report, the crime scene and morgue photos, the coroner's report, the witness interviews, additional detectives' notes, and the final document closing the case.

Bobby carefully reviewed each document until he got to the crime scene photos. He grimaced at the first one—a horrific crime scene shot of the interior of the cabin ravaged by wild animals—and quickly set it aside, disgusted by the gruesome image. He gave each succeeding photo only a cursory glance before putting it down and moving to the next. To Koa's surprise, he never spent more than a few seconds with any of the photos. His lack of attention seemed strange and spoke volumes to Koa.

Koa knew from experience that the best clues to any violent crime were buried in the scene. You needed to study the body's position and the surrounding circumstances, carefully examining every aspect, to understand what had happened. Koa insisted on visiting actual crime scenes to bring all his senses to bear and rarely relied solely on photographs. When attending the location wasn't an option, he poured over every pixel of photos from edge to edge and top to bottom. No detail was too small or insignificant. He knew that visual analysis was essential to reconstructing the movement of the deceased and the wrongdoer if there was one. In a possible suicide case, any alternative theory must, of necessity, find its roots in the crime scene.

Bobby, Koa realized, lacked both the experience and the stomach to analyze the gruesome pictures. Odd. As a lawyer with a criminal defense firm, Bobby should have expertise in examining evidence. Yet, the kid didn't pause to study the rope marks on Hazzard's neck nor the gash on the side of his head. He made no effort to distinguish between animal claw or bite marks and injuries that might have been inflicted by another human being. As he sped through the photos, he seemed unwilling or unable to look at his grandfather's crumpled body or consider its relationship to the surrounding objects like the fireplace tools.

In their discussion, the kid hadn't proposed an alternative theory. Now Koa guessed he would remain hopelessly behind the curve. In the absence of a credible indication of foul play, there would be scant basis to challenge the coroner's finding of suicide. The kid's quest was beginning to look like an exercise in futility, and Koa felt some semblance of relief. Maybe he would get through this nightmare after all.

When Bobby finished with the photographs, he turned to the other materials. The coroner's report noted the strangulation marks caused by the noose still around Hazzard's neck when hikers found the body, consistent with the determination of suicide. After reading that report, Bobby made notes on his iPad. Zooming in a touch, Koa saw that Bobby had also noted the names of the three main witnesses the police had interviewed. Since Koa knew they had subsequently died, their names were unlikely to yield any new insights into Anthony Hazzard's death.

Koa was disappointed, but not surprised, to see Bobby make a note of the investigating detective's name. Retired Detective Ronnie Kaohi had been the only person to raise any doubt about suicide. He would be Bobby's best, and perhaps only, source of additional information.

Koa wondered whether he should alert the old detective. After some thought, he decided against it because it might make him appear too interested in Bobby's inquiry. A savvy cop like Kaohi had a nose for anything odd, and Koa couldn't afford to raise suspicions. Besides, the chances were strong that Kaohi would reach out to Koa before talking to Bobby. Most police officers, even retired cops, were wary of strangers digging up old cases.

When Bobby got to the materials about the unidentified fingerprint, his reaction troubled Koa. The discovery that some unknown person had been in the cabin seemed to charge Bobby up, and he pounded the table before making more notes. If he could match the print to a person, that might enable Bobby to get the investigation reopened. The police would then have to determine if that person had been in a position to harm his grandfather.

Koa knew that the print wasn't his and thought it posed no immediate danger to him. Still, it was an unknown. Sure, the police had run it through the FBI fingerprint identification system, but that system had been far less sophisticated in 1989. The bureau had added millions of prints to the database in the past thirty years, and its print-matching algorithms had become faster and more accurate. Koa could only hope that the old fingerprint would remain a mystery. Yet, he couldn't discount the possibility that the bureau might find a match.

CHAPTER ELEVEN

THE DISCOVERY OF Baldwin's doctored personnel file and her car's odd sale created a dilemma for Koa. He had to find out what was going on at X-CO but knew he needed to coordinate with the chief, who'd already expressed displeasure with his visit to the defense contractor. Worse, X-CO was a political lava pit. Senator Chao, the governor, and other big shots sat on the board, and everyone was on edge about the upcoming AI seminar.

Before confronting the chief, Koa wanted to explore beneath the surface to learn as much as possible about X-CO. Experience had taught him that thorough preparation enabled him to outmaneuver, or at least neutralize, his boss. He knew from his recent chance meeting with Makaiao outside X-CO that its people had traveled to the Army's Pōhakuloa Training Area, the center of military activity on the Big Island. The training area, widely known as the PTA, was the largest US defense facility in the Pacific. It occupied 109,000 acres in the mile-high Humuu'la saddle area between Mauna Loa and Mauna Kea, the two 14,000-foot volcanoes that formed the island's backbone. Military units from all over the Pacific practiced the arts of warfare there. Tanks attacked mock targets, helicopters fired missiles at dummy vehicles, artillery batteries blasted supposed enemy strongholds, troops practiced on firing ranges, and combined arms teams held war games.

If a defense contractor on the Big Island had a relationship with the Army, Koa's friend Jerry Zeigler, commander of the military police detachment at Pōhakuloa, would know the score. Koa and Jerry had a long history, working together on criminal investigations and civilian relief efforts after earthquakes, tsunamis, and hurricanes. Both had grown up poor, and both were into sports, links that brought them together as friends as well as law enforcement colleagues.

Jerry, who'd grown up in South Dakota, had learned to skate about the same time he'd learned to walk. He'd been a high school hockey star and suffered so many injuries that his men called him "stick face." Having grown up in the middle of the Pacific, Koa wasn't into hockey. He favored traditional Hawaiian canoeing and treasured his role as the caller on a prize-winning, six-man outrigger racing team. Both expert marksmen, Zeigler and Koa competed against each other in island-based shooting competitions. Fierce rivals when trophies were on the line, they regularly practiced together.

Considering the chief's qualms about his X-CO visit and the secrecy surrounding the company, Koa guessed he'd get more information in a face-to-face meeting with Jerry. A scheduled target practice session the following day on one of the PTA's small arms ranges provided the perfect opportunity to get some background on X-CO.

Just after dawn, after kissing a sleeping Nālani on the forehead, Koa drove up the winding Saddle Road to the PTA. He and Jerry always met early to avoid the harsh midday sun and heat on the exposed mile-high lava plain. Tourists liked Hawai'i's coastal roads with vast ocean vistas, beach access, and occasional glimpses of waterfalls, but Koa found the Saddle Road more dramatic. Starting at sea level in rain-soaked Hilo, it rose through dense forests of ferns and ʻōhiʻa trees, which shrank in height with increasing elevation and decreasing precipitation until they became dwarfs or disappeared altogether. Passing through alternating bands of foggy mists and bright sunshine, Koa emerged into the saddle. At 5,600 feet in elevation, the road left the Mauna Loa lava flow from 1855 and crossed to the 1935 flow while skirting the ʻĀinahou sanctuary for nēnē, the unique and endangered Hawaiian goose.

Off to his right, Mauna Kea, wreathed in clouds, soared to 14,000 feet, topped by some of the world's most sophisticated telescopes. To his left lay Mauna Loa, nearly equal in height, but farther away and seemingly shorter because of its elongated triangular shape and gently sloping sides. A classic shield volcano. In between, lava's overlapping flows told the story of the Big Island's expansion over the millennia since it first arose from the sea. The Hawaiian in Koa thought of the richly toned brown and blackish terrain between the two volcanoes as a history book written by *Pele*, not unlike the fire goddess's recent destruction in the Puna district and her extension of the eastern side of the island.

Koa's girlfriend, Nālani, likened the ragged charcoal and rust-brown lava to seized chocolate. The metaphor always made him smile. Thinking of Nālani affected him like an elixir. They'd been together for nearly four years, sharing his Volcano village cottage. Trained stateside as a biologist, she treasured her position as a park service ranger. Bright, independent, and athletic, she accepted his long, frequently irregular hours. Yet, every moment they were together was a precious gift, a kind of magical escape from the tawdry side of being a police detective.

Passing the turnoff for the Mauna Kea access road on the right, Koa sped by Puʻu Huluhulu, a dramatic Mauna Kea volcanic cinder cone, on his left. A short distance ahead, he reached one of his favorite parts of the drive where the road skirted giant *puʻus*—Puʻu Nēnē, Puʻu Omaokoilī, and several smaller cinder cones—whose colors shifted with the changing weather and sunlight. In the distance, a giant red flag wafting in the wind warned Koa he'd entered the PTA and that military units were actively engaged in live-fire exercises. He drove another four and a half miles, past Mauna Kea State Park, to the PTA's main gate. A guard checked his credentials and waved him through.

He met Zeigler, dressed in desert fatigues, at the military police command post. Together, they took Zeigler's jeep over a gravel road cut into Mauna Loa lava flows, which pre-dated recorded history. Scattered *māmane, naio, ʻōhiʻa,* and *pūkiawe* shrubs abounded except where the Army had cleared land for training purposes.

"How's Nālani?" Zeigler asked. He'd met her on several occasions after the Park Service had assigned her to assist the Army's efforts to protect rare and endangered plants, including the *ʻĀnunu*, a kind of gourd, that once grew wild in selected areas of the PTA.

"She's great," Koa responded, "and sends her regards."

"You're a lucky man," Zeigler said with just a touch of envy in his tone.

"You got that right," Koa responded.

In the distance, tanks, firing their main guns, supported by helicopters launching rockets, blasted training targets in the PTA's impact area. The sharp crack of tank canons followed by the cacophony of exploding shells and rockets rolled across the high desert lava plain and echoed off the mountains.

"The troops are out early this morning," Koa remarked.

"Yeah," Jerry responded. "We've got two units in for training. It's the Army against the Marines. They were at it most of the night. Nobody got much sleep."

Koa rolled his eyes. "Already dreaming up excuses for losing today's match with your fancy gun?"

"Ouch." Jerry mimed a flinch. "You'd better put 'em all in the center ring, buddy."

They parked behind a small-arms range and carried their weapons to the firing line. As usual, Zeigler brought his $5,000 Ans 54.30 match-grade rifle with a 1918 aluminum stock. The magnificent competition firearm was one of the few things Koa envied. He'd purchased his Remington 40x CPM used from a gun dealer for less than a fifth of what his friend had laid out for his gem.

Zeigler walked fifty meters downrange to place the paper targets. Koa shot first, executing the ISSF 50-meter rifle event, firing forty rounds from a prone position. Jerry, using a spotting scope, called each shot while Koa chambered the next round. Despite his inferior rifle, Koa usually scored better but knew by his sixth shot that he hadn't achieved the mental focus required to outshoot his friend. His thoughts repeatedly drifted to Tiger Baldwin and X-CO, rather than the target. Closing his eyes, he cleared his mind, resettled his position, and concentrated, letting his vision narrow to his single objective. Breathe and squeeze. Finally, he began to score, putting round after round in the bull's-eye.

When his turn came, Jerry put nearly all his shots on target, and their scores were unusually close. "You're a bit off today," Jerry remarked as they cleaned up their brass. "You got something on your mind?"

"What, you're a psychic now?"

"Your head wasn't into the game, especially at first, so I know something's bothering you."

Koa turned to face the military policeman. "You ever heard of X-CO?"

Koa caught a momentary flash of surprise before Jerry responded with a question of his own. "What's your interest?"

Koa wanted to get a feel of the situation before sharing the more troubling facts and simply responded, "I'm investigating the murder of one of their employees."

Jerry appeared concerned. Most people would have taken Jerry's reaction as expected. Only a psychopath would relish hearing about a murder. Yet, Koa read something more in the officer's expression and knew he'd touched a sensitive topic. "Who?" Jerry asked.

"Woman named Tiger Baldwin."

Jerry said nothing for several seconds, but Koa caught the tiniest tightening in his expression. When Jerry spoke, Koa could tell he was choosing his words carefully. "X-CO is a defense contractor, working with the Army on a top-secret project. It's got a high-powered board, including Senator Chao, the governor, and a whole lot of other bigwigs."

It didn't escape Koa that Jerry had avoided responding to Tiger Baldwin's name. Jerry came across as evasive, but Koa was on a mission. Perseverance had helped him power his way to chief detective, and he wasn't about to slow up now. "Let me make this more complicated." He laid out the discovery of Tiger Baldwin's body and the search for her identity, ending up with her doctored X-CO personnel file.

"Jesus." Taken aback, Jerry was quiet and appeared to be digesting what he'd just heard. Koa sensed the Army officer struggling to respond. Finally, Jerry said, "Look, what you're telling me is troubling. I get it, but I can't say anything more."

Surprised by Jerry's response, Koa pressed, "You know something, but you can't tell me?"

"Yeah. I do, but I can't talk about it. It's complicated. Give me a day to check with some people. Maybe then I'll have something for you."

Jerry's language struck Koa as odd. The MP didn't say he needed to talk to his commander but to some ambiguous "people." That wasn't Jerry's usual direct style. It was weird. Frustrated, Koa said, "*Maybe* isn't going to help me solve Baldwin's murder."

"As I'm sure you've figured out, you're digging into some highly classified shit. I've got to get the okay before I tell you more."

Koa believed in maintaining the momentum of investigations and hated roadblocks. Annoyed by his inability to make sense of the mysteries surrounding Baldwin's death, Koa tried again. "We're talking about a nasty murder. The killer cut off her fingers to obscure her identity and buried her body in a remote graveyard, where wild pigs made a meal of her leg." Koa's vehemence reflected his frustration.

Jerry paused but remained unmoved. "Sorry. You'll just have to wait. And I can't promise anything."

Jerry knew something, something vital to the investigation. Every bone in Koa's body wanted to push for more information, but he knew it would do no good. Pressing his friend to violate his government secrecy obligations would only damage their friendship.

Something was terribly wrong, but Koa was in the dark.

CHAPTER TWELVE

KOA FOUND THE discrepancy between Baldwin's payroll records and her bank deposits, the hurried clearing of her apartment, and the sale of her car by an impersonator troubling. So close to her murder, the timing suggested a coordinated effort—a conspiracy—to conceal her death, her identity, and the killer's identity. And X-CO stood dead center of the mix.

Despite his instincts, Koa's hard evidence was thin. The payroll discrepancy could turn out to be a clerical error. He hadn't identified the people who'd moved Baldwin's furniture and had no way to tie them to X-CO. He had a surveillance video of the man who'd pretended to be Tiger Baldwin and sold her car using Baldwin's vehicle registration for identification but not the imposter's real name. Koa needed more evidence before talking to the county prosecutor or pursuing the matter with the chief.

Mulling over the possibilities, he thought about showing the imposter's picture around or getting Professor Diaz's colleague to run the man's image through facial recognition. Yet, questioning people with the picture might alert the wrong people to his inquiries, and facial recognition would take time. There might be a more straightforward way.

Koa had a hunch and decided to pursue it. With Makanui's help, he set up an observation post with rotating shifts of officers positioned on the roof of the building across the road from X-CO. A parapet around the top provided concealment while giving his officers a good view of employees coming and going from the X-CO facility. Koa provided his team with enhanced pictures from the surveillance video of the man who'd impersonated Baldwin.

Officer Johnnie Maru spent a boring eight-hour shift on the roof with nothing to show for it. Then late in the day during Officer Horita's watch, he spotted the subject coming out of the X-CO complex and getting into his car. Not just any car, but a Tesla Model S with a sticker price of more than $95,000. When Koa got the news, he wondered whether the man had been in the facility all night or if Maru had missed him. With a screwup like Maru, anything was possible.

A DMV inquiry on the Tesla revealed the imposter's name—Kirk Snelling, a thirty-eight-year-old resident of Hilo, employed as a security guard at X-CO—and confirmed his ownership of the pricy, high-tech car. Maybe the man had inherited wealth, but Koa still thought it unusual, if not downright odd, for a security guard in Hawai'i to own such a luxury car. A further records check revealed no criminal history, not surprising for an employee at a classified defense facility.

Having discovered that Snelling had impersonated Baldwin, Koa wondered if he had also supervised the removal of Baldwin's furniture. Following his gut instinct, he took Snelling's picture to Baldwin's condo. Both Leilani Craig, Baldwin's former neighbor, and the resident agent recognized Snelling as one of the movers who'd cleared out Baldwin's place. Koa thought it likely that other X-CO employees had helped Snelling with the move.

The fog, Koa thought, was lifting off an opaque conspiracy. Someone at X-CO had doctored Baldwin's personnel file to hide her professional qualifications, position, and salary. As a computer AI specialist, she wouldn't have been a secretary, and she would have earned more than a secretarial salary. Snelling, an X-CO security guard, driving a super-luxury car, had impersonated Baldwin and sold the dead woman's Honda. Snelling, holding a supposed authorization from Baldwin and the keys to her apartment, had cleared out her belongings, again after her death. Someone at X-CO had probably created her phony resignation letter. X-CO, it seemed, had tried to erase all traces of Tiger Baldwin, just as her killer had tried to conceal her corpse and her identity.

For Koa, those facts spawned more questions. Had Snelling killed her? Had he desecrated and buried her? Had he altered her personnel records? Had Snelling, Koa wondered, forged her resignation letter? The motive was most mysterious of all. Why had Baldwin been killed, and why had someone associated with her employer tried to hide her death?

Uncovering Snelling's activities gave the investigation direction. In impersonating Tiger Baldwin, Snelling had falsely signed her name to a contract to sell the vehicle. That in itself amounted to forgery, a felony under Hawai'i law. In Snelling, Koa had identified a potential inside witness and had a hammer to hold over his head. Time, he thought, to ratchet up the pressure.

Before hunting down Snelling for questioning, Koa thought it wise to brief the county prosecutor. Zeke Brown, in his sixth term as Hawai'i county prosecutor, had a long oval face, wide-set eyes that missed nothing, and a thick bush of somewhat unruly black hair. He held the most powerful position on the island with the possible exception of the mayor. He and Koa typically worked significant criminal cases together and frequently served as sounding boards for each other. This time Koa also had an ulterior motive in reaching out to the prosecutor. Zeke pursued criminals of every stripe from the most powerful to the humblest and disliked political interference. Zeke, Koa well knew, would push back if the police chief persisted in steering the investigation away from X-CO.

Koa found Zeke in his office, leaning back in his chair with his boots propped atop his desk, listening to an assistant practicing her closing argument in a criminal trial. Except in court, when he donned a sports jacket, considered formal attire in Hawai'i, Zeke lived in jeans, a *paniolo* shirt, and black buffalo hide Lucchese cowboy boots. He had a friendly, easy going manner with friends and voters, but could be as hard as lava when the situation warranted. Criminal defendants and their defense counsel crossed him at their peril.

When the mock legal argument finished, and the assistant left, Koa filled the prosecutor in on the discovery of Tiger Baldwin's body, along with his efforts to determine her identity and the time of her death.

"Damned clever," Zeke commented when Koa explained his collaboration with Professor Diaz's colleague using facial recognition software to identify Baldwin.

"Credit for being clever goes to Georgina, who suggested using Professor Diaz. Georgina also found Baldwin's DNA in Baldwin's empty apartment despite a thorough professional cleaning," Koa responded. "Did you know she's taking a forensic pathology class at UH Hilo?"

"No, I hadn't heard that. Good for her," Zeke responded. "So, you've got a positive ID?"

"Yeah. But then it gets tricky." He explained Baldwin's sudden disappearance, the removal of her belongings, his visit to X-CO, the sale of Baldwin's car, Baldwin's UH Hilo adjunct professorship, and the surveillance to identify the seller. "So," Koa summarized, "turns out that an X-CO employee named Snelling moved her stuff and sold her car after she was dead. And Wingate, the boss man at X-CO, misrepresented her position, gave me phony payroll data, and provided what I believe is a phony resignation letter."

It was hard to surprise Zeke, who'd seen it all, but Koa came close. With eyebrows raised, the prosecutor's weathered boots dropped off his desk as he sat bolt upright. "You serious? X-CO, the defense contractor with an all-star board of directors. They gave you phony payroll records and a fishy resignation letter?"

"Sam Napaka at First Hawaiian says there's no match, not even close, between the X-CO records and Baldwin's direct salary deposits."

"That's damn strange," Zeke said. "You have the bank records?"

"No. Napaka needs a subpoena. And we can't find Baldwin's cell phone, so we're going to need phone company subpoenas and Google location data. That's why I'm here giving you all this background. We need subpoenas. Can you handle that and let Makanui know? I want her to hand-deliver them to expedite matters."

"I'll take care of it," Zeke responded. "By the way," he asked, "how's your new detective working out?"

"Great," Koa responded. "She's savvy, a real quick study, and tough."

"You checked out why she left the HPD?" Zeke asked.

Jesus, Koa thought, nothing happened in this county without Zeke getting wind of it. "Yeah, I got the real skinny. Someday I'll tell you the story."

They were both quiet for a moment before Zeke asked, "You question this Snelling character?"

"Not yet," Koa responded.

Koa, famous for pushing inquiries as fast as possible, saw the surprised look on Zeke's face.

"I drove up to Pōhakuloa to get Zeigler's reaction to Baldwin's death and some background on X-CO. He says the company's got some kind of highly classified deal with the Army, but then he got cagey telling me he'd have to talk to 'people' and might have more in a day or two. I'm positive he knew more than he let on."

"So, your Army buddy is holding out on you?" Zeke said.

"Yeah. Big-time," Koa responded. "And I'm hoping he gets what he needs to open up."

"You're waiting to hear back from Zeigler before leaning on Snelling?"

"Yeah. Thought I'd give it twenty-four hours."

CHAPTER THIRTEEN

KOA WASN'T SURPRISED when the call came from retired detective Ronnie Kaohi. Someone had contacted him about an old case. "This fellow, he wants to talk to me about an old murder case, yeah. Don't know what his angle is. Thought I ought to check in, yeah." Kaohi spoke loudly like many people with hearing loss and had adopted the pidgin practice of adding "yeah" to the end of his sentences to make sure you were listening.

"This fellow have a name?" Koa asked, guessing it must be Bobby Hazzard.

"Hazzard, said his name was Hazzard. Same as the old case, yeah. Something about his grandfather. You know anything 'bout 'im?"

"He's the grandson of Anthony Hazzard, one of the old sugar barons who hanged himself. It was thirty-plus years ago. He's—"

"I remember now," Kaohi interrupted. "Kids hiking found the remains in some off-the-grid huntin' cabin somewheres up in the Kohala Mountains, yeah. I remember."

Since Kaohi was the only official who doubted that Anthony Hazzard had taken his own life, Koa wanted to tease out his current sentiments about the case. "That's the case. Hazzard's grandson is digging into the family history, and raising questions about what happened."

"It's a bit late for that, yeah. Hell, if I remember right, feral pigs and rodents rooted around in that cabin for days. Probably more than a week, yeah. Ugly scene, yeah. Piss and shit everywhere. Smell was horrific. You don't forget a scene like that one."

"Coroner ruled it a suicide," Koa prompted.

"A guess. Good as any, but still a guess, yeah. No way to tell."

"You going to meet with the grandson?" Koa asked.

"Don't see no harm in it, unless you tell me not to."

Koa would have preferred no meeting, but he didn't want to raise suspicions by telling Kaohi to beg off. Not with Senator Chao and Kāwika Keahi backing young Hazzard. Koa wasn't going to do anything that might come back to haunt him, but he could plant the seeds of caution in the old cop's ear. And maybe get some protection. "Young Mr. Hazzard seems to think the cops investigating his grandfather's death were incompetent."

"Is that so?" Kaohi responded. "We'll see about that. We will, yeah."

"Mind if I sit in? This young man has some high-powered mentors."

"No problem."

"Where and when?" Koa asked.

"Tomorrow afternoon at the burger joint. You know. The old cop hangout. Quarter to two, after the lunch rush, yeah?" Kaohi responded.

* * *

Kaohi had already settled at one of the burger joint's Formica-top tables, beer in hand, when Koa arrived. The old cop had aged. His hair had turned white, and his face bore deep wrinkles from years of sun damage, but his perfect white teeth retained their pearly sparkle. His eyes still had the wariness that comes from years on the street. Once a street cop, always a street cop. Instead of a uniform, he now wore jeans, sandals, and a loud Hawaiian *aloha* shirt, emblazoned with a repeating sea of *hula* dancers.

"*Aloha*," Koa greeted him. "I haven't seen you since the police picnic a couple of years ago."

With his hands on the table, Kaohi pushed himself awkwardly to his feet, and they shook hands. "Took a fall a while back. Gets harder to bounce back as I git older, yeah. But I'm still lookin' down, not up, at the ground." After shaking hands, Kaohi sat back down. Plainly, he was more comfortable sitting.

Bobby Hazzard, in a new preppy getup, this one in shades of beige, came through the door and approached the two men sitting at the table. He took his place on an empty plastic chair and put his iPad on the table, scowled at Koa, and without an *aloha* or other pleasantries, spat, "Why are you here?"

Kaohi seemed taken aback by the unfriendly question, and Koa wondered what was behind Bobby's apparent hostility. Koa smiled and, adopting an air of calm, said, "The chief doesn't want any complaints from Senator Chao or his aide, so I'm here to facilitate things."

Nodding tersely at Koa, Bobby turned to Kaohi and, again without preamble, abruptly began, "I'm Bobby Hazzard. My grandfather was Anthony Hazzard. You investigated his death."

Kaohi was old Hawaiian, deeply steeped in the *aloha* traditions that smoothed the rough edges of a multicultural society. He stuck out his hand. "*Aloha*. I'm Ronnie Kaohi. Nice to meet you, Mr. Hazzard."

Oblivious to the gracious cultural gesture, Bobby briefly shook hands and pressed on in his interrogating style. "You investigated my grandfather's death."

Kaohi stared directly at the young man, and Koa wondered if he was thinking of pulling the plug on the meeting. Finally, speaking loudly, he said, "Yeah, I investigated Anthony Hazzard's death a long time ago, long before I retired."

"Did you ever get in touch with his brother?"

Koa could see from the look in Kaohi's eyes and the downturned corners of his mouth that he chafed at Bobby's overbearing approach. He'd come to the meeting as a courtesy, and Bobby had not reciprocated. Koa couldn't understand Bobby's aggressiveness. The kid was a Harvard-educated lawyer who'd interned for a politician. Yet, he displayed none of the tact or subtlety one would expect from his training; instead, he projected arrogance that rubbed Kaohi the wrong way.

An adage Zeke often quoted popped into Koa's mind: The lawyer who represents himself has a fool for a client. Bobby was emotionally involved, letting his frustrations over his grandfather's death overwhelm his better judgment. He'd get less information for that failing, and that was fine by Koa.

"I don't remember knowing he had a brother," Kaohi responded.

"So, you didn't notify next of kin?"

Kaohi fixed the younger man with an unfriendly look and spoke slowly, controlling his annoyance. "If I remember correctly, the sugar mill records identified his mother as next of kin. She turned out to be deceased, and if you are saying there were other relatives, your grandfather must not have updated the records. So, I'm not sure how we could have identified other kin."

"He was supposed to fly back to New York about a month after his death. His brother called the mill when he didn't show up."

"I wouldn't know. The mill never informed me about it."

"But you knew he planned to go to New York?"

"We found his airline tickets. That I remember, yeah."

"Why would a man planning a trip buy first-class air tickets and then kill himself?"

Koa watched Bobby alienate Kaohi, the sole investigator who had doubted Hazzard's suicide. It was counterproductive, and Koa wondered if his presence had upset Bobby, triggering the man's apparent animosity. Whatever the cause, it served Koa's purposes. Bobby was unlikely to get anything useful from the ex-cop.

"I have no idea," Kaohi responded, "but in twenty-five years as a detective, I've seen people doing a whole bunch of inexplicable things, yeah."

"But you didn't think it was suicide, did you?"

Kaohi hesitated again before responding. "That ain't right. The scene in your grandfather's cabin was a nightmare, yeah. A broken rope was hangin' from a rafter, and there was this noose around your grandfather's neck. It looked like a suicide, yeah. Feral pigs and rats had been runnin' wild in there for a week, maybe more, gnawin' on your grandfather's body. There was shit and piss all over the place, insects too, making it a hard scene to process, yeah. One of the ugliest I'd ever seen. I couldn't be a hundred percent sure, and friends of your grandfather doubted he killed himself, so I just wanted to leave the case open."

"But you did close the case," Bobby said accusingly.

"The coroner said it was suicide. His call, not mine."

"So, you just let it go?" Bobby said disparagingly.

"No, that ain't right," Kaohi responded, his voice tinged with anger. "We had a meeting, me and the chief. The chief back then. He had the coroner's report, and he asks me did I have some other theory to track down. And I told him I had nothin' to go on, yeah. Then he asks me if I'm gonna develop another theory. What could

I say? The crime scene was all fouled up with pig shit, rats, and bugs, yeah. Worse than an outhouse. Nobody was ever gonna prove much of anything from what we saw in that cabin. All I had was an airline ticket and a couple of business friends doubtin' suicide. Nothing else. The chief closed the case. Period. End of story."

"The coroner didn't do the standard tests," Hazzard insisted.

Hazzard had managed to get Kaohi's back up. The old detective glared at Hazzard's grandson. "Son, you ever seen a corpse chewed up by feral pigs?"

"No," Hazzard answered.

"Or a body that's been dead in the wild for more than a week?"

"No," Hazzard answered again.

"Well, maybe you should take another look at the crime scene and them morgue photos before you go judgin' the coroner too harshly, yeah."

Koa would never have approached the old cop with such an attitude and was shocked at Hazzard's lack of finesse. He'd gotten nothing useful and had only reinforced the case for suicide. He should have given up, but the obnoxious kid plowed ahead.

"You found an unidentified fingerprint?" Hazzard asked.

Kaohi scratched his head, and his recollection seemed to falter for the first time. "Maybe. I just don't have a clear recollection."

"It's in the police report," Hazzard snapped.

"If you say so," Kaohi responded indifferently.

"And you didn't follow up?"

"If we found a print, we put it through the system, and if we got a hit, we pursued it. Of that, I'm sure."

"How come you didn't fly to New York to talk to the family?"

Kaohi looked at the kid with undisguised contempt. "We sent a notice to the NYPD telling 'em Hazzard died along with the name we had for next of kin. That's how we found out his mother had passed. The Hawai'i County Police in 1989 didn't have the budget to fly an officer to New York without a damn good reason. And we had no such reason."

And with that, Kaohi ended the meeting. Putting both hands firmly on the table, the old cop slowly rose, levering himself to his feet, and walked out, turning his back on Bobby Hazzard.

CHAPTER FOURTEEN

A DAY AND a half had passed with no word from Zeigler, so Koa decided to act. He waited until late in the day when Snelling was likely to be home before grabbing Makanui and heading for the security guard's place. Once in the car, Koa planned to ask Makanui about her participation in the raid on the Abu Sayyaf camp, but she beat him to it.

"I'm guessing you're curious about the Abu Sayyaf raid in the Philippines."

"You guessed right."

"The damn Philippine Army wouldn't let me go in the with the raiding party. Said they couldn't risk an American getting killed. So, I talked my way onto the medical team sent in to care for any hostages who were still alive."

"You went in after the assault?"

"Yeah, with a Philippine medical team. We helicoptered into this jungle shithole of a camp. Mostly lean-to shacks and tents. Horrible damp and smelly place. We found six hostages in bamboo cages barely big enough for a medium-sized dog. None of them could stand up straight, and three of them couldn't walk. Those three, a French couple and a nun, were in a really bad way. Sick with parasites and dysentery, dehydrated, and living in their own filth.

We got all six of them out and to a hospital in Manila. The nun had been traumatized. Never uttered a word before she died a couple of weeks later."

"Sounds like hell."

"Worse than your most horrific nightmares."

"You keep in touch with any of the hostages?"

"A couple. The rest can't stand to be reminded of the horrors they endured, and I respect that."

"Any idea how much the terrorists collected in ransom money?"

"Millions. International agencies figure more than forty hostages went through that stinkhole, and many paid hundreds of thousands of dollars in ransoms."

The address on Snelling's driver's license led them to a high-end oceanfront condo in Hilo's tallest building. In the western sky, the setting sun turned the long feathery clouds high above Hilo Bay pink and gold. Pulling into the condo's parking lot, they spotted Snelling's Tesla Model S. That the complex was way too upscale for a security guard only heightened Koa's suspicion. They knocked at a third-floor apartment on the ocean side and announced themselves as police officers.

Snelling, barefoot, and wearing only boxers and a wifebeater tee-shirt, opened the door. Of average height, he had the well-toned muscular body and the crew cut of a military recruit. "Who are you, and what the hell do you want?" he asked with an attitude.

Koa identified himself and Makanui.

"I've got nothing to say," Snelling snapped and started to close the door before Makanui body blocked it.

"You can talk to us here or down at the station. Your choice," Koa said.

Snelling's face turned red with indignation before resignation slowly replaced his hostility, and he reluctantly opened the door. The two detectives followed him into a living room sparsely outfitted with cheap modular furniture. Imitation Ikea, Koa thought reflexively. A giant picture window overlooking Hilo Bay provided the only pleasing element to an otherwise drab room. The evening panorama featured fishing boats returning with the day's catch trailing wakes across the bay's calm waters in proximity to an oil tanker gliding out of the inner harbor past the breakwater and out toward the sea.

"Nice view," Makanui said.

"You're not here for the view," Snelling grumbled. He grabbed a chair from around a wooden table, reversed it, and straddled its seat. When he failed to offer them seats, the two cops ignored the discourtesy and sat in chairs across the table from the security guard.

Snelling made no effort to conceal his hostility. "What the fuck is this all about?"

Koa, who had studied micro-expressions, watched the man's face. For an instant, Snelling's eyebrows drew together, and his eyes bulged, an indication of anger. Koa ignored the security guard's crude remark. "You work at X-CO?"

"Yeah. In security. What of it?"

The man's rancor was apparent—so apparent Koa thought it might be nothing more than a tactic—because he saw no sign of fear or nervousness. No tension in his lips. No shifting on the chair. Snelling, Koa decided, was more complex and controlled than he let on. "Want to tell us about Tiger Baldwin?" Koa asked.

"She's a friend," Snelling responded quickly, too quickly. Koa sensed he'd expected the question and knew exactly why the police had knocked on his door.

Koa thought he might rattle the man, and Snelling had offered the perfect opening. "You mean before someone shot her?"

Snelling's eyes opened wide in disbelief, but there was something forced and unnatural in the reaction. Koa couldn't tell whether it was real or a ruse. Several seconds passed before Snelling spoke. "You're kidding. When? How?"

They were questions an innocent man might well ask, but Snelling, Koa thought, had waited too long to ask them, reflecting calculation, not spontaneity. "We're asking the questions, Mr. Snelling," Koa responded, and paused just long enough for Makanui to start their tag-team approach.

"How and when did you meet her?" Makanui asked.

"At work," Snelling responded.

"When?" Makanui asked.

"Maybe a couple of years ago. Could be three or four years. Shit, lady, I don't remember," the security guard responded with a smirk.

The man, Koa thought, had a bad attitude toward women. Makanui, he figured, would fix that.

"You remember how long you've worked at X-CO, Mr. Snelling?" Makanui asked, displaying her own touch of attitude.

"About two years, I guess."

"So," Makanui closed the loop, "if you met her at work, it was within the past two years, right?"

"Yeah."

Thinking of the banker's reaction to Baldwin's payroll records, Koa asked, "And what kind of work did she do?"

"She was just a secretary."

Snelling was giving them the same crap as X-CO's managing director. They didn't know that Koa had learned of her computer expertise, checked with her bank, and knew that her skills and pay suggested a far more senior role. "Secretary for whom?"

"For the executives. They don't have individual assistants."

Working in a secretarial pool, Koa thought, made it even less likely she'd be highly compensated.

"When did you last see her?" Makanui asked.

Snelling paused to gather his thoughts. "About ten days or two weeks ago, just before she left to return to the mainland."

"What did you talk about?" Koa asked.

Snelling's lips curled into a sarcastic smile. "I didn't say we talked."

Koa had just about reached his limit. "*Did* you talk with her?"

"Yeah, I did. Sometime around then."

Koa became warier. Snelling exhibited an arrogant, almost reckless attitude. The man showed none of the tensions typical of people in police interviews. It was as though Snelling was toying with them.

"And what did the two of you talk about?" Makanui asked.

"Her car."

Koa, exasperated with this slow waltz, stood up and said, "It's time to take this downtown, Mr. Snelling."

"Okay, okay." Snelling held his hands up in a gesture of surrender. "She asked me to sell her car, and I said I'd do it."

Koa sat back down. "Why would she do that?"

"She was hot to get back to the mainland and didn't have time to get her money out of her wheels."

"So, you sold her car?"

"Yeah. To that Kimo guy. Didn't get much of a price, but she was in a hurry."

"What did you do with the money?"

"Put it in her bank account."

Koa hid his surprise. Unless Snelling was lying, the reason for his annoying self-confidence had become apparent. He might have a reasonable explanation for his conduct. A woman planning a quick departure from the island might well ask a friend to sell her car for her.

"You signed her name?" Makanui asked.

"Yeah. With her permission."

If true, Koa thought, that eliminated a forgery charge.

Makanui followed with the obvious next question. "You have proof?"

"Yeah, I do," Snelling snarled. "I got her email about the car, and I got the deposit slip for her account. Hope that satisfies ya."

"Let's see them," Makanui said.

Snelling made an exaggerated show of picking his cell up off the table, placing his thumb over the home button to unlock the phone, and showing them an email from Baldwin. In it, she asked him to sell her car and provided her bank's name and account number for him to deposit the proceeds. He retrieved a deposit ticket for cash and a check to Baldwin's First Hawaiian Bank account from a make-shift desk across the room and slapped it down on the table. "Check it with the fucking bank, if you don't believe me."

"We will," Makanui responded. She had Snelling forward a copy of the email and took the deposit slip. Opening her own phone, she studied the forwarded email before looking back up at Snelling. "Baldwin asked you to sell her car on June 1, and you waited until June 15 to sell it. Why wait two weeks?"

Snelling gave Makanui a condescending smile. "She needed her car to get to work."

Makanui nodded and turned her attention to the deposit slip. "And you didn't deposit the proceeds for another two weeks." She held up the deposit slip. "Why the delay?"

Snelling hesitated, causing Koa to wonder if the question had surprised him. "I was busy," he finally responded.

"Doing what?" Makanui asked.

"Classified stuff," Snelling responded with a self-satisfied sneer.

"Classified stuff?" Makanui asked skeptically

"That's right, lady."

Koa guessed that Snelling would have an equally plausible defense for moving Baldwin's stuff from her condo. "You do anything else for your friend?"

"Yeah. She asked me to put her junk in storage, and I got a couple of guys to help me do it."

"Proof?" Koa asked.

This time Snelling seemed less sure of himself. "She gave me her credit card number for the storage facility." Again, he worked the email app on his phone until he found another email from Baldwin.

Koa asked him to forward the second email, and Snelling obliged. "And the storage facility?" Koa asked.

"Hakido's," Snelling responded.

Koa didn't let his disappointment show. He'd come to Snelling's place sure he would find evidence connecting the man and X-CO to Baldwin's murder. Now, he'd be leaving less confident than when he arrived. It wasn't the first time he'd experienced a reversal in an investigation, but it was aggravating all the same. "Don't leave town, Snelling. We may want to talk to you again," Koa said as the two detectives left Snelling's apartment.

In the parking lot, Koa turned to Makanui, who had a keen sense for people with several years as a cop under her belt. "You believe him?" he asked.

She hesitated. "His documents might be persuasive, but there's something off about him. He's too cocksure of himself like he's constructed what he thinks is an airtight story. That classified stuff was bullshit. And he doesn't like women. You saw the way his face changed, and he got snarly when I questioned him."

Koa nodded in agreement. "And he described Baldwin as a secretary. If they were close enough for her to ask him to sell her car, he'd have known she was more than a secretary."

CHAPTER FIFTEEN

KOA SMILED WHEN Bobby Hazzard called the following morning with yet another request. He wanted to interview the coroner—not Reggie Ruiz, the coroner who'd examined Anthony Hazzard's body; Ruiz had passed. Bobby instead wanted to talk to the current coroner, Shizuo Hori. Bobby couldn't have appreciated that Hawai'i County still had no qualified medical examiner. A local doctor had historically filled the coroner's role, and that practice had not changed. In this case, the coroner was a seventy-nine-year-old obstetrician who owed his job to the cronyism rampant in the Hilo government. He hadn't opened a medical text in forty years, knew little about forensic pathology, and screwed up most autopsies. It would be, Koa knew, the incompetent questioning the incompetent.

Shizuo was also a classic narcissistic prick, who claimed far more knowledge and sophistication than he possessed. Always quick to take offense, he would likely provide Bobby with plainly erroneous information. Under other circumstances, Koa might have worried that Bobby would complain to his mentor, Senator Chao, or maybe Kāwika Keahi about Shizuo's ignorance and attitude. In this case, Koa didn't care. He'd been complaining about Shizuo for nearly a decade and would welcome any help the senator or his aide might offer in getting rid of the incompetent quack.

Bobby's request was easy for Koa to honor. After determining that Shizuo had returned to Hilo and calling to schedule a meeting later that day, Koa emailed the doctor a copy of the thirty-year-old coroner's report.

At the appointed time, Koa met the kid in the lobby of Hilo Memorial Hospital, and they walked together to Shizuo's office. They had to wait twenty minutes before the coroner arrived in his delivery room scrubs. Shizuo seemed surprised to see them. Like he'd forgotten the appointment Koa had made on Bobby's behalf. Koa, who'd often been stood up by the pretend coroner, wasn't surprised, but the doctor's "why-are-you-here" approach annoyed Bobby Hazzard, who frowned. So much the better, Koa thought.

They took seats in Shizuo's cramped office, and Bobby began, "I'd like to ask you about a report your predecessor did thirty years ago."

"Wouldn't know about that," Shizuo responded with his usual "can't-be-bothered" attitude.

"I thought maybe you'd read the report in preparation for this meeting," Bobby suggested.

"I have patients to see. Why would I waste time with an old report?"

Koa suppressed his reaction. Shizuo was a caricature of himself and would soon start waffling. That, Koa thought, would drive Bobby over the edge.

"Well, let me ask you." Bobby tried a fresh approach. "Aren't tests for asphyxiation normal in possible suicide cases?"

"It depends," Shizuo responded curtly.

"On what?" Bobby asked with rising irritation.

"On lots of things. You wouldn't understand."

Bobby chewed his lip in a sign of his growing annoyance. "Well, suppose there were doubts about the cause of death?"

"It would be complicated," Shizuo insisted.

"What about blood tests?"

"Same answer."

"What if the deceased had a head injury?" Bobby's voice rose half an octave, and Koa could tell he was barely able to control his anger.

"Lots of possibilities. Let's not talk in hypotheticals," Shizuo said dismissively.

"If you'd read the report, I could ask about the specifics," Bobby snapped.

"Well, I haven't read it," Shizuo responded unapologetically.

Bobby paused, fighting to control his anger and searching for some gap in Shizuo's intransigence.

Struggling to maintain his composure, Bobby changed tacks. "What do you know about your predecessor, Doctor Reggie Ruiz?"

"That was a long time ago," the coroner responded.

"Did you or didn't you know him?" Bobby demanded.

Shizuo raised his voice in turn. "Don't be rude."

Again, Bobby paused, trying to keep his temper in check. "I simply asked if you knew him."

"He was not my predecessor. There were two others after him."

"So, you didn't know him?" Bobby asked.

"I didn't say that. We played poker together, a group of us."

Koa clamped his teeth tight to keep from reacting. Poker was central to Shizuo's existence. Losing big bets in hand after hand during the mayor's Thursday night smokers had earned Shizuo his appointment as coroner. Long-time Mayor Tenaka and his council buddies gladly took Shizuo's cash, and the coroner continued losing because it was his ticket into Hilo's political elite. Koa knew that Shizuo wasn't the only mayoral appointee who benefited from similar corrupt practices.

"So, what did you think of Doctor Ruiz?"

Shizuo seemed oblivious to Bobby's rising anger. "He wasn't such a good player."

"His forensic skills?" Bobby snapped.

"Oh, he was a great doctor for someone with a European medical education."

Shizuo's beeper sounded, and he went off to deliver another baby. Bobby, angry at having accomplished nothing, stomped off down the hospital corridor. Koa breathed a sigh of relief that he'd survived another round in Bobby's hunt to exonerate his grandfather. Secretly, he hoped Bobby would complain to Senator Chao and Keahi. Working with Professor Diaz was a lot more rewarding than dealing with Shizuo.

CHAPTER SIXTEEN

CONFUSION CLOUDED KOA'S thoughts that evening as he drove south on Highway 11 toward the cottage he shared with Nālani. Often when he faced uncertainty, he contemplated *Reptiles*, the M. C. Escher lithograph that hung on his office wall. People, like the creatures in Escher's imagery, where lizards undulated in and out of different spatial planes, often inhabited impenetrable underworlds filled with secrets. He'd pegged Snelling as one of those people who morphed with their surroundings and had his doubts about the man's story.

Makanui verified the authenticity of the bank deposit slip. Still, they knew that anyone with access to Baldwin's computer or smartphone could have created the emails authorizing Snelling to sell the car and put her things in storage. And the timing was peculiar. Maybe Snelling's work schedule delayed his banking, but bank deposits weren't time-consuming. And, Snelling hadn't deposited Baldwin's funds until after Koa and Makanui had visited X-CO. Koa suspected their visit had prompted Snelling to cover his tracks.

Stranger still, Makanui had canvassed the airlines flying from Hawai'i to the mainland without finding a reservation for Tiger Baldwin. If, as Snelling asserted, she had been "hot" to get back to the continental US, she would have made a reservation. Koa was increasingly confident that her supposed resignation was a sham.

As he neared their Volcano cottage, his thoughts turned to Nālani, and he put the case out of his mind. In four short years, she had become his soul mate and an unending source of wonderment. With a coy look or a well-timed tease, she could send his heart racing. After parking, he found her standing in the doorway and greeted the love of his life with a kiss. Dressed in skinny jeans and a white blouse that offset nicely her bronze skin and long black hair she'd tied back in a ponytail, she seemed lovelier than when he'd kissed her goodbye that morning. "*Aloha*, my *ipo*," he said softly using the Hawaiian term of endearment, and kissed her again, this time letting their lips linger.

He changed into hiking clothes, and they drove a short distance into Hawai'i Volcanoes National Park. As a park ranger, Nālani had seen the many changes wrought by the May 2018 eruptions, but for Koa, this was his first opportunity to see *Pele*'s most recent handiwork. Less than two months earlier, an explosive eruption had rocked the crater, projecting ash more than 30,000 feet into the sky. That initial event triggered tens of thousands of subsequent earthquakes and repetitive collapses of the crater floor as a billion cubic feet of magma drained away down the east rift zone. In a way, Koa thought he was back to where the whole Tiger Baldwin investigation had started with an unusually disruptive earthquake.

They parked near the visitor's center and walked hand in hand along a trail to the edge of the Kīlauea caldera, where Koa gasped at the incredible sight. Parts of the caldera floor had imploded so that Halema'uma'u, the former pit crater within the caldera, now covered more than a square mile and plunged to a depth of 1,500 feet—deeper than the height of the Empire State Building. Gaseous steam and smoke rose from vents near the bottom of the abyss. Even as they walked, another small quake rumbled beneath their feet.

"I need to talk to you about Taharu," Nālani said as they passed through wisps of steam drifting up from the Kīlauea's sulfur banks.

"He's one of your *keiki mākua ʻole*," Koa responded, referring to the group of orphaned and troubled teens in a local group home where Nālani volunteered twice a week. "He's the little guy, the one who nearly tipped over the canoe on our last outing?" After Nālani had started volunteering, she and Koa had taken "her kids," as she referred to them, on several adventures, including two overnight canoeing trips. Their shared commitment to helping less fortunate islanders was one of the things Koa cherished most about their relationship.

"That's him. I think he's headed for trouble."

"Drugs?" Koa asked.

She nodded. "I'm seeing the usual signs—flushed cheeks, evasive behavior, lack of interest. All the signs are there. You've seen it in kids."

"You talk to him about it?"

"Yeah, but I don't think I got through to him."

"He denied using?"

"Not really. He kind of hedged and wouldn't look me in the eye. I told him I cared about him and tried to pump up his self-esteem. Told him he didn't need to do that stuff to impress anyone and emphasized the risks. But he just sat there looking blankly down at the table with deaf ears. It was like talking to a stone."

"You want me to talk to him?"

"I thought about that, but he's into the sovereignty thing, and my instincts tell me he'll see you as police, and you'll just get his back up. I don't want to lose him."

"Well, who else could talk to him?"

"I don't know. You had this kind of problem with your brother when he was growing up. You find anything that worked?"

Koa's brother, Ikaika, had a troubled youth and many run-ins with the law before becoming a career criminal. For years, Koa had tried to talk to him, helped him find employment, lent him money, and visited him in jail, all to no avail. Only when Ikaika had collapsed in prison had Koa discovered that his brother had a rare brain tumor that affected his ability to control his behavior.

Koa looked out at the now gently smoking crater of the collapsed volcano and thought about Nālani's question. He realized that although none of his overtures had done much good in the short term, his efforts may have had some long-term effect. "I can't say that anything I did had much immediate effect, but I guess I did manage to keep a line of communication, and maybe that helped in the long run."

He paused, reliving those awful years when Ikaika used cocaine, amphetamines, and god only knows what other chemical substances. "It was different with my mother. She always had a place in her heart for Ikaika and never lost faith in him. Looking back on it, she kept him alive. Without her, he would have overdosed or died in some back-alley knife fight. So, to answer your question, I'd say communication and perseverance are the only things that made a difference. Keep talking. Make it clear that even though you disapprove of his drug use, you still care about him and will always be there for him. Don't break the bond. That bond is Taharu's lifeline."

"I see what you're saying, but there has to be somebody we could ask to weigh in with him. Somebody he'll respect and relate to." She hesitated. "I was wondering whether I should get one of the sovereignty protesters to sit down with Taharu. What do you think?"

"I don't know. Makaiao would be good, but what about 'Aulani,'" Koa suggested. "The pictures of her blocking the road during the Thirty Meter Telescope protests give her serious sovereignty creds, and she's worked in county anti-drug programs counseling teens. She'd also be more likely to follow up than Makaiao, who's spread thin these days."

"That's a great idea. I'll talk to her."

He slipped an arm around her and pulled her close. "You mean everything to me, *ipo*. Your generosity gives me hope and makes me a better person. You know that, don't you?"

"It's mutual," she whispered just before they stopped to kiss.

Surrounded by full darkness, they walked back to their car. Koa turned for one last look at the crater. "I miss the red glow of lava boiling inside the crater."

"It'll come back," Nālani responded.

"When?"

"Only *Pele* knows," she responded, with an impish smile.

*   *   *

Koa was sound asleep later that night when the phone rang. Never a good sign in the middle of the night. He answered and heard Zeigler's voice. "Sorry to wake you, but there have been developments on the X-CO front. Can you come up to Pōhakuloa?"

Koa looked at the clock. "Right now? It's four thirty a.m."

"It'll be reveille by the time you get here."

Koa groaned. He hadn't heard the military wake-up call since his soldiering days. Easing himself out of bed to avoid disturbing Nālani, who'd turned over and gone back to sleep, he dressed, grabbed a cup of coffee from the kitchen, and headed for the saddle. Darkness gave way to first light as he left Hilo and headed up the Saddle Road toward Pōhakuloa at 6,800 feet above sea level. Approaching the 4,000-foot level, he entered a cloud bank that shrouded the surrounding forest in an eerie mist. Barely able to make out the yellow dividing line down the center of the curvy highway, he slowed to a crawl. Eventually, he climbed above the clouds, where the foggy air gave way to clear skies. The road leveled out and crossed overlapping lava flows from Mauna Kea and Mauna Loa where there were fewer trees, leaving only shrubs or nothing on the jagged brown landscape.

Curiosity consumed Koa as he turned into the Pōhakuloa Training Area. He secured a pass at the security gate and drove to the military police headquarters. Zeigler, dressed as usual in military camo, met him in the parking lot. "What's this all about, buddy?" Koa asked.

"You'll see," Zeigler responded, motioning Koa toward a military police jeep. Zeigler took the wheel, and they drove half a mile to a blockhouse-type structure surrounded by a separate fence with armed security guards. Once inside, Zeigler cleared them through a high-tech guard station and led the way to a conference room, where five people—two women and three men—waited.

Zeigler introduced Rachael Goodling, a lawyer from the Division of National Security of the US Department of Justice, her colleague Tony Ige, and FBI agents Cesare Moreno, Fred Carvelli, and Linda Somes. "Moreno and Somes are from the bureau's cybercrimes unit. Carvelli is from the bureau's espionage unit," Zeigler added. Goodling and Ige stood to shake hands with Koa, but the three FBI agents, who remained seated, offered only brief nods. Moreno's expression appeared conspicuously dour.

National security, cybercrimes, and espionage—something heavy was going down. Given Koa's earlier meeting with Zeigler, it had to relate to Baldwin, but he couldn't imagine how. On top of that, an air of heightened tension, like an electrical charge, seemed to permeate the room. Moreno, in particular, radiated displeasure with whatever was about to unfold. Koa guessed that the DOJ and the FBI were not on the same page. That put Koa on edge. He'd have to watch his footing with the bureau.

Goodling took the lead. "Thanks for coming up here on short notice." Strikingly tall at close to six-feet, she had black hair, chiseled features, and a dusky complexion. She wore no jewelry and dressed conservatively in a white blouse and dark blue pants. With her height, a Glock semi-automatic in a shoulder holster, and a DOJ badge fastened to her belt, she cut an imposing figure. The surprisingly deep tone of her voice only added to her commanding presence. "I've reviewed your extraordinary military service record and heard good things about you from the US Attorney in Honolulu and Coast Guard Admiral Cunningham."

Koa had worked extensively with both the Honolulu US Attorney and Admiral Cunningham, most recently on a case involving a young astronomer. While Goodling might have intended her words to make him feel comfortable, he got the message that she'd thoroughly checked him out. Her next words left no doubt. "It's not everybody who can get a temporary top-secret security clearance in less than forty-eight hours."

Koa, who'd held a top-secret clearance during his days as an Army Special Forces officer, understood the extensive background checks necessary to obtain such a security classification. That Goodling had reactivated his security clearance in the past forty-eight hours signaled both her clout and something of extraordinary importance. Hell, Koa thought, the Justice Department and the FBI would send five officials to the Big Island only for a matter of national urgency.

Goodling nodded toward Moreno. With a long face, dimpled chin, and thick, dark, wavy hair, Moreno was shorter than the stereotypical FBI agent, giving him a pugnacious appearance. The FBI agent opened a briefcase, withdrew a paper, and slapped it down on the table. His hostility could not have been more evident as he shoved the security clearance form towards Koa.

"You need to review and sign that before we can proceed," Goodling said. "What we're about to share is top secret with additional restrictions."

Koa read the document, signed, and handed it back to Moreno, who unceremoniously retrieved it. Moreno, Koa thought, was not happy with his presence.

"The Army has a contract with X-CO," Zeigler began, "to create the communications software for a new, fully automated cyberweapon, called Deimos, after the Greek god of terror. It's the most sophisticated and deadly ground-based weapon ever developed, and it's being tested here at Pōhakuloa."

Zeigler began activating programs on the laptop in front of him while Somes, who seemed to be the most junior of the group, killed the lights. Suddenly, a massive hologram appeared hovering at the other end of the room and startled Koa. The eerily transparent floating image of a sizable camouflage-colored vehicle seemed real enough to reach out and touch. With a flat top, slanted front, rear, and side panels, it looked like an elongated, chopped-off pyramid topped off with a giant dome. The image slowly rotated, allowing Koa to view all sides. Then the apparition tilted forward until a top-down view revealed an asymmetrical depression in the top of the dome. The thing had an ominous, otherworldly appearance.

"That's Deimos," Zeigler said. "Completely autonomous, it needs no human operator. It's armor-plated, but more importantly, generates an electromagnetic field that deflects incoming shellfire, rockets, and bombs, making it virtually indestructible. The science is super-highly classified, but it can also generate a particle field that renders enemy weapons inoperable and can be tuned to destroy both enemy personnel and equipment. In short, putting nuclear weapons aside, it's more powerful and deadly than anything science fiction writers have ever conceived." As Zeigler described Deimos, Koa found himself mesmerized by the stunning holographic image rotating before him.

Zeigler continued. "We've run dozens of tests. Nothing in our arsenal can touch it, short of a nuclear detonation. Except, of course, another Deimos." He paused, letting Koa absorb the flood of unfamiliar information. "Unfortunately, we've got one monumental problem."

"A problem?" Koa queried.

"Yeah," Zeigler conceded. "There's a flaw in the communications software that permits an enemy hacker to take control. Watch."

The hologram disappeared, and an eight-foot digital panel on the far wall lit up. The Army Ordnance Corps insignia filled the screen before the video switched to a shot of one of Pōhakuloa's training ranges. An aerial view showed a Deimos vehicle sitting on open ground, surrounded by a small convoy of military vehicles. A voice-over on the video announced, "The Deimos is protecting the military convoy around it."

The camera switched to a wide-angle view showing an array of offensive weapons, including tanks, artillery, and rocket batteries, surrounding the Deimos and its convoy at a distance of about a thousand yards.

One by one, the offensive weapons opened fire on the Deimos and its convoy. Koa watched in amazement as the shells and rockets seemed to evaporate in midair before getting anywhere near the Deimos or the vehicles it protected. Then suddenly, all the surrounding weapons fired simultaneously, sending a wall of

projectiles at the Deimos. Incredibly, the barrage simply disappeared in vaporous puffs before any of the ordinance reached the
Deimos or the convoy.

"A single Deimos can protect a battalion-sized armor or infantry
unit, but it could also guard a harbor, a military base, an oil field, or
an aircraft carrier. This version has a range of ten miles, but the next
version, Deimos Two Point Zero already on the drawing board, will
have a range of fifty miles," Zeigler explained. "It can protect not
only against traditional military strikes but also satellite, laser, and
other virtual weapons. Field deployment of the Deimos technology
will revolutionize the nature of warfare, enabling us to protect any
valuable site against any kind of enemy attack at a minimal cost.
Deimos is everything President Reagan ever dreamed about achiev-
ing with his Star Wars technology and more."

"So, where's the problem?" Koa asked.

"Keep watching," Zeigler said. "Our US government hacker is
about to take control of the Deimos."

This time the weapons in the outer offense ring released a swarm
of small drones. The small unmanned aerial vehicles flew toward the
Deimos unobstructed, striking several convoy vehicles and crashing
into the Deimos, releasing puffs of red smoke to mark their hits. A
moment or two after the last of the UAVs struck their targets, the
Deimos emitted a rumbling sound, and the convoy vehicles around
it began to vaporize as the Deimos turned its incredible power on
its own protectees.

The video demonstration left Koa filled with questions, but first, he
wanted to understand why the feds had invited him to this show. "So
how," he asked, "does this connect with me and my investigation?"

Goodling removed a sheet of paper in a plastic sleeve from her
briefcase. "The DOD inspector general received this note a week
ago." She handed it to Koa. It read:

"The Deimos communications software program has been
sabotaged with hidden hack points. Look at code lines 3,768,742
to 3,779,905 in command.op, inside veh.sys, inside the comm.
control module and the interrupts within the driver protocols.
There's more. Will be in touch. *Aletheia*"

The message, Koa noted, was typed or computer-processed in a
standard font on what appeared to be ordinary printer paper, except
for the handwritten signature. "Who's *Aletheia*?" he asked.

"The Greek goddess of truth—*Veritas* by her better-known Ro-
man name," Goodling answered. "The Defense Department might
have treated the note as a hoax except for the writer's intimate
knowledge of the Deimos software program structure. There was
more than enough data in the note for DOD experts to discover a
back door into the program that led to the demonstration you just
watched."

Although unfamiliar with the computer lingo, Koa understood
the essential point. Still, that didn't explain why he'd been given a
security clearance and invited to this meeting. Baldwin was somehow the key. He'd told Zeigler about Baldwin, and the military policeman had initially declined to engage but had now invited him to
this meeting with the feds. Then suddenly, it hit him. "You suspect
that Tiger Baldwin wrote that memo?" he asked.

Goodling nodded affirmatively. "And was killed to prevent her
from naming the saboteurs or revealing further faults in the Deimos
command and control programs."

"What makes you think the note came from Baldwin?" Koa
asked.

"Several things," Goodling responded, "none of which are conclusive but together are pretty compelling. First, there is the name *Aletheia*. She's the Greek goddess of truth. Baldwin used the goddess's

image on her Facebook page while she was at MIT. Its use on the note could, of course, be a deliberate deception, but we don't think so. Second, while the single word *Aletheia* isn't enough for a definitive handwriting comparison, we checked all the possibilities at X-CO, and Baldwin's handwriting comes closest. Third, the author of the *Aletheia* note had to have an intimate knowledge of the Deimos communications software. Baldwin was one of the few systems experts at X-CO who had that knowledge."

"That's pretty thin," Koa responded.

"There's more," Goodling continued. "Tell him, Moreno," she directed in a firm voice that permitted no rebuttal.

Moreno looked as uncomfortable as a chastised schoolchild and hesitated before speaking. "We figured Baldwin was *Aletheia* and wanted more from her, so we tried to set up a meeting. An agent left a message at her apartment—just the name '*Aletheia*' and a phone number. We hoped Baldwin would call. Instead, twenty-four hours later, she was gone. Just disappeared." He stopped, took a deep breath, and swallowed before continuing. "We checked her apartment and found a spy camera hidden in the hallway. There's . . . there's a possibility . . . a real possibility we got her killed."

Koa said nothing. At least he understood Moreno's hostility. Koa, too, had lost people he should have saved—and felt the remorse and shame of failure.

Zeigler, Goodling, Moreno, and their colleagues remained quiet, giving Koa a chance to digest the enormity of what he'd just learned. The FBI's screwup, likely costing Baldwin her life, was awful, but he put that aside and focused on the present. Knowing there was a saboteur, why hadn't the feds already raided X-CO? What possible reason might they have for delay? "Why," he asked, "don't you just raid the place and close it down?"

"It's not so simple," Goodling responded. "There are a lot of factors in play. If Baldwin was, in fact, the whistleblower, the saboteurs killed her before she could tell everything she knew. We haven't identified the people who corrupted the program, and we can't arrest everybody. The defense department has spent billions on this project. Any premature action against X-CO would set the project back years and double or triple the cost." After a moment, she added, "And there are other restraining factors."

Goodling didn't explain the other factors, but Koa guessed that elements of the Deimos software were transferable to other weapons systems, including drones, fighter aircraft, and ships. He felt a chill run down his back as he realized that Baldwin might have prevented America's enemies from seizing control of all of the nation's next generation of superweapons.

"Aren't you afraid the saboteurs have or will steal the whole Deimos concept and adapt it to their arsenal?" Koa asked.

Goodling nodded as though she'd expected the question. "It's a good question. Against that possibility, DOD compartmentalized the Deimos program from the outset. Different companies conceived, designed, and built the guidance, analysis, weapons, motorization, and communications modules. X-CO provides only the communication software, and doesn't have access to the other components."

"If I understand correctly, X-CO provided just the communications software, but none of the weapons components. So, the problem is with the controls, not the weapon itself," Koa reiterated to be sure he understood.

"You got it right," Goodling acknowledged.

Koa looked around at Zeigler, Goodling, Moreno, and the others. "So, why do you need me?"

Again, Goodling took the lead. "We want to put Moreno on your police team so we can use Baldwin's murder as cover for our espionage investigation. It has to be discreet, so we don't tip off those responsible inside X-CO. He can be a new hire or someone borrowed from the Honolulu force. Whichever way you want to play it as long as X-CO doesn't know he's FBI."

Goodling implied that Moreno was on board, but so far as Koa could tell, Moreno was unenthusiastic, if not hostile. Koa's military service had taught him a lot about interservice and interagency rivalries. He'd been burned before and had no desire for more of the same. He debated letting things develop before raising the issue but decided to attempt to clear the air. "I get the feeling that not everyone buys your plan."

"You got that right," Moreno said, standing up to add emphasis to his words.

Goodling laser-focused her stare on Moreno. "I thought we'd had an understanding. The DOJ is running this investigation with bureau support. I can call the director and request your replacement."

"Okay . . . okay," Moreno responded begrudgingly. "It's just risky to bring in locals . . . increases the likelihood of a leak or a screwup." Still standing, he looked accusingly at Koa. "We already know your police chief has loose lips."

Moreno's knowledge of the chief's unfortunate habit of off-the-record briefings for the mayor and even some councilmen on sensitive police matters surprised Koa. He glared back at Moreno and parsed his words carefully, speaking slowly, emphasizing each word. "There will be no leaks from my end."

"Okay, enough," Goodling said, pointing a finger at Moreno. "We've vetted the chief detective, and he's in."

Moreno acquiesced, but Koa was not so naive as to think Goodling had resolved their conflict. Moreno would be looking for any opportunity to undercut the local police. Koa thought about walking out, but curiosity, patriotism, his friendship with Zeigler, and maybe an element of pride kept him in for the moment.

"So, you'll help us?" Goodling asked.

Considering the audacity of the idea, Koa paused to analyze the obstacles to such a plan, not the least of which would be managing the chief. "Supposing for the moment I agreed, I see at least three potential hurdles. First, I'd have to clear your involvement with my chief, who will be unlikely to agree to anything that would upset the political rock stars on X-CO's board. Second, we'd need the county prosecutor's cooperation so we'd have to bring him into the loop. And third, the evidence against X-CO isn't as strong as I thought and may not get us a search warrant."

Goodling's eyebrows arched at Koa's third point. "What about the evidence?"

Koa explained how he'd identified Snelling, detailing how the man had reacted to the police and provided emails from Baldwin. "So," Koa said, "at least superficially, he presented a plausible explanation for the sale of her car and the storage of her belongings. Most importantly, he provided a bank deposit slip showing that he put the proceeds from the sale of her car in her bank account."

"And you believe him?" Moreno asked, not bothering to hide his skepticism.

"I have doubts," Koa responded. "The bank deposit slip is genuine, but there's something not right with Snelling, and the time gap between the sale of Baldwin's car and the bank deposit raises flags."

"We still have Wingate and Snelling describing Baldwin as a secretary, along with payroll records to that effect?" Goodling said.

"Yes," Koa responded cautiously, "but only a banker's word about the discrepancy between the company's payroll records and the corresponding bank records. The prosecutor has subpoenaed the records, but we don't have them yet. We've also discovered that Baldwin was some kind of computer expert who taught an artificial intelligence seminar at UH Hilo."

"That's interesting," Goodling said. "How'd you come by that little gem?"

"She didn't show up for a teaching assignment, and the department head reported her missing," Koa explained. "According to her department head at UH, Baldwin was supposed to teach all summer. And, Baldwin never made an air reservation to go back to the mainland. Makes me think X-CO forged her resignation letter."

Turning to Moreno, Goodling directed, "Give him the bank records." Moreno, deferring to Goodling, reached into his briefcase, pulled out a sheaf of papers, and handed them to Koa.

"You now have her bank records showing Baldwin's annual salary of roughly \$210 K," Goodling said.

"Two hundred ten thousand?" Koa said, surprised at the amount.

"Yeah," Goodling said. "Baldwin was a senior programmer, an expert in the architecture of artificial intelligence software, not a secretary. With that, you should have enough to get a search warrant."

Two hundred ten thousand dollars was a lot of money, especially in Hawai'i. It explained Baldwin's upscale apartment. "How?" Koa asked and then caught himself. "Patriot Act?" Although not an expert, Koa knew that the USA Patriot Act allowed the FBI to issue national security letters demanding the production of many kinds of financial, computer, and customer records without ever seeking judicial approval. Those letters also imposed secrecy on the entity providing the information, which explained why Napaka hadn't told Koa that the government had already demanded Baldwin's bank records.

Goodling nodded.

Goodling was right. The bank records proved that Wingate had produced phony payroll records. Unless X-CO paid two hundred ten grand for a secretary—a most unlikely happenstance—the records also confirmed that both Wingate and Snelling had lied. The salary data also dovetailed with what he'd learned from Professor Alfonzo at UH Hilo about Baldwin's professional skills. With those facts and the likelihood that X-CO had faked her resignation letter, the county prosecutor should have no trouble in getting a search warrant. "And the other issues I mentioned?" Koa asked.

"We can have the US Attorney in Honolulu talk to Zeke Brown, your county prosecutor. That's not a problem. They've worked together in the past," Goodling responded. "But your chief does have loose lips, and that *is* a problem." She emphasized the word "is." "We'll just have to scare the shit out of him. The US Attorney and I can probably handle that."

They were right about the chief's tendency to discuss police matters with the mayor and council members, but Koa doubted that they could successfully browbeat Lannua. They didn't understand the depth of the chief's protective instincts when it came to the mayor. The mayor, after all, had appointed Lannua and controlled his budget. Koa tried to imagine a meeting where Goodling and the US Attorney attempted to enlist the chief's agreement while simultaneously threatening him under the Patriot Act if he leaked information to the mayor. It wouldn't go well. The chief would likely balk and order Koa not to facilitate their subterfuge.

There had to be a better way, and it suddenly came to Koa. In the past, the county prosecutor had appointed Koa an assistant prosecutor. He could do the same for Moreno. "Suppose," he suggested, "we go around the chief. Instead, Zeke Brown could designate Moreno as an assistant prosecutor to assist in the execution of the search warrant."

Goodling cracked a tiny smile, the first break in her poker face. "I like it. I like it a lot."

Koa thought of another problem. "How do you plan to get around the fact that everything at X-CO is classified? They're not going to let the local cops just walk in."

"Peter Romero, the contracting officer, appointed by the Secretary of Defense to administer all the Deimos contracts, plans to visit X-CO next week. It's a routine inspection trip scheduled months ago. He'll be inside when you serve the search warrant, and he'll instruct X-CO to cooperate fully with the police investigation. With Romero inside, whoever is behind this won't be able to destroy evidence."

Goodling and her colleagues had devoted a lot of time and thought to setting up this operation. Pretty impressive, Koa thought, given that he'd alerted Zeigler to the discovery of Baldwin's body less than seventy-two hours ago.

Goodling turned her focus on Koa. "Are we good to go?"

Koa nodded. "I'm on board."

Driving back to Hilo from his meeting with the feds, something occurred to Koa, something he hadn't thought to discuss with Goodling. Having executed many search warrants, he knew judges typically limited them to specific items or categories of things based on the police representations in the affidavit supporting the warrant. In this instance, the feds would need a broad search of X-CO to seize computer data showing access to and modifications of the Deimos software. Koa wondered if they had enough to support a warrant that broad.

CHAPTER SEVENTEEN

KOA SENT MAKANUI and Piki to the police impound lot to supervise the forensic search of Baldwin's car. Although Makanui had been with the department for months, she and Piki had not worked together. "I checked you out," Piki said. "You had quite a rep in the HPD, being in the anti-terror unit and all."

Makanui didn't want Piki or anyone else digging into her background, so she responded flatly, without elaboration, "It was a job."

Piki, oblivious to her tone, asked, "Well, why'd you leave?"

"I had my reasons."

Undeterred, Piki persisted, "What'd you do after you quit?"

"What is this?" Makanui retorted. "Twenty questions?"

"Sorry. Didn't mean to pry."

"You could've fooled me," Makanui snapped.

"I'm sorry." Piki sounded embarrassed, most likely because he realized he'd overstepped. "Really, I am. Can we start over?" Piki pleaded.

"Sure."

They parked outside the garage, and Piki hurried around to open Makanui's door. She eased herself from the vehicle. Looking him squarely in the face, she said with an edge in her voice, "You haven't worked with a female detective before, have you?"

Taken aback, Piki responded, "Can't say I have."

"Well, save the chivalrous shit for your girlfriend," Makanui responded wryly.

"Just being polite," Piki said awkwardly.

"Polite is a distraction. You cover my back. I'll cover yours. That's how we operate. Okay?" she said coldly, leaving Piki behind and heading toward the open garage bay door.

"Okay," he mouthed sarcastically to her back before following her inside.

Inside, Mickie Durban, the department's vehicular forensics guru, had the green Honda's back hatch open and its hood up.

"So, what do you have for us?" Makanui asked.

"A couple of things," Durban said. "There're a few spots of blood in the back." He grabbed a UV light from a workbench and shined it into the vehicle's rear, revealing several dime-size spots and one larger black stain.

"We ought to send a sample over to Professor Diaz for a DNA test to determine if it's Baldwin's blood," Piki suggested.

"Agreed," Makanui responded, "and ask him if he can use Raman spectrography to determine when the blood got there."

"Raman spectrography?" Piki asked.

"Yeah," Makanui responded. "It uses reflected laser light to ID drugs and other substances, and there's research suggesting it can date blood samples."

"You learn that in the anti-terror unit?" Piki asked.

Makanui didn't respond.

"We found some hair, too." Durban pointed to several blond strands on one side of the rear compartment. "Right color. Could be Baldwin's."

"Send a sample of that, too, to Professor Diaz and another to the state lab, same as the blood sample," Piki directed.

"Another thing," Durban said, leading them around to the front of the car, where he pointed to an open electrical box just under the windshield. "The GPS data has been wiped."

"Shit," Piki said. "That means we can't tell where the car has been."

Makanui pointed her Maglite at the control box to read the brand label before turning away to make a call on her cell. After a couple of minutes, she returned with her phone still to her ear. "Hey, Mickie," she said, "can you read off the serial number on that GPS box?"

Durban did so, and Makanui repeated it into the phone. After another short wait, she reeled off a police department email address. Ending the call, she re-holstered her cell phone. "The GPS data for this vehicle is stored in the cloud. They're sending it to Cap Roberts in tech support."

"Why didn't I think of that?" Piki asked.

"Good question," Makanui said.

*   *   *

Three hours later, Makanui walked into Koa's office with a self-satisfied expression on her face. Koa guessed his newest colleague had scored a hit in the Baldwin investigation. "What's up?" Koa asked.

"Blood, hair, and locations," Makanui responded, "from Baldwin's green Honda."

"Her hair and blood?" Koa asked.

"Yeah. Traces of her blood in the back of her Honda. Professor Diaz got a DNA match. Recent, too," Makanui responded.

"How do we know it's recent?" Koa asked.

Makanui explained the Raman spectrography test.

"Clever," Koa conceded. "So, what else do we know?"

"The bloodstains suggest the killer transported her body in the car. That alone doesn't tell us much. The only fingerprints they found match Baldwin's prints we got from the FBI, so whoever moved her body wore gloves or wiped it down like a pro. Then there's GPS data."

"And," Koa prompted.

"Baldwin's wheels, like lots of modern cars, had a GPS tracking system, but someone disabled that system and wiped the memory clean sometime shortly before Snelling sold it to Kimo."

"So, there's no historical data?" Koa asked, letting his disappointment show.

"There's no historical data on the unit, but some of these systems have cloud backup. I checked with the manufacturer, and we got lucky. I had 'em download the data, and one of Cap Roberts' people in tech support figured out how to decode it."

Koa began analyzing Makanui's discovery. "If someone transported her body in the car and we have tracking info, we should be able to tell where he killed her."

"Maybe," Makanui agreed. "The car went from home to work at seven a.m. the morning of June 14, then arrived back home at nine twenty p.m.," Makanui explained, reading from the GPS data downloaded to her phone. "From Baldwin's home, someone, most likely the killer, drove to Volcano and stopped near the graveyard at ten eleven p.m., and then at eleven sixteen p.m. drove back to Baldwin's home."

"That would suggest the killer shot her at her home," Koa said.

"Possibly. I see the logic, but I'm not convinced," Makanui responded.

Koa liked challenges. It forced him to analyze all the possibilities. "Why? What am I missing?"

"Several things," Makanui responded. "Let me explain. According to the GPS data, Baldwin routinely worked from seven a.m. to six thirty or seven p.m., although she sometimes worked much later. So, seven a.m. to around nine p.m. was a relatively long day for her."

"Not exactly your usual secretarial hours. But okay. What else?" Koa questioned.

"Given that she was shot twice and bled profusely, the small amount of blood in the back of her Honda means the killers must have bagged her before they transported her."

Koa, now listening intently, said, "That makes sense."

"Assuming a drive time of forty or forty-five minutes from her home to the graveyard, that leaves only five to ten minutes at her condo. Doesn't seem like enough time to kill her, mutilate her fingers, tape the plastic bags together, bag her body, and load it in the car." Makanui paused. "So, I think she was killed and bagged at work."

Koa turned toward the window and the view of Hilo Bay, digesting all that Makanui had said. "If she was killed and bagged at the office, how come we found blood and hair in the back of her Honda?"

"The crime scene team found quite a bit of blood inside the plastic bags. Some probably leaked along the taped seams. The hair could have adhered to the bag when the killer wrapped the body. Maybe it came loose in the back of her Honda. Or maybe it got there when Baldwin used the rear compartment months ago. There's no way to tell with hair," Makanui replied.

"And," Koa added, "nobody at her apartment remembers hearing any shots. Cutting off her fingertips to thwart identification would have made a bloody mess, and no one complained about blood when they cleaned Baldwin's apartment." He paused, thinking. "If the killer or killers murdered, mutilated, and bagged her at the office, why drive to her house?"

"Maybe to get something . . . maybe something she was killed for or something that incriminated her killer?" Makanui suggested.

"Could be," Koa acknowledged, but his mind raced in another direction. "How accurate are the GPS locations?"

"To within about three meters. What are you thinking?" Makanui responded.

Koa ignored the question. "And the car went straight from the X-CO parking lot to Baldwin's house. No stops?"

"Correct."

"So, the killer had to be an X-CO employee or someone else allowed inside the compound."

"Most likely," Makanui agreed. "I suppose the attack could have occurred in the parking lot, but it seems unlikely that someone could have killed her, mutilated her hands, and bagged her body in plain sight."

"Great work, Detective. You just solved a big problem. We got probable cause to believe Baldwin died inside X-CO, and that should give us a solid basis for a broad search warrant."

CHAPTER EIGHTEEN

LATER THAT SAME afternoon, Bobby Hazzard appeared in Koa's office dressed as his usual preppy self, this time in black pants and a tan polo shirt emblazoned with an eponymous logo. Koa wasn't happy to see him and liked what the young man had to say even less. With the same lack of *aloha* he'd displayed with retired detective Kaohi and the coroner, Bobby dispensed with the pleasantries.

"How come you never told me you knew my grandfather?" Bobby asked.

Koa felt like a lightning bolt had struck him. He hadn't expected Bobby to make the connection between his father and the mill manager, and Koa fought to conceal his surprise.

Once when he'd been out ocean canoeing, his tiny hull had been surrounded by a shiver of large sharks circling with their supersensitive eyes trained on his little vessel. Koa had guessed that several were "granders," weighing at least a thousand pounds. Sharks attacked small boats more often than most people realized, and Koa's tiny craft wouldn't survive an onslaught from an angry or curious shark. He'd been frightened. One misstep, and he'd be eaten alive. He felt that way now and played for time to think and find out how much Bobby knew. "What are you talking about?" he asked.

"Yeah," Bobby continued. "Kāwika Keahi, the senator's aide, suggested that I check the old newspaper archives at the Hilo library for information about my grandfather. So, I went looking and came across an article about your father's death. He died in one of my grandfather's sugar mills. Up on the Hāmākua coast. Some kind of bizarre accident."

"So?" Koa responded, still playing dumb.

"Didn't you meet my grandfather when he came to express his condolences?"

In his agitated state, it took Koa a moment to realize the assumption inherent in Bobby's question. The kid had assumed, albeit erroneously, that Hazzard had talked to Koa about his father's death. After a slight hesitation, he responded, "It's true my father died in a mill accident, but I don't recall your grandfather ever expressing his condolences. Not to my mother or me."

Bobby appeared visibly deflated. "Oh."

Koa went on. "My father was a lowly sugar worker, a factory hand, on the bottom rung of the sugar business. Some of those mills, like the ones on the Hāmākua coast, were more than a half-century old and in pretty desperate condition. My father wasn't the only laborer to die in a mill accident. I doubt your grandfather took much notice."

"You sound bitter," Bobby said.

"It was a long time ago and another era with different standards," Koa responded before steering the conversation in a different direction. "You haven't lost a parent, have you?"

"No," Bobby admitted.

"It's one of life's tough passages . . . one of those times when you discover you're alone in the world."

Bobby was not distracted. "I guess you're saying you never met my grandfather?"

Avoiding an outright lie, Koa opted for evasion. "When I was a kid, my father took me to the mill a few times, but I don't think he introduced me to your grandfather. I think I would have remembered that."

"Hmm." Bobby seemed to have missed the lack of a direct answer and approached from another direction, an even more dangerous one. "I was talking to Kāwika Keahi, and he said there was a lot of labor unrest back in the 1980s when the mills were consolidating or closing. Was your father involved in that?"

Koa felt the sharks were getting closer. He wasn't sure why he'd become fixated on sharks. Maybe because one of the human variety was in the room. Maybe because, just a few days earlier, a shark had attacked and killed a man off the Kohala Coast. It happened from time to time, mostly when tourists swam in the ocean at twilight. Koa felt sweat form under his arms. Control yourself, he told himself. He took a deep breath and forced himself to sit back in his chair, assuming a more relaxed posture, if only for show. He decided on an oblique response. "My father, not unlike other laborers in the sugar and pineapple fields, wanted better wages and working conditions."

"But your father was never a leader in the labor movement?" Bobby followed up.

Koa again deflected the question. "He never held a union position, like shop foreman . . . or anything like that."

"Okay." Bobby got up to leave. "I saw the old newspaper stories and thought I'd ask. I'm going up there to the Hāmākua coast. See if I can find one of these old sugar workers. See what they remember about my grandfather."

Koa sat quietly after Bobby left, regaining his composure and reflecting on the visit. He thought he'd dodged immediate disaster. He'd gotten past Bobby's questions without lying. Evading, but not lying. The kid had seemed satisfied with his answers. Still, the sharks were circling. He had no idea whether Bobby could find an old sugar worker or what any of them might say. He had no confidence that his father's confrontations with the mill manager wouldn't resurface and trigger suspicions that Koa himself had killed Hazzard. Koa's secret was, after all, the alternative theory that Bobby sought.

Senator Chao's role also nagged at him. The senator and his aide seemed too involved, too supportive of what Koa saw as Bobby's obsession. He worried that the senator or his aide somehow suspected Koa's role in Anthony Hazzard's death. Yet, that seemed improbable. How could they possibly know? The senator had lived on Oʻahu back then, while Koa and Keahi had been childhood friends and fishing buddies.

Suddenly, he wondered if the senator or his aide had put Bobby up to this whole inquiry. Yet, why would they do that? It didn't make sense. Once again, his paranoia was getting the best of him. Bobby's family supported the senator's campaigns, and the senator had reciprocated by hiring the young man as an unpaid summer intern in his senate office. There could be no other motive.

CHAPTER NINETEEN

PREPARATIONS FOR THE search warrant raid on X-CO proceeded but not as fast as Koa, who believed in momentum, would have liked. On Friday, the Honolulu US Attorney brought the county prosecutor, Zeke Brown, into the loop. Koa then met Zeke to share what he'd learned about X-CO and Deimos and warned Zeke about Moreno's reluctance to cooperate with local authorities. He was about to tell Zeke about Makanui's discovery of the GPS data, when an assistant ushered Goodling and Moreno into the conference room, interrupting Koa's report.

Koa introduced the feds to Zeke. After the usual pleasantries, Zeke pivoted to Koa's concern about Moreno. "Mr. Moreno," the prosecutor began, "I'm prepared to appoint you an assistant prosecutor, but I want your assurance you'll play by our rules." Zeke hung a leg over the arm of his chair, letting his black buffalo hide boot dangle in the air. "I'm the only cowboy in this office. Do we understand each other?" Koa expected an explosion from Moreno, but he got only a quick smile and a nod. Zeke had a way with people.

Zeke then explained the process of preparing an affidavit in support of their request for a search warrant before concluding, "Getting a search warrant won't be a problem. Given the phony Baldwin personnel file, her bank records, and the X-CO lies about her position, there's plenty of ground for a warrant, but it could be quite limited."

"Why?" Goodling asked.

"With X-CO's high-powered board and the public hoopla over the upcoming artificial intelligence seminar in Hilo, the judge will be cautious. He'll likely limit the warrant to personnel records, and maybe just Baldwin's records."

"But we need access to emails—Baldwin's, Wingate's, and Snelling's, plus records of access to the computer system to track down the source of the rogue code," Goodling responded.

"That's a tall order," Zeke responded in his usual loud voice.

Koa started to respond, but Moreno interrupted.

"This local warrant stuff is all bullshit," Moreno interjected. "We shouldn't be farting around with the local cops. The Patriot Act gives us everything we need. That's what we should be doing."

So much for détente, Koa thought.

Goodling glared incredulously at Moreno, visibly annoyed. "Oh, right. I get it. We bust in like cowboys, alert the perps, all for the sake of a little evidence that won't ID the saboteurs and will set the Deimos program back a decade." She paused for emphasis. "Remember our primary objective, Moreno."

Silence filled the room as the two feds stared each other down. In that interval, Koa realized that he didn't fully understand the government's primary objective. Was it as simple as identifying the saboteurs or uncovering all the Deimos hacks? Or was there something more profound happening—something underlying the tension between Goodling and Moreno that he'd sensed from his first meeting with them?

Finally, Moreno said, "Have it your way."

"I was about to say," Koa interjected, "that I don't think there'll be a problem getting a broad warrant."

The others looked surprised.

"Why not?" Moreno asked.

"We had a breakthrough last night." Koa shared what he'd learned from Makanui about the cloud-based GPS data detailing the movements of Baldwin's car on the night of June 14–15. "So, we have probable cause to believe that Baldwin was killed, mutilated, and her body bagged inside the X-CO compound. The killer or an accomplice loaded her into her car at X-CO. From there, the killer or killers drove to her home, and then to the Volcano cemetery."

"That's a game changer," Zeke agreed.

Goodling nodded in agreement. "One more thing," Goodling added, looking at Moreno. "Tell 'em."

Moreno sighed. "Earlier today, when I contacted the DOD contracting officer supervising X-CO, I learned that the company's government contract requires it to give notice within forty-eight hours of all employee hirings, firings, and resignations so that the government has a record for security purposes. X-CO failed to give timely notice of Baldwin's resignation."

"Let me guess," Koa interrupted. "They gave notice sometime after Baldwin's death on June 14th or 15th."

"Yeah. On June 15th, saying she resigned on May 27th."

"That's a two-week gap. X-CO have an explanation for the delay?" Koa asked.

"None," Moreno answered. "Putting that fact together with your timeline, the whole resignation story, along with the emails to Snelling, have got to be bogus."

"Okay," Zeke said, "I'll go see the judge first thing Monday, and we should be good to go Tuesday a.m."

"If your local yokel judge signs the warrant," Moreno added caustically.

Koa ignored the comment, but Zeke turned on Moreno. "That local yokel will break your balls if you cross him."

Koa suppressed a smile and broke the awkward silence by asking, "Will the contracting officer be here by then?"

"He's got meetings this weekend but will be flying in on Monday and ready to go on Tuesday," Goodling responded.

Staying behind while the feds left, Koa and Zeke hammered out the affidavit that Koa would sign to support the search warrant. With Koa's suspicions, the contracting officer's statement that X-CO had failed to report Baldwin's resignation, and the GPS evidence showing that Baldwin died at the X-CO compound, Zeke felt confident the judge would grant them a broad search.

"You worried about blowback from a search with all the big egos associated with X-CO?" Koa asked.

"Oh, they'll scream like pigs in a trap. They'll try to quash the subpoena. But they're not going to stop a murder investigation. Not on my watch. Besides," Zeke added with a smile, "a little controversy is like exercise. It gets the heart pumping."

*   *   *

Both Zeke and Koa were in Zeke's office before sunrise on Monday morning, finishing the last of the paperwork they needed for their warrant. By nine, they were ready. "I want you to come with me," Zeke said, slipping his sports jacket on over his white *paniolo* shirt. "The judge knows you from a bunch of appearances, including your last big murder investigation. He respects your judgment. You being there might just make the difference."

"You got it," Koa responded.

"You know the drill," Zeke continued as they left the prosecutor's office and walked across the parking lot to the courthouse. Disregarding the elevators as was Zeke's habit, they climbed the stairs to

Judge Hitachi's chambers. "I'll present the request for the warrant. You take the fact questions."

Meleana, the judge's secretary, nodded to Koa but greeted Zeke like a second son. "You coming to the surprise birthday party for the judge this Friday?" she asked, disengaging from their embrace.

"Wouldn't miss it. All the defense lawyers, you know, the bad dudes who wear black hats and represent crooks, they'll be there, trying to curry favor with the judge. So, somebody's got to stand up for the good guys," Zeke said in a down-home, good-old-country-boy voice.

Meleana laughed. "I suppose you'll be wearing your white hat?"

"You bet. My white Stetson on top and my black boots on the bottom," Zeke said with a bow and a grin.

Meleana laughed. "I just love those boots." She buzzed the judge on the office intercom.

Koa and Zeke entered Judge Hitachi's chambers. Like the courtrooms in the modern courthouse, his office was functional with narrow windows on the outside wall and a floor-to-ceiling bookcase behind a more than ample desk in richly grained local wood, adding a warming touch to the otherwise sterile room. A handsome man of Japanese heritage, Judge Hitachi had on a casual shirt. As was his routine, he wore dark slacks and dress shoes so he could don his robe and head to his courtroom formally attired.

"*Aloha*, gentlemen. Zeke, what have you brought me this time? It must be unusual if you need Detective Kāne's help," the judge added with a wry but friendly smile.

"*Aloha*, Judge," they responded.

"It's a bit sensitive," Zeke began. "It arises from the gruesome murder of a young woman, named Tiger Baldwin, who worked for X-CO, the defense contractor, here on the Big Island. We have evidence that someone at X-CO killed Ms. Baldwin, mutilated her body to conceal her identity, bagged her in plastic, and buried her in an abandoned Volcano village cemetery. When questioned, X-CO provided the police with inaccurate payroll records, and two X-CO employees misrepresented Ms. Baldwin's position at the company. X-CO claims that Baldwin resigned, but the company failed to report her resignation to its government contracting officer in a timely fashion as required by its contract. We're requesting a search warrant to obtain all records, including emails, payroll information, work history, job performance, and any other materials related to Ms. Baldwin and the X-CO employees who made the false representations. Finally, we've drafted the warrant to cover all evidence relevant to Ms. Baldwin's job and death. Detective Kāne has prepared an extensive affidavit and can walk you through the full basis for a search warrant."

Zeke had drafted the warrant carefully. Because of Baldwin's actual job as a senior systems architect, the phrase "all evidence related to Baldwin's job" would give the search team access to the X-CO computer system so the feds could trace any unauthorized modifications to the Deimos software.

Zeke handed the affidavit and draft search warrant to the judge. Koa led the judge through each significant step of the police investigation. He laid out in detail the GPS data, the sale of Baldwin's car, and the removal of her possessions.

The judge asked several clarifying questions and considered the matter for several minutes before asking, "How do you plan to deal with the confidential nature of X-CO's work for the government?"

As Koa had seen so often, Zeke took the potentially difficult question and turned it to his advantage. "Before joining the police force, Detective Kāne served in the military where he held a top-secret security clearance. In light of the need for this search, we have been in contact with the Justice Department, which has temporarily renewed his security clearance. In addition, a representative of the FBI, who has an appropriate security clearance, will accompany Detective Kāne during the search."

Not for the first time, Koa marveled at Zeke's savvy. In one stroke, Zeke had answered the judge's question, underlined the importance of the search, and assured the court that there would be no recriminations from the federal government.

Zeke then deftly addressed another potential problem. "Judge, as you can see in the warrant, we've included a provision requiring all personnel involved in the raid to keep it secret until after we're finished."

Koa had expected the judge to question this provision, but he just nodded. Outsiders often made the mistake of underestimating Judge Hitachi, but the judge, well acquainted with local politics, was shrewd and understood Zeke's objective. He was ensuring that Chief Lannua had no opportunity to alert the mayor, county council, or X-CO's politically connected management before the police executed the search warrant.

After rereading the affidavit and the proposed warrant, the judge took out his pen, signed the document, and handed it back to Zeke. "Be prepared, Zeke. Given the personalities on the X-CO board, you're going to catch some serious flak."

With the warrant in hand, Koa's instincts told him to round up the team ASAP and head to X-CO to conduct the search. He was famous for pushing cases as hard as he could and didn't like the idea of waiting until morning. But unfortunately, the contracting officer's plane had not arrived, so Koa had to wait.

Thinking he might improve relations with the feds and even ease tensions with Moreno, he invited Goodling, Moreno, and the rest of their group to join his team for a drink that night. Eight of them—the five feds plus Koa, Makanui, and Piki—grabbed two tables next to the wall at the E Komo Mai Lounge on Kuawa Street in Hilo. Koa ordered three pitchers of beer and some *pūpūs*, including *'ahi poke* and *kālua* pork sliders. A little local color, Koa thought, might soften up these mainlanders.

Koa sat with Goodling, Moreno, and Carvelli, while Makanui and Piki huddled with Ige and Somes. Looking across to the other table, Koa saw Piki and Makanui deep in conversation. Piki, Koa knew, harbored intense curiosity about his colleague. The young detective had twice inquired about Makanui's background. Based on his initial experiences with her, Koa figured she'd be at least as good at protecting her secrets as Piki would be at rooting them out with his extraordinary internet skills.

Turning to his table, he said, "Since you've come from DC, I thought you needed some local color. Every town has a couple of police hangouts. This and the Burger Joint are two of Hilo's finest."

"Thanks," Goodling responded. "We've been hitting it hard, so this will be good for us all."

Turning to Moreno, Koa asked, "Tell me about your background. How you got into the bureau."

"Never knew my father. My mom was a plumber. Left me home alone with a computer and some stolen video games. I took computers apart before I was eight and was sneaking into computer class at the local community college when I was ten. I got thrown out of class a dozen times before one of the teachers took pity on me. I became a hacker. Hung for a while with the Anons, you know, the hacker group, busting government computers. One of the other Anons got nailed by the FBI and gave me up. The agent who busted me found out about my hacker-style attacks on kiddie porn sites, sent me to a computer school, and got me a job in the bureau. Normally, a guy with my background wouldn't have a chance at the bureau, but they don't teach hacking at those big East Coast colleges, and the bureau needed my talents. Been there for a decade."

Moreno took a pull from his mug and speared some poke. "I hear you had some tough times in the service?" Moreno said, adding a question mark.

The question put Koa on instant alert. He'd been in the Mogadishu fiasco and lost two good men, including his best buddy, Jerry, who'd taken a bullet intended for Koa. Jerry, who'd always planned to return to Seattle to join its police force, had instead died in Koa's arms. His buddy's death had been the final push that propelled Koa to join the police partly in honor of Jerry's memory. Koa still found it painful to talk about his time in Africa, and he usually resisted doing so. He wondered if Moreno was trying to get under his skin. "Where'd you hear that?" Koa asked cautiously.

"Jeff Edgar. He's with the bureau now."

"I haven't seen Jeff in a decade. Didn't know he was with the FBI," Koa responded.

"Says you saved his ass in Somalia."

Still looking to avoid the subject, Koa said, "So, Jeff's still telling tall tales."

Moreno smiled; the first one Koa had seen from him. "Seriously, I'd love to hear about that op, if you don't mind talking about it."

Moreno's tone seemed conciliatory, and Koa decided to give him the gist of it. "Mogadishu was fucked up from the beginning. Clinton sent us with too few people, shitty intel, and no backup. Our commanders wanted armor, more time, and better intel, but the pols in DC wanted to do it on the cheap. The enemy assholes showed up in force. Too many fanatics with too many AKs and RPGs. Lost my best friend and another good man to snipers. It was touch and go for the rest of us."

Moreno, taken aback by Koa's candor, said, "Sorry about your friend. I didn't know."

After a moment of silence, Koa said, "It's okay. The irony is that he's partly the reason I became a cop."

Goodling, maybe sensing Koa's growing discomfort, changed the subject. "So, tell me what life is like for a senior detective in Hilo, Hawai'i."

"It's not all surfing," Koa responded, happy with the change of subject.

"Seriously," Goodling insisted. "It must be a change of pace after your Special Forces days."

Koa, always cautious in describing his history, chose his words carefully. "This island is in my blood. I was born here, and this is where I belong. With our Polynesian ancestry, checkered history with the US, our ethnic polyglot, and the economic upheaval following the death of the sugar and pineapple plantations, Hawai'i's a lot more complex than you'd think based on tourist posters."

"I understand," Moreno interrupted, "there's a sovereignty movement."

"True," Koa responded. "It's deeply rooted in Hawaiian culture and the history of US exploitation."

"So, you support sovereignty?" Moreno asked.

"No, but I understand and empathize. Westerners brought diseases that killed off the vast majority of the native Hawaiian population. Then, the US stole the islands in much the same way it overran the American Indians, and there is little doubt that native Hawaiians have suffered severe economic exploitation."

"Sounds to me like you support the sovereignty movement," Moreno said. "I hear you've got activist friends."

Koa gave Moreno a sharp look. The man *was* trying to provoke a dispute. "I don't like economic exploitation in any form, and it's an undeniable historical fact that a bunch of wealthy Western merchants staged a *coup d'état* against the legitimate Hawaiian government. But that was a hundred and twenty-five years ago, and we can't undo history. Restoration of sovereignty now would be a disaster. Yet, the consequences of that wrongful act persist, and I try to forge relationships with activists who use peaceful means to make the lives of the native Hawaiian people better. Besides, as police officers, we're often in the middle, and it's useful to have friends on both sides."

So much for improving relations with Moreno. Having delivered his rebuttal, Koa decided to ignore Moreno and instead focus on Goodling. "What about you? How'd you get into protecting the national security?"

"I grew up in New York in the Bronx, got into Princeton on a scholarship, and then got my law degree from the University of Virginia before clerking for a federal judge and joining a private law firm. When I was a young lawyer in private practice, I got assigned to a case defending a Chinese spy. We ultimately pled him guilty, and he ratted out a couple of associates. It seems I impressed the justice lawyer on the case, and when he got promoted, he asked me to join the department. I've never looked back."

Koa raised his glass. "Well, here's to national security and success in tomorrow's raid."

"Yeah, right," Moreno mumbled.

"And to Tiger Baldwin," Goodling added. "Without her, we might never have known about the Deimos deception."

CHAPTER TWENTY

WITH THE SEARCH warrant in hand and Peter Romero, the DOD contracting officer responsible for government oversight of X-CO's Deimos operations, on-island, Koa and Goodling marshaled their forces to execute the search warrant. The team consisted of six officers—Romero would ensure access, Koa and Moreno would search, and Makanui with two uniformed, cops would provide backup. Romero had given them a floor plan of the building, designating precise areas with relevant files, so each officer would know where to go.

Although Koa had supervised many warrant searches in his twelve years as a detective, this one held a special meaning. Like most men who'd been in the crucible of combat with fellow soldiers, he regarded turncoats as beneath contempt. He couldn't shake the image of the Deimos destroying the convoy it was supposed to protect, like a rogue soldier killing his buddies. Fragging had become all too common during the Vietnam War, especially to young, inexperienced officers. Still, Koa knew the raid might not yield the evidence they needed to get to the bottom of the Deimos treason, so he tried to keep a lid on his adrenalin rush.

Romero, a huge ex-Marine who served as the federally appointed DOD contracting officer, entered the complex at 7:45 a.m. After routine introductory interviews with X-CO executives and a tour of the facilities, so everyone would recognize him and his authority, he was in a position to facilitate access. He alerted Koa with a text, and at 9:15 a.m., Koa and Moreno drove into the X-CO parking lot. Makanui and two patrol officers followed in a separate car.

At the gate in the chain-link fence surrounding the facility, Koa and his team waited less than thirty seconds before being admitted by a guard who escorted them into the building. Romero met Koa and Moreno in the lobby, just outside the biometric security door protecting the secret part of the facility. With Wingate, wearing his usual white dress shirt and tie, watching, Romero made a show of examining the search warrant and papers verifying that Koa and Moreno had the requisite security clearance. Romero then gave Wingate the documents and informed him that the police were conducting a search related to Baldwin's death. He directed Wingate to open the security door. Wingate reluctantly acquiesced and accompanied Koa and Moreno into the secure area. Makanui stopped at the security door, holding it open so she and the two backup officers could enter if needed to enforce the warrant.

Snelling, in his security guard uniform armed with a Glock, confronted Koa in the hallway just inside the secure area. He bore a hostile expression and stood blocking the search team's way forward. "You can't barge in here," he said in a loud voice. "This is a secure facility. You don't have clearance."

"We have a search warrant for these premises and the requisite clearances," Koa said evenly. "Your CEO—" Koa pointed to Wingate, who trailed just behind Koa—"has already reviewed the warrant signed by Judge Hitachi, and your DOD contracting officer has verified our security clearances. We'll arrest anyone who resists."

Snelling started to protest, but Romero cut him off. "Your contract with the DOD requires adherence to all lawful requirements. You'd better not resist."

Snelling dropped one hand to his holstered gun, and, looking to Wingate, he asked, "You want me to send 'em back outside?"

"I suggest you take your hand away from that weapon," Koa said. "There are three armed policemen just outside the entry door ready to arrest you for obstruction and haul you down to the lockup."

Wingate waved a hand to signal Snelling to back down and, glaring at Koa, raised his voice. "You are making a mistake, Detective. You know who sits on our board? They're powerful people, and they'll have your badge before you go home tonight."

Koa returned Wingate's harsh stare. "Don't threaten me, Mr. Wingate. Now, move out of the way, and do *not* attempt to interfere with this search."

"It's your career," Wingate growled.

Pissed and projecting attitude, Wingate and Snelling stepped aside. Following the X-CO floor plan from Romero, Koa walked past them and headed to the human resources area. Moreno hurried toward the computer data center. The contracting officer used the building-wide public address system to explain that a police search was in progress and warned all employees to cooperate.

The Human Resources area consisted of the HR director's office, an interview-conference room, and a records room with desks for two employees. Nameplates identified them as Kimberly Ward and Haukea Kapule. Kimberly, middle-aged and conservatively dressed, was a gray-haired *haole*. Haukea, a Hawaiian in black leggings, dressed in hipper garb and couldn't have been more than twenty-five. Both seemed concerned, if not frightened, when Koa identified himself and informed them of the warrant.

Kimberly, the more seasoned of the two women, responded efficiently to Koa's requests, copying personnel files and payroll records for Baldwin, Wingate, and Snelling onto a flash drive Koa had brought with him. Koa also demanded backup records showing the date and time when each of the personnel files had been entered or modified. Because he wanted immediate access to Baldwin's history with X-CO, he instructed Kimberly to print all those items. Several dozen sheets of computer paper spooled off a nearby printer.

Working quickly, Koa examined Baldwin's files and found them identical to those provided by Wingate during Koa's first visit. There had to be more. Looking up from the Baldwin documents, Koa asked if there were, or had been in the past, other files related to Baldwin. The two women looked at each other before Haukea started to speak, but Kimberly interrupted. "You have everything," she said.

He looked at Haukea. "You were going to say something?"

She hesitated, glanced again at Kimberly, and said, almost inaudibly, "Just what Kimberly told you."

Koa recognized the dynamic between the two women and knew they were withholding information. He guessed that Haukea had been about to reveal that there were indeed more documents before Kimberly shut her down.

Koa knew obstruction when he saw it and considered how to proceed. He could separate the two women and question them individually. Haukea might open up, but inside the office, she'd be reluctant, fearing retribution from her colleagues. He'd likely be more successful interviewing her at home, away from the office, and any possible intimidation by her coworkers.

Koa turned back to Kimberly. "It's a crime to obstruct a police investigation. Are you sure you've given me everything, past and present, related to Baldwin?"

"Yes," she replied curtly.

"And Wingate and Snelling?" Koa asked.

"Yes."

Frowning with disapproval, Koa placed the files in a secure box, locked it, and carried it out to one of the uniformed officers with Makanui for transfer to a secure conference room at the prosecutor's office. As he returned to check on Moreno, Haukea emerged from a restroom. Passing close to Koa, she slipped him a note scribbled on a slip of paper. With a glance, Koa saw a phone number before he stuck the paper in his pocket. Koa had guessed right. Haukea had something she wanted to tell him outside the presence of her coworkers.

Moreno spent four hours in the computer center, gathering up more than a dozen boxes of files, commercial disk drives, pieces of computer hardware, modems, printouts, and other materials before moving to search different areas. While they worked, Koa took a call from Zeke. X-CO's lawyers had filed a motion with Judge Hitachi to quash or withdraw the search warrant. "You've got X-CO stirred up like a mother hog protecting her young. They've hauled out the big guns with affidavits from Senator Chao and a statement from the governor."

"Wow, that was fast," Koa responded.

"Yeah. Suggests to me X-CO's got something big to hide," Zeke responded.

"You're right about that. Do we need to stop the search?" Koa asked.

"No, not until the judge decides. The hearing starts in ten minutes."

"What are the chances the judge will reaffirm the warrant?"

"Pretty good. I'll call you as soon as we get a ruling."

At that moment, Wingate approached Koa. "Listen, Detective, our lawyers have just filed papers to overturn your warrant. You need to halt the search right *now*!"

"Sorry," Koa responded, "the warrant is valid until the judge says otherwise."

Wingate swore. "You son of a bitch. We're going to sue your ass . . . sue you for everything you're worth when the judge overturns your warrant," Wingate snarled before turning away.

Koa, used to threats, found Wingate's over-the-top reaction revealing. X-CO had to be hiding something . . . something momentous, like the sabotage of Deimos, and Wingate was afraid the search team would stumble on evidence to prove it.

Shortly after that, Koa noticed Snelling and Wingate standing off to the side of the open-plan working area observing. They were, Koa thought, oddly inseparable. Why, he wondered, would the company's highest executive hang with a security guard? In Koa's mind, the unusual pairing suggested that Snelling was more than just a guard. To Koa, it also meant that Wingate likely had an intimate knowledge of Snelling's activities, like his sale of Baldwin's car and the removal of her belongings from her apartment. Both men, he concluded, would bear greater scrutiny.

The search went on for another hour. Wingate's face, which had earlier reddened in anger, became near apoplectic with each new box of materials that Koa's team carried out through the biometric door to their van. Koa figured Wingate's blood pressure must be in the stratosphere. He once again sensed that much more was at stake than just the execution of a search warrant.

The team had nearly finished when Koa spotted Wingate and Snelling in a heated conversation. Wingate wore an air of defeat, and Snelling appeared angry, more genuinely angry than when Koa and Makanui had first interviewed him. Moments later, Koa's cell rang. It was Zeke. Judge Hitachi had denied the motion to halt the search.

Koa walked over to the two X-CO men, who stopped talking as he approached. He took pleasure in reporting, "Just thought I'd let you know that Judge Hitachi denied your motion."

Wingate's face fell further, but he didn't give up. "Our lawyers will appeal or go to federal court."

"Good luck," Koa responded.

A short time later, the team finished and left, their van loaded with seized materials.

In planning for the raid on X-CO, Koa had anticipated the likely reaction. As Zeke had predicted, X-CO had tried to upend the subpoena, but the prosecutor's quick response and the court's ruling had shocked X-CO's legal team. Koa and Zeke were certain that Wingate would raise hell inside X-CO and that its politically connected management would explode into orbit, bringing their political clout to bear. Koa and Zeke decided to strike first, and less than an hour after completing the search, they were in Police Chief Lannua's office.

Even before pleasantries, Zeke abruptly announced, "Koa and a special agent from my office just served a search warrant on X-CO. I expect you'll shortly be hearing complaints."

"You did what?" Lannua roared. "Why didn't I know about this?" Then, before anyone could respond, he pointed a finger at Koa. "You told me you had finished with X-CO."

Zeke, who usually had the loudest voice in any room, spoke softly. "You didn't know because the judge ordered complete secrecy in advance of the raid. And the map changed dramatically after Koa last briefed you."

The chief reacted to this slight with increased anger. "How? What changed? I run this department. Why the hell wasn't I told?"

Zeke, who had a long and tumultuous history with the chief, reacted to the outburst with practiced calm. "We developed proof that Baldwin was killed, mutilated, and bagged inside the X-CO compound. Its executives lied and created phony documents to cover up her death."

Lannua appeared stunned by this news but recovered quickly. He banged his fist on his desk, a glass paperweight crashed to the floor, and the sound reverberated. "The X-CO people will go crazy. Their chairman will call the governor. Senator Chao will be in here. The mayor will have a coronary. This is going to be a disaster for the AI Seminar coming later this week."

Koa knew from personal experience that no one intimidated Zeke. The county prosecutor, elected by and accountable only to the Big Island voters, had prosecuted governors, police chiefs, and some of the island's heaviest hitters. "Tough shit," Zeke responded. "X-CO obstructed a murder investigation and got caught."

"Easy for you to say. You don't have to deal with Zhou Li, Senator Chao, Kāwika Keahi, the governor, and the mayor," the chief screamed.

"That's exactly what I do want. I want them to deal with me. Tell them you had nothing to do with the search warrant, it's out of your control, and they can complain to me," Zeke replied.

The chief shook his head. "You must be a masochist . . ."

A ringing telephone interrupted the chief. He picked it up, listened for a minute, and said, "The prosecutor is here now. I'll put you on speaker."

"What the hell is going on?" Senator Chao yelled. "Just had a call from Arron Zhou Li. The police barged into X-CO and upset the whole place. Zhou Li is hopping mad and ready to chop some heads."

"Good afternoon, Senator. Zeke Brown here. You can tell Chairman Li to chop some heads in his own outfit. His people are obstructing a murder investigation, and I'll indict them if they're not careful."

"Christ, Zeke," the senator responded, "you'd better know what you're doing. Li's got connections from the governor to the White House. He'll have your head."

"Better men have tried and failed."

Silence prevailed for several seconds before the senator said, "C'mon, Zeke. I've got to tell Zhou Li something."

"Tell him to instruct his people to stop stonewalling," the prosecutor replied.

"Zhou Li is going to be here later this week for the big AI seminar. You can give him that message," the senator responded.

Senator Chao had barely hung up when Mayor Tenaka stormed into Chief Lannua's office. The short, stocky former Army lieutenant colonel was hopping mad. He stopped in the doorway, stared briefly at each man, and began yelling. "What the hell are you assholes doing? You've upset the X-CO people just before the AI seminar. Goddammit. Don't you understand it's critical to Hilo's future to increase tech investment?"

Zeke, who often dealt with the mayor, remained unfazed by his outburst. "We *assholes*," Zeke emphasized the word, "are enforcing the law against murder."

"Murder?" Tanaka yelled. "What murder?"

"An X-CO employee was murdered, mutilated, and bagged in plastic inside X-CO, and the company's employees are playing cover-up," Zeke said.

"What's your proof?" Tenaka demanded, dialing down his anger.

"They gave Koa phony payroll records and lied about the employee's position. And that's just for starters."

"Jesus." Tenaka paused. "This is going to ruin the AI seminar. Couldn't you have waited until afterward?"

"You know better than to suggest that," Zeke said softly, giving his response more menace than if he'd yelled.

"Jesus," Tenaka repeated. "You know Zhou Li and half his board of directors are coming in later this week."

"Yeah, I know," Zeke responded. "I'll have subpoenas waiting for them."

"What?" Tenaka screamed.

"Just kidding," Zeke responded with a smile. "At least for now . . ."

CHAPTER TWENTY-ONE

KOA WAS AT his desk later that afternoon when the duty sergeant called. "I got a guy named Akira Sato on the line. Wants to talk to you. Says it's about your father."

The name Sato was vaguely familiar, and Koa took the call. "*Aloha*, Mr. Sato, how can I help you?"

"You probably don't remember, but my father, Shiro, and your father were friends way back in the '80s at the mill."

The name Shiro triggered a memory, and Koa recalled a grizzled old Japanese laborer who'd worked alongside Koa's father on the cane crushing line at the Hāmākua Sugar Company. Shiro was one of the men who'd told Koa how his father had confronted Anthony Hazzard over the mill's unsafe conditions. It had been Shiro, Koa remembered, who'd shared what he knew about Hazzard's role in Koa's father's death.

"Yes," Koa responded cautiously, "I remember my father talking about Shiro. He must be quite elderly now."

"He passed several years ago," Sato said, "but—"

"Sorry about your father," Koa interrupted.

"He'd been ill for a long time, like a lot of sugar workers. He's in a better place now. But that's not why I called. There's a guy says he's Hazzard's grandson. He's up here in Honoka'a askin' questions."

"Questions. What kind of questions?"

"About how his grandfather died. Whether somebody killed the old bastard."

"You talk to him?"

"Yeah, told him his grandfather was a mean son of a bitch. Told him how the bastard bought and sold people like cattle and treated them worse than hogs. Told him the scumbag must have hung himself outa remorse for all the bad shit he'd done," Sato responded without any attempt to hide the contempt in his voice.

For Koa, this was useful intelligence, but nothing Sato had said involved Koa, so he didn't yet understand why Sato had called. "How'd he react?"

"Said I didn't know his grandfather, so I told him he was the ignorant one. He had no idea what an evil bastard he had for a grandfather. Then he asks me if I knew whether you'd ever talked to old man Hazzard. I thought that was pretty odd. So, that's why I'm calling. I mean, Hazzard didn't know anyone's name, let alone their kids' names. And anyway, he wouldn't have given a shit unless he thought they'd be strong enough to work in the cane fields."

"You told him that?"

"Yeah, and he didn't like it one bit."

"He talk to anyone else?"

"Well, he showed me a list on some fancy political paper with a bunch of old-timers' names. Most of them died years ago, lots of 'em from the epidemic of kidney disease among the sugar workers. But a couple of the younger ones, they're still around."

The words "political paper" caught Koa's attention. "You said a political paper, what kind of political paper?"

"It said 'United States Senate' across the top and something about committee or subcommittee on the side. Somethin' like that."

It must, Koa thought, have come from Senator Chao or more likely Koa's friend, the senator's aide. One of them had researched the old sugar cane employees and given Bobby Hazzard their names. Chao and Keahi seemed unusually invested in Bobby's crusade to disprove his grandfather's suicide. But why? Koa had previously written off their support of Bobby as an effort to curry favor with his father, a significant campaign contributor. Now, Koa had his doubts. His instincts told him he was missing something, but what exactly eluded him.

"So, this guy talked to a couple of other old-timers?" Koa asked.

"Maybe. I know Kimura told this dude to go to hell. I'm not sure if he ever talked to Ikeda."

"Thanks," Koa said. "I appreciate the call. Let me know if you hear anything else."

"You got it. We're all sugar family even if the work's gone."

Koa had just put his office phone back in its cradle when his cell rang. The screen said Kāwika Keahi, and Koa answered. "What's up, brah?"

"Just wanted to give you a heads-up. You really stepped in it at X-CO. Chairman Zhou Li has been on the phone with the senator and has him all riled up. Chao's talked to the governor, and he's arranging for Zhou Li to talk to the president. Get your rain slicker on 'cause shit is gonna come pouring down."

Koa, annoyed as always by political interference, responded curtly, "Tell the senator to deal with Zeke and Judge Hitachi. I had a warrant and served it by the book."

"Bullshit, Koa. The senator knows who's driving this investigation, and it's not Zeke. So, look out for yourself."

The tenor of the call bothered Koa. There was something off about Keahi's over-the-top warning. He could understand how Zhou Li might be upset, but couldn't see either the senator or the governor making an overt effort to interfere with a murder investigation. And,

Koa thought, there was no way the President would stop an inquiry run by his own Justice Department into potential sabotage of a top-secret defense department weapons program.

*   *   *

At six p.m. that evening, when he thought she'd be home from work, Koa called the number on the slip of paper Haukea had passed to him in X-CO's offices. He identified himself and asked, "Was there something you wanted to tell me?"

"Yes," she said softly, her voice hesitant . . . almost faltering. "Can you meet me?"

"Sure," he responded. "When and where?"

She hesitated, apparently thinking of a place. "Tonight at nine at the tower on Coconut Island. Okay?"

Koa hesitated. It was an unusual place for a nighttime meeting. Coconut Island, or Mokuola as Hawaiians called it, was a speck of land in Hilo Bay, connected to the shore by a causeway. In ancient times, it had been a *puʻuhonua* or place of healing. According to legend, the sick could be cured by swimming around the island three times. The tower on the seaward side of Mokuola, actually a stone diving platform with multiple levels, had been rebuilt many times following devastating tsunamis that swept over the tiny islet.

"Nine o'clock. I'll be there," he responded.

Although he had no reason to distrust Haukea, Koa didn't like the isolated meeting spot, so he took Makanui as a backup, and they arrived before sunset. They parked and walked through Li-liʻuokalani Park on the edge of Hilo Bay. Named after the last ruling monarch of the Kingdom of Hawaiʻi, and built in the early 1900s, the 24.5-acre oasis was the most spacious authentic Japanese ornamental garden outside Japan. Koa and Makanui passed several century-old banyan trees, pagodas, and a classic Japanese footbridge before crossing a modern causeway to the tiny island where he would meet Haukea.

He left Makanui in the deep shadows behind one of the bath-houses and continued along the stone path to the tower. He sat on a rock wall, watching twilight fade and darkness creep over the bay. Birds in the nearby trees gradually stopped chirping, and the night grew quiet save for the sound of waves lapping against the base of the tower. The smell of the ocean soothed him, and he tasted its salty tang. The sea air made him think of being out on the ocean and then his latest outing with Nālani and the young Hawaiian kids they took on weekend canoe outings. Koa's thoughts turned to Bobby Hazzard, and he wondered if swimming three times around the lit-tle islet would rid him of the young man and his inquiry into his grandfather's death.

At precisely nine o'clock, he heard footsteps and saw Haukea ap-proach, illuminated in the soft glow of a red-filtered flashlight. After spotting him, she looked around to be sure there was no one else in sight before sitting next to him. After a moment, she turned the light off, leaving them in the pale light of a quarter moon.

"I'll lose my job if anyone from the company sees us together," she whispered.

He wanted to ask why, but she seemed nervous, and he didn't want to heighten her anxiety. Remaining neutral, he said simply, "I appreciate your coming."

"You're from Laupāhoehoe. Your mother is a healer." It was a statement, not a question.

He hadn't recognized her surname, so she surprised him with her knowledge of his family. "How do you know my family?"

"I'm from Pāpaʻaloa. Your mother once blessed my father with her *lāʻau lapaʻau*, her medicine."

Seeking to reinforce his connection with her, he said, "So we were neighbors."

"Yes." Without further preamble, she turned to look at him and said, her voice less hesitant, "Kimberly lied to you."

"About the Baldwin file?" he asked.

"Yes. That and other things."

In interviewing cooperative witnesses, Koa was never sure what would come out and so liked open-ended questions. "Like what?"

Her words tumbled out, hurried by her nervousness. "Kimberly works for Snelling and spies on the . . . on the employees." Haukea's voice cracked, but then all restraint disappeared, and she spoke in a torrent. "They put apps on people's phones to track their movements and record their calls. They set up video surveillance on some employees. They put trackers on people's cars. They follow employees, and keep secret files on everyone."

"How do you know all this?" Koa asked.

"Kimberly had me create some of the files. She told me the government required the company to monitor its employees, and would prosecute me if I ever disclosed anything."

"They were monitoring Baldwin?" Koa asked.

"Yes. There were three files on Baldwin—her original personnel file, a phony one that Snelling gave to Kimberly, and a monitoring file on her."

"Tell me about the phony file."

"It was a replacement for the real one they purged."

"Purged? Who's *they*?"

"Kimberly and Snelling." Haukea spoke Snelling's name with distaste, struggling to contain her dislike for the man.

"Why?"

"I'm not sure why. They switched the files a day or two after Baldwin stopped coming to the office. I kind of assumed it had to do with her departure."

"How do you know about the file switch?" he asked.

"I heard Kimberly and Snelling talking about Baldwin's records. Their conversation seemed odd, so I checked the file and saw they'd altered it."

"What happened to the old file?" he asked.

"Kimberly trashed it, but you know nothing digital ever disappears completely, and in big companies, there's almost always a backup somewhere. I copied one of the backups, and snuck it out of the building."

Koa could hardly believe his luck or this young woman's guts and her sense of right and wrong. "You have the copy?"

She held up a small flash drive. "I didn't think it was right when Kimberly lied to you, especially after you warned her. I used her name as the password on this drive. It's Kimberly, spelled backward with a capital K at the end."

He took the flash drive. "What about the monitoring file on Baldwin. Have you ever seen that file?"

"Yes. I copied it, too. It's on the drive I just gave you."

"Thank you. Just a few more questions. You don't appear to care for Mr. Snelling. Is there a reason?"

"He's a creep, always watching me. I try never to be alone with him."

Her complaint sounded like sexual harassment, so he asked, "Has he harassed you?"

"He's tried touching me a couple of times before I threatened to complain. Now he mostly just watches me," she responded, "like he doesn't trust me."

"Do you know anything about what happened to Baldwin?"

"No. Just that she stopped coming to work."

"Last question. You wanted to meet out here because they're watching you?"

"Yes, but I'm not using my own phone. It's one I borrowed from my friend Malia. That's the number you called. And I left my phone, the one with the company app, at home. They'll think I turned it off and went to bed early."

"Okay." He circled his cell number on one of his cards and handed it to her. "Call me if you learn anything more or have any trouble at work."

She took the card, nodded, rose, and turned the red mini-light back on. He watched her walk along the path toward the causeway and disappear into the Japanese gardens. Haukea's parents, Koa thought, should be proud of her. He dealt with too many citizens who, if they didn't cheat themselves, closed their eyes to the wrong-doing of others.

After racing back to the office with Makanui, Koa put the flash drive into his computer, selected it, clicked on the only folder, and entered the password Haukea had given him, careful to type the capital K at the end. Inside, Koa found an eye-opening series of document files. According to her employment application, Tiger Baldwin had attended Stanford, then MIT, and had been recommended to X-CO by Hawai'i Governor Akoni, who sat on the company's board. Koa thought her connection to the governor noteworthy and decided to ask Zeke to make discreet inquiries.

He also verified Baldwin's employment as a senior computer systems architect at a salary of $210,000 per year. That conformed with the First Hawaiian Bank records Koa had gotten from Goodling. Unsurprisingly, Baldwin had glowing performance reviews and had been promoted twice in a short span. Koa read through all the material and, as he expected, found no resignation letter. Someone at X-CO had forged that little gem after Baldwin's death.

When Koa turned to the monitoring file on Baldwin, he found the contents surprising and disturbing. X-CO had tracked Baldwin's daily movements for months and recorded her telephone calls, creating transcripts of those deemed significant. A memo described several of those calls to a friend at a California defense contractor as "suspicious," and suggested that Baldwin might be leaking proprietary X-CO data to a competitor.

Digging deeper into the Baldwin surveillance file, Koa found that X-CO had planted spy cameras in the hallway outside Baldwin's apartment. One of those cameras had captured pictures of FBI agent Linda Somes sliding an envelope under Baldwin's door. Moreno had been right. The FBI's ham-handed attempt to reach Baldwin might well have gotten her killed.

The following morning, Koa briefed Zeke, and the two of them met with Goodling and Moreno around the conference table in Zeke's office. Koa described his Coconut Island rendezvous with Haukea and provided printed copies of the materials from the flash drive he'd received from the young woman. "We've learned five things," he explained. "Kimberly works for Snelling in security; X-CO spied on its employees, including Baldwin; the company suspected her of working with a competitor; her resignation letter was definitely phony; and," he added, looking directly at Moreno, "they had pictures of Somes's visit to Baldwin's apartment."

"Shit," was all Moreno could say.

"What about this claim of sharing proprietary information?" Koa asked. "What do we know about her friend in California?"

"It's not an issue," Moreno responded. "After we ID'd Baldwin as *Aletheia*, we got her phone records and checked up on her friend in California. They were college friends. Nothing more."

The way Moreno quickly volunteered the information made Koa suspicious that he wasn't getting the full story, probably because the feds' "checkup" had gathered information through national security letters and maybe even wiretaps under the Patriot Act. Yet, Koa thought it was only tangentially relevant, and he let it go.

Goodling, who been studying Baldwin's original personnel file, interrupted Koa's train of thought. "According to this stuff, X-CO promoted Baldwin twice to a position even more senior than we thought. She would have been in the perfect position to spot any tampering with the Deimos software."

Koa nodded. "That just makes the murder and cover-up all the more disturbing. You'd think X-CO's management would have rewarded her, not killed her. Makes me think the traitorous termites inside X-CO who hacked the Deimos program control the heart of the organization. Maybe you feds should just move in and shut it down."

"Not yet," Goodling said. "We've got to identify all the termites, as you call them, before everyone lawyers up."

"Your call," Zeke acknowledged.

Following their discussion of Baldwin's personnel files, Moreno detailed his analysis of the computer files seized under the search warrant. "Those emails Snelling gave you about Baldwin's car and belongings; they're bogus. Came from Baldwin's computer and were generated after she was already in that graveyard."

"No surprise there," Koa responded. "What about the Deimos program tampering. Learn anything about that?"

"A little. The bad code sections are sophisticated. Our cyber-experts figure a group of top-flight programmers using the latest techniques and equipment spent months assembling and testing the hacks. Someone then loaded the bad code into the Deimos program in blocks, along with several patches to other parts of the program."

"Okay," Koa said, "I get that it was complicated, but what's that mean for our investigation?"

"It means a couple of things," Moreno responded. "First, no one inside X-CO wrote the hack code. A single programmer or even a small group simply couldn't have both written and tested it. The hack code is almost certainly the work of a state-sponsored cyber team. Second, there had to be two-way communication."

"I'm not sure I understand," Koa said.

"Yeah," Zeke added, "put some red meat on that carcass."

Moreno obliged. "To insert a block of code, you have to know where it goes and how it connects to the rest of the program. The same is true for each of the patches. For each inserted part, you need the connecting code. Someone on the inside of X-CO must have provided the hackers with a lot of information about the program to enable them to write and test the hack code. Then, they smuggled the bad code blocks and patches into the X-CO facility."

"So, if I have this right," Zeke said, "before the bad code was smuggled in, some of the good code was smuggled out."

"Exactly," Moreno agreed.

"But we don't know who stole the good code?" Koa asked.

"Right."

"Do we know the whereabouts of the hackers who wrote the bad code?" Koa asked.

"We don't know for sure," Moreno responded, "but we're talking about a state-sponsored group with access to highly sophisticated equipment. That limits the possibilities. I'd say China." He hesitated. "But it could be North Korea, Russia, or even Iran."

The way Moreno hesitated before adding the last three countries made Koa think they were red herrings, added to obscure a topic Moreno didn't want to discuss. "But you think it's China, right?" Koa pressed.

"Yeah," Moreno admitted grudgingly.

"Why?" Koa asked.

"We have our reasons," Moreno responded.

There was something, Koa realized, that Moreno didn't want him to know. He was about to pursue it when Zeke interrupted.

"So how does this two-way communication happen?" Zeke asked.

"There are only three ways," Moreno explained. "The key code sections could be transmitted over the internet, transported on a drive, or sent directly point to point."

"Explain point to point," queried Zeke.

"Could be by radio, telephone, or some kind of advanced system like a laser," Moreno explained.

"What's most likely?" Koa asked.

"The bad code sections are substantial, so the easiest and safest way to insert them would be on a drive. That would greatly reduce possible transmission errors. Once the outsiders understood the architecture of the Deimos program, the hooks—that is, the code surrounding specific insertion points—could be easily transmitted to Hawai'i by modem, but would still have to be put on a drive to be inserted."

Koa envisioned a nearly impossible task. "You mean we're looking for one outgoing phone call and one incoming drive? That'll be like looking for a penny in a lava field."

"No, no." Moreno shook his head. "We found at least eight blocks of bad code uploaded over a period of several months. We don't know the number of outgoing communications, but there had to be quite a number, especially since programmers inside X-CO were constantly updating and refining the software."

"Any pattern?" Koa asked.

"What are you looking for?" Moreno responded.

"I'm not sure. Maybe a day of the week, a time of day, a source workstation, call records, or an IP address. Anything that might help us narrow the search."

"Not yet, but we're still checking," Moreno responded.

"So how do we identify the culprits and their communication routes?" Zeke asked.

"Maybe we start with Snelling?" Goodling suggested.

"Snelling is number two on my list. I want to take a crack at Kimberly Ward first," Koa responded. "She lied to me, failed to comply with the search warrant, and obstructed our investigation."

"Think a grand jury subpoena might loosen her tongue?" Zeke asked.

Koa thought for a moment. "An arrest warrant would be better."

"Want me to call the judge tonight?" Zeke asked.

Koa nodded and answered with an emphatic, "Yes."

At ten p.m. that night, Koa and Makanui arrived at Kimberly Ward's apartment complex to find a police vehicle, its flashing blue lights alternatively illuminating buildings on either side of the street. "What's happening?" Koa asked a young cop just getting out of his cruiser.

"Reports of shots fired," the officer responded, pointing toward Kimberly's building.

Koa, Makanui, and the officer ran toward the main door to the complex. When they entered the hall, a resident opened the door, saw a police uniform, and said, "Thank God. We heard shots upstairs, maybe twenty minutes ago, toward the back of the building."

Reaching the top of the stairs, Koa spotted an open door at the far end of the hall. With their Glocks out, he and Makanui moved to the open door and stepped inside. The apartment was in shambles, as though hit by a whirlwind, and Kimberly Ward, bleeding profusely from a gunshot wound, lay on the floor under a window on the far wall. Koa checked the bedroom, and Makanui cleared the kitchen. When they were sure no one else remained in the apartment, Koa knelt next to Kimberly's body. While Makanui called for an ambulance and a crime scene team, Koa checked for a pulse but felt none.

Kimberly Ward was dead. Burn marks on her face and arms suggested torture. A trail of blood across the carpet indicated that Ward had survived the initial bullet wound and crawled across the room. Koa looked around for a phone or a gun—anything that might have drawn the dying woman, but saw nothing and wondered what had motivated Ward's final struggle. Maybe she'd just been trying to escape her tormentor.

Had her killer sought to keep her from talking? That was a possibility, especially given what Haukea had said about Ward's role in security. Yet, burn marks reflected torture. Her condition, combined with the surrounding tornado of overturned bookcases, displaced drawers, and shattered artwork, told Koa that Kimberly Ward had kept secrets—secrets that her killer tried to pry from her. The search of her home suggested that she had secreted incriminating evidence. What secrets, he couldn't guess. Nor could he know whether Kimberly's killer had found what he or she was seeking.

Ronnie Woo arrived to shoot official photos, followed by Georgina Pau with her crime scene team, and finally, Ernesto Diaz, substituting for Hawai'i County's usual coroner. When they eventually moved Kimberly's body, Koa spotted something odd on the wall next to where she'd died. Several bloody spots. Someone with blood on their hands had touched the wall. He checked Ward's fingers and found blood. She'd been touching the wall.

Koa knelt and leaned in close. That's when he made out the letters, less than an inch tall, written in blood: "TB = Thief." Koa stared at the message trying to decipher its meaning. TB most likely referred to Tiger Baldwin, and theft probably reflected the suspicion, recorded in the Baldwin X-CO surveillance file, that Baldwin had engaged in industrial espionage with a friend at a California defense contractor. Kimberly must, Koa realized, have exhausted the last of her energy to leave this dying declaration. But why? Why this message and not the name of her killer?

CHAPTER TWENTY-TWO

LOOKING AROUND AT the disarray in Kimberly Ward's apartment, Koa focused on the why of her murder. Her torture and death had to be X-CO related. Any other explanation would be too coincidental. He could search Ward's apartment for anything the killer had missed, or he could accelerate the investigation by interrogating Snelling, who was next on his list. Koa was eager to question the man, especially in the wake of Ward's death. As usual, his instinct to keep the investigation racing forward prevailed. He left Georgina in charge, instructing her to conduct a no-stone-unturned search of Ward's apartment.

Koa and Makanui headed for Koa's SUV and Snelling's apartment on the Hilo waterfront. As they turned off the highway approaching Snelling's complex, they saw headlights come on in the parking lot. Moments later, a Tesla Model S peeled out. In the light from a streetlight, they spotted Snelling at the wheel. The man was so intent on getting somewhere fast that he failed to notice the two law officers.

"Where's he going in such a hurry?" Makanui asked.

"No idea," Koa responded, "but I think we ought to find out." He turned the car around and dropped into the traffic several cars behind Snelling. They'd tracked him south across town past the airport road when it started to rain—one of Hilo's nighttime showers. The Tesla turned left on to Leilani Street, and Koa dropped farther back in the lighter traffic before Snelling turned right toward the Pana'ewa Drag Strip. "I think he's headed toward the waste transfer station," Koa guessed.

Koa pulled off the road and parked just before the entrance to the waste station, grabbed his night-vision binoculars from the glove compartment, and focusing through the rain, began describing Snelling's movements to Makanui. "He's pulled up to one of the waste shoots. He's getting out . . . he's got a plastic bag in his hand. It's small and reddish-brown . . . not a full trash bag . . . he's tossing it into the shoot . . . he's getting back in the car . . . and now he's leaving."

"Why would he drive all the way out here to get rid of a single small bag of garbage?" Makanui asked.

"To get rid of something he doesn't want us to see," Koa suggested.

Turning to Makanui, Koa said, "You take this vehicle and trail him. I'm going to get Piki out here and see what he just trashed." Koa grabbed a rain slicker and a Maglite from the back of the SUV before Makanui left to follow Snelling. Koa called Piki while he walked up the road to the waste transfer station. Fifteen minutes later, Piki arrived with two coils of rope. Looking at Piki, Koa grinned. "You just won a free dumpster dive."

Piki grimaced. "You're kidding, right?"

"I'm not." He explained that they needed to retrieve a small reddish-brown plastic bag that Snelling had discarded down the trash shoot.

"Shit," Piki protested.

"Probably not . . . just garbage, but it's wet, so don't go sliding around," Koa warned.

Piki fastened the rope around his waist and took Koa's flashlight. Koa supported him as he walked backward down the shoot into the truck bed positioned below to catch the refuse. He sank to his knees in the stinking debris and floundered around following the beam of the Maglite for a minute before coming up with the small reddish-brown plastic bag Snelling had dumped.

"That's the one," Koa said as he hauled a soaking wet Piki out of the stinking pit.

With Piki watching, Koa opened the bag. Inside, he found a puzzling collection of odds and ends—a phone charger, a leather-bound desk calendar, a boars bristle hairbrush, a Mont Blanc pen, a tortoiseshell hair clip, a fancy makeup case with a brand logo, and an empty but expensive leather business card case.

"What the hell," Piki said. "Who throws away that kind of shit?"

It was, Koa thought, a good question. Checking to make sure he had everything from the bag, he pulled out an additional item, a blue-gold ceramic pencil holder. Koa stared at the handcrafted pottery. There was something familiar about it. Then he remembered the collection of ceramics in Leilani Craig's apartment. Her words came back to him—she "helped me with my ceramics." Maybe Leilani Craig had made this pencil holder and given it to Tiger Baldwin. A quick call to Leilani confirmed his guess.

Snelling had trashed stuff belonging to Baldwin, probably items taken from her X-CO workplace. Why, he wondered, would Snelling be hot to toss Baldwin's belongings? Then it hit him. Had she resigned and returned to the mainland, she would have taken these things with her. As happened so often, criminals somehow couldn't resist destroying evidence, which often led to their downfall. The discovery provided yet another link between Snelling and the murdered woman. The fact that Snelling had tried to hide Baldwin's property in a remote waste station suggested guilty knowledge.

Koa next called Makanui, who had trailed Snelling back to his oceanside condo and was parked outside. Asking her to wait, Koa had Piki drive him back across town to Snelling's place. Koa had initially planned to question Snelling about the phony Baldwin emails and his whereabouts when someone murdered Ward. He would still do that, but the guilty knowledge reflected in Snelling's surreptitious disposal of Baldwin's things would change the outcome. Snelling was going to spend the night in jail.

After sending Piki back to the station, Koa and Makanui knocked on Snelling's door. He opened up, took in the two detectives, and started to close the door. "I got nothing to say to you pigs."

Makanui stopped the door from closing with her foot, and Koa pushed it open. "You want to talk here or downtown?" Koa asked.

"I ain't saying shit without a lawyer," Snelling responded.

"Then we'll do this down at police headquarters. You can call your lawyer after we book you."

"Book me?" Snelling raised his voice. "For what?"

"Obstruction of justice," Koa informed the security guard. "Turn around and put your hands behind your back."

With exaggerated slowness, Snelling complied, and Makanui fastened cuffs on the man, wrenching them down tight. Koa guessed she felt a little jab of pleasure when Snelling complained.

Koa wanted to search his apartment but needed a warrant, so they took Snelling down to police headquarters, booked him into the jail, and called Zeke to initiate a request for a search warrant.

They had Snelling on obstruction and evidence tampering charges, and Koa suspected the man had murdered both Baldwin and Kimberly Ward. He was eager to question Snelling, but when brought up to an interrogation room, the man lawyered up and refused to say a word. It was close to ten p.m. before Koa and Makanui returned to Snelling's apartment with a warrant. Their search turned up his Glock, stashed under a floorboard in the bedroom, but nothing else relevant to the investigation. Koa had the weapon test-fired for a ballistics comparison against the bullets taken from Baldwin and Kimberly Ward.

After a night in the lockup, Koa transported Snelling to the courthouse for his bail hearing. Deputies typically accompanied prisoners, but in this case, Koa wanted to see for himself Snelling's reaction to the surprise Zeke had planned for the X-CO security guard.

Snelling had hired Plato Tripi to represent him. The tall, bearded lawyer regularly appeared in Hilo's criminal courts, mostly representing drivers in DWI cases. Koa regarded him as competent, but not top-flight. Given the charges against his client, Tripi undoubtedly expected to get Snelling released on bail. Zeke, Koa knew, had other ideas.

When the court clerk called the case, Snelling pled not guilty, and the judge asked for the state's position on bail. Zeke surprised the defendant by saying, "The state requests that Mr. Snelling be denied bail and remanded to custody. He is charged with conspiracy, obstructing a police investigation, and tampering with evidence. More to the point, we suspect him of murdering a woman named Tiger Baldwin."

"Your Honor," Tripi responded, "the evidence against Mr. Snelling is insubstantial, and there's no evidence that he had anything to do with Baldwin's death."

"Yesterday evening," Zeke responded, "the police observed Mr. Snelling surreptitiously disposing of property belonging to the deceased woman."

Tripi, embarrassed by his misstep, stood to make a further argument, but the judge cut him off. "Enough, gentlemen. Mr. Snelling is remanded for forty-eight hours. If he's not indicted within that time, bail will be $50,000 cash or bond."

Koa caught up with Zeke on the way out of the courtroom and asked, "What do you think?"

"Tripi has never tried a murder case, so one of two things will happen," Zeke predicted. "If Snelling pulled the trigger, he'll have a new lawyer within forty-eight hours. If he's not the shooter, Tripi will come sniffing for a way out."

Two hours later, Tripi sat across from Koa, Makanui, and Zeke at the prosecutor's conference table. "You can't prove my client murdered Baldwin," Tripi argued.

"Oh, I think we can," Zeke responded. "We've got a strong circumstantial case. He tried to cover up Baldwin's disappearance by selling her car and clearing out her apartment. To facilitate those acts, he created bogus emails and lied to the police. He ordered Ms. Kimberly Ward to alter Baldwin's personnel files and substitute false information. And he trashed her personal belongings."

"He didn't do it," Tripi responded.

"So he says," Zeke replied disparagingly. "And if he didn't kill Baldwin, he knows who did."

Tripi pressed his hands together in a pyramid and paused for a long moment. "Hypothetically, suppose he could tell you exactly what happened. What's in it for him?"

Not for the first time, Koa marveled at Zeke's savvy. The situation was playing out as Zeke had predicted.

"Depends on what he tells us and what he has in the way of proof," Zeke responded. "But if he's truthful and helps us, it'll go a lot better for him."

"He wants immunity," Tripi said.

"Maybe for a hat trick," Zeke responded. "Let's hear what he has to say."

Koa called Goodling, asking her to come to police headquarters and bring Moreno. So far as Koa knew, X-CO was not aware of the federal espionage investigation, and the feds wanted to maintain that appearance. So, when Goodling and Moreno arrived, he put them in an observation area next to the interrogation room to observe without being seen.

Koa, Makanui, Zeke, and Tripi entered the interrogation room. Koa had Snelling brought from the lockup. Handcuffed and dressed in a baggy orange jumpsuit, he appeared unshaven with purple bags under his eyes. The X-CO security guard, Koa could see, had not enjoyed his time in jail. That might knock some of the cockiness out of him. Koa had the guard remove his cuffs and pointed to a chair. "Sit."

"Tell us about Tiger Baldwin," Zeke said.

The security guard looked at Tripi, who nodded. Snelling then began talking. "Wingate called me into his office. This would have been in the middle of June. When I got there, Wingate told me he'd had a confrontation with Baldwin. He said there'd been an accident."

"An accident? Like two gunshots at close range? That sort of accident?" Zeke said with palpable sarcasm.

"Yeah. That's what Wingate said—an accident."

"And you believed him?"

"Wingate's the boss. You don't question what he says."

"What kind of confrontation?" Koa asked.

"He didn't say."

"Go on with your story," Zeke said.

"Wingate told me he shot her."

"What happened to her body?

"I don't know. I never saw her body."

"Why didn't you or Wingate go to the police?" Zeke asked.

"Wingate wouldn't allow it."

"And that's your story?" Zeke asked incredulously.

"Yeah, and then the next morning, Wingate tells me to sell her car and empty her apartment. Then he gives me this thumb drive and tells me to trash her personnel records and replace them with the ones he gave me. I wasn't sure exactly how, so I got Kimberly Ward to do it for me."

"When did you fabricate the phony emails?" Koa asked.

"After he showed up at the office." Snelling pointed to Koa. "Wingate told me I'd better cover my tracks."

"Where's Baldwin's computer?" Zeke asked.

"Wingate told me to get it from her apartment. He's got it."

"The things you trashed at the waste transfer station," Koa asked. "They were from Baldwin's desk in her office at X-CO?"

"Yeah."

"Why trash her stuff?"

"Wingate told me to."

It was, Koa thought, a strange story, but no matter how they questioned him, Snelling didn't deviate, so they took a break to confer with Goodling and Moreno, leaving Snelling and Tripi in the interrogation room.

"You believe him?" Zeke asked.

"Not a fuckin' word," Moreno said. "He fabricated evidence and lied to the police. I'm guessing he'd wouldn't know the truth if it strangled him."

"I don't know," Koa responded. "His story's weird, but the real question is whether he murdered Baldwin. Zeke got us a search warrant, and last night Makanui and I searched his apartment. We found his Glock and had it test-fired. It's not the murder weapon. He could have another weapon, but we've found no trace of it."

"So, where do we go from here?" Zeke asked.

"Think you can get him to wear a wire?" Goodling asked.

"Don't know," Zeke responded. "Have to break his loyalty to Wingate first."

"How are you going to do that?" Moreno asked sarcastically.

"Well," Zeke responded, "if you don't ask . . . for sure you won't get."

Zeke, Koa, and Makanui returned to the interrogation room where Snelling and Tripi waited while Goodling and Moreno again watched through the interrogation room's one-way mirror.

"You think Wingate's gonna admit killing Baldwin?" Zeke asked Snelling when they were once again seated.

"No," Snelling responded. "I told you he said it was an accident."

"Two bullet holes at close range . . . that's no accident." Zeke let his words sink in before continuing. "Wingate's going to finger you. And he's the boss. You don't question what he says." Zeke quoted Snelling's words back to him. "A jury won't question what he says. He's going to be drinkin' martinis while you're doing life."

Koa saw the change in Snelling. His tough cookie exterior seemed to crack as Zeke's prognosis sank in. Much of the self-assured cockiness he'd shown earlier vanished. He didn't tremble but became subdued as he saw his future playing out precisely the way Zeke described.

"You ever been in a cell?" Zeke asked. "A ten-by-ten space with bars on one side?"

"N . . . no," Snelling replied with a slight hesitation.

"They let you out for an hour a day . . . if you behave."

Zeke paused before speaking slowly in a soft, menacing voice. "Years go by . . . you don't walk on the beach . . . you don't get much sunshine . . . you don't have many visitors . . . you don't eat steak . . . you don't drink martinis . . . you don't drive your Tesla Model S . . . it's just you and the walls . . . for the *rest of your life*." Zeke's tone hardened with his emphasis on the last four words.

"That ain't right. I didn't kill her."

"You're going to have to prove it," Zeke said.

"How? How can I prove it?" Snelling asked, a hint of desperation in his voice. He looked to Tripi, but his lawyer had nothing to say.

"You're going to wear a wire, meet with Wingate, and get him to spill everything on tape."

*   *   *

The following day, Koa, Zeke, and Makanui spent hours preparing Snelling for his meeting with Wingate. Koa had worked with a lot of informants over the years. Some were motivated by money. Others by fear of going to jail. Anger propelled a limited group. A few acted out of remorse or shame for their past deeds. And some for their ideological beliefs. Figuring out an informant's motive offered clues to his or her reliability.

Zeke hammered Snelling with the prospect of spending the rest of his life in jail, but Koa sensed no genuine fear in the man. Resignation maybe, but no fear. They weren't paying him, and he exhibited not the slightest sign of remorse. Snelling was in many ways inscrutable, and that gnawed at Koa.

Snelling began by playing dumb. "What am I supposed to say?"

"Draw Wingate out. Get him to talk about what happened to Baldwin," Koa responded.

"What if he knows I'm wired?"

"He won't, as long as you act naturally, the way you normally do," Koa promised.

"You don't know him. If he says it was an accident, then it was an accident. You don't cross him. He's ruthless, and he'll fire me." Snelling pleaded loyalty and fear at the same time, but Koa saw none of the telltale signs of fear. Snelling didn't sweat, his breathing remained even, his hands stayed steady, his facial expressions unchanged. He sat still as a stone monolith. Snelling, Koa decided, was a cold fish, but whether Snelling was an *ono*, a flaky white fish, or a *manō*, a shark, Koa couldn't tell.

"We'll be listening. We won't let it get out of hand," Koa responded.

"Do I have to do this?" Snelling asked.

"The evidence points to you as Baldwin's killer," Zeke said. "You'll go down for murder unless you produce evidence that someone else killed her."

"It's not fair. I didn't kill her," Snelling rebutted.

Zeke stared hard at the security guard. "I don't believe you, and neither will a jury."

They worked with Snelling for another two hours. He vacillated between claims of innocence and assertions of loyalty to Wingate. Koa couldn't tell which, if either, really mattered to Snelling. In the end, they wired him up and sent him back to X-CO the following morning, less than confident in his ability to pull off a successful deception.

They figured Wingate would be suspicious if Snelling initiated a conversation about Baldwin, so they'd instructed him to go about his usual routine, hoping Wingate would contact him. They'd set up a command post in the warehouse across the street from X-CO and took turns listening throughout the remainder of the day. Nothing happened until the end of Snelling's shift when Wingate finally summoned him into the executive's office. Koa listened intently while a machine recorded the conversation.

"I hear the police picked you up," Wingate began.

"Yeah, they think I faked the emails about Baldwin's car and furniture, but they can't prove it. I showed them the deposit slip, showing I put the money in her account. Really helped me."

Wingate paused unnaturally long before responding, and then his words came out slowly, carefully, and with some hesitation. "I'm glad it worked out for you."

Koa was encouraged. Wingate was talking. Maybe, just maybe, he thought, Snelling might pull it off.

"Yes, sir," Snelling responded. "Remember the morning you called me into your office."

Wingate remained silent, and Koa held his breath, wondering if Snelling had gone too far too fast. Maybe Snelling had spooked his boss. The silence stretched, and the longer the quiet extended, the more certain Koa became that Snelling had blown it.

Wingate finally spoke. "Yeah."

"It's a shame your plan didn't work. No one was ever supposed to know," Snelling said.

Koa let out a long, slow breath, not saying a word even though Snelling and Wingate couldn't hear him. They were talking and getting closer to the jugular, but so far only in vagaries. The "plan" could be killing Baldwin and hiding her body, or something else entirely. Nothing yet tied the conversation to Baldwin's murder.

"Nobody could predict a thing like that," Wingate responded.

Koa supposed they were talking about the earthquake that exposed Baldwin's body, but their words could have many meanings, and he couldn't be sure.

"That's for sure," Snelling said.

"Yeah," Wingate responded. "But, it created a big problem for us."

Koa waited for details. It looked like Snelling might get Wingate to talk about Baldwin.

"Couldn't be helped, not after you caught her accessing the Deimos program," Snelling said.

Koa was taken aback. Snelling had previously fingered Wingate, as confessing that he alone had confronted Baldwin. Snelling had denied knowing more, but now he was changing his story, asserting that Baldwin had been accessing the Deimos program, whatever that meant. Snelling, it seemed, thought Baldwin guilty of wrongdoing.

Another seemingly interminable silence ensued before Wingate spoke. "Yeah."

"I saw her pointing a gun at you, boss. Damn near killed you, too," Snelling said.

Confused, Koa wondered if he'd heard right. Snelling had previously claimed that Wingate had summoned him to the executive's office only the morning after Wingate's confrontation with Baldwin. In this *tête-à-tête*, Snelling was acknowledging being present during the encounter with Baldwin. Worse, he painted Baldwin as the aggressor, claiming to have seen her holding Wingate at gunpoint.

"It was self-defense. Pure self-defense," Snelling continued.

Koa swore. Snelling was double-crossing them, setting the stage to exonerate both himself and Wingate. It wasn't the first time a cooperating witness had pulled such a stunt, and it shouldn't have surprised Koa, given Snelling's ambivalence during their prep. Koa kicked himself for being taken in and wondered just how far Snelling would go.

"Absolutely," Wingate agreed. "Baldwin gave us no choice."

"All because the stupid bitch pulled a gun," Snelling said.

"Y-e-a-h," Wingate responded slowly, drawing out the word.

"A little .38 special, a lady's piece, for god's sake," Snelling said.

Koa shook his head in disgust. Snelling now admitted that he'd witnessed the shooting. He'd previously lied to the police. There could be legal repercussions for that, but nothing like a murder rap.

Koa tried to separate fact from fiction. Wingate had been present during the shooting. He was admitting it. Snelling, too, had also been present, and he now admitted it. Wingate was the shooter, and that seemed consistent with the test ruling out Snelling's gun. But there were gaping holes in the picture. What had Baldwin really been doing? Why had Wingate shot her? Had she really had a gun? Had Wingate murdered her or acted in self-defense?

"Yeah, the damn gun." Wingate raised his voice. "Without that damn gun, she wouldn't have gotten away."

Koa banged his fist against the wall. Gotten away? They didn't know the police had the GPS data proving that Baldwin had died at X-CO. They were play-acting . . . working together to confuse the facts . . . concocting a fairy tale . . . establishing a phony defense . . . and painting Baldwin as a wrongdoer. Wiring up Snelling was turning out to be a disaster, a fucking disaster.

"Maybe we should have gone to the police," Snelling suggested, "but the government would have shut us down."

"Yeah. And destroyed the company. No way." Wingate hesitated. "The government would have shut us down for damn sure if they'd known Baldwin had compromised the program with her friend in California. I'd be out of a job. You'd be out of a job. And Zhou Li would have had our heads."

"Yeah, you saved the Deimos program and the company."

"That's right, but Baldwin's still a problem," Wingate added.

"I doubt the cops will be able to prove anything in the end," Snelling responded.

The conversation ended with the bang of a door closing.

Koa cursed.

CHAPTER TWENTY-THREE

THE CALL TO see the chief came unexpectedly, and Koa wondered what was going down. Things became apparent when he entered the chief's office. Senator Chao, Kāwika Keahi, and Bobby Hazzard sat around the chief's conference table. Koa nodded to Bobby, shook hands with the senator, and high-fived his friend Keahi.

"I understand you've been helping Bobby," the senator said. "I do appreciate your assistance."

Koa didn't miss the senator's casual use of Bobby's first name. It reflected familiarity and, from Koa's unique perspective, raised the stakes.

"We're always glad to accommodate you," the chief responded before turning to Koa. "Mr. Hazzard would like to visit his grandfather's old cabin, and I thought it would be nice if you accompanied him."

So, Koa thought, the senator leaned on the chief who was leaning on his chief detective. He caught himself wondering if his boss had some inkling of his involvement in Hazzard's death but dismissed the idea as paranoia. The chief was simply sucking up, as he always did, to a powerful politician.

Koa knew the way to the cabin. The treacherous ten-hour trek back from Anthony Hazzard's remote mountain cabin, located deep in one of the nearly inaccessible, steep-walled valleys on the northern coast of the Big Island, had been part of the most trau-matic event in his life, and the centerpiece of many a nightmare. He shivered at the thought of going back.

Although Hazzard's death had indelibly branded its location into his psyche, Koa had no intention of letting on that he'd ever been anywhere near Anthony Hazzard's old cabin. "Where exactly is this cabin?" Koa asked.

"I've got an old map my grandfather sent my parents." Bobby un-folded a yellowed paper and flattened it on the table.

Koa studied the crude drawing, probably more than fifty years old and out of date, although not much had changed in that part of the island. It showed the series of steep-walled valleys on the island's northwestern coast. Someone, probably Anthony Hazzard, had marked a rough trail west of the small former sugar town of Hono-ka'a through the Waipi'o Valley, across the Muliwai Trail, into the Waimanu Valley, and finally up the Waimanu River to the old Haz-zard cabin.

"You sure this cabin is still standing? I doubt anybody's lived there since your grandfather died."

Bobby hesitated. "I honestly don't know."

"Only one way to find out," Keahi said, adding with a grin, "Should be a fun outing. The Waipi'o Valley is a historic cultural gem, and the views from the Z-Trail up the far side of the valley are stunning. And the waterfalls in the Waimanu Valley are among the tallest in the world."

"Keahi's right that the northwest corner of the island has some gorgeous country, but the ground's rough and the hiking trails are among the toughest in the state. And this map lacks the detail to get us there," Koa said. "We'll need a guide to show us the way."

"I'm sure one of the old trail hands up in Waipi'o can get you there. You might even go in on horseback," the chief suggested.

"Couldn't you use a police helicopter?" the senator asked.

Koa shook his head. "According to this map, the cabin is way up the Waimanu Valley. A chopper would have to land on the beach, and then we'd need horses for the last few miles. Better to pick up horses in the Waipi'o and go up the Z-Trail to the Muliwai Trail over the ridge into the Waimanu Valley. I'll find us a guide and some horses." Turning to Bobby Hazzard, Koa added, "It'll be a rugged overnight trip through pretty brutal terrain, and you can't be sure the cabin will still be standing. Sure you want to do this?"

"I'm sure," Bobby said, but without much enthusiasm.

"Tomorrow morning? We should have good weather. Early start?"

"How early?" Bobby asked sheepishly.

Koa wondered if the kid was planning to sleep late. "About five a.m.," he responded.

Bobby was not pleased but wasn't in a position to object. "Okay."

As the meeting broke up, Senator Chao walked out with Koa. "He's a good kid. Take care of him," the senator said. Then, as an apparent afterthought, the senator added, "You created a bit of a stir out at X-CO."

Koa's antenna instantly went up. The chief had registered his displeasure with Koa's initial visit to X-CO based on a complaint by the senator's aide. The senator had then objected to the search warrant raid. When Zeke had rebuffed that complaint, Keahi had warned Koa that the senator had reached out to the governor and maybe even the president. Now the senator was following up. Koa responded cautiously. "As Zeke Brown said, we're in the midst of a murder investigation, and the company was uncooperative." Then hoping to learn more, he added, "I don't suppose you ever met Baldwin?"

"No, afraid not, but I can tell you that this whole situation has made Zhou Li hopping mad. He's considering whether to cancel the AI seminar."

Koa worried that the senator's last sentence was a threat to retaliate if the police continued investigating. Nothing pissed him off like political interference. He chose his words carefully. "I guess he's free to cancel the seminar, but that won't stop the investigation."

* * *

Koa wasn't thrilled about a two-day babysitting excursion into one of the most inaccessible places in the entire state, and he didn't like losing two days he needed to keep pushing the X-CO investigation. Nor did he want to be away from Nālani any more than necessary. Yet, the chief and the senator had left him no alternative. So be it. He assembled his camping gear, adding his D.J. Russell belt knife, Savage Arms Axis, 6.5 mm Creedmore hunting rifle, and binoculars, along with his regular Glock pistol. He knew there would be no cell coverage in the Waimanu Valley, and checked a satellite phone out of the police equipment inventory. He didn't want to be in the wilderness with no way to communicate if something went awry. They would pick up food and extra water in the morning on their way to the Waipi'o.

As promised, Koa picked Bobby up before dawn the following morning. They drove north along the coast, past Koa's birthplace at Laupāhoehoe and through the historic sugar town of Honoka'a, where they bought supplies, to the edge of the Waipi'o Valley. They stopped at the overlook, giving Bobby his first look at the deep green lowland more than a thousand feet below, bordered at its ocean terminus by a broad black sand beach, lapped by frothing ocean waves. The idyllic sight never failed to impress, and Bobby oohed and aahed like the typical tourist.

From the overlook, Koa steered them down the steep, narrow, winding one-lane road to the valley floor. At sea level, he made a sharp U-turn onto a muddy track leading to the black sand beach. Wild horses grazed in the shade of towering pines, but close up, the rock-strewn beach looked more treacherous than idyllic. They met up with Naomi, their Hawaiian guide, and three somewhat aged trail horses. The short, slim woman was middle-aged, but her white hair, wrinkled face, and sun-weathered hands made her appear older.

"So, ya bin wantin' to see da old Hazzard 'ohana?" she asked in a mixture of English, Hawaiian, and local pidgin.

"You know it?" Bobby asked.

"Yeah, yeah, I bin there . . . dat place not da kine," she responded. "Long ride . . . nothin' to see."

"I want to see whatever is there," Bobby said.

"Okay . . . okay, you da boss," she responded, shaking her head the way people do when asked to do foolish things.

Naomi adjusted the saddles on the horses, and they mounted. Koa had ridden since childhood and often with Nālani, and being on horseback made him think of her. He quickly developed a feel for his old horse. Bobby, however, had trouble mounting, and once astride, appeared uncomfortable. His signature hiking boots were ill-fitted for the stirrups. His horse sensed his nervousness and shied and backed. Koa kept his eyes on the kid, knowing the chief would blow a gasket if Bobby got hurt. With Naomi in the lead, they waded slowly across the mouth of the shallow Waipi'o River. Their route took them along the black sand beach toward the western side of the valley where a cliff shot up nearly perpendicularly to a height of almost two thousand feet above the valley floor.

Mostly to distract young Bobby from his nervousness, Koa explained that the Waipi'o had been the home of *ali'i* or Hawaiian royalty for centuries and housed the ruins of some of the island's most sacred *heiau* or ancient Hawaiian temples. "The whole valley floor, as far as the eye can see, was once covered in taro fields," Koa explained. "Many ancient artifacts, along with the graves of *ali'i*, are hidden in caves deep within the valley walls. And the *LuaoMilu*, a door to the underworld, is supposed to be here in the Waipi'o."

"Spooky," Bobby responded.

"In more modern times," Koa added to lighten the mood, "this is where the characters in the 1995 movie *Waterworld* found dry land."

"It's beautiful even if it's spooky," Bobby exclaimed. "Why don't more people live here?"

"Tsunamis triggered by Alaskan earthquakes," Koa responded. "The valley's funnel shape focuses tsunami waves that surge miles up the valley. Those waves have killed thousands over the centuries, destroyed the original Hawaiian settlements in the valley, and pose an ever-present danger to those who remain." Bobby stiffened, obviously concerned about the potential threat. The young lawyer was way out of his element. "The valley's isolated nature," Koa continued, "also makes it difficult for residents to get their children to school or purchase supplies. As a result, the population today is a fraction of what it was before the Westerners arrived in the islands."

They soon found themselves climbing the narrow zigzagging Z-Trail up the cliff that separated the relatively accessible Waipi'o from its more remote companions to the west. Time and heavy rains had carved several valleys into the northern face of the Kohala Mountains, including the Waimanu Valley, where Hazzard had built his cabin. There were no roads and few trails in these valleys. Again and again, as they climbed the steep path, they stopped to rest the horses and look back at the magnificently verdant Waipi'o. Majestic ocean views rewarded them at nearly every turn. At one of these stops, Koa pointed out toward the ocean. "The Battle of the Red-Mouthed Guns, the first naval battle in Hawaiian history, took place out there. That's where King Kamehameha defeated two other *ali'i* and began his conquest of the other islands."

After nearly two hours, they crested the cliff's top and started across the headland plateau on the Muliwai Trail, where they entered a wholly different terrain. Thick forest alternated with near jungle concealing the ocean off to their right. They crossed one gully after another, several with small perennial streams. After another hour, they started down a steep switchback trail, this one even steeper than the Z-Trail they had followed coming up from the floor of the Waipi'o. It was slow going, and the track became so treacherous that they had to dismount and walk their horses. After catching occasional glimpses of the ocean, they finally neared the floor of the Waimanu Valley.

By midafternoon, they were back at sea level, where Naomi brought the group to a stop for a short rest. She pointed to a small hillock and explained that it used to be Wilford Mock Chew and his father's home. "Him and his da, they bin in da house when the 1946 tsunami, she come in da valley . . . da wave she carried 'em out to da bay . . . an' den da next wave she carried 'em back . . . an' dey lived. Dey say da water was ten times da size of a man an' went fifteen miles up the valley. Da gods blessed Wilford and his da."

Bobby looked out at the ocean, trying to visualize the sixty-foot wall of water crashing through the valley. The kid paled as though startled by an apparition. It was, Koa thought, an eerie place with a tortured history. He wondered if Bobby was beginning to regret this sojourn.

"Want to turn back?" Koa asked. "Otherwise, we'll be spending the night camped out."

Koa thought Bobby might abort, but the kid shook his head and responded, "I need to see the cabin. I need to see this through."

A short time later, they reached the Waimanu River and, still in their saddles, used a safety rope to wade across the chest-deep, rapidly flowing water. They emerged soaking wet but, except for their soggy boots, dried quickly in the warm sunshine. Once on the river's west side, they turned south, paralleling the west valley wall on their right and the river on their left.

The poorly maintained trail was rough going, but a dozen magnificent waterfalls, many over five hundred feet high, cascading off the cliffs, buoyed their spirits. They stopped at an enormous crystal-clear pool near the base of Wa'ilikahi Falls to rest the horses and wash up in the ice-cold water. During their stop, Naomi picked guavas from the surrounding trees. She judged their ripeness perfectly, and they snacked on the delicious pear and strawberry pulp.

"Dey used to be da kine Sandalwood all ova dis valley," Naomi said.

"What happened to it?" Bobbi asked.

"Dey cut 'em all down an' shipped 'em to China by da boatloads. No more nothin' hea anymore."

By the time they reached the site of the old Hazzard cabin, the sun had dipped below the lip of the western valley wall, casting the land into deep shadows. The ruins of the old log cabin sat in a modest clearing atop a small rise with a commanding view of the Waimanu River, which meandered toward the ocean far in the distance. In the ethereal light of the fading day, the place was both more beautiful and more ominous than Koa remembered. When they dismounted, Bobby caught his foot in the stirrup and nearly fell. He was, Koa could see, spooked by the place.

Although the spirits of the departed figured prominently in Hawaiian mythology, Koa had never believed in ghosts who returned to avenge their tormentors. Yet, he couldn't escape the feeling that Anthony Hazzard's spirit lingered nearby like a malevolent force, condemning him for what he had done so long ago. The presence of the man's grandchild only intensified Koa's sense of dread.

While Naomi took care of the horses and Bobby sat resting on a fallen log, Koa walked the perimeter of the area, passing an old well and what little remained of the outhouse, which had crumbled into a pile of rubble. Not far away, empty food cans and a discarded condom memorialized hikers, who'd likely camped or frolicked there.

In his mind, he replayed the eventful evening from his past. He remembered the long wait in the dark forest outside the cabin, occasionally peeking through a window while Hazzard drank himself blind. The man had finally used the outhouse before staggering back, barely making it into the cabin. That's when Koa had struck. He could almost feel his arms around Anthony Hazzard's neck. Once again, he heard the sound of Hazzard choking and felt the man go limp. He relived his surprise when the mill manager turned on him as soon as he released his grip. He sensed the pain he'd felt where the older man had hit him, leaving bruises. He remembered his paralyzing fear when he realized that Hazzard was bigger, stronger, and far more dangerous than he'd imagined. He heard the man's bellow again as he charged Koa with murder in his bloodshot eyes. Most of all, he recalled the splitting sound of the iron poker connecting with Hazzard's skull.

Koa stopped by the old stump, now mostly rotted, where Hazzard had chopped wood. The outcropping of rock where he'd hidden and watched Hazzard drink himself into a stupor stood less than a dozen feet away. Memories of that night paraded through his mind, welling up within him, and spawning waves of remorse. He'd killed a man, a man with a son and grandchildren. The horror of his actions was more real today, having met Bobby and learned about Hazzard's family, than it had been thirty years ago. His pride in what he'd accomplished in the intervening years, his military service, his work as a detective, the cases he'd closed, the people he'd helped, it all paled in comparison to the awful crime he'd committed. He'd been so young, so stupid, and so reckless.

The loud cawing of a crow interrupted Koa's recriminations, sending a shiver down his neck. The ʻalalā, or Hawaiian crow, was infamous in Hawaiian legend for carrying souls of the departed to the underworld. These unique Hawaiian crows had become extinct in the wild before being reintroduced and were still seldom seen or heard. Koa couldn't resist thinking that Anthony Hazzard had sent the bird in search of Koa's soul.

By the time Koa had completed his circuit around the cabin, Naomi had unsaddled, tethered, and fed the horses. Bobby still sat on the log, where Koa had left him, staring at the dilapidated structure. Grunting and snorting noises erupted from the nearby brush. "Wild pigs," Naomi warned. "No go off alone. Da pigs, dey kin kill a man, like dat." She snapped her fingers. The brush moved at the edge of the clearing, and two bright eyes glimmered in the dim light. Koa checked his Glock, chambering a round in case he had to shoot a charging boar. Bobby Hazzard stared wide-eyed at the animal with a look that said he'd rather be almost anywhere else in the world. Koa wondered if he, too, could feel the presence of his long-dead grandfather.

He had no idea what the young man had expected to find, but to Koa, he appeared disappointed. Maybe his grandfather had exaggerated the magnificence of his personal retreat. Perhaps the utter loneliness of the place, bathed in the valley's weird twilight, lent credence to the possibility of suicide. Maybe Bobby hadn't appreciated the cabin's remote location and now understood how days could have passed before anyone discovered his grandfather's death. Perhaps the presence of wild boar in the area gave substance to the notion that animals had ravaged his grandfather's body almost beyond recognition. Whatever was going through his mind, Bobby sat transfixed by the broken cabin as though willing it to give up its secrets.

"Dey's ghosts all ova dis valley," Naomi said, "ghosts of da old *ali'i,* da old kings, and dey's guarded by da marchers in da night. When dey come, dey come wid lighted torches, torches burnin' in da night, and den ya more bettah be still like ya is dead, else da marchers dey take ya 'way to da other side thru da *LuaoMilu*."

Bobby turned toward the old woman. "Do you believe that stuff?"

"Shhhh. No talk like dat," Naomi warned.

It was close to dark when Bobby finally turned to Koa. "I need to have a look inside." He rose and turned toward the ruin. The shell of the old log building had survived without its door, windows, and chunks of its roof. Vines had overgrown one wall. Mold stained the rotting timbers. Parts of the chimney had collapsed, leaving a pile of rustic bricks. A small tree had sprung up inside along with assorted weeds and debris. A mongoose scurried out of the derelict building. The sound of an owl hooting in the distance echoed across the valley. It was a forlorn and desolate place, eerie as the fog on a moonless night.

Koa pulled a flashlight from his pack and led the way, while Naomi remained outside. Inside the remnants of the cabin, Bobby and Koa found the rotting floor rancid with animal droppings and small animal carcasses. An overpowering stench burned their nostrils. The flashlight beam revealed rusted bedsprings, a broken table, the seat of a chair, smashed crockery, and broken liquor bottles littering the floor.

When the light fell on a corroded fire iron near the cracked stone hearth, Koa suddenly felt light-headed. That commonplace tool— that very one—had saved his life and killed Hazzard. He could almost feel the metal in his hand and hear, as he had so often, the crack of the iron against Hazzard's head. He owed his life and his guilt to that poker.

Only when Koa turned the light upward did they see the remnants of a frayed rope hanging from one of the rafters. Bobby gasped, and for a moment, Koa thought the kid might collapse. Koa imagined Hazzard's body swinging to and fro, casting weird shadows on the walls, but blinked the image away. He wondered if Bobby had pictured a similar scene.

Bobby looked stunned and ready to heave. After turning around twice to take in the whole horrific setting, Hazzard's grandson stumbled back outside. Koa followed him. Bobby crossed the open area around the cabin and sat back down on the same log, staring off into the night. His shoulders slumped, and Koa heard a sob. Despite his own concerns and personal dislike of the young man, in that instant, Koa felt sorry for the grandson of the man whose life he'd snuffed out.

Naomi built a blazing fire in a clearing a couple of hundred yards from the cabin, and the three of them ate dinner in its warmth and light. The sounds of forest animals and the proximity of the place where his grandfather died weighed on Bobby, and he withdrew into himself. Koa and Naomi chowed down, but Bobby barely touched his food. After dinner, they unrolled sleeping bags. Koa slept on and off, but Bobby found no rest. Twice, Koa saw him sitting beside the dying embers of the fire, staring off into space.

They rose before dawn and packed for the journey back. Koa offered Bobby a chance to revisit the cabin, but the young lawyer declined. Bobby remained subdued, maybe even morose, on the ride back along the Waimanu River to the valley's mouth. Not even the magnificent waterfalls fed by overnight showers at higher elevations could distract him from his thoughts. Two hours after their start, they reached the wide valley floor not far from the beach, where they would again cross the deep, fast-moving flow of the Waimanu River before heading toward the Muliwai Trail.

Suddenly, Koa's horse jerked and stumbled. Simultaneously, he heard the crack of a high-powered rifle. Having been under fire in combat, he reacted instinctively, grabbing his rifle and clearing the horse as it faltered and fell from the bullet that hit its hindquarters. Koa dove and rolled coming up behind a small boulder. He yelled for Bobby and Naomi to take cover. They were slow to react, remaining exposed for way too long. Koa feared for their lives, but they both made it safely to cover.

The attacker had picked a perfect spot for an ambush, and they were in a difficult tactical situation. The shooter occupied higher ground with clear lines of fire toward the open areas between their position and the Waimanu River. They'd be easy targets if they attempted to get to the ford and across, yet they had to get to the other side to reach the Muliwai Trail. They could reverse direction and go back past the Hazzard cabin to the head of the Waimanu Valley. There they could cross through the 2,000-foot high Waimanu Gap into the upper reaches of the Waipi'o Valley to get help or escape. But with a gunman on their tail, that long, dangerous trek would be too risky. Alternatively, Koa, armed with a rifle and a handgun, could go after the gunman, but that would leave Bobby unprotected and vulnerable.

They were trapped, but not entirely without options. Koa's satellite phone gave him an advantage the shooter couldn't have anticipated in the remote valley known for its lack of cell service. Koa could call for help. Since they were close to the beach, reinforcements should arrive quickly, maybe even fast enough to capture the gunman. He dialed HQ, got the dispatcher, and had police officers running for a helicopter in less than eight minutes.

While he waited, Koa scanned the slope from which the shot had come. C'mon, he thought, show me where you're hiding, you bastard. Twice he saw movement, each time followed by a bullet ricocheting off a rock near his position. Even with an unobstructed shot at Bobby or Naomi, who'd been slow to dismount, the gunman hadn't fired at them. Koa realized that he alone appeared to be the shooter's target.

Moving stealthily, Koa slipped behind a tree and dropped into a sheltered prone position at the edge of an outcropping of rock. He aimed carefully at the spot from which he thought the shooter had fired and waited. The wind came up, and Koa adjusted his aim. He saw movement and fired, but he'd overcompensated, and the bullet kicked up fragments of rock less than a foot from the shooter's position. Although he missed, his shot would make the attacker more cautious and keep him from rushing their position. He saw a muzzle flash, and another round zinged off the boulder above Koa's head. He returned fire.

They had achieved a stalemate. The shooter might think he could wait them out. Maybe even keep them pinned down until dark when he would have an even greater advantage. Little did this asshole know that a standoff with the police helicopter on the way was precisely what Koa had hoped to achieve.

Inexplicably, Bobby jumped to his feet and started hoofing back up the trail toward his grandfather's cabin, presenting his broad back to the shooter. A perfect target.

"Down! Get down!" Koa screamed, but Bobby kept running.

Shots—one, two, three—in rapid succession rang out, but again the bullets struck close to Koa. The shooter had chosen not to go after Bobby, who, after an agonizingly long minute, disappeared around a bend in the trail. Koa and his attacker exchanged intermittent fire over the next twenty minutes, but neither moved. Koa had achieved a continuing standoff.

Koa heard the faint sound of helicopter rotors out over the ocean, growing louder as the chopper neared the valley. His satellite phone chirped, and he began coordinating with the incoming police chopper. As the rotor sound increased, Koa again spotted movement on the hillside. He aimed and fired. His adversary had heard the chopper and was withdrawing up the slope, dodging around trees and boulders, putting distance between himself and the valley floor. Koa sent two more bullets after the assailant, encouraging his retreat. Two minutes later, he knew the man was out of rifle range. Koa reported the activity to the chopper pilot. He didn't want the chopper to take fire. The pilot, with a better vantage point than Koa, reported seeing a man fleeing over the ridgeline to the west. Still, out of an abundance of caution, the helo came in fast and low over the surf to a hot landing on the beach. Four policemen in tactical vests armed with automatic weapons swarmed out and took up defensive positions.

With the shooter gone, Koa raced up the trail to collect Bobby, whom he found cowering behind a thicket of *hāpu'u* ferns. "C'mon out. It's safe now."

Bobby emerged from his hiding place, his face flushed with anger. "You were supposed to protect me!"

Koa stared at the young man. "Relax. You're okay even though you ignored my warnings."

"I didn't sign up for this . . . for dealing with wild pigs and getting shot at."

"Didn't sign up? What are you talking about?"

Bobby hesitated and seemed to get control of himself. "Never mind."

Not understanding, Koa started to press Bobby but was interrupted by shouts from police around the chopper. He walked Bobby to the police helicopter. To his surprise, the chief climbed out and approached. "Bobby, are you all right?" the chief asked anxiously.

"He's fine," Koa responded. "It seems I was the target."

The chief, Koa, and Bobby boarded the helicopter, leaving Naomi to care for the horses, and the four police officers waiting for the chopper to return for them. While the police helicopter whisked Koa back to Hilo, two thoughts were foremost in his mind. First, he needed to warn Nālani. The odds were slim that anyone would attack her, but they had been threatened before and understood the risks. They had long since agreed upon protective measures. Second, he had to figure out the who, why, and how of the ambush.

He borrowed a cell phone and called as soon as the chopper landed. Nālani took the news calmly and, as a law enforcement pro, began to analyze the situation. "In the Waimanu Valley?" she asked. "That's pretty remote. Are you sure you were the target?"

"Positive. The first bullet barely missed me and hit my horse. After that, Bobby—that's the kid I was escorting—was slow to dismount. The shooter had maybe thirty seconds to take him out. Would have been an easy shot. But instead, he trained all his fire on me. The same thing happened when the kid got scared and bolted."

"How'd this shooter know you'd be there?"

"I haven't got a clue. Only a handful of people, mostly in the police department, knew I was taking this kid to his grandfather's cabin. I can't imagine any of them trying to get me killed."

"Maybe the kid told someone?" Nālani suggested.

"I suppose that's possible."

"What about the guide? You set that up in advance?" Nālani asked.

"You know Naomi. She guided us on your birthday outing into the Waipi'o. What possible motive would she have to take me out?"

They were both silent for a time.

"Strange," she said. "Any progress on capturing the shooter?"

"The police are looking, but it's not likely. He fled west over the ridge toward the Honopū'e Valley. That's wild country. A man could hide in there for years."

CHAPTER TWENTY-FOUR

THE FOLLOWING MORNING, Koa, Zeke, and Goodling gathered in Zeke's office to take stock of the investigation and decide upon the next steps. Koa began by briefing Zeke and the feds on the ambush in the Waimanu Valley. He had spent a long, fitful night replaying the shootout and thought it wise to share his experience in detail. "I don't know whether it's related to our investigation, but somebody tried to kill me. I suggest you all take precautions until we sort it out."

"Jesus," Zeke said, "that place is pretty isolated. Who knew you'd be up there?"

"That's the odd part," Koa responded. "Just the kid, the guide, a few police officers, Senator Chao, and his aide. That's all, and I don't think anyone of them is out to kill me."

Pivoting back to their investigation, Koa updated the group on the particulars of Kimberly Ward's death and the strange message "TB = Thief" written in blood beneath her body. He tied the message to X-CO's surveillance of Baldwin and Snelling's assertion, backed by Wingate, that Wingate had caught Baldwin surreptitiously accessing the main X-CO computer. They were deep into the discussion when Zeke's secretary announced that Georgina was outside with an urgent message.

"Sorry to interrupt," she began, "but you need to see this." She held up a cassette-sized metal box in a clear evidence pouch. "It's a computer drive. We found it behind a wall in Ward's apartment. I don't know what it contains, but the fingerprints on it match the Baldwin prints we got from the FBI."

"Let me check out that drive," Moreno said, reaching out to take it from Georgina.

"Just suppose," Koa said, "we're wrong about Baldwin. Could she have been stealing the Deimos code, or worse, sabotaging it?"

"That's preposterous!" Moreno said. "We know *Aletheia* sent the warning letter to the FBI."

"Yes," Koa acknowledged, "but what if *Aletheia* wasn't Baldwin?"

"We've been over this," Moreno responded. "Let's not waste time."

"Hear him out," Goodling ordered.

"First, I want to know what's on that drive. If it was Deimos code with Baldwin's fingerprints, she was up to something. Second, X-CO traced Baldwin's movements and suspected her of providing secrets to her friend in California. Why would they make that up? And why would Ward accuse Baldwin of theft in her dying declaration if it weren't true? Even courts allow dying declarations into evidence despite the hearsay rule because people facing death have little reason to lie."

Goodling turned to Moreno. "How long will it take you to check the drive?"

"A couple of hours," Moreno responded.

"Do it," Goodling ordered.

Moreno and his people did the analysis, and two hours later, when the team regrouped, they had their answer. The drive—covered with Baldwin's fingerprints—contained not an unauthorized download of Deimos software but a block of code permitting unauthorized control of Deimos. That blockbuster discovery set off an internal debate. Moreno, instantly reversing his position, argued that Baldwin was the saboteur. Koa wasn't so sure. He suspected Moreno had an ulterior motive. If Baldwin were the saboteur, that would mean Moreno's ill-advised efforts to contact her, possibly triggering her death, wouldn't be so horrific.

Koa's instinctive paranoia kicked in. He'd fooled the cops investigating Anthony Hazzard's death by planting false evidence. He'd seen criminals do it in other cases. Now, within the space of three days, Snelling and Wingate had accused Baldwin, Ward had labeled Baldwin a thief, and the drive with Baldwin's fingerprints had turned up hidden in Ward's apartment. Wasn't it all a little too convenient? This new image of Baldwin as the saboteur also seemed inconsistent with the cover-up of her death. If Snelling, Wingate, and Ward had known that Baldwin was the thief and had the drive with her fingerprints to prove it, why had they concealed her body and covered up her disappearance? The pieces didn't fit. Koa knew he was missing something.

Keeping those thoughts to himself, Koa said, "Granted, the drive contains unauthorized code, but we have only fingerprints to tie it to Baldwin. We don't know when or how she touched the drive. It's a pretty slim reed."

"There's got to be some way to be sure," Goodling said.

"Maybe that drive wasn't the first or only one," Koa said.

"Couldn't have been the first," Moreno responded. "Our cyber-team analyzed the stuff we got in the raid and verified that the Deimos program was compromised months ago—by February for sure, and someone added bad code multiple times after that. So, if Baldwin was the saboteur, she uploaded bad code into the computer more than just once."

"She probably would have used the same technique each time," Goodling added. "And she might have kept the drives she'd used."

"Where would they be?" Koa asked.

"Her stuff?" Goodling suggested.

Although they considered it a long shot, Koa and Goodling decided to go through the boxes and furnishings Snelling had cleared out of Baldwin's apartment and moved into storage. Drafting Moreno and Makanui to help in the search, the team located the self-storage facility on Railroad Avenue in south Hilo. Situated in a shabby warehouse area across from a heavy equipment yard, it didn't seem like a place Tiger Baldwin would have chosen. Still, Koa reminded himself that Snelling, not Baldwin, had made the arrangements.

An ancient Thai woman from the front office led them down a gravel drive between long sheds with roll-up doors for each storage unit until they reached unit E-20. Armed with another warrant Zeke had secured, they broke the locks. Furniture and boxes crammed the space from floor to ceiling. They were in for a long day with only a faint hope they would find anything relevant to the investigation. Koa figured they were on a fool's errand. It took two hours to remove and search the boxes before they could even get at the furniture. After four hours, they had nearly finished combing through the furniture, and only Baldwin's desk at the back of the storage unit remained. Goodling was tired, and Moreno had called it quits, so Koa and Makanui tackled the desk.

"Hey," Makanui exclaimed, pulling two hefty red-rope folders from the back of a filing drawer in one of the desk's pedestals.

"What have you got?" Koa asked.

"Something heavy." Makanui set the packages on top of the desk, unfastened the bindings, and opened the flaps to reveal six more drives, identical to the one Georgina had found in Ward's apartment.

Koa, peering at the irrefutable physical evidence, said, "Score one for Moreno."

"Damn," Goodling swore. "We need to get those to the cyber team, but it sure looks like our assumptions about the identity of the whistleblower were wrong. I was sure Baldwin was *Aletheia*. Never occurred to me that she might be the saboteur."

Three hours later, federal computer experts confirmed that the drives contained unauthorized Deimos communications code. Koa added up the evidence—Wingate's and Snelling's statements, X-CO's surveillance, Ward's dying declaration, the drive from Kimberly's apartment, and now these six drives. Altogether, it made for a damning case. Yet, ultimately, it all came from X-CO, and that bothered Koa. Someplace in the back of his mind, he feared that he and the feds were being played.

That concern evaporated when Goodling, who'd been on the phone with her superiors, walked into Zeke's office with a long face and a sheet of paper. "We blew it. The DOD inspector general just got another communication from *Aletheia*."

"Fuck," Moreno exclaimed.

Goodling handed the paper, fresh off a fax machine, to Koa. It read: "Tiger Baldwin tampered with the Deimos software," and was signed "*Aletheia*."

Koa found the discovery depressing. His need to pursue justice, buried deep in his psyche, derived in no small measure from his connection with and empathy for victims. Tiger Baldwin—shot, mutilated, and discarded in a desolate cemetery—had triggered his empathy. Her ghost had motivated him to pursue her killer. He found it hard to change gears and view her as a saboteur rather than a victim.

Yet, there was no contesting the facts. There might be doubts about everything else, but the message from *Aletheia* was irrefutable. Tiger Baldwin's status changed from heroine to traitor. Someone else at X-CO had tipped the government and had now blown the whistle on Baldwin.

In the shower the following morning, Koa was still kicking himself for misjudging Baldwin. The feds had relied on thin evidence
and jumped to conclude that Baldwin was *Aletheia*, the whistleblower, and they'd been wrong. The mistake made him think of
ancient Polynesian mariners, sailing double-hulled canoes across
thousands of miles of hostile ocean. While early researchers believed
these explorers drifted on the winds and currents, the truth is far
more complex. Polynesian sailors understood the movement of the
stars and, lacking a written language, passed their knowledge from
generation to generation in detailed chants. They read the ocean
currents and swells. They knew bird migration patterns and had
identified which birds wandered the oceans and which always returned to land. After they crossed more than twenty-six hundred
miles of inhospitable ocean from the Marquesas, the first Hawaiians
then followed *'ua'u* birds, dark-rumped petrels, to the Hawaiian Islands where those birds nested and bred.

Nor was the Polynesian voyage of discovery to the Hawaiian Islands an isolated event. Modern archeologists uncovered evidence
of two-way trade routes across vast stretches of the Pacific and multiple migrations from South Pacific islands to Hawai'i. Spectro-
graphic analysis of stone tools demonstrated that adzes and other
implements from quarries in American Samoa found their way to
Hawai'i and other parts of the Pacific. As Koa well knew, even Hawaiian geographic names memorialized travel between Hawai'i and
Tahiti. The channel between Lāna'i and the Kaho'olawe islands bore
the name *Kealaikahiki*, meaning "pathway to Tahiti."

Koa, long familiar with ancient Hawaiian navigation techniques,
drew upon his lifelong devotion to *heihei wa'a*, outrigger canoe racing, and from a two-week stint aboard the *Hōkūle'a*, the Polynesian
Voyaging Society's modern replica of an ancient double-hulled canoe. Friends in the society had invited him to join a voyage to *Rapa*

Nui, Easter Island. Lying on the deck studying the stars, listening to the navigators explaining, and sometimes debating, the natural signs, feeling the immense power of the ocean, and confronting the uncertainties that challenged ancient seafarers had been life-altering for Koa.

Finding the speck of *Rapa Nui* more than a thousand miles from its nearest neighbor without modern navigation tools had been a daunting experience. For a voyager at wave height on a canoe deck, the earth's curvature limits the unobstructed sightline to about three miles. Sailors could see a ship or an island at a greater distance depending upon its height, but a voyager could sail past a low-lying island without ever seeing it. Koa had seen for himself the mirages that often tricked sailors. It was devilishly hard to distinguish between a low cloud bank on the horizon and an island.

Tiger Baldwin, the patriot, had turned out to be an illusion. Like a distant low-lying cloud bank, she had steered all of them off course. Koa had been misdirected in previous investigations before recovering his footing, and he knew what they had to do. They had to go back to the beginning, and rethink every step, reevaluate every piece of evidence. He had to reexamine every detail in the light of what they had now discovered. Unlearning the assumptions they had all internalized would be demanding.

Baldwin's treachery changed the entire focus and the time frame of the investigation. Baldwin's death was now only the endpoint of their inquiry. They needed to go back in time and discover how and when she'd become an enemy agent, why X-CO had hired her, her movements since her arrival in Hawai'i, and her contacts. In short, her whole life history. Only then could they hope to learn how, and with whose assistance, she'd hacked the Deimos software.

The discovery of Baldwin's perfidy added credibility to Snelling's and Wingate's story that they'd caught her engaged in unauthorized access to the computer. Still, it left Koa, Zeke, and the feds in a quandary. They had Snelling's testimony, seemingly confirmed by Wingate, that Wingate had killed Baldwin, but they hadn't found the weapon that fired the kill shot. Both said that Baldwin had drawn her "lady's gun," but that gun, too, was missing.

Both men asserted self-defense, but Koa had his doubts. People who killed in self-defense usually went to the police. Instead, Snelling and maybe Wingate had conspired to mutilate Baldwin's fingertips and conceal her body—felonies irrespective of how she died.

Then there was Wingate's excuse for failing to go to the police—his fear that Zhou Li would fire him and the government shut the Deimos program down. To Koa, it didn't compute. Wingate's actions would have let a severe security breach go unreported without checking to see if Baldwin had previously stolen or compromised the program. In Koa's world, no patriot would risk giving away his nation's military secrets just to save his job. That Wingate would do so suggested to Koa that the X-CO executive was hiding something else.

The following morning brought a torrent of wind and rain from a tropical depression coming from the east. The lousy weather darkened Koa's already bleak mood. The Deimos investigation was growing ever more convoluted while Bobby Hazzard's investigation threatened to upend his personal life. Trudging through the downpour from his SUV to the prosecutor's office, he wanted to hang both Wingate and Snelling.

Peeling off his dripping slicker, he met Goodling and Moreno in Zeke's reception area, where together they went into the prosecutor's office and gathered around his conference table.

"We should charge both Wingate and Snelling with murder," Koa proposed after they exchanged gripes about the weather.

"That'll fuck up our national security investigation," Moreno responded, letting his hostility loose. Moreno had made his objection to Koa's involvement plain from the outset, and their relationship had only grown worse with the snafus they'd encountered.

Zeke, directing himself more to Koa than the others, said, "I can't charge them with murder based on what we've got. They're not going to admit willfully murdering Baldwin, and they're both going to claim self-defense. Then there's the claim that she managed to get out of X-CO that night. Put that together with Baldwin's betrayal, and we'll be up to our eyeballs in reasonable doubt. Hell, the judge might not even let the case go to trial."

"They mutilated her body and dumped her in a graveyard for God's sakes," Koa shot back, immediately thinking better of his hostile tone.

"That's probably true, but there's no forensic evidence. Hell, what little evidence we've got is all circumstantial."

"We have the GPS data and the Snelling tape. He says Wingate shot Baldwin."

"Yeah, but Snelling claims she shot first with the lady's gun, and Wingate shot back in self-defense. He also says she escaped. We have no proof that either one of them killed Baldwin."

Koa felt the stress of the Hazzard case warping his usual good judgment but knew he shouldn't give up. "We know Snelling had the keys to Baldwin's car. The GPS shows that the car went from X-CO to Baldwin's home to the graveyard. We could get Snelling for the unlawful desecration of a corpse. Plus, we can prove he forged Baldwin's emails so we could get him on the theft of her car and furniture."

"Koa." Zeke looked hard at his friend. "You don't have the evidence. You don't know where and when Baldwin died. She could have driven herself home. She could have met her end there. She could have given Snelling a spare set of keys. There are too many unknowns. And no jury is going to convict Snelling of theft when he put the proceeds of the car sale in her bank account and stored her furniture in a warehouse unit rented in her name."

"And we're not going to expose our espionage investigation for a weak theft case against a lowly security guard," Moreno said, ending the argument.

"So, we just let these two snakes roam free?" Koa asked.

"For now," Zeke responded. "We don't have a choice."

CHAPTER TWENTY-FIVE

LATER THAT SAME day, after Koa had returned to his office, he answered his cell. After exchanging greetings, Zeigler, who said that Goodling was also on the line, explained the purpose of their call. "We've got one of your native activists in custody. My MPs caught him in the restricted area with heavy-duty surveillance gear spying on our classified trials."

The news puzzled Koa. While native hunters sometimes trespassed along the PTA boundaries, most didn't venture too far inside the restricted area for fear of triggering unexploded ordinance. More than one trespasser had lost a limb or worse to an old artillery shell. Besides, few if any natives had or could afford sophisticated surveillance equipment.

"He may have blown our cover," Goodling added, concern evident in her voice.

"How?" Koa asked.

"He recorded a Deimos test, one in which the cyber weapon turned on its own protectees."

"If you caught him and have his equipment, you must have the pictures he took," Koa reasoned.

"Yeah," Goodling acknowledged, "but he had satellite Wi-Fi gear. We think he forwarded the photos as he took them."

"Forwarded to whom?" Koa asked.

"We don't know, and this guy isn't talking. If X-CO got those photos, then they know we know about the sabotage. I'm afraid the saboteurs are going to bail before we can ID them."

"Want me to send someone up to get him?" Koa asked. The Army had court-martial jurisdiction over military personnel but turned civilian offenders over to the local authorities.

"Yeah, and get the truth out of him," Goodling said.

"That may be easier said than done," Koa warned.

Koa had a patrolman bring the trespasser back to an interrogation room at police headquarters. Two hours later, Koa and Goodling stared through the observation window watching Chase Sana, a young Hawaiian from Nāʻālehu in the southern part of the island. A bulky guy, he sported black bands of geometric tattoos on his neck and arms, typical body art among young Hawaiians, and a braided necklace from which a white fishhook dangled.

"He doesn't look real smart," Goodling said.

"He's not." Koa had pulled his record. "Never graduated from high school. Suspected gang affiliation. A dozen arrests. Burglary, drugs, assault. Two stints inside."

"Somebody outfitted him with the binos, a high-performance video camera, and sophisticated satellite Wi-Fi gear," Goodling said.

"Yeah. Either that or he stole the stuff. He didn't buy it . . . that I'll guarantee," Koa responded.

"What's that plastic thing around his neck?" Goodling asked.

"A fake *lei niho palaoa*. In ancient times, *aliʻi*, Hawaiian royalty, wore real ones, made of human hair and whalebone as symbols of rank. A lot of young hoods wear plastic replicas as a sign of disrespect for their elders."

"Nice." Sarcasm dripped from Goodling's voice. "Think he's going to tell us where he got all his fancy equipment?"

"Not a chance," Koa responded. "He won't say a word. When we arraign him, one of the activist leaders will rail against the Army for stealing his native birthright to unrestricted access on what were once native Hawaiian lands. The judge will tell him to stay out of the PTA and let him go. That's why we rarely bother to prosecute native trespassers."

"Damn. We got to find out if X-CO put him up to spying, and I doubt we'll get an answer by tracing the serial numbers on the stuff he had." Goodling's tone underlined her disappointment. After a pause, she added, "Maybe I should arrest him for espionage."

"Which you don't have the evidence to prove?" Koa asked.

Goodling sighed. "Isn't there some way to get him to talk?"

Koa paused to think before answering. "Maybe . . . just maybe."

An hour and two phone calls later, Koa introduced Goodling to an exceptionally tall native Hawaiian man with ebony hair, sparkling white teeth, and an ugly facial scar. "Ms. Goodling, this is Makaiao."

Goodling, who was six feet tall, had to look up at Makaiao. "I've seen your picture somewhere in the news."

"Trying to keep *haole* people from destroying the whole planet," he responded with a smile that robbed the words of their hostility.

"We're hoping you might help us," Koa said by way of introduction before explaining Sana's arrest and their need to understand who had put him up to spying on the Army.

"Why should I help you, *hapa haole* man?"

Koa ignored the racial slur intended to denigrate the legitimacy of his Hawaiian roots. "When we last met, you were protesting outside X-CO. There's something peculiar going on at X-CO and—"

"You got dat right, brah," Makaiao interrupted.

"Which," Koa continued, "it might be in our mutual interest to resolve. Besides, you'd get credit for bailing Sana out. You'd do him and the community a favor in straightening him up and making a man of him."

Makaiao paused, apparently giving the proposition some thought. "Sana is one *ʻōpio lawehala*."

"Juvenile delinquent," Koa translated for Goodling. "That's true, and one of these days he'll wind up doing serious time if someone doesn't knock some sense into him. I can't do that, but you can."

"No blowback?" Makaiao asked.

Koa knew they had a deal. Makaiao just wanted to be sure his activist friends didn't learn he'd helped the police.

"No blowback," Koa promised.

"And he walks with me even if I tell you nothing?" Makaiao pushed.

Koa nodded. "We'll turn the sound off while you talk to him."

Makaiao rose, and they led him to the interrogation room door. Goodling and Koa observed through a one-way mirror. It was like watching a silent movie, as Sana's face paled at the sight of the well-known Hawaiian activist. Makaiao sat opposite the young punk, staring at him in silence for several minutes. Sana squirmed in his seat as the silence went on and on. The kid appeared to shrink like a wet animal when the older man spoke. Then with cobra-like quickness, Makaiao's long arm flashed across the table to tear the fake *lei niho palaoa* from the boy's neck. Makaiao snapped the plastic fishhook in his huge hands and tossed the broken ornament to the floor. A serious conversation ensued.

An hour later, when Sana and Makaiao walked out of the room, the older man had his arm around the kid's shoulder. Koa hoped Makaiao could work his magic on the young delinquent and save the county the cost of future crimes, trials, and incarceration. He also hoped that Makaiao would tell them what the kid had been doing in the PTA. Yet, he knew he'd have to wait because Makaiao would never let the young Hawaiian radical see him reporting to the police.

*   *   *

The following morning brought cool, sunny weather—perfect for the long-anticipated AI seminar. The mayor and the police chief insisted that Koa attend because native sovereignty activists would be out in force. They wanted Koa available to defuse any confrontation. They'd seen him use his influence time and again to calm a potentially explosive situation. The activists might disparage him for joining the police force, but he still commanded a measure of their respect, enhanced by his weekend classes in canoe racing for native teenagers and his other work with Hawaiian community groups.

Koa would have attended the seminar in any event to observe the interactions between the big shots who dominated X-CO's management and board of directors. Wingate and Snelling would be present, as would their corporate bosses, and Koa remained curious about the dynamic between his two principal targets and their superiors. He didn't expect an epiphany, but experience had taught him never to miss an opportunity to watch his suspects interact.

The crowd in town for the event left the police shorthanded, and they scrounged for additional officers, borrowing from the sheriff's department and the National Park Service. As a park ranger, Nālani was a federal law enforcement officer, having attended the US law enforcement training center in Glyno, Georgia. Koa had mixed motives in arranging for her to participate in the seminar. She was a pro and a valuable addition to the security forces, and she could also help Koa keep an eye on the X-CO executives who would be attending the conference. Koa's targets, who had no reason to know of her connection to Koa, might be less guarded in her presence.

Arriving at the Hilo college campus for the seminar, Koa and Nālani agreed upon their surveillance strategy. They separated, each moving in different circles while watching X-CO personnel prepare for the centerpiece event, the presentation by their chairman, Zhou Li. Koa immediately noticed that X-CO had heeded his advice. The event coordinators had cordoned off an area for the activists, provided water and snacks, and set up a live television feed from the main event space and several seminar rooms. A couple of dozen Hawaiian protesters walked back and forth in their designated zone carrying placards condemning *haole* companies, military contractors, and other assorted real and imagined oppressors. Everything looked peaceful. Lucia Bianche, Zhou Li's US representative, had kept her promise when she had overruled Wingate's lawless approach. It was, Koa thought, a hopeful sign.

An hour later, Wingate came strolling through the campus, followed by Snelling. Making the rounds of the police security team, Koa kept an eye on the X-CO executive and his security man. While Wingate checked on preparations for the seminar and greeted some of the attendees, Snelling hovered close by, protecting his boss. From what, Koa couldn't imagine. Nothing on the UH Hilo campus posed any threat. Native activists demonstrated peacefully, and other seminar attendees, including Lucia Bianche and several corporate CEOs, senior to Wingate, came and went without visible bodyguards. The sizable police presence seemed like overkill. Still, Wingate and his body man were inseparable, like conjoined twins. Maybe Wingate was paranoid. That would, Koa thought, be consistent with his over-the-top reactions to the activists.

Koa and Nālani tag-teamed the two X-Co executives. Koa would watch for a while and text Nālani. Then, he'd walk away, and she'd observe Wingate and Snelling, usually from the opposite direction.

They traded off like a well-rehearsed duet, making Koa think, not for the first time, what it would be like to team up with Nālani as a fellow police officer. Smart and intuitive, she'd make a great detective. That dream faded when he thought of the dangers cops faced. He'd be devastated if anything ever happened to her. Besides, Nālani loved her position as a national park service ranger and was much safer in that role.

Each time Koa checked on the X-CO pair, sometimes from a distance and other times close up, he sensed something amiss. He studied them, watching their movements, trying to figure what had triggered his antenna. The nagging sensation of something out of kilter gnawed at him, but he couldn't pinpoint what bothered him.

As the day wore on, the protesters became more lethargic, and their ranks thinned. Koa stood watching the protesters when Lucia Bianche, billionaire Zhou Li's American representative, appeared by his side as if by magic. He hadn't heard her approach.

"I want to thank you for your advice, Detective," she began.

He turned to face her. Dressed in a white linen pants suit, she wore a *lei pūpū*, a string of tiny, pastel-colored Niʻihau shells that glowed against her white outfit. Having bought a similar artisanal necklace for Nālani, Koa couldn't help but recognize the superb quality of Bianche's double strand. "About the protesters?" he guessed.

"Yes. The live video feed was a brilliant idea. Letting the protesters see the working group sessions and the main stage presentations appears to have taken the mystery and menace out of our gathering. The most common reaction seems to be boredom."

Koa chuckled. "I'm sure that's right. I watched a little of the system architecture seminar and didn't understand a word. The participants appeared to be talking a foreign language."

"I doubt that, but thank you for your sound counsel."

Koa decided to use the unexpected meeting to his advantage. "I confess, I was surprised by Wingate's over-the-top reaction to the protesters. It wasn't productive and gives X-CO a bad reputation."

She hesitated, and Koa sensed she was choosing her words with care. "Chairman Li met Wingate at Beijing University in China where he was conducting research. The Chairman subsequently bought the X-CO technology from Wingate and put him under contract. He's the genius behind the company's products, but like a lot of entrepreneurs, he goes off in all directions and doesn't always show the best judgment."

Her words left no doubt about where the power lay in the X-CO organization, but Koa had already sensed that from the way she'd shut Wingate down at the pre-conference security meeting. He decided to probe deeper. "Have Wingate or Snelling said anything about Tiger Baldwin, the murdered former X-CO computer systems architect?"

Bianche kept a poker face, but Koa thought he detected the faintest flicker of surprise at either Baldwin's name or his description of her former position. He couldn't tell which. "We've had reports on the police investigation from them and the company lawyers, and we've instructed them to cooperate," she responded.

Koa upped the pressure. "Moving to overturn our search warrant wasn't exactly cooperation."

"I apologize for that. Wingate hired and instructed the lawyers before talking to us. We've told the lawyers to drop the appeal."

Having seen Wingate in action while executing the search warrant, Koa wanted to understand the man's aggressive reaction. "He seems particularly paranoid about our investigation."

"He's extremely secretive, always afraid somebody's out to steal his technology." She paused and looked at her watch. "I'm due back in the main arena for a meeting with the Chairman. Again, thank you for your advice." She turned away.

Like clockwork, a late morning downpour sent the remaining activists running for cover. Makaiao, who'd been with the protesters throughout the morning, took advantage of the lull in the demonstrations to approach Koa on one of the campus's covered walkways.

"How's my *hapa haole* brother today?" Makaiao asked without rancor.

"Each serves our heritage in his own way," Koa responded with a half-smile. "You straighten out the young *'ōpio lawehala*?"

"*He Malanai wale nō kēia?*" Do you think I'm some sort of sorcerer?

Koa chuckled at the old Hawaiian phrase. "I guess it will take some magic to clean up Sana's act."

"A project requiring strong spirits and much patience," Makaiao responded before turning serious. "The security man, the one following the X-CO boss man around today. He offered Sana a hundred bucks to take pictures on the PTA. Gave him the camera and showed him how to use it."

"*Mahalo.*" Koa acknowledged Makaiao's help.

"No blowback," Makaiao said.

"No blowback," Koa assured him as the big Hawaiian walked away.

Makaiao's disclosure left Koa puzzled. As a principal software contractor for the communications package on the Deimos project, X-CO had direct access to the results of the Army trials. Such access would be essential to improving the software. Why would anyone from X-CO need to spy on the Army? Unless, Koa thought, someone at X-CO feared the Army was withholding information . . . like the discovery of the software hack. That had to be it. Something had made Wingate suspicious, and he'd ordered Snelling to check it out.

Koa pulled out his cell phone to call Goodling, who answered on the second ring. "I just got the skinny on our activist friend with the spy gear. Snelling put him up to it," Koa reported.

"Damn," Goodling responded. "That means that X-CO knows the Army is on to the sabotage."

"Yeah," Koa responded. "But how much do you think they know? I mean, we've kept Justice and the FBI in the background. They don't know about *Aletheia* or how far the investigation has advanced."

"From your lips to God's ears," Goodling said before hanging up.

The rain gods retreated, suddenly vanquished by bright sunshine. The trade winds blew the rain in and then whisked it away—typical Hilo weather. Walking back toward the auditorium, Koa spotted Snelling with Lucia Bianche. For once, Wingate was nowhere in sight. Koa stepped into the shadows of a banyan tree to observe the security man with Zhou Li's top American representative. From his vantage point, Koa could see Snelling's face, but not Bianche's. Their conversation went on for several minutes, during which Snelling gestured emphatically. His face registered intense interest, if not a hint of distress. Koa couldn't be sure.

Odd, Koa thought, that one of Li's senior executives would have a serious rendezvous with someone so far down the corporate ladder. Had Wingate dispatched Snelling with a message, or was Snelling acting on his own? Maybe Snelling was Bianche's eyes and ears inside X-CO. A part of Koa wished he'd had a long-distance eavesdropping device, but, absent a warrant, Hawai'i law required the consent of at least one party to a conversation, and Koa had neither a warrant nor a listening device. He was left guessing.

After lunch, the luminaries arrived for the day's highlight, the keynote address by Chairman Zhou Li. Koa followed the crowd into the main auditorium, where Li was to speak. Zhou Li, reported to be worth a half a *trillion* dollars, was one of the world's leading artificial intelligence experts. He also ran one of the world's largest venture capital firms and had billion-dollar investments in the world's leading tech companies. His seminars were sometimes called the Davos of the artificial intelligence world. Everyone wanted to curry favor with the man, and accordingly, CEOs and other senior executives packed the auditorium.

Koa stood at one side near the front where he could see the stage and still scan the faces in the audience. The CEOs of Facebook, Amazon, Apple, Netflix, and Google, all of whom Koa recognized from TV, sat in the front row. They were eager to support their largest outside investor and lay the foundation for joint ventures with Mister AI, as some newspaper accounts referred to Zhou Li. Of greater immediate interest, Koa spotted the governor; Senator Chao; his aide, Kāwika Keahi; and Mayor Tenaka, all of whom sat with Wingate, also in the front row. He guessed that the other front-row attendees, whom he did not recognize, were mostly other X-CO board members.

Unlike the technical discussions that dominated the conference's early part, Chairman Zhou Li delivered a simple message. Now in its infancy, AI would revolutionize the world, eliminating millions of jobs, upsetting the social order, and energizing revolution unless lawmakers around the world enacted laws enabling all elements of society to share in the benefits of this extraordinary new technology. Koa found Li's predictions sobering.

Later, when Koa stood in the entryway to the UH Hilo main auditorium, he suddenly noticed a security camera fastened to the ceiling opposite the entry door. He stared at the camera and then kicked himself for not having paid more attention to the university's security system. He'd been distracted by Bobby Hazzard and hadn't scoped out the AI seminar venue. Still, it wasn't too late. Retracing his steps through the seminar area, he identified five security cameras and photographed each of them with his smartphone.

He called Makanui, who answered on the second ring. "Can you get a team together to review the CATV footage from some UH Hilo security cameras? I'm about to text you pictures of the relevant ones. Have the team flag every sequence involving Wingate or Snelling." He paused before adding, "And Lucia Bianche, too. Find a place to work on the campus and text me the location."

"I'm on it," Makanui responded.

Two hours later, Koa met Makanui, Piki, and two other police department employees in a cramped room next to the campus security office. Koa began reviewing the video the others had isolated showing Wingate, Snelling, or Bianche. The police team worked until after five, and Koa found nothing of particular interest, except a snippet that captured Snelling and Bianche in the same conversation that Koa had witnessed, but in this case from the opposite angle, recording Bianche's face. Koa watched the segment several times, but Bianche kept turning her head, making it difficult for him to decipher her words. He asked Makanui to take the Snelling-Bianche segment to Professor Atkins, a lip-reading expert at UH Hilo whom Koa knew and had occasionally consulted.

Koa left the security office a little after five and ran into Kāwika Keahi. Both men were headed across the campus toward the parking lot and fell into step together. "Good to see you, brah," Keahi said.

"You, too," Koa responded.

"Look at you, a kid from Laupāhoehoe who made the big time. You as Chief Detective. Pretty amazing, huh, brah?"

Koa thought he detected a hint of bitterness. "It's been quite a ride," he responded before remembering the funeral he'd attended two months ago. "Hey, I wanted to tell you again how sorry I was that your mom passed. She was great. I'll never forget the taste of her homemade *kūlolo*." He referred to a native Hawaiian pudding made with grated taro and coconut cream.

"Thanks. I miss Mom, but I guess she's in a better place."

Koa thought he saw an opportunity to gather a bit of intelligence as the two men walked and switched topics. "Mind if I ask you a question?"

"Ask away . . . I'll tell you anything except I won't confess my many sins," Keahi responded, smiling.

"You and your boss have been backing Bobby Hazzard, who's out here asking about a thirty-year-old murder. What's the deal with that?"

Keahi stopped walking, and the two friends faced each other. "It's a long story. Buy me a beer, and I'll tell you the sorry tale."

Koa realized he might have stumbled onto something and jumped at the opportunity to pursue it. "You're on. Cronies?"

"Sure."

Koa texted Nālani to let her know his plans. Twenty minutes later, he and Keahi were seated in the red and blue glow of multiple TV screens at Cronies Bar & Grill. Both were into Hawaiian craft brews, and Koa ordered a Mauna Kea Pale Ale, while Keahi chose a Humpback Blue. Keahi took a long pull from his mug and set it back on the table. "I never knew my father. When I got older, I asked my mother, but she said he wasn't part of our lives."

Koa had no idea where Keahi was going with his story or how it connected with Bobby Hazzard, so he just nodded an acknowledgment.

"After my mom died," Keahi continued, "I went through her papers, and I discovered a trust fund set up in 1975 at the First Hawaiian Bank. That's the year I was born. I visited the bank and got access to the declaration of trust, along with a letter from my mother." Wetness welled in the corners of Keahi's eyes. "In it, she told me about my . . . my father. The father I never knew." Keahi took another swig of beer, a long one.

"My mother was fourteen, and he was much older when they met sometime back in 1974 or early 1975. He was wealthy and powerful, and she was just a girl, not more than a child. She said they had an affair in her letter, but I bet he just took advantage of her. We've both seen it happen to a lot of young Hawaiian girls." He paused, fiddling with a circular charm on a leather cord around his neck. "Anyway, within a year, she got pregnant and had me."

In a flash of intuition, Koa thought he knew the ending, but it was not possible. Not even *Pele* could throw such an ugly lava ball. Yet, with a sinking feeling, he somehow knew he was about to get the shock of his life.

"Anyway, this dude was married and didn't want the notoriety of a bastard child, so he set up this trust and dumped my mother." Bitterness dripped from Keahi's voice. "Mom never named the bastard in her letter, but I pressured the bankers for details. They claimed confidentiality obligations, but the senator called one of the senior guys. They identified the sorry son of a bitch as Anthony Hazzard. The dirtbag died about thirty years ago. Hanged himself, according to the police. May he burn in hell."

Koa felt like he'd been stabbed. It couldn't be. It wasn't possible. He couldn't have killed his best friend's father. And Keahi looked nothing like Anthony Hazzard; there was no physical resemblance. Koa felt his face redden and his heart pound. Picking up his beer to cover his shock, he fought to maintain his composure.

Keahi didn't seem to notice. "After I found out about my "dad—" Keahi put the word in air quotes—"I figured he must be a relative of this Bobby Hazzard guy who was an unpaid summer intern in the senator's office. Imagine my shock learning that his father and I are half-brothers, making Bobby my nephew. And he doesn't know his grandfather got my underage mother pregnant and dumped her. Of course he doesn't know. My 'nephew'—again, Keahi used air quotes—grew up in a ritzy New York apartment surrounded by sterling silver and fancy oil paintings. He wouldn't stoop to using our family outhouse." Sarcasm dripped from Keahi's words.

Upset as he was with Keahi's awful revelation, Koa couldn't help reacting to the anger and bitterness in Keahi's demeanor. He'd never seen this side of his childhood friend. The shock of discovering the circumstances of his birth had wounded Keahi, leaving a profound scar.

"Bobby's hung up on his grandfather's suicide . . . can't believe one of his esteemed relatives pulled the pin. He wants to dig up his grandfather's past. So, I say, what the hell. Let him dig. I got the senator to help him. Maybe he'll find out what a slimeball his grandfather was."

"Jesus," Koa muttered. "That's some screwed-up history."

"Yeah. Hard to believe, isn't it?"

After he left Keahi outside Cronies, Koa sat alone in his SUV for what seemed like an eternity. Keahi's tale was too much. He simply couldn't absorb his awful luck. He'd killed the father of his best friend. True, the man had been a murderer and a statutory rapist, but that did nothing to reduce Koa's shock or minimize this cruel turn of fate.

After a time, he got control of himself, and his mind veered in another direction. What bearing, he wondered, did this new horror have on Bobby Hazzard's quest. How could Bobby Hazzard ever learn the truth about his grandfather, and what would he do if he were to discover that his grandfather had fathered the senator's aide with an underage girl?

* * *

When Koa finally reached his Volcano cottage, he felt burned out and wanted to put Keahi's revelation, Bobby Hazzard, and the

Deimos investigation out of mind for the evening. He kissed Nālani and changed into jeans and a tee-shirt before the two of them retreated to the kitchen to make dinner together. She prepared salad, while he chopped and parboiled *hōʻiʻo*, a native fern-like thin asparagus, for a pot of simmering risotto.

"So, what did you think of the seminar?" Koa asked.

"A bit different than a day at the park," she responded. "I enjoyed it. It was fun working with you. The seminar itself was also a treat, especially Zhou Li's speech. I'm glad you arranged for me to help." She blew him a kiss.

"Same here," he responded.

"That Li guy was impressive, but his message is scary. You think he's right that this AI stuff will leave half the world's workforce unemployed?" Nālani asked.

"Maybe, but I don't see robotic park rangers," he joked, returning her air kiss.

"I'm serious," she insisted.

"Well, factory robots are already pretty common, so I'd guess things will only get worse for workers, but it'll take time. Big changes always take longer than people think."

She nodded her agreement before switching to a new subject. "Those two guys you asked me to watch are a strange pair."

"Wingate and his bodyguard?"

"Yeah. Except I'm not so sure Snelling is a bodyguard."

Koa turned toward her, still stirring the rice dish. "Why do you say that? They were together almost all day . . . like twins."

"That's the point. They were together, but Snelling wasn't acting like a bodyguard. He wasn't checking the surroundings looking for external threats. He was mostly just watching Wingate. He rarely took his eyes off the man, almost like he was guarding a prisoner."

Koa went over what he'd observed—Wingate going about the seminar, greeting people, directing staff, playing the managing director role with Snelling always in the background. For him, the anomaly had been Snelling's eyes. Like Nālani, Koa realized he'd never seen Snelling searching for external threats, never once sweeping the crowd or checking out newcomers. No, Snelling's eyes had invariably focused on Wingate. Koa wanted to kick himself. He and Nālani had both seen the same pattern but processed it differently. He had sensed something out of kilter but hadn't understood its significance. Nālani, with fresh eyes, had seen beneath the surface.

Koa went over his past interactions with Wingate and Snelling. On his first visit to X-CO, Wingate had introduced himself as managing director of X-CO. Later, the police had ID'd Snelling through his driver's license as a security guard employed by X-CO. Snelling himself had confirmed that role when Koa had confronted him in his apartment, and during his second interview, Snelling had told them, "Wingate's the boss. You don't question what he says." It all hung together like a million-dollar painting, but maybe it was just an illusion.

Snelling's surveillance of Wingate suggested a different kind of relationship. Koa recalled Lucia Bianche's words—Wingate was "the genius behind the company's technology, but like a lot of entrepreneurs, he goes off in all directions and doesn't always show the best judgment." Suddenly, it all made sense. Zhou Li and Bianche needed Wingate, but they didn't trust him. He was like the precocious child you never let out of your sight for fear of what he or she might do. So, they'd installed Snelling as his shadow. That observation triggered a different recollection, one of Snelling in earnest conversation with Lucia Bianche. Koa then thought of the pre-seminar planning meeting in which Bianche had shut down Wingate in a curt display of superior power.

Pursuing this new line of thinking, Koa reflected on the case with an entirely new focus. As the man in charge, Wingate shouldn't have had to consult others before releasing Baldwin's personnel file. Yet, during their first meeting at X-CO, he'd had to check before giving Koa Baldwin's phony materials. But with whom? Had he consulted Snelling? Or Bianche?

Koa had replayed Snelling's taped conversation with Wingate more than a dozen times—always thinking of Wingate as the top dog and Snelling as an underling. Their conversation had seemed odd, even stilted, but made far more sense if Wingate took his cues from Snelling. It was Snelling who'd said that Wingate had caught Baldwin tampering with the computer, and it was Snelling who'd first mentioned self-defense. It was also Snelling who'd referred to Baldwin's "lady's gun" and Snelling who'd alleged that Baldwin had escaped.

He, Goodling, and Zeke were under the impression that they were using Snelling to bring pressure on Wingate, the boss, but what if Wingate was just high-priced talent while Snelling or Bianche called the plays from the sidelines?

CHAPTER TWENTY-SIX

WHEN BOBBY HAZZARD asked the police to run the single finger-print initially found in the Hazzard cabin in 1989 through the FBI IFIAS database, Koa had reached his limit. With Senator Chao's interest in the young man, Koa knew he would need the chief's okay to stop Bobby's probe, so he took the request to Lannua's office.

"We've wasted too many resources on this kid's fantasies about what happened to his grandfather," Koa told the chief. "It's time to send him home."

The chief looked skeptical and reacted predictably. "What will the senator say?"

"I'd guess he was just helping the son of a friend. Senators do things like that all the time. If we get blowback from Chao, we can explain that we've already made extraordinary exceptions to normal procedures in giving him access to the file. Then we took him out to Hazzard's old cabin, facilitated his interview with former detective Kaohi, and even set up a meeting with the coroner. The senator will understand. I mean, it's a thirty-year-old case, properly closed in light of the coroner's report and the lack of any alternative theory." Koa knew he was taking a calculated risk in being so direct, but felt he had little choice.

"What's the big deal about running a single fingerprint?" the chief asked.

"Think about it, Chief," Koa began. "Even if we get a hit, it won't prove anything. The fingerprint might have been there for years. It could belong to anyone, like a friend who stayed there, a curious hiker, or a hundred other legitimate sources. But we'll still have to reopen the case and waste precious police resources investigating a thirty-year-old event. It doesn't make sense. The department's resources are already stretched too thin. You've seen the overtime numbers." Koa knew that budget issues frequently swayed the chief, and added, "We already need more manpower, and you know how hard it is to pry money out of the county council."

Lannua was quiet for several seconds, flexing the fingers of one hand against those of the other hand, something Koa had often observed when the chief was puzzling through a problem. "I see your point," he said finally, "but the fingerprint was unknown thirty years ago. What are the chances we'd get a hit now?"

"Impossible to say, but there are way more fingerprints in the system, and the matching techniques are far better than thirty years ago. So, anything's possible."

"But unlikely?" the chief asked.

"Why run the risk of having to reopen an ancient dead-end case?"

"It's a small risk. Let's talk to the senator," Chief Lannua decided.

Shit, Koa thought, the chief is such a political animal. He's afraid to decide even obvious issues for fear of offending a goddamn politician. So, they called the senator's office. After getting past an administrative assistant and two congressional staff aides, the chief got Senator Chao on the phone, and together they explained their predicament.

The senator answered, lowering his voice and speaking without a trace of his usual accent. "I'm not going to tell you how to run the police department. That's your job. But Bobby is a bright young man. He's explained his theories, and they make sense to me. I appreciate the help you've given him and anything more you can do to assist."

Koa's heart sank. The senator's words were conciliatory, but their meaning and tone were definitive, at least in the eyes of a chief who curried political favor whenever possible. They would have to acquiesce to Bobby's request and process the unidentified fingerprint. Koa felt strangely nervous about the outcome.

He kept telling himself there would be no match, and that would put an end to Bobby Hazzard's flights of fancy, but his nagging premonition of disaster would not go away. Just as he'd felt at the remote Hazzard cabin, he imagined Anthony Hazzard pointing an accusing finger at him. A strange foreboding gripped him. He felt his carefully constructed life fraying and in danger of coming apart. His cases had taught him that the past had a way of curling back and catching up with the present. History, coming from an unexpected direction like this young upstart mainlander, blindsided you. After his buddy Jerry had taken a bullet intended for Koa in Somalia, Koa had honored his best buddy's memory by becoming a cop as Jerry himself had always planned. Koa had devoted his life to pursuing criminals and dragging them to the bar of justice. Now justice seemed to be catching up with him. Bobby Hazzard was forcing him to pursue himself.

CHAPTER TWENTY-SEVEN

HAVING LOST THE argument against sending the lone fingerprint from the Hazzard cabin to the FBI, Koa returned to his office discouraged. Despite his disappointment, he knew he couldn't lose focus on the Baldwin investigation. Sorting through his inbox, he found an envelope from Makanui. Opening it, he found a note and transcript from Professor Atkins, the lip reader at UH Hilo.

The note read, "Did my best. Subject turned. Angles bad." The transcript set forth Bianche's side of the Bianche-Snelling conversation Koa had witnessed at the AI seminar. As he'd seen from the university's security tape, Bianche had only occasionally faced the camera, so the transcript had numerous gaps. Still, the gist of her message was clear— "Li paid a half a billion dollars for X-CO to get Wingate's patents and [unintelligible word]. His security algorithms are critical to the Army contract. [unintelligible sentence] Without him, the company is worthless. Your job is [unintelligible]."

Koa was rereading the partial transcript when the desk sergeant called. "Detective Kāne , I've got a young woman down here with a message for you. Says she'll only give it to you."

Puzzled, but curious, Koa said he would be right down. At the desk, the sergeant pointed out a young Hawaiian woman dressed in running gear. Koa introduced himself, and she responded, "I'm Malia." He recognized her name. She was Haukea's friend, the one from whom Haukea had borrowed a cell phone. He became more curious and led her into the corridor away from the officers and other civilians around the reception desk. "What can I do for you?" he asked.

"My friend Haukea gave me this envelope last night." She pulled a plain white envelope from her waist pack. "She asked me to give it to you and only to you. She said it was important." She handed him the envelope.

"*Mahalo*. Did Haukea have any other message for me?"

"No. Just the envelope."

Returning to his office and opening the envelope, Koa removed an unsigned note and what appeared to be a screenshot from a computer. The note read: "Copied and decrypted from the X-CO executive server." The screenshot captured a message from Snelling to Wingate, time-, and date-stamped three hours before Snelling had recorded his conversation with Wingate. It read:

You are vital to the successful completion of the Army contract and the future of X-CO. Given what happened the other night, we must protect you at all costs. The police think I am cooperating. I will come to your office with a hidden recording device. I will take the lead. You follow. We will discuss the event much as it happened, adding that I was there, she had a gun, you shot in self-defense, and she left the room alive. I will take steps to support that version of events.

After reading through the message, Koa sat back in his chair. The email confirmed that Snelling had played them, staging the whole exchange in Wingate's office. The keywords were in the next-to-last sentence. In their staged discussion, Snelling and Wingate planned to describe what had happened, adding four falsehoods. Snelling's presence, Baldwin's gun, the idea of self-defense, and Baldwin's alleged escape were all fabrications. Everything else about the Snelling-Wingate conversation was, to quote the message, "much as it happened." That meant that Wingate alone had caught Baldwin surreptitiously accessing the Deimos program and killed her. Baldwin had died inside the X-CO facility. Then, either Wingate or Snelling or the two of them together had mutilated and buried her body.

The last line of the message intrigued Koa. What "steps," he wondered, had Snelling taken "to support that version of events." Koa felt a chill as he recalled the sequence. Just two days after Snelling had taped his conversation with Wingate, someone had ambushed Koa in the Waimanu Valley. Had the security guard somehow learned of his trip with Bobby Hazzard? Had Snelling, who'd exhibited a propensity for lawless behavior, tried to kill the chief investigator or maybe have him killed?

Suspicious as always, Koa considered whether there might be authenticity issues with the potentially explosive message in the screenshot. Because it was just a picture of a message, he had no metadata, but he saw no reason to distrust Haukea. She had previously delivered verifiable information, and more critically, the Snelling-Wingate message made logical sense in the context of everything else he knew.

Satisfied that he could rely on Haukea's info, Koa directed his attention to determining the two men's location at the relevant times. Such information could come from two different sources—the phone companies who recorded call metadata, including cell tower routings, and internet providers, like Google, who collected GPS cell phone location data. Koa had already received and reviewed the phone company records. Because cell towers covered wide angles and broad areas, tower data was often useless in determining the precise location of a phone at the time of the call.

Internet location information collected through satellite GPS coordinates was far more precise. Zeke had already subpoenaed such information about Baldwin's, Snelling's, and Wingate's cell phones, but Koa had not yet received that information. He called Zeke to check on it.

"Came in last night," Zeke responded. "I'll email it to you."

Moments later, Koa began poring through the data looking for two things. He wanted to know where Snelling, Wingate, and Baldwin had been at each of the exact times when someone added bad code to the Deimos program. It took him over an hour, but the Google location data showed a perfect match. All three had been at X-CO every time someone had uploaded corrupt code to the main computer. It didn't prove that any one of the three was the culprit, but it made them prime suspects.

Koa then scoured Wingate's and Snelling's phone location data the night Baldwin disappeared. Wingate had remained at X-CO, but Snelling had been on the move. At 9:00 p.m., Snelling was at X-CO, but by 9:15, he was roughly halfway between X-Co and Baldwin's condo. At 9:20 p.m., the data put him at Baldwin's condo, and from 10:11 to 11:16 p.m., the data placed him at the Volcano cemetery. The data matched that from the GPS unit in Baldwin's Green Honda. "Gotcha, you bastard," Koa exclaimed. Even if Wingate killed Baldwin, the data unequivocally tied Snelling to the disposal of her body.

Just as a double-check for consistency, Koa also verified that Baldwin had been at X-CO the night she'd perished. In that process, Koa realized that someone had compromised the Deimos program that night. Strange, he thought. If Wingate had caught Baldwin accessing the computer, hadn't he ascertained what she'd been doing? Wouldn't he have discovered the corrupt code?

Koa tried to picture the scene, imagining a mini-movie in his head. Wingate walks in and sees Baldwin with a disk plugged into the main computer. He realizes she's up to something and calls her on it. A confrontation follows. Wingate pulls a gun and kills Baldwin. He says it was an accident. Wingate, of course, can't see what's on the disk, but he doesn't check, and so doesn't learn that she's uploaded corrupt code. Maybe he's too upset by Baldwin's death or too involved in disposing of her body to follow up.

Koa supposed it *could* have happened that way, but aspects of the picture seemed wrong. Why did Wingate have a gun? Koa had seen no evidence that he usually carried one. Maybe Wingate had suspected Baldwin of theft based on X-CO's security surveillance of her. Perhaps that's why he had a gun. But why kill her? Why not merely escort her out, terminate her employment, or turn her over to the police? Could there really have been an accident? Could Wingate have shot unintentionally? Maybe once, but twice? Frames were missing from Koa's imaginary movie.

Koa picked up the phone to call Goodling. A premonition stopped him, and he dropped the phone back into its cradle. With their vast computer savvy and Patriot Act powers, the feds would have had the Snelling Google data for days, long before Zeke could get it through the cumbersome subpoena process. The feds would also have analyzed it and recognized that Snelling disposed of Baldwin's body. Yet, they hadn't shared that knowledge. In a flash of anger, he realized the *feds had been holding out on him*. They'd sat through his meeting with Zeke without revealing evidence that would have supported his push to arrest Snelling. He recalled Moreno's outburst and now appreciated its significance. The feds feared that arresting Snelling would alert the saboteurs before they could roll up all the participants and document the full extent of the damage. That's what Moreno had said, but was it the whole story? Once again, he sensed he was missing something.

He couldn't blame the feds for their priority on national security. With the next generation of super weapons at risk, the stakes were astronomically high. Still, he had a different mission—taking killers off the streets. Besides, the saboteurs were already suspicious, if not fully aware, that the feds were on their tail. Why else, he asked himself, would Snelling arrange to spy on the Army Deimos trials?

An hour later, Koa was in Zeke's office. He prepared himself a cup of pure Kona coffee from the prosecutor's fancy machine and joined Zeke at his conference table. Koa laid out what he and Nālani had seen at the seminar and handed Zeke copies of the lip reader's partial transcript of the Snelling-Bianche conversation. He added the screenshot of the Snelling message to Wingate provided by Haukea. He then went over what he'd learned from the Google records Zeke had subpoenaed.

"When I put it all together, it looks like Wingate is the indispensable brains behind X-CO and critical to the company's ability to fulfill its Army contract. On the evening of June 14, he discovered Baldwin tampering with the Deimos software and killed her. The powers at X-CO then decided to protect Wingate no matter what. Snelling ditched Baldwin's body. Then he and others at X-CO tried to make it look like she returned to the mainland."

Zeke leaned back in his chair, looking up at the ceiling. It was a classic Zeke posture Koa had seen many times when the prosecutor was deep in thought. "Except *Pele* intervened to disinter the lady's body, and they didn't figure on you stirring the pot."

"Right," Koa responded, "and Snelling has been trying to keep this cover-up together ever since."

"You think he's that smart?" Zeke asked.

"I'm sure he's more than a security guard. The location data proves he was at the Volcano village cemetery the night Baldwin disappeared. Alone or with help, he buried Baldwin where no one would ever have found her absent a freak earthquake, and he made it difficult for us to ID her. He sold her car and stored her things, gave us phony emails authorizing those actions, and then after we started asking questions, put the proceeds from the car sale in Baldwin's bank account. And I have to admit that he outsmarted us in the taped conversation. Instead of giving us a case against Wingate, he created doubt whether Baldwin died inside X-CO and set up a self-defense claim. He's a major actor in this scheme, but I'm still unsure whether he's the planner, the brains, behind it all. That could be Bianche or even Zhou Li."

Koa took a slug of coffee and set the cup back on the table. "One thing is bugging me, though. That night—the night Baldwin died—is one of the dates when someone uploaded bad code. If Wingate caught her tampering with the computer, why was he armed? Why did he kill her? And most critically, why didn't he catch and stop the sabotage?"

"Good questions. Maybe," Zeke responded, "he didn't realize what she was actually doing."

"I guess, but that's hard to swallow. He's supposed to be the mastermind behind X-CO success," Koa said.

"Okay, suppose what you laid out is accurate." Zeke leaned forward, elbows on the table. "What do we do about it?"

Koa had already thought through the next steps and didn't hesitate. "We've got to bring Wingate in . . . get his story."

"I agree," Zeke responded, "but given all the politicos associated with X-CO, I think we'll invite him in for a chat. No harm in starting nice."

Following Zeke's suggestion, they invited Wingate to an interview. That courtesy produced no harm but provided no benefit. Wingate's counsel called to say that his client would decline Zeke's request for an interview and would, if necessary, assert his Fifth Amendment right not to speak to the police.

CHAPTER TWENTY-EIGHT

KOA TOSSED AND turned in the twilight at the edge of sleep. A resemblance of Wingate's face floated behind his eyes only to morph into Snelling's features. The image of Kimberly Ward's bloodied body appeared and faded. Snelling's voice rattled through Koa's semi-consciousness slowly overlaid by Wingate's impervious tones and, then, Zeke's overly loud voice, until he could no longer identify the source. The investigation that had consumed his waking hours had now invaded his sleep.

A sound, maybe the creaking of the old Norfolk pine behind the house, brought Koa out of his half-sleep. He lay in the dark, his mind chewing on the evidence against Baldwin and the concern he'd voiced to Zeke. Why, if Wingate had caught Baldwin tampering with the computer, hadn't he discovered the sabotage?

Unable to sleep, Koa quietly dressed and left Nālani, who had long since dropped off into a deep sleep. Dressing in running gear and slipping out the front door, he walked down the drive and began to jog. The crisp night air invigorated him and stimulated his thinking. His training had taught him to focus foremost on motive. Why had Wingate killed Baldwin? Had she somehow resisted? Snelling's communiqué to Wingate made it clear that they had fabricated the idea that she'd had a gun. There was no other evidence of resistance. Surely, Wingate had not killed her simply because she was accessing the computer.

Snelling had said, not once but three times, that Wingate had caught Baldwin accessing X-CO's central computer. Koa suddenly realized that Snelling and Wingate were the *only* sources for that assertion. What if it were a lie?

Still, overwhelming evidence pointed to Baldwin as the saboteur, and thus she must have accessed X-CO's central computer. He ticked off the evidence in his head—the drives, X-CO's surveillance file, Ward's dying declaration, and most damning of all, the second note from *Aletheia*. Could all that evidence be false? It seemed unlikely.

When he ended his predawn jog back at his cottage, Koa felt too mentally wired to go back to sleep, so he showered, dressed, kissed his still sleeping *ipo*, and headed for Hilo. He had nearly reached the office when Georgina buzzed his cell. The crime scene technician sounded excited. "I've been doing some checking and found something. Can we meet?"

When Georgina found something, it was usually significant. "Sure," he responded. "I'll be in my office in ten. Meet you there."

Koa found Georgina at his desk poring over a set of glossy photographs—enlargements of each separate letter in Ward's dying declaration. "What do you see?" she asked, pointing to each of the photos in turn.

"Letters in Ward's blood," he responded.

"And what don't you see?" she asked.

He puzzled over the pictures before giving up. "C'mon, Georgina, tell me."

"You don't see even the tiniest trace of a fingerprint."

He scrutinized each image a second time—studying the smooth red letters. Georgina was right. There was no evidence of a fingerprint anywhere in any of the pictures. "Okay, I see that."

"I got a pint of blood from the hospital and tried more than a hundred times. It's *impossible*—" she emphasized the word—"to make those letters with a fingertip and not leave traces of a fingerprint."

The significance of her efforts dawned on him. "You're saying that Ward didn't write that message?"

"Right. Whoever wrote Ward's dying declaration wore gloves, probably medical gloves."

"So, you think Ward's killer wrote the message but wanted us to believe it was from Ward?"

"That's my guess."

Koa kicked himself. At the scene in Ward's apartment, he'd wondered why a dying woman would leave such a message, but he hadn't followed up. Thirty years ago, he'd created false clues suggesting that Anthony Hazzard had committed suicide. After becoming a cop, he'd promised himself that he wouldn't let false clues mislead him, but this time he had let it happen. A nightmare come true. Only Georgina's excellent work had saved him. "Great work, Georgina. I owe you a case of your favorite brew."

"That makes four cases. When are you going to pony up?" she asked.

"Touché."

Koa considered the implications of this new information. People didn't typically create false clues to tell the truth. If it was false, that meant the message had to be untrue. So, TB was not a thief. Did that mean she wasn't the saboteur? He thought about the most damning evidence—the second note from *Aletheia*. That could be a false clue only if X-CO had known about *Aletheia*, and they could only have learned of *Aletheia* through Moreno's botched attempt to reach Baldwin using that name.

Koa went to his computer to reexamine the X-CO surveillance file on Baldwin. He began with the material he'd received from

Haukea and found the picture of Somes in the hallway of Baldwin's apartment building, but no reference to *Aletheia*. He then went through the similar file Georgina discovered on a flash drive in Ward's apartment. Although page for page, it mirrored what he'd gotten from Haukea, he found one page that had been missing from the Haukea file. It was a copy of Moreno's note to Baldwin bearing only the name *Aletheia* and a phone number. X-CO had known about *Aletheia* and could have faked the second note!

Then it hit him. What if Wingate *himself* was the saboteur, and Baldwin had caught *him* tampering with the Deimos computer? Suddenly, everything made sense. Wingate might well carry a gun when engaged in sabotage. He'd want to protect himself if someone caught him in the act. In that event, Wingate would have a powerful motive to kill. And having killed Baldwin, Wingate couldn't afford to face the inevitable questions, which would have revealed the sabotage. Wingate had to make Baldwin disappear, and Snelling was the man for that job. Everything else followed as Snelling raced to sustain the cover-up of Baldwin's murder as it slowly unraveled under police scrutiny. It had been right in front of Koa. Why hadn't he seen it? Because the big lie was always the hardest to penetrate.

Koa was confident he'd nailed the truth, but his theory lacked evidentiary support. Zeke would call it speculation run wild. He needed evidence to give credence to his logic. For the second time in forty-eight hours, Koa ripped up his mental portrait of Baldwin. First, he'd seen her as a patriotic whistleblower, then as a saboteur, and now recognized that she might indeed be the patriot whistleblower as he'd initially thought. It was, Koa realized, a series of hairpin turns to rival the infamous road to Hāna on Maui. As so often happened when an investigation took a new direction, he needed to back up and rethink everything he knew.

As was his habit, he went to Zeke's office to brainstorm with the prosecutor and outlined his latest theory of the case. "Tell me I'm not crazy."

Koa watched Zeke's face as the prosecutor evaluated what Koa had just laid out for him. Countless jury trials had trained Zeke to control his reactions, but Koa knew Zeke well and could tell that the prosecutor was intrigued.

"It's an ingenious theory," he said, "but the evidence is bubble thin, and you don't have a motive. Why would Wingate sabotage his own program? Not for money. Not if Zhou Li paid him handsomely for the company."

"That's an issue," Koa acknowledged. "You're right, he's not likely motivated by money, but it could be ideological. The FBI thinks China is behind the sabotage, and Wingate has a China connection. According to Bianche, Wingate ran a research program at Beijing University, where he first met Zhou Li. Think about it, Zeke. An American doing high-tech research in Beijing must have come to the attention of the Chinese securities services. I know the evidence isn't strong, but no other scenario accounts for the known facts about what happened the night Baldwin died."

"Okay," Zeke agreed. "Let's go with your theory. You ID'd Baldwin through facial recognition software run by some professor at UH Hilo. What do we know about her background, independent of her X-CO employment records and her UH Hilo teaching?"

"Not much," Koa responded. "We've never found her documents. They didn't turn up in the X-CO search and weren't in the storage unit, so we have no birth certificate, no tax returns, credit card statements, or other financial records. Not even a passport."

"I'm surprised," Zeke said.

"Maybe Snelling took them," Koa suggested.

"Either that or she stashed them somewhere. Whether she was a saboteur or a whistleblower, she might have needed to run at a moment's notice. She'd have wanted 24/7 access to her papers, credit cards, and money," Zeke said.

"Okay. Let's assume for a moment that Snelling didn't take them. Where would they be? They'd have to be someplace close and always available, but where no one would think to look."

"You didn't find them in her car," Zeke recalled.

"Right," Koa responded. "The crime scene techs took it apart and didn't find any documents." Koa ran his mental checklist of their investigatory steps, this time focusing on places—her apartment, her X-CO office, UH Hilo. He stopped. "Baldwin taught classes at UH Hilo. I wonder if she had an office or a locker there."

He called Makanui. The two of them drove to the university, parked, and headed down a covered walkway to the Computer Science and Engineering Department, where they once again hooked up with Professor Adriana Alfonso.

"You're back, Detective. Interested in a computer class?" the bronze-skinned professor asked with a smile. "We've taught several police officers over the years."

"Not today," Koa responded. "Not sure I'd be a good student. I can barely use a keyboard."

"Oh, I doubt that," she replied.

Koa asked if Baldwin had occupied an office or used a locker, and the IT professor answered "no" to both questions. "The school doesn't provide much in the way of facilities for adjunct faculty."

Koa shook his head, disappointed but not surprised they'd struck out.

"Nice lady," Makanui commented, on the way back to Koa's SUV. "Reminds me of my grandmother."

Makanui's reflection made Koa think of another grandmotherly woman. Was it possible? He asked himself why a whistleblower or a saboteur would spend time cultivating an elderly neighbor. To ensure that she had an accessible place to hide something where it would be hard to find? It was plausible. "C'mon," he said, "I've got a hunch."

Koa and Makanui drove down Kamehameha Avenue, turning onto Kalanianole Street toward Baldwin's former apartment complex. When they got there, Koa led Makanui, not to Baldwin's old apartment, but Leilani Craig's home next door. He knocked, and she greeted them seated in her wheelchair.

"Come in, come in, Detectives," she said enthusiastically. Koa suspected the lonely woman welcomed all visitors, even cops. "Can I offer you some tea?"

"No, thank you, Ms. Craig," Koa responded, and Makanui did likewise. "How are you getting along?"

"I'm getting by, but I do miss Tiger. She was such a nice lady," Leilani said wistfully.

Koa had accepted her assessment of Baldwin when he'd first met Leilani, but Baldwin's possible treachery had changed his opinion. Baldwin's kindness, he was now sure, had been driven by self-interest. "We stopped by to see if Tiger Baldwin might have left something with you, an envelope, or a box, maybe."

"Why, yes. Funny you should ask. She had me store a small lockbox. I'd forgotten about it. It's in the spare bedroom."

Koa felt a tinge of excitement. Baldwin had been smart. Few people would suspect that she'd secreted materials with an elderly neighbor. "Could we see this box?" he asked.

Leilani wheeled her chair around and down a hall, led them into a sparsely furnished bedroom, and pointed to a closet. Koa slid the door open to reveal a large square box on the floor. More like a small safe than a lockbox, the black cube was about eighteen inches on a side. The door had a combination dial.

"I don't suppose you have the combination?" Makanui inquired.

"Sorry," Leilani responded. "Tiger didn't share it with me."

"We need to take the box with us," Koa said.

"As long as you're sure that Tiger won't object," Leilani responded.

"Don't worry," Makanui responded. "We'll take good care of it."

On the way back to headquarters, Makanui called Bernie Kūkiʻo, a lock and key man often used by the police. At the station, Bernie fiddled with the combination and had the box open inside twenty minutes. Inside, they found a few thousand dollars in currency, several credit cards, a passport, a bunch of personal financial documents, and a notebook. Makanui examined and inventoried everything except the journal.

Koa opened the notebook, which appeared to be some sort of diary, and began reading. Only partway through, he realized he'd uncovered a bombshell. Incredulous at its contents, he dialed Goodling, who answered on the third ring. Koa identified himself and said, "You'd better get to Zeke's office as fast as you can. And bring Moreno."

When he got to Zeke's office, Koa caught the prosecutor leaning back in his chair with his boots atop his desk, engrossed in a legal brief. "Get your legal lightsaber, Counselor . . . we're gonna nail Darth Vader," Koa announced.

Zeke swung his boots to the floor, dropped his papers onto his desk, and moved across the room to the conference table where Koa spread out Baldwin's notebook. Koa gave Zeke a preview while they waited for the feds.

Thirty minutes later, Goodling and Moreno arrived. Neither looked happy, and Moreno scowled. His contempt for local authorities had reached new heights. Too bad, Koa thought, relishing the prospect of informing the feds that X-CO had again outsmarted them.

Koa began by outlining Ward's death, her fabricated dying declaration painted in blood, the flash drive Georgina had found in her apartment, and the screenshot provided by Haukea.

Moreno interrupted. "Why the hell didn't you fill us in along the way?"

Koa started to respond, accusing Moreno of holding out, but Zeke interceded. "I suggest you curb your hostility and listen. You might learn something."

Moreno's eyes went wide, and he opened his mouth to protest, but Goodling silenced him with a wave of her hand. "Go on," she said. "Let's get this over with so we can go back to work." Like her colleague, she was pissed at not having been involved earlier, but professional enough or maybe just curious enough to hear what Koa had to say. Moreno rolled his eyes.

When Koa presented his theory that Baldwin was, in fact, *Aletheia*, Moreno went postal. "That's fucking absurd. She couldn't be *Aletheia* unless she sent the second message from her grave, and dead people don't send messages." He stood up and waived to Goodling. "Let's bag these loonies and go back to work."

Koa, under pressure from the Hazzard investigation, had reached his limit with Moreno. "X-CO sent the second message because you tipped them to *Aletheia*'s identity and probably got her killed," Koa said in a low, but firm tone.

"You bastard!" Moreno screamed, jumped up, and walked out, slamming the door with a resounding bang.

Goodling, looking at Koa, said, "That was unnecessary," and gathered her belongings to follow Moreno.

"If I were you, I'd stay and hear what Koa has to say," Zeke said in a soft but decisive voice.

Goodling hesitated and resumed her place at the table.

When Koa suggested that Baldwin might have caught Wingate inserting the corrupt code into the computer, Goodling reacted skeptically. "That seems unlikely. Wingate is the genius behind Deimos. It's hard to believe he'd deliberately screw it up."

Koa ignored her. "Zeke and I started wondering why we hadn't found Baldwin's passport or any of her financial records. I checked UH Hilo, where she taught, but had no luck. Then I asked myself why Baldwin had spent so much time with her elderly neighbor. I mean, whether she was a whistleblower or a saboteur, it seemed like an odd friendship. Turns out the neighbor, Leilani Craig, kept a small safe for Baldwin. We brought it back to police HQ and had a locksmith open it. Along with Baldwin's passport and some financial records, we found this inside." He pushed Baldwin's notebook to the center of the table and flipped it open to the first of several pages he'd marked with little yellow Post-it stickies.

When Goodling had failed to follow Moreno out of the room, he'd gotten cold feet and returned, standing against the wall just inside the door.

Koa ignored his reentry and went on uninterrupted. "It's Baldwin's diary. In it, she describes how she discovered a section of bad code in the Deimos program, how she followed up, found more bad code, and then wrote an anonymous letter to the Defense Department. There's a copy of her letter to the DOD Inspector General in the diary. I think you'll find it identical to the letter you showed me when we first met. It's signed, *Aletheia*."

Moreno's mouth hung open. "Holy shit," he exclaimed.

"There's more," Zeke said, tweaking the feds. "The best is yet to come."

Koa continued. "According to her diary, Baldwin continued to investigate after she blew the whistle." He turned several pages in the notebook to the next entry flagged with another sticky. He read: "There's a pattern—bad code invariably added to the Deimos software late at night—usually around eight p.m. Few people working then, creating a small pool of possible suspects."

"Somehow," Koa continued, "Baldwin got access to the sign-in records and ID'd Snelling and Wingate as present on every night when the tampering occurred. Baldwin also made a note of seeing Wingate coming out of the computer room one night with a drive in his hand." Koa pointed out the relevant diary entry.

"I don't believe it!" Moreno seemed at a loss for words.

Koa flipped through several more pages to the last of the entries he'd flagged. "Then, there's this. It reads: 'Wingate gets the code from someone outside the company. Waited outside in the parking lot and followed. Lost him near Pāhala. Next day saw him in the computer room with a drive.'"

"That confirms what we suspected. Wingate didn't act alone," Goodling said. "Somebody fed him the unauthorized code and put him in position to sabotage Deimos." She turned to Moreno. "Tell them what we've learned."

The FBI cyber expert didn't look happy, but complied. "We analyzed the drives. They were created on a specially designed Fujitsu mainframe computer using specialized software."

"Okay," Zeke said, "why is that important?"

"It means—" Moreno leaned forward, getting into his teacher mode—"bureau cyber experts were able to determine that the contents were copied onto a physical disk and not sent electronically to Hawai'i."

"You mean somebody brought them here?" Koa asked.

"Probably, but not for sure. They could have been mailed or sent by air express, but that would involve risk, so I'm betting the drives were hand-carried," Moreno responded.

"If I recall correctly, there would have been at least eight deliveries since February," Koa said.

"Right. The Deimos program was compromised at least eight times, so there had to be at least eight drives," Moreno agreed.

"All smuggled by the same person?" Zeke asked.

"Wouldn't have to be," Moreno said, "but if I were planning to sabotage a major U.S. government program, I'd want someone I trusted to carry the parts essential to my plan."

"Then we're looking for someone who's been to Hawai'i at least eight times in the last six months," Koa said.

"That's my best guess," Moreno agreed.

"Any candidates?" Zeke asked.

Moreno looked at Goodling as though appealing her order to share.

Rejecting his subliminal plea, Goodling said, "Tell 'em."

"Using airline and other transportation data, we've got a list of about three hundred people who arrived in Hawai'i at least eight times since February. We're trying to narrow it down, but it's tough."

Koa couldn't resist the dig. "Especially if you're not familiar with local people and their patterns. Maybe you could share the list."

Goodling nodded. "Okay."

Moreno didn't scowl this time.

Koa summarized. "Bottom line, Baldwin built a powerful circumstantial case against Wingate. For whatever reason, she must have tried to catch Wingate in the act. Or maybe she made a mistake, and he caught her following him or snooping." Koa thought of stopping but couldn't resist. "Or maybe, after X-CO discovered the message Moreno left for Baldwin, Wingate figured Baldwin for a whistleblower. Whatever happened, something went wrong and got her killed."

"I can't believe it," Moreno said again. Still, he lacked the grace to apologize for his previous skepticism.

"Combined with the GPS data, Wingate's statements, and Snelling's other actions, everything points to Wingate as Baldwin's killer. At first, he and Snelling tried to hide the killing, and then after we discovered her body, they framed Baldwin first as giving data to her friend in California and then as the saboteur," Koa concluded.

"I can't believe it," Moreno repeated for the umpteenth time. "But Wingate sold the company to Li for five hundred million dollars. He's rich. Deimos is his baby. Why would he sabotage it?"

Koa stared at Moreno, taking pleasure in the agent's discomfort. "Given what we've discovered about Wingate, I suspect he's hidden parts of his personal history. When you dig deeper into his background, I'm betting you'll find lots of inconsistencies. Try a biopsy into his time at Beijing University."

When Koa had finished laying out the facts of Wingate's duplicity and Baldwin's actual role, Zeke guided the discussion toward the next steps, signaling to Koa to take the initiative. "We've got more than enough to arrest Wingate, and we need to get him in custody before he kills someone else."

"No can do," Moreno responded. "Getting to the bottom of the Deimos sabotage is our highest priority. We know from Baldwin's notebook that Wingate is getting the drives from someone on the outside. If we arrest Wingate, he'll lawyer up before we nail the rest of this ring."

"If Wingate kills again, that won't be much comfort to the next victim's family," Koa responded with more than a little bite in his voice.

"That's a risk we have to take," Moreno said.

Already short-tempered from the Hazzard investigation and thoroughly fed up with Moreno, Koa lost patience. "Maybe you have to, but we have a responsibility to protect our citizens, and we don't need federal approval to arrest a murderer."

"Goddamnit," Moreno began. "We're running this—"

"Enough," Goodling interrupted. "We understand the need to prevent another murder, and I'm sure you understand the federal government's imperative to catch all the saboteurs. If it helps balance those objectives, I can tell you that we already have both Wingate and Snelling under blanket electronic surveillance—mikes and video at home and office, taps on their phones, trackers on their vehicles. We can intervene at the first hint of a threat."

Koa nodded. He'd already guessed as much. The feds had Patriot Act powers allowing them to conduct warrantless, no-knock searches in secret, and with Deimos at risk, they would not be shy about using them. Still, it wasn't enough for Koa. "The first hint of action is likely to be when Wingate pulls the trigger. That'll be too late."

"Christ," Moreno swore, "I said it from the beginning. We should never have trusted—"

Goodling held up a hand to cut off the exchange. "We're asking you to hold off on Wingate. We can have the secretary of defense call your governor, if necessary, but I hope it won't come to that."

Her threat to involve the secretary of defense set off a silent alarm in Koa's head. Something clicked. The feds *were holding out.* "There's something—something critical—you're not telling us. You're going to have to come clean if you want us to hold off arresting Wingate."

The look of consternation on Goodling's face provided all the confirmation Koa needed. She appeared stressed, and he understood that she was struggling to balance her secrecy obligations against her mission objectives. "You're right," she said, tacitly acknowledging that she couldn't achieve her goals without forfeiting secrets. "What I am going to tell you does not leave this room. *Understand?*"

Both Koa and Zeke agreed.

"People at the highest levels of our government—the very highest levels—have reliable information that a highly placed foreign spy is directing the Deimos sabotage—a traitor who has already done enormous damage to our national defense. We *must* identify this traitor, and getting to the bottom of the Deimos sabotage is our best, maybe our only, chance."

It took Koa a moment for the import of her words to sink in. Protecting Deimos, as critical as that might be, was only a secondary objective. The government had sent Goodling and her colleague along with three FBI agents to the Big Island, backed up by God only knows how many others, to catch a spy, a spy who posed an enormous continuing threat to the US. No wonder they'd refused to shut down X-CO.

Dead silence filled the room, broken only by the sound of an ambulance somewhere in the distance. Tension filled the room, like steam in a sauna. Zeke, staring hard at Goodling, finally responded, "You're asking us to leave a killer on our streets. That's not a risk I'm prepared to take for long. You've got seventy-two hours before we arrest Wingate." Zeke skipped a beat before adding, "And a call from the President himself won't buy you more time."

"Damn," Moreno muttered.

"What about Snelling?" Koa said. "He's at least an accessory to murder and may have killed Ward."

"No!" Moreno repeated. "You don't get it. That'd be like hanging out a sign telling the spy we're after to run."

"You're the one who doesn't get it," Koa responded, hotly. "We're talking about human beings . . . about their lives."

Moreno started to speak, but Zeke cut him off. "Koa's right. You've got seventy-two hours. And if Wingate or Snelling kills again, their victim's death will weigh on your conscience."

CHAPTER TWENTY-NINE

A WHIRLWIND OF worry consumed Koa. Wingate and Snelling still walked the streets. Koa wished Zeke hadn't given the feds seventy-two hours. He also feared the revival of the old Anthony Hazzard investigation, adding even more stress. Why, he fumed, were the senator and his aide supporting Bobby? The case was closed and should stay dead. He'd tried to paint the resubmission of the old fingerprint to the FBI as a waste of police resources and failed. He kicked himself for not having argued more forcefully to let well enough alone.

He knew he was conflating separate problems and letting his emotions get ahead of his judgment, but he couldn't help it. After rising to become the chief detective and finding the love of his life in Nālani, it was suddenly all at risk. He wanted to blame his precarious position on Bobby Hazzard, a rich kid with powerful friends researching his family history. But a small voice inside his head reminded him of the painful truth that no one ever escaped their past misdeeds. He thought of the killers he'd put away decades after their crimes. He now risked a similar fate.

Wracked with fear and tension, he was in a sour mood by the time he reached his Volcano cottage that night. Nālani immediately sensed something amiss and asked, "What's wrong, my love?"

He dismissed her concern with a quick kiss and a wave of his hand. "Just a work problem." Her inquiry only added to his insecurity. His relationship with Nālani had grown progressively richer over the three years they'd been together. They shared hopes and secrets and became so entangled in each other that they often anticipated one another's thoughts. Yet, he'd concealed the most searing event in his life—the killing of another human being—which had shaped who he was and fueled the passion with which he pursued his career. He'd often worried his secret past would infect his relationship with Nālani. Now, what he feared was happening. Throughout dinner, his mood remained dark as he silently brooded on the possibility that the Hazzard case might be reborn. Damn, he thought. Just when life was at its best, it might crash and burn.

Nālani, who'd been biding her time throughout dinner, tried again. "Talk to me. Something's bothering you. It's pretty obvious."

In his foul humor, her persistence annoyed him, and he snapped at her. "I'm okay. Stop bugging me!"

His outburst was out of character and devastated her. He realized he'd hurt her deeply. His fears were doing the damage he dreaded. He couldn't let that happen. "I'm sorry . . . so sorry, *ipo*. I'm just under too much pressure at work."

"Want to talk about it?" she asked, her voice soothing.

"I can't."

She was near tears. "I'm not going to share what you say with anyone. You know, I always keep your secrets."

Of course, she was right, but he'd be asking too much of her to keep his criminal past secret, and even if by some miracle she did, just knowing what he'd done would inevitably affect their relationship. What woman wanted to sleep with a killer?

"I know I can trust you, and I love you for it, but this one is complicated and involves government secrets," he responded. At least that was mostly true whether he meant the Deimos matter or Bobby Hazzard's pet project.

"I helped you the other day at the AI seminar. Let me help you now."

He shook his head. "I'd love your help, but I can't. Not right now."

She rose from the table and circled behind his chair to envelop him in her arms. "You know I love you very much. I don't like seeing you upset, and it hurts when you shut me out."

He stood and returned her embrace, squeezing her tight. "I'm sorry. I love you, too."

She took his hand. "C'mon. Let's go for a walk, and then I'll take you to bed." For a moment, her mischievous grin cheered him, but then he thought of her horrified reaction when she learned that her lover had killed a man.

CHAPTER THIRTY

KOA'S WORST FEARS materialized with the receipt of a message from the FBI. The IAFIS, the FBI fingerprint identification system, had matched the lone fingerprint from Hazzard's cabin to the prints on file for one ʻAnalū Kāliʻi. A records check revealed that Kāliʻi lived on the Big Island and, at age forty-nine, was old enough to have been Anthony Hazzard's killer thirty years back. Worse still, he had a long rap sheet for vandalism, brawling, assault, burglary, and attempted murder. He'd been in and out of jail half a dozen times. Even the translation of the man's Hawaiian name—Kāliʻi referred to a spear-throwing ritual—suggested violence. Any uninvolved policeman would regard Kāliʻi as an ideal suspect. For Koa, who knew the man was innocent of Hazzard's murder, Kāliʻi's history only added to the nightmare of Bobby Hazzard's quest.

Koa would have to lead the department's reopening of the Hazzard murder investigation. They'd learn everything there was to know about ʻAnalū Kāliʻi. Koa could only hope that the investigation eliminated Kāliʻi as a suspect. He could not fathom the alternative and knew he couldn't let an innocent man pay for his crime.

He had Makanui start with Kāliʻi's criminal history. The file revealed Kāliʻi to be a big man. Over six feet tall and two hundred fifty pounds. Plenty strong enough to have subdued Hazzard. His mug shot showed a Hawaiian with long jet-black hair and widely spaced, unfriendly black eyes, wearing a *palaoa* on a black cord around his neck. Like the punk Snelling had hired to spy on the Deimos at Pōhakuloa, this guy wore a cheap plastic replica of the hook-shaped, whalebone necklace worn by Hawaiian royalty, making Kāliʻi a poster boy for rebellion against authority. Just the sort of juvenile delinquent, Koa thought, who thirty years ago would have taunted a *haole* like Anthony Hazzard.

Vandalism, brawling, and even assault were typical of troubled Hawaiian youth, but the burglary charge sent Koa's head spinning. In 1988, Kāliʻi had broken into Hazzard's plantation house home, apparently expecting to find it unoccupied. Instead, he'd awakened the sleeping sugar baron who had confronted Kāliʻi and chased him out of his house before filing a police report. Hazzard's subsequent testimony had put Kāliʻi in jail less than a year before Hazzard's death. He'd served nine months and been out of prison at the time of Hazzard's death. Kāliʻi had a powerful motivation to seek revenge.

By 1995, Kāliʻi had served three years in prison for the attempted murder of another Hawaiian, but then seemed to have gotten his life together. His parole reports recorded his regular appearances, steady employment, and marriage to a young Hawaiian woman. They'd had a child, a daughter, and Kāliʻi had stayed out of trouble, at least so far as official records revealed.

After additional inquiries produced nothing of significance, Koa had Kāliʻi brought into the police station for questioning. Koa studied him through the one-way glass of the interrogation room. Kāliʻi looked older than in his mug shot and had a band of Hawaiian warrior tattoos around his neck. Prison ink, Koa guessed. Not the kind of defendant likely to win over a wavering jury.

Koa would have liked to have questioned Kāliʻi alone but knew that, in this case, above all others, he needed to follow protocol to the letter. He had Piki sit in on the interview. Koa began slowly, eliciting Kāliʻi's family situation, his job in a Walmart warehouse, and his membership in a fundamentalist church. Despite his criminal history, Kāliʻi seemed unconcerned by Koa's questions, probably because the man had lived a lawful life during the past twenty years.

Koa turned to the guts of the matter. "Ever known a man named Anthony Hazzard?"

"Yeah. Nasty buggah. Beat up friends who had work for him, and den ratted me out years ago. But I wen clean up my act."

Koa cringed inwardly. The animosity in Kāliʻi's answer only reinforced his revenge motive. "So, you didn't like the man?" Koa asked.

"No way. No, no one like dat buggah."

"Why not?"

"He was a mean bastard . . . treated his workers like cattle."

God, Koa thought, he's making it worse by the moment. "Ever been in the Waimanu Valley?"

"Where's dat?" Kāliʻi asked.

"Immediately west of the Waipiʻo Valley," Koa explained.

"Naw, never bin there. I bin in the Waipiʻo and the valley way over toward the west, the Pololū, but never in none of 'em other valleys."

Kāliʻi's answer dashed Koa's hope that the man could explain away his fingerprint in Hazzard's cabin. Instead, Koa thought he'd locked himself into a lie. The fingerprint proved that Kāliʻi had been in the cabin, so denying it made Kāliʻi a liar. Reluctantly, Koa made the lie abundantly clear. "So, you've never been to Anthony Hazzard's old cabin a few miles into the Waimanu Valley?" Koa asked.

"Naw. Never knew about no cabin up there." A quizzical look came over Kāliʻi's face. "Hey, what's this all about anyway?" he asked.

Koa ignored Kāliʻi's question. "So, how'd your fingerprint come to be in Anthony Hazzard's Waimanu cabin?"

"I ain't got no idea." Kāli'i paused and then asked again, "What's this about?"

"It's about Anthony Hazzard's death thirty years ago," Koa said flatly.

A light suddenly illuminated in Kāli'i's eyes. "You're trying to hook me up for his death?" Kāli'i asked, and then added, "I want a lawyer."

"Jesus, he did it," Piki said enthusiastically, as the two officers left the interrogation room. "We cracked a thirty-year-old case."

*　　*　　*

The following day, Koa and the prosecutor had just finished reviewing the evidence in an unrelated rape case when Zeke said, "I hear your guys cleared a thirty-year-old murder case."

Koa stiffened, suddenly concerned about Zeke's intentions. "You're talking about the old Hazzard case?"

"Yeah," Zeke responded.

"We reopened the old case, but I wouldn't say we've cleared it," Koa responded cautiously.

"From what I hear, it's pretty airtight," Zeke said.

Although Zeke had sources in almost every Hawai'i County office, Koa hadn't involved the prosecutor's office in the Hazzard investigation and wondered where Zeke had gotten his information. "What makes you think it's airtight?"

"Senator Chao and his aide, that Keahi guy, were in to see me and laid out the details."

Koa should have guessed. Chief Lannua must have reported the details of the investigation to Senator Chao.

Zeke continued, "The senator says you've got this guy 'Analū Kāli'i by the short hairs. The bastard tried to rob Hazzard and got caught.

Hazzard had him prosecuted, so he wanted revenge. Even admitted to a grudge during his interview, so there's powerful evidence of motive. He's a big, strong brute with a record of violence, including assault and attempted murder. His fingerprint puts him inside Hazzard's cabin, but he denies being there. That makes him a liar. Sounds to me like a layup for a conviction."

The strength of Zeke's summation shocked Koa. The prosecutor was serious about going after Kāliʻi. Koa's worse fear—that an innocent man would do time for Koa's crime—was becoming ever more a reality. He needed to dissuade Zeke, but, like Koa, the prosecutor was rabidly persistent in pursuing wrongdoing. Koa took a deep breath before summoning his best argument. "Aren't you forgetting that the coroner ruled Hazzard's death a suicide? Won't that alone be enough to create reasonable doubt?"

"That's a problem, but I talked to Kaohi, the retired police detective who investigated the crime." For once, Koa wished Zeke hadn't been so thorough. "Kaohi was never comfortable with the suicide finding but didn't have an alternative. He'll testify that, if he had known about ʻAnalū Kāliʻi, his confrontation with Hazzard, and his fingerprint in the cabin, he'd never have bought the suicide notion. And we can back that up with Hazzard's plans to visit his family in New York and his purchase of a first-class air ticket."

Koa felt his heart sink and wondered what he should do. Maybe he should confess. Tell Zeke the dirty secret he'd been hiding for thirty years. Confess to manslaughter, or maybe Zeke would think murder. He'd lose his job. He'd lose Nālani. He'd go to jail. Despite his anguish at the prospect of standing by while an innocent went to prison, Koa could not bring himself to fess up to Zeke.

He wondered if he could somehow exonerate ʻAnalū Kāliʻi, although he couldn't imagine how. Perhaps there was an explanation for the fingerprint. Maybe Kāliʻi had an alibi. Yet, as the chief detective, Koa couldn't even talk to Kāli'i. After Kāli'i asked for a lawyer, the court had appointed a public defender who had advised Kāli'i not to speak to the police. Koa could see no way to fortify the man's defense or prove his innocence.

Koa left the prosecutor's office and walked through Wailoa Park. Images from that awful night at Hazzard's cabin filled his head, distracting him. He stumbled and nearly fell. The pictures in Koa's head were now of Kāli'i. Kāli'i in the interrogation room. Kāli'i at the defense table in a courtroom. Kāli'i crumbling under Zeke's cross-examination. The jury returning a guilty verdict. Kāli'i in a jail cell.

Koa saw his life unraveling. His efforts to redeem himself all for naught. His struggle to get an education. His military service. His successes as a detective. The Pōhakuloa case. The two murdered loners living off the grid. The KonaWili school disaster. His magical relationship with Nālani. The respect he enjoyed in the department and the community. All his good deeds overwhelmed by one terrible act.

He'd murdered a man and was remaining silent while another man—an innocent man—paid for his sins. Overwhelming guilt for the crime he'd committed and the renewed duplicity of his ongoing silence weighed upon him.

At home later that night, Koa found himself drowning in fear—fear of losing Nālani, his job, his reputation, and his freedom. He had trouble concentrating. At dinner with Nālani, he fought to control his anguish. Nālani made his favorite dish—seared nori-wrapped 'ahi—but he only picked at it. He had lost his taste for food.

Unwilling to see Koa suffer through a second evening in distress, Nālani pressed, "What's wrong, Koa?"

As he had the night before, he tried to put her off, but she persisted. "Talk to me, ipo. Whatever it is, we'll get through it. Please don't shut me out."

He had to say something but still couldn't bring himself to tell her about Hazzard. Instead, he said he'd become entangled in a highly political matter angering the chief and Senator Chao. Without giving her names or details, he confessed that the issue could cost him his job.

Nālani wrapped her arms around him and tried to comfort him, but it was no use. Her love and support felt hollow when he couldn't share the truth with her.

When they crawled into bed, he couldn't sleep. His mind raced. He had half-conscious nightmarish dreams of Hazzard's death, Kāliʻi on trial, the judge sentencing Kāliʻi to life in prison. He tossed and turned and awoke drenched in sweat. After a sleepless night, he felt exhausted.

Dragging himself to the office, he went through the motions. Less than thirty-six hours had passed since Zeke had set a deadline for Wingate's arrest. Koa disagreed with the delay, but he couldn't override Zeke, at least not without a damn good reason. He tried to take comfort that the FBI had trackers on Wingate's and Snelling's cell phones and cars, but he somehow knew it would not be enough.

Trying to be productive and push away thoughts of the Hazzard fiasco, Koa reviewed the list of possible couriers who might have transported the Deimos hack software to Hawaiʻi. Although he tried to concentrate, the names blurred before his eyes, and the letters morphed into faces from his nightmares. His heart raced, and he felt a sharp pain in his chest. God, was he having a heart attack? He tried to stand up but felt light-headed and dizzy and slumped back in his chair.

When he next became aware of his surroundings, he looked at the clock on his office wall. Had a whole hour passed? Had he been unconscious or asleep? The idea of losing consciousness scared him. He got himself a glass of water, thinking that he'd ignore the strange lapse, but concern for his health gnawed at him and he called his doctor. The receptionist scheduled an appointment for him later that afternoon.

*   *   *

Doctor Reginald Sart, whom Koa had known for more than a decade, greeted him warmly. In his office, the thin, bespectacled doctor listened attentively as Koa described what he thought was a blackout. In response to the doctor's questions, Koa admitted to being severely stressed, which he attributed to a difficult case, described his flagging appetite, and owned up to sleepless, sweat-drenched, nightmare-filled nights.

After they chatted, the doctor took his vitals and did a full medical exam. Although he still needed lab results, Sart shared his conclusions. "I'm pretty sure you had a classic anxiety attack. Your body is telling you it needs sleep. I'm going to prescribe an antianxiety med and something to help you sleep." He scratched out two prescriptions. "What you need is a vacation. Take a couple of weeks off."

"I can't, not right now," Koa responded.

"That's what patients say until they have a breakdown or a heart attack. You're demanding more from your body than it can sustain. It'll catch up with you if you don't listen to what your system is telling you. Take some time off."

Koa left the doctor's office relieved that he hadn't had a heart attack, but his thoughts quickly returned to Kāliʻi. There was nothing he, as a policeman, could do to help the accused man, but if he couldn't help, maybe someone else could. Someone like Alexia Sheppard, the best criminal defense lawyer on the island. She'd done a terrific job for Koa's wayward brother keeping him out of jail numerous times before his brother's violent temper had finally made any defense impossible. She was smart and creative. If anyone could help Kāliʻi, it was Alexia.

Having hit on the idea, he turned to the logistics. He couldn't just ask Alexia to represent Kāliʻi. She'd want to know why he, the chief detective, was trying to help a man credibly accused of murder. Whatever he told her, she'd be suspicious of his motives. Worse, if it ever came out that he hired her to defend Kāliʻi, he'd be in deep shit with the department and the prosecutor. People would ask questions he couldn't afford to answer.

Maybe he could hire Alexia anonymously. That way, he wouldn't have to ask her for a favor or expose himself to her questions. It would take money, a lot of money, but he'd lived frugally and had decent savings. The more he thought about it, the more he liked the idea.

He kept a thousand dollars in a small safe at home. He cashed two thousand-dollar checks at different banks and hit four ATMs for five hundred dollars each. He always used gloves or avoided touching the bills. He doubted that anyone would try to trace the money, but he took no chances. That gave him a total of $5,000, enough to get Alexia started.

He drafted and redrafted a letter to Alexia, purportedly from a friend of ʻAnalū Kāliʻi. The message had to spark Alexia's interest and appeal to her sense of justice. Koa thought he knew how to frame the request. Alexia hated political interference in the administration of justice, and Senator Chao's role in pursuing ʻAnalū Kāliʻi would infuriate her. When he finally finished the letter, it read:

Aloha, Miss Sheppard:

The police have charged my friend ʻAnalū Kāliʻi with the thirty-year-old murder of Anthony Hazzard. He is innocent of this crime. In 1989, hikers found Mr. Hazzard's ravaged and decomposed body with a hangman's noose around his neck in his Kohala Mountain cabin. The original police investigation found no evidence of foul play, and the coroner ruled Hazzard's death a suicide.

Anthony Hazzard's grandson cannot accept that his grandfather committed suicide and is pursuing a vendetta to identify and prosecute someone—anyone—so he can remove the stain of suicide from his family history. Mr. Kāliʻi's only connection to the crime scene is a single fingerprint found in Hazzard's cabin. There is no evidence as to how or when it came to be there. Despite evidence of Kāliʻi's animus against Anthony Hazzard, there is no proof that he ever acted on that hostility. Senator Chao supports the grandson's vendetta and has pressured the police department and the prosecutor's office to charge and convict Kāliʻi. Kāliʻi's conviction would represent a grave miscarriage of justice. He needs a defense attorney who will dig into the facts and challenge the evidence.

I beg you to contact Kāliʻi and offer to represent him. He cannot afford to pay you, but I have included a $5,000 retainer to cover your initial fees.

ʻAnalū Kāliʻi's friend

Koa put the letter, typed on one of the computers in the public library, together with the money in a manila envelope, and slipped it under Alexia's office door in the middle of the night. Having done what he could, he held his breath and waited. Late the following day, he got a call from Zeke. "Surprise, surprise. Your lady lawyer friend, Alexia Sheppard, has entered her appearance in the Kāliʻi murder case." After putting down the phone, Koa let out a long sigh. He had started the ball rolling. Now at least Kāliʻi had a chance.

CHAPTER THIRTY-ONE

KOA TOOK THE pills his doctor had prescribed and awoke the following morning from a drug-induced sleep feeling groggy. At least he'd slept. Although the antianxiety medication had calmed him, it couldn't resolve the dilemma he faced with Kāliʻi on trial. Two cups of coffee, some breakfast, and a long hug from Nālani got him ready for the office.

Once in the office, he set out to trace the spy who controlled Wingate and through him the Deimos sabotage, pulling together everything that might be relevant. He had Baldwin's diary where she'd written, "Wingate gets the code from someone outside the company. Waited outside the parking lot and followed. Lost him near Pāhala. Next day saw him in the computer room with a drive."

According to Baldwin's diary, Wingate had meetings with someone, most likely his handler. One of Baldwin's notes put the location of at least one of those meetings near Pāhala, the tiny former sugar settlement fifty miles south of Hilo. If, Koa mused, Wingate got the drives full of bad code from an outsider, then there would have been several meetings, each roughly corresponding with the times when someone had inserted bad code. Maybe all of those meetings had taken place in the same location.

He'd already been through the phone company and Google location data from Wingate's phone but only for the night of Baldwin's murder and at the times when someone had uploaded corrupt code to the Deimos program. Now he went back to that data looking to see if Wingate had traveled to or through Pāhala. Strangely, he found no indication that Wingate had ever been anywhere near Pāhala—not even on any date around the time of Baldwin's calendar entry. Weird.

Sure that he'd missed something, Koa went back over the data a second time. Only then did he notice that there were gaps in the data—periods showing no location at all, most likely when the phone had been off. Printing blank calendar pages off his computer, he began the laborious task of filling in Wingate's general location each day. As he worked, Koa saw that Wingate typically went back and forth between his home in the Hilo hills and X-CO's offices or elsewhere in Hilo, probably to shop, eat, or drink. Still, a distinct pattern of blanks also became apparent.

The gaps in Wingate's movement always occurred late at night and at roughly ten-day intervals. The common practice of turning off one's phone at bedtime might explain the gaps, but it was hard to imagine a phone subscriber who turned his cell phone off only every tenth night. And the gaps started when Wingate was at the office, not when he was at home. The gaps, Koa thought, could mean only one thing. The son of a bitch knew his cell could be tracked and was up to something he wanted to hide. If Koa was right, those data gaps could represent dates when Wingate met the person or persons who directed him. If Wingate was the Deimos saboteur, then his handler was likely feeding him the bad data drives late in the evening roughly every tenth day.

Sensing he was on to something, Koa dug out the list of dates he'd gotten from Moreno—times when someone had modified the

Deimos program. He overlaid those events on his calendar. There it was! Another pattern. The data gaps typically preceded the Deimos program alterations by one or two days. Koa was now pretty sure he'd reconstructed the timeline when Wingate received drives containing unauthorized code.

Next, Koa realized he needed to match those dates against the list of people who had visited the Big Island eight or more times since February. With 300 names, it was a huge task, and he enlisted Piki. They divided the list and began scratching off people whose visits to the Big Island did not coincide with the dates when Wingate had gone dark. The list slowly dwindled until they were down to twenty names.

Of these names, Koa recognized only seven—Bianche; Senator Chao; Kāwika Keahi, Koa's childhood friend, and now the senator's aide; Mayor Tenaka; Colonel Tripplet, commander of the Pōhakuloa Training Area; Harvey Reid, an X-CO director; and Chief Lannua. Koa was surprised that his chief had been off-island so frequently but figured he'd been to Honolulu, probably half for police business and half for politics. Then again, with such a politically ambitious chief, he was likely sucking up to his political cronies. Bianche and Reid were intriguing, but Chao, his aide, Tenaka, and Tripplet all had legitimate reasons for their travel. As a US senator, Chao regularly traveled in and out of the state, frequently with his aide, and Tenaka and Tripplet often went back and forth to Honolulu for business.

Koa assigned Piki to research the other fourteen frequent travelers using the internet, Facebook, and other law enforcement databases. Even for an internet wizard like Piki, it was slow going, and Koa wasn't sure the effort would yield anything.

While Piki worked, Koa called Goodling. "Hi. I've got a question. How long have you guys been tracking Wingate's vehicle?"

"About three weeks," she responded.

"Any indication that he's traveled out of Hilo?"

"No. We've been watching, and he hasn't left the Hilo area. Why? What's your angle?"

"Not sure. I'll get back to you if it goes anywhere." After hanging up, Koa stared out the window, trying to understand the discrepancy. Ten days previously, there'd been a gap in Wingate's location. If the gaps represented Wingate's trips to meet his contact, then the FBI tracker on his car should have recorded them. Maybe Baldwin had been wrong in guessing that Wingate's meeting took place near Pāhala, or perhaps Pāhala had been a onetime thing. The more he thought about it, the more Koa felt that he'd missed something—something just beyond his grasp.

His years on the force had taught Koa to trust his hunches, and the gaps in the location data triggered those instincts. He needed some way to check his suspicions, and thought maybe the old-fashioned way—physical surveillance—could give him the confirmation he sought. The last gap in the location stats was nine days back, so if Wingate maintained roughly the same schedule, it was time for another meeting. Koa asked Makanui to reestablish their original stakeout on the X-CO headquarters from the roof of the building across the street. "Have the cops watch for Wingate. Have them follow him when he moves and call me if he goes anywhere besides home," Koa directed.

His timing turned out to be perfect. At ten p.m. that evening, Makanui called. "Just heard from Horita on the stakeout. Wingate came out of the building and got on a motorcycle. He's headed south on the Belt Highway toward Volcano."

Koa felt a rush of adrenalin. It appeared he'd been right about the location gaps. Wingate was likely on his way to meet his handler. The motorcycle, Koa realized, also explained the failure of the

FBI-installed tracker on Wingate's car to detect his out-of-town movements. The feds didn't know that Wingate had a motorcycle, likely registered in another name. Wingate could turn off his phone, disappear, meet with whomever, and leave no trace.

Koa thought for a second. If Wingate planned to travel toward Pāhala, he'd have to pass by Volcano, less than two miles from Koa's cottage. There was a chance that Wingate might go elsewhere, but after previously doubting Baldwin, Koa now trusted her diary entry. If she'd lost him in Pāhala, that was the place to start. "Have Horita follow him but discreetly," he told Makanui. "Have him call me and stay on the phone. I'm going to get ahead of Wingate and pick up surveillance in Pāhala. Have Horita alert me when he gets close."

Thirty-five minutes later, Koa was sitting in his SUV just off the highway a quarter-mile north of Pāhala when Horita reported, "He's a mile north of town." A minute later, a motorcycle flashed past, and Koa took up the tail.

Wingate turned off the highway at Pāhala and then turned again on Wood Valley Road. Given the lack of traffic in the rural area and the red taillight on Wingate's motorcycle, Koa was able to stay well back, driving without lights. Wingate gave no sign that he'd spotted the tail. Four miles later, Wingate turned into Nechung Dorje Drayang Ling, otherwise known as the Wood Valley Temple, a world-renowned Buddhist monastery and retreat. Koa drove past and pulled off two hundred yards farther along. He grabbed binoculars and a long-lens camera from his surveillance pack and cut through the woods back toward the monastery on foot.

With a history dating back to 1902, the Wood Valley Temple compound occupied twenty-five partially manicured woodland acres, with a brightly colored Tibetan temple at its center. The site housed a Buddhist monastery, educational center, and retreat where the Dali Lama had once taught. Eucalyptus, palms, and bamboo surrounded the formal gardens, and jasmine scented the air. Brilliantly feathered peacocks wandered the ground during the day. Trails through the forest behind the temple gave the resident monks an idyllic place to walk and meditate. It was, Koa thought, an odd, out-of-the-way place for clandestine meetings, but maybe that made it a perfect choice.

He surveyed the area in the light of the waning moon. The monks' dormitories were dark and quiet this late at night, as were the guesthouse visitors' quarters. Nothing moved on the monastery grounds. Even the forest sounds seemed muted. Wingate's motorcycle stood in the parking lot close to the ornate Buddhist temple, beside a late model, black Toyota Prius. Koa snapped pictures, capturing both vehicles' license plates.

He trained his binoculars on the temple's vibrant red, yellow, and green pagoda-like structure. Two highly stylized *shishi*, Chinese lion-dog statues, one male with a foot resting on a ball, and a female whose foot rested on a lion cub, guarded the entrance. A gong hung from the temple rafters, and two pairs of shoes lay on the steps. Koa focused on the temple's double doors. Although the glass panes in the temple doors should have been dark this late at night, soft, flickering golden candlelight glowed from within.

Judging from the number of vehicles in the parking lot and pairs of shoes, Koa guessed that at least two people were inside. Wingate had to be one of them. A shadow moving across the dimly lit glass panels confirmed someone's presence inside. Koa watched, hoping to see the shadows of two people together, but never saw more than a single silhouette at a time.

Sensing he was alone outside, Koa risked creeping slowly forward into an Asian garden about a hundred feet in front of the temple. He thought about moving still closer but knew he couldn't get close enough to hear what was going on inside without risking discovery.

So, he settled behind the garden's short rock wall that provided concealment and adjusted his position to observe the temple through a gap in the stone bulwark.

He waited. The moon drifted lower. A breeze rattled the forest trees on either side of the compound. Other than the wind, the distinctive little barks of geckos, the whine of coqui frogs, and the occasional hoot of a *pueo*, an owl, the night was quiet. Minutes passed. If there was a meeting inside the temple, it was taking quite some time. For an instant, Koa wondered if Wingate had come to pray, but quickly dismissed the idea. Wingate didn't strike Koa as the type, and people didn't go to such great lengths to hide their prayers.

Twenty minutes later, the temple door opened, Wingate emerged, slipped into his shoes, and descended the steps. Koa snapped multiple photos before the man mounted his motorcycle and rode off. He briefly considered following but knew Wingate would be long gone before Koa could get back to his vehicle. Instead, Koa had a more critical objective—identifying Wingate's contact. He assumed the person was still inside the temple, a guess the remaining pair of shoes seemed to confirm.

Another thirty minutes passed, and Koa began to worry that Wingate had been alone when the candlelight inside the temple went out. Moments later, the temple doors opened, and a man stepped onto the porch. He stood still, barely illuminated by the scant moonlight, scanning the night for danger. Muscular like a bodybuilder, he appeared to be in his thirties with a brutal, sun-damaged face under a shock of unruly black hair. He wore stained jeans and an ill-fitting sweatshirt. Koa didn't recognize him, and he was not at all what Koa expected. Koa snapped a dozen photos before the stranger put on his shoes, moved down the short flight of stairs, got into the Prius, and drove off.

Koa thought about waiting until morning to brief the feds but decided against any delay. He'd just achieved a major break in the investigation, felt an urgent need to identify the stranger who'd met with Wingate, and didn't want to hear Moreno complaining about being out of the loop. On his way back to Hilo, Koa called Goodling, awakening her for the second night in a row to summon her to a post-midnight meeting in Zeke's office. She wasn't happy, but she and Moreno appeared for the three thirty a.m. conference. Bringing them up to speed, Koa explained the gaps in Wingate's location data and the renewed surveillance of the X-CO facility. "I'll be damned," Moreno conceded when Koa described Wingate's late-night motorcycle ride and Koa's tracking starting in Pāhala.

Using an office copier, Koa had downloaded and printed the digital photos he'd taken. Passing copies to the feds, he explained that they showed Wingate leaving the temple, followed thirty minutes later by a second person who left in the black Toyota Prius.

"Who is he?" Goodling asked.

"Don't know," Koa responded. "The plates on the black Prius came off a wrecked vehicle reported stolen months ago. I rousted an IT professor at UH Hilo out of bed, and he's running the dude's picture through facial recognition software. I figured you guys might also try your sources."

"How come you didn't follow him?" Moreno asked with more than a touch of annoyance.

Koa wasn't in the mood for criticism from Moreno, but responded, "Couldn't." Then somewhat conciliatory, he added, "I was too far from my wheels."

Zeke made coffee while the feds transmitted pictures of the stranger to their colleagues to help identify the unknown man. Koa checked in twice with the IT professor, only to hear that his software was grinding through the county's DMV database. Two hours passed before Koa got word. When the name of Professor Diaz's colleague popped up on his cell, Koa put the caller on speaker. "We got a hit. Your man is Kūʻula Kai."

"*Kūʻula Kai*! You're kidding," Koa exclaimed.

"No, I'm not kidding. That's the name attached to the DMV photo," the IT professor responded.

Koa walked to Zeke's computer, signed in to his police account, and queried the DMV database. A picture popped up, and there it was. The face of the man he'd photographed coming out of the Wood Valley Temple. His name was indeed Kūʻula Kai. He listed his occupation as a fisherman and his home address as a commercial fishing vessel named *Mea Hoʻopaʻi*, the *Avenger*, moored in the Wailoa Boat Harbor.

Kūʻula Kai, Koa explained to the feds, was a mythological Hawaiian fisherman with a magic fishhook giving him mystical powers to control fish in the sea. "I've never heard of a real person with that name. If it's not an alias, this guy's parents had one wicked sense of humor."

"How do we get a handle on this fishhook man?" Moreno asked.

Koa knew who to ask. Hook Hao, his fisherman friend, knew everyone worth knowing on the Hilo waterfront and frequently updated Koa on waterfront activities. Turning to the rest of the group, Koa said, "I'm going to pursue a couple of leads on this guy. I'll be back in an hour. In the meantime, see what the bureau has on this dude."

Leaving Zeke's office, Koa stepped into the beginnings of sunrise and knew Hook would already be on his second or third cup of uber-strong java. He called to tell his fisherman buddy he'd be stopping by the *Kaʻupu*, the *Albatross*, Hook's big ocean going trawler. Ten minutes later, Koa stepped off the quay onto the stern of the

Ka'upu. Moving around to the side of the wheelhouse, Koa entered to find the old fisherman in his chair behind the chart table with a steaming cup of Kona coffee.

"You're up early," Hook said in greeting. "Help yourself to a cup."

Koa poured himself a coffee, enjoying its fragrant aroma as the dark liquid slowly filled his cup. "Need to ask you about a fellow fisherman—a guy named Kū'ula Kai."

"Sea trash," Hook snorted, surprising Koa with his vehemence. "Crime must be at an all-time low if you're chasing a bottom-feeder like Kai."

"How so?"

"Holds himself out to be god's gift to fishermen like his namesake, but he can barely bait a hook."

"Then how's he make a living?" Koa asked.

"Smuggling, I'd guess."

"Based on?" Koa pushed.

"He sails way beyond the twelve-mile limit. Says he's hunting deepwater *'ahi*, but the couple of times I've seen the *Mea Ho'opa'i* out there, she's been alongside a freighter. Had to be transporting contraband one way or the other."

Of course, Koa thought to himself. A Hawaiian fishing vessel connecting offshore with a freighter would be a perfect way to smuggle a computer disk onto the island. "You ever catch the name of one of these freighters?"

"Nope." Hook shook his head. "But I remember them flying an Indonesian flag."

If China were using ships to smuggle materials into Hawai'i, they would not, Koa figured, use China-flagged vessels, but they might use an Indonesian vessel. China and Indonesia, he knew, were significant trade partners. In other cases, he'd checked ship registries, but wasn't sure whether any website tracked ship movements the way they traced plane flights. He called Makanui and asked her to see what she could find. He then headed back to headquarters.

By ten a.m., the police-FBI team had assembled a dossier on Kūʻula Kai. The high school dropout had never filed a tax return despite ownership of an old, but serviceable, oceangoing trawler and a five-figure bank account with numerous $2,500 deposits. A review of the credit card charges linked to his bank account disclosed payments for boat maintenance, a gym membership, and numerous bar bills, but little else of interest. Oddly, they could find no evidence that he sold fish despite frequent trips into deep water east of the Big Island. Nor did he appear to be otherwise employed.

Makanui had checked international shipping registries and discovered that the *Bumi*, a freighter owned by a Hong Kong shipping company and flying Indonesian colors, had passed fifteen miles off the eastern coast of the Big Island at least ten times in the past year. Koa told the feds what he learned from Hook, along with the shipping data compiled by Makanui. Extending Makanui's research, Moreno dug into his files and confirmed that the *Bumi* had been near the Big Island before each of the dates when someone had inserted corrupt code into the Deimos software. Koa and the feds figured they'd found the saboteurs' pipeline.

Despite their confidence that they'd identified the supply chain, they still didn't know who was really behind the Deimos sabotage. None of the team, not even Moreno, pegged Kūʻula Kai as anything more than a delivery boy. He'd barely made it through junior high school, never had a passport, and so far as records revealed, had never been out of Hawaiʻi. His relatively modest cash bank deposits corresponding with his probable rendezvous with the Indonesian-flagged ship supported their conclusion that he was just a courier. Based on his history, neither Koa nor the feds would ever have suspected him of international espionage. His superiors had chosen well.

They debated arresting him. Moreno wanted him in an interrogation room, but Goodling and Koa resisted. "He'll lawyer up, and we'll get nothing," Goodling argued. "Better to leave him on the street and watch him."

"I agree," Koa responded, "especially since he's just come from a meeting with Wingate and could have a message to pass on."

They put Kūʻula Kai under maximum surveillance—phone tap, car and boat trackers, sound and video, as well as physical eyes on. He slept on his trawler until twelve thirty p.m. when he left carrying a gym bag. Gyms, Koa knew, were ideal places for clandestine meetings. He called Moreno, who checked Kai's credit card records and reported that Kai belonged to Shaka Fitness, a run-down sports club in south Hilo. Figuring Kai would hit his gym for a workout, Koa called Piki. "Looks like Kai is heading for Shaka Fitness. Pick up some special gear from the bureau and go for a workout."

With their access to a plethora of high-tech gadgets, the feds armed Piki with a camera and recording device concealed in a pair of phony eyeglasses. Slightly heavier than regular eyeglasses and far more capable than the highly publicized, but commercially unsuccessful, Google glasses, Piki couldn't help feeling a little like James Bond. That put a spring in his step.

Kai stopped at a nearby greasy spoon for a classic Hawaiian *loco moco* lunch of white rice, topped with a spam slice and a fried egg, passing on the usual topping of brown gravy and opting instead for ketchup. An hour and a half later, he hit the aging Shaka Fitness located in a shabby commercial space. Piki was already inside on a stationary bike with a clear view of the entrance and the exercise floor. He snapped pictures of Kai coming in and working out on the weights. True to his physique, the man could bench press 250 pounds.

While working out, Kai repeatedly checked his watch and occasionally scanned the gym. Piki figured he was waiting for someone.

About forty-five minutes into Kai's workout, another man entered the gym and headed straight to the locker room. Piki knew he'd seen the newcomer somewhere in Hilo but could not put a name to the face. Kai stopped his workout, returned his weights to their racks, and headed for the lockers. Piki gave him a two-minute head start and then followed. Although there were only a handful of men in the locker room, Kai and the man who'd just entered the club stood at adjoining lockers.

Kai and the newcomer did not appear to speak, but Piki sensed they were coordinating their movements. Both men stripped and headed for the showers. Kai's clock-watching, the two men's odd choice of lockers, and their strange lack of overt communication made Piki suspicious. He stripped, leaving his glasses on, and followed the two men into the open-plan showers. The two men stood close together, soaping up.

Kai and his contact stepped under a cascade of hot water. Piki could see that they were talking, but was too far away to hear anything over the shower noise. The thick steam and the other men in the showers gave Piki some cover, enabling him to move closer to his targets without arousing suspicions. Activating both the camera and the recorder in his phony glasses, Piki photographed them through a curtain of steam. Given the roar of water from multiple shower heads, Piki doubted that his miniature recording device would catch much of their conversation.

Piki wasn't the world's best photographer and didn't have a professional camera. Yet, the pictures he transmitted back to Koa left no doubt about the identity of the man who'd met Kai in the showers of a sleazy Hilo fitness club. He was Kāwika Keahi, Senator Chao's aide.

Koa found it hard to believe his childhood friend and aide to a powerful US senator was a traitor to his country. Koa wracked his brain for an innocent rationale for the meeting, but couldn't think of one. It hurt to reveal his childhood friend's betrayal to the feds, but Koa had no choice. They needed to know about the Keahi-Kai meeting to protect critical defense secrets. He would need their intelligence sources and Patriot Act powers to investigate how, when, and why Keahi had become a foreign agent.

"*Senator Chao's aide!*" Moreno yelled, unable to hide his astonishment. Goodling, too, expressed shock. Like Koa, they sought an innocent explanation, but the sketchy recording Piki had captured put a quick end to any effort at exoneration. The tiny audio recording device had captured little given the heavy background noise, but they heard the word "Deimos" twice in the garbled recording. That highly classified word left no room for doubt.

Koa's shock at Keahi's treachery slowly faded, replaced by consternation and outrage. How could someone he'd known like a brother for most of his life be a traitor? The magnitude of Keahi's deceit astonished Koa. *Deceit.* Koa focused on the word. A traitor was the ultimate deceiver. If he lied about his loyalty, he could lie about anything and everything. Everything about a traitor—every word he'd ever uttered—was suspect.

Koa began digging into Keahi's history. Starting at the beginning with Keahi's birth certificate, he found the first lie. That led to the discovery of other deceits. Koa only wished he'd investigated earlier. Maybe, just maybe, it was not too late.

CHAPTER THIRTY-TWO

THE CALL FROM Wingate's wife came into the police switchboard at four p.m. that afternoon. It seemed Wingate had left for the X-CO offices at seven a.m. but hadn't returned her calls all day. When she finally got hold of one of his colleagues at X-CO, she'd learned that he'd never arrived at work, and she was frantic. The news reached Koa minutes later. He swore and called Goodling. What, he asked, did their surveillance tracking show?

Goodling paused, and Koa heard her ask someone in the background for an update on Wingate. Following more muffled voices, Goodling said, "His car is in the X-CO parking lot."

"Something isn't right," Koa responded. "His wife just reported him missing."

"Meet you at X-CO," Goodling responded, urgency evident in her voice.

Koa raced for his SUV, phoning Makanui to join him. They made it to the X-CO building in less than seven minutes. Wingate's car was nowhere in sight. Goodling and Moreno arrived a short time later. For once, Moreno moved more slowly and with less self-assurance. Using a handheld device, the feds located the tracker that should have been on Wingate's car. They found it on the ground in an empty parking space.

"Think it fell off?" Koa asked, sarcastically.

"Hell no," Moreno responded. "Not in a million years. Someone had to have pulled the sucker off."

Moreno, Koa thought, was almost certainly right. How, Koa wondered, had the perp known about the tracker? If he knew about the tracker, what else did he know about their surveillance? Was he smart enough to leave the tracking device where it might plausibly have fallen off, casting a sliver of doubt? Absent a witness, they might never know for sure what had happened.

"What about his cell? You're tracking that, too, aren't you?" Koa asked.

"There's no signal. It must be off," Goodling responded.

It was a bad sign for Wingate, Koa realized. A terrible sign. Their inability to monitor Wingate's whereabouts suggested foul play. Who, Koa asked himself, would benefit from Wingate's demise? He considered Snelling, but that didn't seem right. Snelling, it appeared, had repeatedly protected Wingate and seemed to have nothing to gain from his death. Maybe Kai? It was possible. Wingate could finger him as his go-between with Keahi, but it seemed unlikely that he'd go after Wingate. No, he realized that Keahi, the senator's aide, had the most to gain. Wingate could almost certainly expose him as a traitor.

So much for the government's vaunted surveillance. Koa wanted to take his frustrations out on Moreno but held his tongue. There'd be time for recriminations. He needed to focus on finding Wingate if it wasn't too late. He called the dispatcher and ordered an APB on Wingate's car. He started for the X-CO building to ask if anyone inside knew of Wingate's whereabouts when his cell buzzed.

He answered, and the dispatcher reported that a park ranger had found Wingate's car abandoned near the ocean on Chain of Craters Road in Hawai'i Volcanoes National Park. The ranger had seen no sign of Wingate and suspected a possible suicide. Koa passed this information to the others. Makanui called for a police helicopter to transport them to the scene and a police boat to scour the adjoining shoreline.

The chopper carried the four of them—Koa, Makanui, and the two feds—over the meandering brownish-black lava flows from the recent eruptions in the lower east rift zone, then farther south past the now-dormant volcanic cone at Pu'u Ō'ō before making a rough landing between two park police vehicles blocking the Chain of Craters Road. They climbed out of the aircraft into shafts of sunlight cutting through fluffy white clouds, racing overhead in stiff trade winds.

They'd landed near the ocean on the eastern side of a vast lava delta. To the west, naked lava rose in steps back to a massive *pali* or cliff rising a thousand feet to another sloping plain of old lava flows. Aside from ruins of a few ancient Hawaiian settlements and the two-lane asphalt road leading back toward the *pali* and Kīlauea Crater, the landscape was barren. Civilization lay more than twenty miles away.

To the east, the delta ended just off the road at a rocky cliff edge poised above a restless, white-capped ocean extending to the horizon. Waves thundered against the black *pāhoehoe* lava threatening to break it into chunks and carry it away.

Wingate's gray BMW SUV sat half on and half off the narrow asphalt roadway, not more than fifty feet from the cliff at the edge of the ocean. The driver's door stood open, rocking in the wind. Before checking the vehicle, Koa walked to the edge and peered down at a tiny black sand beach between a rocky outcrop and a sea arch. Eight-foot waves repeatedly swept over the inaccessible shoreline and broke against the cliff in a blizzard of frothy white spray. Koa didn't expect to see Wingate's body. If the man had jumped, been pushed, or thrown over, the waves had carried him away.

Troubled by the turn of events, Koa turned back toward the car. He spotted Jimmy Kahana, whom he knew from HVNP events he'd attended with Nālani. The two men acknowledged each other, and Koa shook hands with the tall, broad-shouldered national park ranger. "*Aloha*, Jimmy. What's your take?"

"The driver could be off hikin', but . . ." The round-faced ranger shook his head. "Who leaves the driver's door open . . . 'specially with the wind whippin' it? Naw. I'm thinkin' suicide. People have done it before. You jump off that cliff, and you belong to the ocean. There ain't no comin' back. *E nui ke aho, e ku'u keiki, a moe i ke kai, no ke kai lā ho'i ka 'aina.*" Koa translated the old saying about suicide— "Take a deep breath, my son, and lay yourself in the sea, for then the land shall belong to the sea."

"More likely murder," Koa said.

Jimmy looked shocked. "Murder?"

"The driver's a key witness in a murder case," Koa explained. "What can you tell me about the car? When did it enter the park? Who was driving? Assuming there was a second person, how'd he get out of here?"

"You're serious," Jimmy said, unhooking a radio from his belt. He contacted the park service employee at the entry gate, described the BMW, read off the license number, and listened for a few seconds before disconnecting and turning back to Koa. "Kawelo is going to check the video at the entry kiosk and call me back."

"If he turns up a picture of the driver, have him text it to me," Koa instructed.

"Will do," Jimmy said.

While he waited for answers, Koa joined the others around the BMW, taking in the angle of the wind rocking the open car door, the keys in the ignition, the gearshift still in drive, the emergency brake unset, just the way a man rushing to suicide might have left it. A perfect suicide scene. Too perfect, Koa thought.

He popped the back hatch and checked for visible bloodstains. He found a fresh oil stain on the floor, but nothing that looked like blood. He went over the back seat, looking for evidence that a second person had been in the car. Again, he found nothing out of the ordinary. He scanned the area around Wingate's BMW, checking for signs of a second vehicle that might have parked nearby. No luck.

Makanui, who'd been on the phone running down the GPS data from the BMW's security system, reported that Wingate's BMW had entered through the HVNP's main entrance a little over two hours earlier. The vehicle had turned left on to Crater Rim Drive, left again on Chain of Craters Road, and driven seventeen miles down to the ocean.

Moments later, Koa's phone pinged with an incoming text attaching a grainy picture of a man behind the wheel of the gray BMW at the park's entry kiosk. The driver might have been Wingate, but a baseball cap and sunglasses obscured most of the face, and the image was so fuzzy that Koa couldn't be sure. Although neither the floor of the back seat nor the rear compartment was fully visible, Koa saw no evidence of a second person in the car. An additional check with the gate attendant confirmed that the driver had been alone in the BMW, and no other vehicle had entered the park within the ten-minute window before and after Wingate's entry.

Something about the scene still seemed incongruous. Koa walked across the road and climbed a small lava outcropping to get an overall view. Bracing himself against the stiff breeze, his sense of contradiction grew, but it took him a minute to figure out why. Then it came to him. The road dead-ended less than a mile away, so Wingate's car must have come from his right, just as the GPS data indicated. Yet, the vehicle now pointed back in the direction from which it had come. The driver had turned around. It was a small detail, but a significant one. The car next to the ocean, driver's door open, the keys in the ignition, gear shift still in drive, emergency brake unset created the impression of a man in an all-fired hurry to fling himself into the ocean. Yet, this driver—or someone else—had taken the time to turn around on the narrow, shoulder-less asphalt road, requiring him to back up at least once and more likely twice. Why?

And suddenly, the answer was obvious. The strong trade winds came from Koa's left. If the car had been facing into the wind, the airflow would have shut the driver's door, spoiling the image of a man rushing to his suicide. Someone had staged this tableau. Wingate had almost certainly not taken his own life.

Tentatively ruling out suicide left two alternatives—either an unknown person had killed Wingate and staged the suicide or Wingate himself had arranged the scene and disappeared, leaving both the police and his co-conspirators to conclude that he'd committed suicide. The latter was not a terrible outcome for a man who'd betrayed his country, committed murder, and feared the police were getting too close.

Either scenario required a second vehicle. Koa knew from the many times he and Nālani had visited the park that it took roughly forty-five minutes to drive from the entrance to the ocean and the same amount of time to get back out. Koa asked Jimmy Kahana to have the gate attendant pull video of all vehicles leaving the park, starting an hour after Wingate's BMW entered, and sent Makanui to review the footage.

She found what they anticipated. Almost exactly an hour and a half after Wingate's car entered the national park, a single helmeted rider on a motor scooter sped out the exit lane. The helmet made it impossible to determine the rider's identity. The gate attendant found no record of the motor scooter entering the park or paying the applicable fee. Remembering the oil in the back of Wingate's BMW, Koa guessed the motor scooter had been there when the vehicle entered the park. Had Wingate's body also been in the rear? He went back for another look. Both Wingate and the motor scooter would have fit.

When they ran the license plate on the motorbike, obtained from the park exit camera, they discovered it had been stolen. It turned up later near a waste transfer station. The crime scene team was unable to find a single fingerprint on it. The only prints in the BMW were Wingate's. With nothing more to go on, the investigation of Wingate's disappearance came to a standstill.

CHAPTER THIRTY-THREE

THE MODERN COURTROOM featured an elevated, wood-paneled bench, a jury box, counsel tables, TV monitors, and three rows of seats for spectators. Judge Hitachi, wearing his black robe over a colorful aloha shirt, presided. Zeke sat at the prosecution table with an assistant. Alexia Sheppard sat next to her client, ʻAnalū Kāliʻi, at the defense table. The bailiff called the case: The State of Hawaiʻi versus ʻAnalū Kāliʻi.

It was unusual, but not unheard of, for Koa to attend a trial. He knew it would seem odd for him to sit through the Kāliʻi trial, but he couldn't stay away. In many ways, he was on trial. He could not and would not let an innocent man go to jail. If the jury convicted Kāliʻi, Koa would have to confess to manslaughter, if not murder. When Zeke inquired, he said he'd never imagined the trial of a thirty-year-old murder and wanted to see how it played out. Koa was not the only spectator with a stake in the outcome. Bobby Hazzard sat in the front row with a smug expression. Unlike Koa, Bobby was rooting for a conviction.

After Zeke and Alexia made their opening statements, Zeke called retired detective Kaohi to the stand. Kaohi described the scene in Hazzard's cabin. Hazzard's torn and decomposing body, the noose around his neck, the frayed rope hanging from a ceiling beam, an overturned table, a broken whiskey bottle, loose fire irons, and an unidentified fingerprint. Zeke then led Kaohi through all the reasons the old detective had doubted that Hazzard had killed himself. Kaohi detailed his conversations with Hazzard's colleagues, all of whom denied that Hazzard was depressed and all of whom saw suicide as extremely unlikely. The retired detective also testified that Hazzard's friends had described the sugar baron's plans to visit family in New York and his purchase of air tickets.

Finally, Zeke asked, "Do you believe that Anthony Hazzard committed suicide?"

Kaohi answered, "I was unsure back then, but with what I know now, I'd say no."

"Why not?" Zeke asked.

"A man doesn't plan a family trip, buy expensive air tickets, and then go off into the forest to kill himself. It don't make sense."

The jury seemed to like Kaohi, and Koa saw several of the jurors nodding in agreement. It wasn't a good omen.

Senator Chao entered the courtroom and took a seat in the front row next to Bobby Hazzard. Koa could tell from their expressions that several of the jurors recognized the senator. Koa watched the senator while Zeke continued to question Kaohi. "Did you act on your belief?"

"Yes. I asked my chief to leave the investigation open."

"And did he agree to your request?" Zeke asked.

"No. I couldn't offer a plausible alternative theory, and the coroner ruled Hazzard's death a suicide."

"Would that decision have been different if you'd known that 'Analū Kāli'i had been in Hazzard's cabin?"

It was a hypothetical question, and Koa expected Alexia to object, but she allowed the witness to answer.

"Yes. I believe the decision would have been different had we known the defendant had been in the cabin, yeah."

Senator Chao nodded and smiled at the witness. Several jurors noted his approval. Koa swore under his breath. The senator had come to exert his not so subtle influence on the jury. And Koa feared it was working.

"What would you have done?" Zeke asked.

"We'd have tracked Kāliʻi down, checked out his story, and interrogated him, yeah. Based on what I have learned recently, we'd have discovered his hostility toward Hazzard, his strong motive for murder, and his opportunity to kill Hazzard once he was in the cabin."

When Zeke finished his examination of Kaohi, Senator Chao made a conspicuous display of getting up and leaving the courtroom. The senator was telling the jury he'd heard enough. It was an obvious ploy to signal to the jury that Alexia's cross-examination would be unimportant because Kāliʻi was guilty as hell.

When it came time for Alexia to cross-examine, she approached the retired detective. "Good afternoon, Detective," she greeted him with her characteristically lyrical voice. "You investigated Mr. Hazzard's death nearly thirty years ago?"

"Yes, ma'am," he responded.

"And you still have a good memory of the scene?"

"Yes, ma'am."

"Tell me, Detective, were there any man-made injuries on Mr. Hazzard's body?"

"I don't rightly know."

"You don't know?" she asked with a hint of surprise in her voice.

"The body was so badly mauled by animals and insects that it was impossible to tell," Kaohi responded.

Koa had watched Alexia cross-examine witnesses before and admired her ability to cut their testimony apart with her charm and the nicest of smiles. She was doing it now to Kaohi. "You found a rope around Mr. Hazzard's neck and a frayed rope hanging from a beam, but no evidence that another person had hurt Hazzard. Is that right?"

"Er. Hm. I guess that's right."

Koa felt a surge of relief. Alexia had done severe damage to the prosecution's case.

"You found a fingerprint—one ultimately shown to belong to 'Analū Kāli'i—in the cabin. Is that correct?" Alexia asked.

"Yes, ma'am."

"Where was this fingerprint found?"

"I don't know."

"You don't know?" Alexia asked again in her carefully cultivated manner, letting a bit more surprise creep into her voice.

"One of the crime scene technicians found the print," Kaohi answered.

"So, the fingerprint might have been on a dish or a bottle?"

"I guess."

"Or on a book or a hurricane lamp?" Alexia asked.

"Anything is possible," Kaohi responded.

"Anything is possible. Is that what you said, Mr. Kaohi?"

Koa expected Zeke to object, but the prosecutor remained silent, and Koa realized that he was too smart to add weight to the damaging concession Alexia had extracted from the witness.

"Yeah," Kaohi answered.

"Now, Mr. Kaohi," Alexia asked, "did you determine when this fingerprint came to be in Anthony Hazzard's cabin?"

Kaohi looked confused. "When it came to be? I don't understand."

"Then let me clarify my question," Alexia offered in her most lyrical voice. "Was the fingerprint made the day Anthony Hazzard died or weeks before his death?"

"Oh. I don't know. You can't tell from a fingerprint."

"You don't know," Alexia repeated, slowly shaking her head. After checking her notes, she asked, "Mr. Hazzard died in September 1989, is that correct?"

"Yes, ma'am."

"Did you determine when he went to his cabin?"

Kaohi looked blank, and Alexia added, "You can look at the police report if it helps refresh your memory."

Kaohi looked at the report and answered, "September 1."

"And when did he die?"

"We were never sure, but sometime around September 2, 1989. Maybe September 3, but no later than that."

"And hikers found him ten days later?"

"That's correct," Kaohi answered.

"Now, Mr. Kaohi," Alexia asked in her musical voice, "how did you get to Mr. Hazzard's cabin?"

"We hiked in," he responded.

"Was it a long hike?"

"Yes, ma'am. About ten hours or maybe a little more."

"And ten hours back out?"

"Yes, ma'am."

Movement at the prosecution table caught Koa's eye, and he saw Zeke conferring with his assistant. The prosecutor appeared puzzled by Alexia's last set of questions. Koa, too, wondered why Alexia had focused on the difficulty in reaching the cabin. She undoubtedly had her reasons, but they eluded Koa, and apparently Zeke, too.

Koa knew that Alexia had made a dent in the prosecution's case by getting Kaohi to admit that there was no evidence of man-made injuries on Hazzard's body and by showing that the police didn't know where in the cabin they'd found Kāli'i's fingerprint. He wasn't surprised when Zeke drew Alexia aside during a break and offered to reduce the charge from murder to manslaughter if Kāli'i would plead guilty.

Alexia smiled. "He's innocent, and he's not going to plead."

After the break, Zeke called JD Ricks, another retired police officer. Ricks testified that he'd investigated the burglary of Anthony Hazzard's home and ultimately arrested 'Analū Kāli'i for the crime. He described Kāli'i as an angry young tough who bore a grudge against Hazzard. "Mr. Kāli'i claimed that Hazzard cheated Kāli'i's sugar mill buddies and had them beaten. He swore at Hazzard, calling him *kepalō* . . . the devil."

"Did Kāli'i say anything else about Hazzard?" Zeke asked.

"Yes," Ricks responded, "he said he'd like to kill the son of a bitch."

Koa's heart sank. Ricks' testimony was devastating, and Koa's hope for an acquittal faded.

Finally, Zeke called Detective Piki, who authenticated the tape of Kāli'i's recent police interrogation. Zeke played those portions where Kāli'i admitted his dislike for Hazzard, called him a dickhead, and denied ever having been in Waimanu Valley or at the Hazzard cabin.

"What did you conclude from Kāli'i's statement to you?" Zeke asked.

"I concluded that he lied when he said he'd never been to Hazzard's cabin."

Koa went home that night with a heavy heart. Zeke had put on a compelling case, creating significant doubt about suicide, showing that Kāli'i had a strong motive to kill Hazzard, and worst of all, had threatened to do so. Even Koa, who knew Kāli'i to be innocent, didn't believe his denial of ever having been in Hazzard's cabin.

Koa tossed and turned all night, unable to sleep, fearing the jury would convict Kāli'i. He knew deep down that he would soon have to expose his secret crime to Zeke. He would have to tell the prosecutor, whom he respected and who respected him, that he himself had killed Anthony Hazzard so many years ago.

CHAPTER THIRTY-FOUR

ALEXIA SHOCKED THE courtroom the next morning by calling her client to the stand. Even first-year law students knew that you didn't put a convicted felon on the witness stand. Any competent prosecutor would tear him to shreds.

Koa suffered in despair while Alexia led Kāliʻi through each of his convictions, acknowledging vandalism, brawling, assault, burglary, and attempted murder. After he described the nadir of his criminal life, Kāliʻi told the story of his redemption in marriage and his daughter's birth. He summed up the change in his life, saying, "I thank the gods for giving me a second chance."

"How did you first meet Anthony Hazzard?" Alexia asked.

"In the general store where I worked when I was seventeen. He came in to buy things—tools, lanterns, dishes, that sort of thing," Kāliʻi responded.

"Were these things that you had handled?" Alexia asked.

"Some of them," Kāliʻi responded. "I stocked the shelves, moved things around, and got things down for customers. So, I touched a lot of the merchandise."

"With your bare hands?"

"Yes."

"So, you left your fingerprints on items in the store?"

"Yes. I must have."

"And Mr. Hazzard bought some of these items?"

"I helped him from time to time, so, yes, he bought items I touched," Kāliʻi responded.

When Alexia finished the line of questioning, Koa understood why she'd risked putting her client on the stand. His testimony, together with her cross-examination of Kaohi, had provided an innocent explanation of how his fingerprint had come to be in Hazzard's cabin. She had created reasonable doubt about Kāliʻi's guilt. Maybe one or more jurors would balk at conviction. Koa hoped it would be enough.

Alexia then asked her client, "Where were you on September 2, 1989?"

"On Oʻahu," Kāliʻi answered.

Bobby Hazzard let out a gasp, and stunned silence enveloped the courtroom. Alexia was going to present an alibi. Koa's heart raced. Was it possible that Kāliʻi had an ironclad defense?

"When did you go to Oʻahu?" Alexia asked.

"On August 31, 1989."

"And when did you return?"

"September 6."

Alexia then asked, "Did you tell the prosecutors that you were on Oʻahu from August 31 to September 6, 1989?"

"Yes, but they didn't believe me," Kāliʻi responded.

Alexia approached the witness and handed him a photograph. "Do you recognize this picture?"

"Yes," Kāliʻi answered. "It's a picture of me. My sister took it at Aloha Stadium in Honolulu on the evening of September 2, 1989, during the UH Rainbow Warriors–Tulane football game. It was the season opener. You can see the scoreboard in the background behind me."

Alexia turned to the judge. "I ask that this photograph identified by the defendant be admitted into evidence and shown to the jury."

The judge turned to Zeke. "Any objection?"

Zeke examined the photograph. "No, Your Honor."

The bailiff handed the picture to one of the jurors, who examined it and passed it to the next juror. Several of the jurors nodded or looked up at the defendant after viewing the picture.

Alexia turned and spoke directly to the defendant. "Did you kill Anthony Hazzard?"

"No, ma'am. I did not."

"Were you ever in his cabin?"

"No."

"Do you know how your fingerprint came to be in his cabin?"

"No. I can only guess that it was on some item Mr. Hazzard bought at the store where I worked."

"And you were on Oʻahu when the police say Hazzard died?"

"Yes, I was."

When Alexia sat down, Zeke rose to cross-examine the defendant. He forced Kāliʻi to reiterate each of his crimes and describe the number of times he'd been in prison. "Mr. Kāliʻi," Zeke asked, "what items did Mr. Hazzard buy at the store where you worked?"

"I . . . I don't remember the items. It was a long time ago."

"You don't remember?"

"No."

"Was it one item or more than one?"

"I don't remember."

"And you don't really remember helping Mr. Hazzard, do you?"

"That I do remember. I helped him more than once."

"Is there some particular reason you remember helping Mr. Hazzard?"

"No. I just remember."

Zeke turned to address Kāliʻi's alibi. "You say you were on Oʻahu on September 2, 1989?"

"Right."

"What about September 1st?" Zeke asked.

"I was there on Oʻahu with my sister."

"Do you have proof?"

"Just the photograph," Kāliʻi answered.

"The photograph doesn't prove you were on Oʻahu on September 1st, does it?"

"No, but I was there."

"So you say. Now there were several daily flights between Oʻahu and the Big Island back in September 1989, weren't there?"

"I guess."

"So, you could have flown back and forth and still attended the football game?"

"Maybe, but I didn't do that."

"So you say. So you say." Zeke shook his head, feigning disgust, and sat down.

The judge asked Alexia if she had another witness. She responded in the negative, and the defense rested. Zeke announced that the prosecution had nothing further, and the judge said he would adjourn for the weekend and schedule the closing argument for the following week.

CHAPTER THIRTY-FIVE

HAVING IDENTIFIED KĀWIKA Keahi as the mastermind behind the Deimos sabotage, the feds turned the government's full investigative resources on him. Facial recognition revealed that he had six US and three foreign passports in different names, including one issued by the Chinese National Immigration Agency in the Ministry of Public Security.

Using various aliases, he'd traveled to Panama and the Cayman Islands, where he'd opened illicit bank accounts never reported to US tax authorities. Using the name on one of Keahi's false passports, the feds hacked the CCA Bank in Panama and discovered a multimillion-dollar account belonging to Keahi's pseudonym. They traced the money back through a series of shell companies to a Hong Kong bank account previously identified as financing espionage on behalf of the Chinese Ministry of State Security.

Keahi was no novice at the spy game. He'd obtained the first of his false passports years ago. The earliest financial deposits to his Panamanian account were more than fifteen years old. He'd sold his honor while still in his twenties. After that, his career path, working his way up the ladder in Senator Chao's office and frequent deposits to his offshore bank accounts, meant he'd long been an agent for the Chinese. He'd deposited large sums in his foreign accounts, indicating that he provided highly valuable information to his Chinese handlers.

Koa and the feds had uncloaked a top-level Chinese spy and a major player in the Deimos conspiracy. Only nine months earlier, on a trip to Japan under his own name, Keahi had used an alias to visit Beijing, most likely to initiate the Deimos sabotage project. He'd also made a clandestine trip under a false passport to Tanjung Priok, the giant port in north Jakarta, Indonesia, where he'd probably coordinated trips by the Indonesian-flagged freighter to Hawaiian waters to deliver disks filled with bad code. And in his local bank account, they found a five-figure donation to the Wood Valley Temple. That explained why Wingate and Kū'ula Kai had been able to hold late-night meetings there without interference.

Koa struggled to understand Keahi's motivation. As teenagers, both had been outraged by the US takeover of the islands. They'd been captivated by the Hawaiian sovereignty movement. Koa had learned better while in military service, realizing that, despite historical injustices, the Islands were infinitely better off as the 50th state. Had Keahi harbored a sovereignty grudge and been trying to exact retribution on the US for the last fifteen years? Maybe, but to Koa, that didn't feel right.

An old memory struck Koa. He and Keahi had gone to see a matinee performance of the 1987 film *The Untouchables* with Sean Connery and Kevin Costner at the 1920s Palace Theater in Hilo. After the movie, they'd bought ice cream cones and walked across Reed's Island to the Waikulu River for a swim. When they'd passed the Shipman House, one of old Hilo's most prestigious homes, Keahi had stopped to take in the grandeur of the historic place that had hosted Queen Lili'uokalani, Jack London, Cecil B. DeMille, and Georgia O'Keeffe. Looking up at the round turret, circular portico, and curved glass windows of the mansion, Keahi had said, "I've grown up dirt poor, but someday I'm going to own a house like that." The scene had stuck in Koa's memory because of the glow in Keahi's eyes and his incredible intensity in announcing his ambition. Improbable as it had seemed back then, Keahi could now afford that house a hundred times over. Avarice was all the motive the traitor had needed.

And he was a world-class traitor—one of the few to cause incalculable damage. He'd been a senior aide to one of the most powerful men in the Senate, a man with almost unlimited access to US military and intelligence secrets. Bureau agents in DC had raided Keahi's Washington apartment and found a safe full of top-secret documents stolen from the Defense Appropriations Subcommittee chairman. They included details of the type and location of US nuclear weapons, assessments of Army, Navy, and Air Force operational readiness, US techniques for cyber warfare, materials obtained from US allies and enemies through electronic espionage, and a hundred other highly classified items. Keahi had given China nearly all of the nation's most vital secrets. It would take years to catalog Keahi's espionage and decades to repair the damage to the country.

Like all unexpected and unprecedented developments, it took Koa a while before he internalized the full significance of Keahi's duplicity. Only by degrees did he come to understand that they'd uncovered a virus a thousand times more potent than the Deimos sabotage. Keahi was the Aaron Burr, the Julius and Ethel Rosenberg, the Robert Hanssen of his generation. The traitor of the decade, if not the century.

Keahi's treachery raised another sensitive question: Was Senator Chao also dirty?

"We've got to accept the possibility that Keahi is taking instructions from the senator," Moreno said.

"I agree we have to consider it, but the Chairman of the Senate Defense Appropriations Subcommittee, an operative of a foreign government? That's hard to believe," Goodling responded.

"How would Keahi have learned about the existence of the Deimos program?" Koa asked.

"The DOD would have briefed the senator, but not his aide," Goodling explained.

"There you have it," Moreno responded. "He's a traitor just like his damned aide."

"Hold on," Koa interceded. "Would the senator enlist his own aide? Nothing about this conspiracy has been that obvious. Isn't it more likely that Keahi got the information surreptitiously?"

"You're right," Goodling responded, "but we have to investigate."

Koa knew the feds working with the Department of Justice, FBI, NSA, and CIA would investigate the senator. It would take time, and Koa doubted that they'd find evidence that the senator was a traitor. Still, it didn't really matter. Keahi's crimes would forever tarnish the senator's reputation. He would be just one more victim of Keahi's treachery.

There was no disagreement that the time had come to put the cuffs on Wingate, Snelling, Kūʻula Kai, and Kāwika Keahi. There was just one problem—they had disappeared. Wingate had either committed suicide or gone into hiding. Snelling had vanished from his apartment overlooking Hilo Bay. Kai had abandoned his trawler, the *Mea Hoʻopaʻi,* and no one was home at Keahi's mansion on Kaʻiulani Drive, not far from the Shipman house. None of them had shown up for work. Once again, the targets had outsmarted the federal surveillance gear. Their vehicles with trackers hadn't moved; turned-off cell phones yielded no location data; cameras and eavesdropping equipment yielded nothing. The four men had vanished like the *ʻehu,* the mist, over the Hawaiian mountains.

The team checked everywhere—airports, hotels, bed-and-breakfast places, and even the hundreds of Airbnb and VBRO rentals spread across the island. They visited car rental companies. They interviewed coworkers seeking information about the men's habits. The four men's pictures were distributed to police patrols and wanted posters placed in post offices and other prominent spots. The feds added the four men to no-fly lists. Police observers or federal agents watched the airports and screened every departing passenger. The team combed financial records looking for any property tied to any of the four. Nothing, zilch, zip.

At the same time, Koa searched their homes for clues to their whereabouts. He'd been to Snelling's apartment several times, so he started with the *Mea Hoʻopaʻi*, Kai's trawler, going through the cabin and every locker trying to get the measure of the man. How did he live? What objects did he hold dear? Where had he traveled? Where might he run to hide? Koa didn't know what he was looking for and only hoped he'd recognize something significant when he saw it. Despite the four-figure deposits to his bank account, the fisherman lived a spartan life, wearing cheap jeans or shorts, tee-shirts, and work boots, eating simple Hawaiian food, and drinking cheap beer. Judging from the variety of empty cans in the vessel, Kai bought his beer in quantity and on sale.

The vessel had a GPS navigation system that tracked its movements. Koa reviewed the history going back for six months. The data verified that the *Mea Hoʻopaʻi* had ventured outside the 12-mile limit east of the Big Island on multiple occasions, most likely to meet the Indonesian-flagged freighter, but offered no clue to Kai's hiding place.

The vessel did serve up surprises. Koa found a hunting rifle and a Smith & Wesson handgun in a storage locker. A thorough review of the GPS data revealed that the *Mea Hoʻopaʻi* had been anchored off the northern coast of the Big Island a short distance from the Waimanu Valley when someone had tried to assassinate Koa on his return trip from the Hazzard cabin with Bobby. Koa had little doubt that Kai had been the shooter and wondered whether Wingate or Keahi had ordered the hit. Ballistic tests on the handgun matched the slug taken from Ward's body. Kai had killed Ward and most likely forged her bloody dying declaration. Koa placed a guard on the vessel, but he didn't expect Kai or his co-conspirators to show up there.

Kāwika Keahi's expensive home on Reed's Island told a different story. Filled with luxurious furniture, precious carpets, and pricey art, it confirmed Koa's hunch that Keahi had betrayed his country for money. Koa guessed the fine and decorative arts alone cost hundreds of thousands of dollars. The man had even imported a Maserati Quattroporte GTS with a sticker price of more than $125,000 to decorate his garage. Koa went through every room of the six-bedroom house. Why, he wondered, did a bachelor need so much space? Maybe just to fulfill his dream of owning a home like the Shipman House.

The spacious formal rooms occupied the front of the expensive single-story house while a long hallway gave access to six bedrooms. Koa went through methodically, opening rooms, closets, cabinets, and drawers. He searched the attic and compared interior and exterior dimensions looking for hidden spaces. With the assistance of a locksmith, he accessed a small safe in the master closet. He found two of Keahi's false passports, numerous financial records, and a top-secret briefing paper on the Deimos program. The documents reconfirmed Keahi's status as a traitor but yielded nothing to help the police find the elusive senator's aide.

Koa had walked the hallway to the bedroom wing a dozen times before focusing on a small Buddhist shrine on the back wall. Koa did not recall his childhood friend being religious, although he had a vague recollection of a tiny Buddhist shrine in Keahi's humble home. This shrine was more elaborate, consisting of a finely lacquered, tiered table with a foot-tall bronze Buddha on the top. The next tier displayed a pair of stone lion-dogs and a Chinese *Bùdài* or laughing Buddha. Lower levels held a three-step stone *stupa*—the *stūpa* of complete victory—commemorating Buddha's extension of his life, a small bowl of water, an offering dish, flowers, and a supply of candles.

Koa recognized that great thought and considerable expense had gone into selecting and positioning the traditional objects. The shrine had meant something to Keahi, who might have worshiped before it, replacing the water and flowers, lighting a candle, and making some small offerings. The alter led Koa to a connection he'd missed. He hadn't recognized it at the time, but the round disk Keahi had fingered at Cronies bar had been a Wheel of Dharma, one of the auspicious symbols of Buddha. The image of Keahi wearing his Buddhist charm prostrate before his Buddhist altar contrasted sharply, like a split personality, with the Maserati in the garage and the opulence of the house.

Staring at the shrine, Koa focused on the stone lion-dogs. They were *familiar*. Sure, he'd seen similar objects in pictures and museums, but these were *exact* replicas of something—something he'd seen. He let his mind float into free association. Buddhist . . . lion-dogs . . . shrines . . . money . . . money. Then, it came to him. Keahi had given large sums of money to the Wood Valley Temple, and the lion-dogs in Keahi's shrine were *exact* replicas of the two much larger lion-dogs standing guard at the Wood Valley Temple.

There was no inconsistency between Keahi's avarice and his religious shrine. They were both aspects of the same personality. How ironic—the *stūpa* of complete victory—precisely what Keahi sought for his foreign master in an utter perversion of the Buddhist faith. A man, Koa realized, dressed as a Buddhist monk—who'd donated lavishly—could hide at the Wood Valley Temple complex forever.

Koa had to proceed carefully. Although optimistic, he wasn't sure that his fugitives had holed up at the Wood Valley Temple complex. The monastery was a revered house of worship where the Dalai Lama himself had taught. Koa couldn't go blundering in on a hunch, and any surveillance had to be surreptitious to avoid alerting his quarry if they were present.

Koa thought about approaching one of the monks to inquire about guests arriving in the last few days but rejected that approach. He didn't know any of the monks and worried they might be protective of a major donor like Keahi, who'd contributed thousands of dollars to their charitable foundation.

The complex consisted of the temple, flanked by two peripheral structures that served as living quarters for the monks and the permanent staff. A separate guest house for visitors and retreat participants sat farther back in the forest. Pathways through the woods behind the temple provided an idyllic setting for meditation.

If Keahi or his co-conspirators holed up indoors, they would remain undetected. But Koa was betting on claustrophobia and arrogance. Rather than stay cooped up, their targets would likely walk and exercise in the woodland behind the complex. Rotating surveillance teams in and out of the Wood Valley area posed an unacceptable risk of discovery, so Koa decided to use tiny wireless cameras.

With equipment provided by the feds, Koa and Moreno parked down the road from the temple grounds at two thirty a.m. that night. Although it was a dark and moonless, Koa and Moreno had night vision goggles. They entered the forest and quietly worked their way around behind the monastery. A confirmed urban dweller, Moreno appeared uncomfortable in the unfamiliar forest. When they heard grunting sounds not far away, Koa put his hand on the FBI agent's shoulder to hold him still until the wild boars wandered off in a different direction. It took them two hours to find the optimum locations near footpaths and trails, where they installed a dozen tiny cameras, checking each one to make sure it broadcast properly.

Because the cameras had a limited wireless range, Koa enlisted a rancher friend with a property near the temple. The team moved receivers and communications gear into an unused outbuilding on the ranch property and set up a command and observation post.

Local police and FBI agents took turns monitoring the video feeds. It rained the following day, and there was no human activity on the forest trails. With clearing weather overnight, some of the monks ventured out the next morning. They had short-cropped hair or shaved heads and wore simple brown or dark red, hooded robes, but most left their hoods hanging down. They walked barefoot or in sandals, typically alone or in pairs, along the forest paths, occasionally stopping to meditate at small shrines or water features scattered along the forest trails.

Koa was watching the live surveillance feed when he noticed two monks of interest. They, too, wore flowing dark robes, but unlike the other monks, kept their hoods up, which mostly concealed their faces. One wore black leather shoes, and the other had on running shoes. Unfortunately, the bird's-eye views from the cameras mounted high in the trees made it difficult to make out their faces beneath the hoods. The pair walked a lengthy forest path before returning to the guest quarters but, unlike most other monks, did not stop to meditate.

Sometime later, two similarly dressed monks repeated the exercise. This time one wore boots and was noticeably bulkier and taller than the others who had walked the trails. Once again, they completed their circuit without stopping at any of the shrines. Koa suspected he'd spotted all of the four fugitives, but hadn't made a definite identification and couldn't say for sure.

The team caught a break late on the following day. The robed figures wearing black oxfords and running shoes were back out on the forest paths when an 'io, a Hawaiian hawk, uttered a series of piercing screeches and launched into the air from a treetop. Attracted by the bird's shriek and the movement, both men looked up, almost directly into the lens of one of the fed's cameras.

The one on the right in running shoes was Kāwika Keahi, Senator Chao's aide. The one on the left wearing black leather oxfords was Wingate. The son of a bitch had faked his suicide. Koa's hunch had paid off, and he was now almost sure that Snelling and Kai were also hiding out at the temple complex.

Now they had to formulate and execute a plan to arrest Keahi and his co-conspirators. Moreno wanted to surround the guest house and bust in with guns drawn, but cooler heads prevailed. Given their targets' record of violence and the assassination attempt on Koa, the team could not risk attempting an arrest inside the temple guest house. The risk of collateral damage was too high.

They decided to call in more support, surround the compound, and wait for one or more of their targets to take their next walk in the woods. That way, they could make the arrest safely away from any innocent bystanders without tipping off the others.

The Hilo swat team, with reinforcements from the FBI, surrounded the Wood Valley Temple complex shortly after midnight. Goodling assigned Moreno to supervise the circumference forces, while Koa, Makanui, and Goodling covered the main trail followed most frequently by the monks. Moving as far as feasible from the temple buildings, Makanui hid in a tangled mass of waist-high 'awapuhi, wild ginger. Simultaneously, Koa and Goodling concealed themselves in a thicket of *uluhe* ferns roughly fifty feet farther up the pathway. By separating, they hoped to confront their targets between their positions, cutting off any attempted escape.

The temple bell sounded its heavenly note at four a.m. calling the monks to meditation and prayers. Lights came on in the monks' quarters, and an hour later, the melodious sound of Tibetan chants floated through the nearby forest. Daybreak brought clear skies and chilly temperatures with light trade winds and fleecy white clouds. Breakfast in the monks' kitchen followed at eight a.m., and by nine a.m., a few monks began to walk their forest paths. Because of the cool weather, most wore their hoods, making it difficult to distinguish one from another. Still, at ground level, with powerful binoculars, Koa searched for Wingate's or Keahi's face. Time and monks passed. The temple bell announced lunch. At two p.m., the monks gathered inside the temple for a ceremony where a handful of tourists joined them. Moreno's team watched the parking lot to ensure that none of the fugitives left with the visitors.

In the late afternoon, when Mauna Loa's looming bulk cast a shadow over the forest, two hooded monks came slowly up the forest path. Koa focused his binoculars on their faces and then their feet. He saw Wingate on the right wearing black leather oxfords and the fisherman Kai on the left, plodding along in his knee-high, rubber boots. Koa let them come closer, getting farther away from the temple complex. And still closer until they were deep in the forest far from the temple buildings and past the wild ginger where Makanui hid.

When Koa gave the signal, he and Goodling, guns drawn, stepped out of cover. "Police. Stop where you are! Keep your hands where we can see them!"

Ignoring their warning, Wingate's right hand reached for a slit in the side of his robe.

"Don't do it, Wingate!" Koa commanded.

The X-CO executive froze and slowly raised his hands.

"You are making a mistake," Wingate said. "We can make you rich beyond your wildest dreams."

"If you think we're going to sell out the country, you're a fool," Koa shot back.

Kai suddenly spun around and ran, his rubber boots pounding the forest path.

If Wingate thought the fisherman's sudden break would distract Koa, he was mistaken. The chief detective never wavered, robbing Wingate of any chance to pull the gun concealed beneath his robe.

Forty feet back up the trail, Makanui sprang from her hiding place and tackled the fleeing fisherman, jumped on his back, swept his arms behind him, and fastened her cuffs on him before he had a chance to resist. He could bench press 250 pounds, but he was no match for Makanui.

Koa kept his gun on Wingate while Goodling handcuffed him and took his weapon. "Where is Keahi?" Koa demanded.

Wingate smiled arrogantly, and Koa felt a shiver run down his back. "Gone," Wingate said before adding, "beyond your jurisdiction."

Keahi had slipped away! How? Could Moreno have missed him among the guests departing the earlier ceremony? Koa dismissed the thought. It didn't matter how. What mattered was where. Wingate had said Keahi had gone "beyond your jurisdiction." Not an airport; they were all under surveillance. A private plane? A ship? The traitors had used a ship to smuggle their disks. Keahi might use the same route to escape. Koa took off running, leaving Goodling and the police officers to escort Wingate and Kai through the woods to a plain-wrapper police vehicle hidden on the forest's edge.

By the time Koa reached the road, he had instructed the police dispatcher to get a chopper in the air. While he waited, he called the

Coast Guard. Twenty minutes later, he was airborne flying east over Pāhala toward the open ocean and had established contact with the USS *Kimball*, one of the Coast Guard's newest superfast cutters, operating out of the Coast Guard base in Hilo.

Once over the ocean, Koa spotted a freighter ten miles away near the horizon. He couldn't distinguish its colors given the distance but had little doubt that it flew the Indonesian flag. Moments later, he caught the flash of the foamy white wake trailing behind a speed-boat racing toward the freighter. Koa didn't know whether the Coast Guard could stop Keahi's boat or if they would board an Indonesian-flagged ship in international waters, but he didn't want to find out. He needed to stop Keahi before the traitor could ren-dezvous with the freighter, and he knew it was going to be close. Too damn close.

The speedboat grew in size as the chopper quickly narrowed the distance. Koa saw the freighter slow and begin to turn toward the approaching motorboat. The gap between the two vessels narrowed. Crewmen appeared on the vessel's deck and lowered a rope ladder. Far off to his left, Koa caught sight of the USS *Kimball*, barreling toward the freighter at high speed, but she was too far away to inter-cept Keahi before he boarded the ship.

"Can you stop or at least slow the speedboat?" Koa asked the pi-lot over the intercom.

"Don't know," came the terse reply.

The chopper rocked violently as the pilot swung out to the side before turning back, diving close to water level, and heading into the rapidly closing gap between the freighter and Keahi's boat. The he-lo's downdraft churned up the ocean, throwing up clouds of spray, and making the speedboat jump and bob like a child's toy on the sea's surface. Watching from the chopper, Koa saw Keahi struggling to stand with a gun pointed directly at the helicopter.

"GUN!" Koa yelled, and the chopper began to weave back and forth, trying to avoid Keahi's shots while still roiling the ocean around the speedboat.

The small craft's erratic bouncing forced Keahi back down into his seat, but not before he got off two shots at the police chopper, one of which clanged off the chopper's metal tail somewhere behind Koa. The chopper lurched through a 180-degree turn before racing back into the gap. This time Koa slid open the side door, dropped to the floor, and prepared to fire back at Keahi. He'd disrupt Keahi's aim even if he didn't stop the speedboat.

As the helicopter shot back into the gap, it stirred up mountains of water that tossed Keahi's boat around like a rubber duck in a bathtub. Keahi hung on to a railing while pointing his gun up toward the chopper. Keahi's shot missed. Rather than shoot to kill Keahi, whom he wanted to capture alive, Koa fired three times, trying to disable the craft.

The speedboat veered to the side but continued to race forward, not fifty yards from the Indonesian freighter. "Hold on," the chopper pilot's voice came over the intercom. "I'm going in on top of him."

The helo jerked in a tight circle and dove for the speedboat. Keahi's gun flashed, bullets ricocheted off metal, and the helicopter shuddered. Koa opened fire, pumping round after round into the boat's engine and gas tank. The speedboat barreled ahead—forty yards from the freighter . . . thirty yards . . . twenty yards—before an explosion rocked the speedboat. Flames shot up into the air. Koa watched as Keahi, so close to his destination, abandoned ship and jumped into the churning sea. Seconds later, a second, massive explosion eviscerated the speedboat, sending clouds of smoke and debris into the air around the helicopter.

A loud, electronically amplified voice blasted over the ocean. "Indonesian-flagged vessel *Bumi*. This is the US Coast Guard cutter

Kimball. Turn away. Turn away now." The message repeated over and over.

Koa pulled himself off the floor of the chopper and looked out. He could see sailors manning the forward gun on the *Kimball*. The Coast Guard cutter meant business, and the Indonesian-flagged vessel slowly retreated. Other seamen aboard the *Kimball* scrambled to rescue Keahi from the roiling ocean. Koa had nailed his traitor.

CHAPTER THIRTY-SIX

WHILE KOA WAS chasing Keahi, Makanui set her sights on Snelling. Although the surveillance cameras had initially recorded four hooded monks, leading the team to suspect all four fugitives were at the temple complex, they had not positively identified Snelling. So, Makanui wasn't sure he was on the temple grounds. Keahi had slipped through the police cordon around the facility, and Snelling, if he had been there, might also have eluded them.

Makanui began her search for the X-CO security guard at the temple guesthouse. She was well aware that a confrontation might endanger innocent bystanders, but with daylight fading, she feared her quarry could easily escape into the forest under cover of darkness. She phoned Officer Horita, who was nearby as part of the perimeter force, asking him to join her and back her up as she hunted for Snelling.

The guesthouse, a rectangular, two-story structure, had originally been a rustic plantation temple. It now served as a place for up to sixteen guests, complete with a kitchen, dining *lānai*, and a meditation room dedicated to Tara, the female bodhisattva of enlightenment.

Makanui and Horita approached from the back and hugged the guesthouse's walls, ducking below the windows to avoid detection as they circled to the entry doors on the opposite side of the building. With guns drawn, they entered a hallway running the length of the structure. One by one, they checked the common areas, the four first-floor bedrooms, and the adjoining dormitory, finding unmade beds and clothing in two of the rooms, but no guests.

Moving silently up the stairs to the second floor, the two police officers checked each of the three upstairs bedrooms, finding them empty. A thumping sound drew them toward the meditation space. Approaching the double doors of that room, Makanui motioned Horita to the left while she took the right. On her signal, the two burst into the room with guns at the ready. Inside, they found a man hogtied and gagged on the floor, struggling furiously to free himself. Directing Horita to cover her, she knelt beside the stranger and removed his gag.

"My daughter. You've got to help my daughter. Please. You've got to help her," the man gasped, pleading frantically.

"Slow down. Tell me what happened," Makanui responded calmly while she cut the cords binding the man's hands and feet. "What's your name?"

"I'm John. We're guests, me and my daughter. On a school break. He took her. He's going to hurt her. I know it. You have to help her."

"Tell me what happened," Makanui said, her tone more forceful.

"This guy, some kind of visiting monk, not one of the regular monks. He went crazy. Barging in here. He had a gun . . . tied me up and took my daughter. Lisa's only fourteen, and he took her."

Makanui pulled out a picture of Snelling. "Is this the guy?"

"Yeah, that's him."

"When?"

"I don't know. Half an hour ago. Maybe forty minutes. I'm not sure."

"Did he say anything? Give you any idea where he was going?"

"No. But my daughter, she has her cell phone. And there's an app on it. It's how I keep track of her."

Makanui knew about location tracking apps. The HPD anti-terror group where she'd worked had used them. She realized that they might have caught a break. It depended on whether the girl or Snelling still had the girl's cell and whether it was still on, maybe hidden on her person. "Show me," she demanded.

The anguished father pulled a phone from his pocket, unlocked it, selected an app, and loaded a map on which a location flag blinked rhythmically. Makanui had studied the area around the temple complex intensively while preparing for the police operation and saw the girl's position moving slowly toward the Wood Valley homesteads up the road from the temple. She guessed that Snelling and the girl were on foot, moving toward the remote farm community searching for a car or motorbike he could steal to speed his escape. The police could easily block the only road out of the valley, but there were backroads, dirt tracks, and trails into the surrounding slopes of Mauna Loa where a fugitive might hide for days.

Makanui first called Sergeant Awani, leader of the swat team, and then Goodling. She told the DOJ lawyer that Snelling had taken a young female hostage and appeared to be on foot headed toward the Wood Valley homesteads. "Officer Horita and I are going after him. The Hilo swat team will back us up. Everybody else blocks the road and stays back 'til we figure how to get the hostage out."

Goodling hesitated, but given the primary jurisdiction of the Hawai'i police, had little choice. "Okay, but keep us posted."

Makanui started for the door, but John caught her arm. "I'm coming. Lisa's my daughter."

Makanui recognized that the kid's father might be able to help and nodded. "Okay, but you do what we say, got it?"

He nodded.

She considered having the police dispatcher issue a warning to all the residents of the tiny Wood Valley farming community. Still, she feared losing control of the situation to a group of rural homeowners who undoubtedly owned firearms. It was too risky for both the residents and the hostage.

By the time Makanui had briefed the swat team, and they'd driven up the road to the edge of the homesteads, the location flag on John's phone held steady, indicating that Snelling and his hostage had sought refuge in a farmhouse on the northern edge of the farm community. Coordinating with Awani, she had the swat team surround the house and got the owners' names and phone numbers from the dispatcher. There were two numbers, both cell phones, so they would be useful only if one or both of the residents were home. She sent Horita to the neighbors who reported that the Japanese couple who owned the small farm was in Hilo visiting family.

When she was sure that the swat team was in position, Makanui called Snelling's cell but got no answer. Using a bullhorn provided by the swat team, she tried to open a dialogue with him. "Mr. Snelling, we know you're in the house. You're surrounded and have nowhere to go. I'm going to call your cell so we can talk." She rang his cell, but still no answer.

She saw a shadow in a front window and tried again with the bullhorn. "Your buddies are all in police custody. We know you didn't kill Baldwin. You're not wanted for murder. Don't make it worse. Let Lisa come out, and let's end this before anyone gets hurt."

Another flash of movement at the edge of a window provided Snelling's only response.

Seconds ticked away into a minute and then longer. From her hostage negotiation training at the Federal Law Enforcement Training

Center, Makanui knew Snelling's silence was a bad sign. She needed to get him talking and try to ease tensions. De-escalate—that was the negotiator's mantra.

Unable to reach Snelling and determined to rescue his hostage, she turned to Awani. "I'm going in. Cover me."

He started to protest, but she cut him off. "I'm wearing a vest, and I know what I'm doing."

Back on the bullhorn, she announced, "I'm Makanui. I'm a police officer. I'm unarmed, and I'm coming in." She made a show of handing her Glock to Awani, and, with arms outstretched and hands visible, she started slowly toward the farmhouse. The walk was not nearly as long as her boat ride in the Sulu Sea waiting for the pirates, but the hundred yards or so to the front porch, unarmed and out in the open, seemed to take forever.

She found the front door unlocked and slowly pushed it open. "It's me. Makanui," she said, using her first name to help establish rapport. "I'm unarmed and just want to talk." She heard no resistance to her presence and cautiously stepped into the farmhouse's center hall, noting archways to rooms on each side. Sensing people to her left, she moved in that direction and, before passing under the left arch, repeated, "I'm unarmed and just want to talk."

Stepping into the room, she saw Snelling slumped against the front wall beside a window with his Glock pointed directly at her. Lisa sat curled up in a cushioned armchair across the room, sobbing softly. Unrestrained, she appeared scared but unhurt.

Makanui remained focused on Snelling. Her instincts and training told her he was in a bad way. He appeared drawn with dark circles fanning out beneath his eyes, and several days' growth of facial hair covered his now sallow complexion. Exhaustion etched his face, and his hands trembled like a man having crashed following a manic high. She'd seen similar things in stressed-out amphetamine users. He was in an unpredictable state and might easily do something rash.

"You don't look well. Can I get you some water or some food?" she asked.

"Shut up," he mumbled, his gun still pointed at her.

"Kirk," she said softly, "you don't want to hurt this girl. I can help you out of this mess."

"Really? How?" he asked.

"Tell me what you want," she responded.

"A car. And tell the police to back off."

"I'm afraid I can't do that," she said quietly. "I need to take this child back to her father."

He closed his eyes for a moment in what might have been resignation. The girl started to say something, but Makanui motioned to her, and Lisa remained silent.

Makanui thought about rushing Snelling and trying to disarm him, but she was too far away, and he too likely to shoot. Her only option was to be patient, keep him talking, and slowly wear him down. "You haven't killed anyone. Don't make this worse."

"It's all fucked up. I shouldn't have protected Wingate."

Makanui kept her voice soft and dispassionate. "It's not too late. We can help you."

"Nobody can help me."

"That's not true. You don't want to hurt this child. She's not part of this."

His eyes shifted to the girl, and his gun hand quivered. For a moment, she thought Snelling was going to drop the gun, but his moment of perceived weakness passed, and his weapon steadied back on her.

Although he'd been brazen in kidnapping the girl, Makanui sensed he was ambivalent about the child. He'd taken her but left her unharmed and unrestrained. The lack of restraints was, Makanui thought, a good sign.

"She's just an innocent kid, Kirk. You don't want to hurt her."

Snelling blinked and stared at Makanui, his expression distant and unfocused, seemingly looking right through her.

"Let her go. Let her go back to her father."

He mumbled something she couldn't make out, something about a sister.

Taking a risk because she didn't know the background, Makanui tried to keep him talking. "You have a sister?"

"She's dead," Snelling said with undisguised finality.

Makanui understood. Snelling was telling her that he was alone in the world. He had no one and little reason to live. She feared he was suicidal and would take her and the girl with him. She had to get his gun or at least get the child out before the whole thing went sideways.

"Please, Kirk, give me the gun." She held out her hand but did not attempt to approach him. His gun wobbled, but he remained silent. She wasn't going to disarm him, not without putting herself and the child in mortal danger.

She watched him still slumped against the wall, obviously lost in misery, for another long moment before choosing her words carefully. Again, speaking calmly and spacing her words, she said, "I'm going to take the child outside and back to her father."

He said nothing.

Watching him closely, she took a single sidestep toward Lisa. He made no effort to track her movement, and his gun remained pointed straight ahead into thin air. With Snelling seemingly transfixed, she continued to inch in Lisa's direction. When she extended her hand, Lisa understood the gesture and took Makanui's hand as the girl cautiously rose to her feet. In deliberate slow motion, Makanui led the girl step by step across the room. Snelling watched them through half-closed eyes, but his gun remained fixed in his outstretched hand pointed into space. As Makanui and Lisa reached the archway, Makanui pushed the girl into the hall and quickly followed her.

Once in the hallway, Makanui positioned Lisa in front of her and guided the girl outside. Using her body to shield the child from the house, Makanui walked Lisa toward the street. Halfway there, Lisa caught sight of her father, broke into a run, and fell into his open arms.

Behind them, Makanui heard a gunshot. Depression and exhaustion had worked their revenge on Kirk Snelling.

CHAPTER THIRTY-SEVEN

THE MORNING AFTER arresting Keahi, Koa was back in court when the judge called upon the lawyers to make their closing arguments. Zeke went first and was compelling. He pounded on Kāliʻi's motive, his dislike for Hazzard, and his threat to kill the sugar baron. He repeated the refrain: fingerprints don't lie, but ʻAnalū Kāliʻi lied. Kāliʻi was in Hazzard's cabin. Why Zeke asked, would Kāliʻi deny it? Because he'd killed Anthony Hazzard. "He made the threat, and his fingerprint and his lies leave no doubt that he carried out his threat."

Alexia's closing argument was equally convincing, with its focus on reasonable doubt. The rope around Hazzard's neck, the coroner's suicide conclusion, and the absence of man-made wounds on the body created doubt that anyone had killed Hazzard. Kāliʻi's job at the general store explained the presence of his fingerprint on an object in the cabin, and that fingerprint did not prove that Kāliʻi had ever been in the cabin, let alone killed Anthony Hazzard. "Even before you consider ʻAnalū Kāliʻi's alibi, the prosecutor's case is riddled with reasonable doubt."

Finally, Alexia held up the Aloha Stadium photograph. "Now, ladies and gentlemen, let's talk about Kāliʻi's ironclad alibi. This picture, taken on the evening of September 2, 1989, proves that Kāliʻi could *not* have been at Hazzard's cabin when the police say the man died. You heard the prosecutor try to argue that Kāli'i might have flown back to the Big Island, but that dog won't hunt. Detective Kaohi, the prosecutor's own witness, admitted that it was a ten-hour hike to that cabin and ten hours back out. Add that to the time getting to and from airports and in the air, and what do you get? Analū Kāli'i couldn't have been in Hazzard's cabin during the twenty-four hours before or after the Aloha Stadium football game. He could *not* have killed Anthony Hazzard."

The judge charged the jury and sent them to deliberate at eleven thirty a.m. Koa hoped for a quick verdict of acquittal, but the jury failed to cooperate. The judge had lunch delivered, and the jury adjourned without deciding at five thirty p.m. The following day they deliberated for another eight hours without reaching a verdict.

At ten thirty a.m. on the third day of deliberations, the jury sent a note to the judge, who summoned everyone back to the courtroom. The jury had reached an impasse. They were deadlocked. The judge gave them a shotgun charge, also known as a hammer or dynamite charge:

It is your duty to decide the case if you can conscientiously do so; you should listen, with a disposition to be convinced, to each other's arguments; if much the larger number were for conviction, a dissenting juror should consider whether his or her doubt was a reasonable one which made no impression upon the minds of so many others, equally honest, equally intelligent. If, upon the other hand, the majority were for acquittal, the minority ought to ask themselves whether they might not reasonably doubt the correctness of a judgment which was not concurred in by the majority.

Although the judge's charge was classic legalese, he was, in essence, directing the jury to give it their best shot. There was much chatter in the courtroom as the jury returned to the jury room. The half-dozen spectators seemed about equally divided. Half guessed that most jurors favored conviction, and the other half dissented, believing most jurors favored acquittal.

Koa felt under enormous stress. He had worked through many tense, high-profile cases. He'd sweated jury verdicts involving those he'd arrested and brought to justice, but never before had the outcome of a trial weighed so heavily upon him. Never before had one been so personal. He saw his future as tenuous. He could not, under any circumstance, let an innocent man go to jail for his crime. He wouldn't be able to live with himself. If the jury convicted Kāli'i, he'd have no choice but to confess, losing everything he'd worked to achieve. His job. His relationship with Nālani. His standing in the community. His self-respect.

He'd be locked up. In jail with those whom he caught, arrested, and prosecuted. He knew about cops sent to prison. They got beaten. Most survived only a few months or years behind bars before they went crazy or got knifed. He doubted he could face it.

For the first time, he thought about taking his own life. He'd go swimming off one of Hawai'i's beautiful black sand beaches. Slowly, he'd stroke farther and farther away from land. He'd swim until his muscles gave out ... until he could swim no more, and in a cathartic release gently slip beneath the surface of the sea. It would be a peaceful end. That would be the ultimate irony. He'd never imagined that staging Hazzard's suicide could lead to his own self-inflicted death. He wondered if he could do it. Maybe ... maybe with enough alcohol or the pills he'd gotten from his doctor.

It was, he suddenly realized, the coward's way out. And he couldn't do that to Nālani. She'd blame herself, and that would only magnify

her pain. No, if the worst happened, he'd be a man. He'd look Nālani
and Zeke and all his friends and family in the eye and confess to his
crime. It was the least he could do.

At four p.m., the jury sent another note, and everyone reassembled in the courtroom. The jury reported that it was still hopelessly
deadlocked. The judge had no choice but to declare a mistrial. A
visibly upset Bobby Hazzard stormed out of the courtroom. Koa sat
immobile while others left, stunned by an overwhelming sense that
the ancient Hawaiian gods had come to his rescue. He could breathe
again, and maybe even smile. He wanted to race home, wrap his
arms around Nālani, kiss her, and take her to bed. Then, by degrees,
the reality of the situation seeped into his consciousness. There still
might be a retrial.

Zeke and his assistant hung around. They wanted, Koa knew, to
talk to one or more of the jurors. They wanted to understand how
the jury had come to its impasse. That knowledge would help them
decide whether to retry Kāli'i. A vote of eleven to one for conviction
would almost certainly mean a retrial. The reverse would make that
unlikely.

Koa was dying to know how the jury split but knew he shouldn't
appear too interested in the outcome. He returned to police headquarters after arranging a dinner with Zeke for later that evening.
He'd live with the uncertainty until they met.

They sat out on the veranda at the Hilo Bay Cafe on the waterfront, cooled by a light breeze wafting off the bay. To Koa's surprise,
Zeke ordered a bottle of champagne. The prosecutor had just failed
to win a murder case, a defeat that would typically put him in a dark
mood. If anyone should be celebrating, it should be Koa, who had
at least momentarily dodged disaster. The oddity made Koa uneasy.
"What are we celebrating?" he asked.

"Justice, my friend," Zeke responded, elaborating no further.

They talked politics and other cases until Zeke said, "I hear you arrested Kāwika Keahi, the senator's aide, and his co-conspirators. Everybody but Snelling, that is."

"Yeah," Koa acknowledged. "I'm still in shock that my childhood buddy sold out his country. And tried to get me killed."

Zeke raised his champagne glass. "Well, here's to justice for the traitors and murderers."

They drank. "So, Snelling answered his last roll call?" Zeke asked.

Koa nodded affirmatively. "Seems like he lost it. Went and kidnapped a kid. Makanui tracked him. When she found him holed up in a farmhouse, he wouldn't talk, so she went in. Unarmed. Said he was all messed up, crashing from some sort of high, but she got the kid out."

"Pretty gutsy," Zeke said.

"Yeah. She's tough," Koa acknowledged. "Awani told me she shielded the kid with her body before Snelling shot himself. She's a real find for the department. And for me. I can see us working together on most everything. She sees the job the same way we do."

"I should get to know her better. Send her around to see me. Nothing formal. Just a chat."

"You got it."

"So, Wingate was the top dog inside X-CO?" Zeke asked.

"Yeah, and a traitor to his own company."

"That's what I've heard, but why?" Zeke responded.

"He's a strange bird. The feds are still trying to understand his motives. It turns out he was part of the Chinese 'Thousand Talents' program, where China recruited US scientists to Chinese universities for the purpose of stealing US technology. Wingate was working on secure communications protocols at Beijing University when he met Zhou Li, and they had preliminary discussions about using Wingate's communication expertise for what became Deimos. The

Chinese state security people got wind of their negotiations, and that's when they began turning Wingate against America.

"Remember Wingate's over-the-top reaction to protesters; well, he's a classic, self-absorbed narcissist with a need for unfettered control. The Chinese authorities profiled that flaw and exploited it. They flaunted their rising economic power, the efficiency of their state-run capitalism, and the absence of any concerns about ethics. And, of course, they promised Wingate billions in funding, an un-limited workforce, personal control of every aspect of his research, and fifty percent of the worldwide profits from the sale of his technology—probably more than a hundred times what he received from Zhou Li. All he had to do was take Zhou Li's deal and use it against America. After that, he could bring his technology back to China and become a billionaire. He bought the pitch. Then, when he figured we were closing in, he had one overriding objective—to prevent us from identifying Keahi as the ultimate traitor."

Zeke leaned forward, intent on understanding. "Unpack that for me."

"We had our Manchurian candidate here in Hawai'i. The Chi-nese invested millions and decades in Kāwika Keahi, developing a spy in the office of a leading US senator who served as the chair-man of the Senate Defense Appropriations Subcommittee. In the real world, Keahi was a hundred times more valuable to China than Deimos.

"When Wingate learned that we were closing in on the Deimos saboteurs, he decided, or more likely was instructed by the Chinese, to protect Keahi's role at all costs. He faked his own suicide, figuring that would be the end of our investigation. He apparently believed we'd have no way of discovering Keahi's role, but Wingate made a crucial error. He didn't know that I'd tracked him to Wood Valley and identified Kū'ula Kai as his conduit to Keahi."

"Damn," Zeke swore softly, "the Deimos stuff is bad enough. But Keahi's value as an intelligence asset must have been over the top. He was in a position to give the Chinese everything in our arsenal for years to come." The prosecutor paused. "How'd you figure Wingate was still alive and hiding at the temple?"

"I got my first inkling at the suicide scene he staged on Chain of Craters Road. It was too perfect. There's an irrationality to suicide that's inconsistent with perfection. That was one clue, and then I noticed that the car was facing the wrong way." Koa explained the significance of that anomaly. "I guessed that someone had murdered Wingate or Wingate had faked it. No way was it a suicide."

"That's all you had?" Zeke asked.

"It was enough," Koa responded with a smile.

"And when did you put it all together and figure out where they were hiding?"

"We found big donations in Keahi's bank account to the Wood Valley Temple. Later, I found a Buddhist shrine in Keahi's mansion, just like the temple. That's when I thought he might be hiding out there. When we discovered one of the monks wearing black leather oxfords—like Wingate always wore—we knew. Good police work is all about shoe leather," Koa responded with a grin.

"Brilliant, Sherlock." Zeke raised his glass again.

Koa could finally wait no longer. "Sorry about your loss in the Kāli'i case," he said to prompt a discussion.

"I'm not," Zeke responded uncharacteristically.

Surprised by Zeke's comment, Koa said, "I thought you had a strong case and were gung-ho for a conviction."

"I got pressured into it. It's not a case I'd have ordinarily pursued."

"You, the incorruptible prosecutor, pressured?" Koa responded with a puzzled look.

"I told you that Senator Chao came to see me about the case. I didn't tell you that I also had calls from the attorney general and the governor."

The news stunned Koa.

Zeke took another sip of champagne before resuming. "The senator has serious political clout. He and his senate colleagues pour billions of dollars into the state. Mostly for defense, but Hawai'i also gets more than its share of pork-barrel dollars. When he wants something back from this state, he usually gets it."

Koa felt his heart accelerate for fear the political pressure would ensure a retrial.

"Somebody," Zeke continued, "and I'm guessing it was Kāwika Keahi, got the senator bent out of shape over Bobby Hazzard."

Koa could only hope that the Kāli'i mistrial would end the senator's campaign against Kāli'i. With the arrest of his principal aide on treason charges, the senator should have bigger things to worry about. To test that theory, he said, "I suppose the senator's influence means you're going to retry Kāli'i?"

"Not going to happen," Zeke responded.

Koa struggled to restrain his overwhelming sense of relief. "When did you make that decision?"

"This afternoon. The jury was eleven-to-one for acquittal, but more importantly, after your friend Alexia sprang her alibi defense, and the jury deadlocked, I chatted with her and checked out Kāli'i's story. I tried an innocent man." He paused. "I don't know how Kāli'i hooked up with your favorite lawyer, but he's lucky as hell he got Alexia to represent him. She saved his butt."

"So, it's over?" Koa asked.

"Most likely," Zeke responded. "Before the trial, your friend Keahi said they were trying to get the US Attorney in Honolulu to bring a civil rights case against Kāli'i."

Koa tried to keep the alarm out of his voice. "Will that work?"

Zeke grinned. "A thirty-year-old civil rights case against a poor Hawaiian native for the killing of a rich white sugar baron. In Hawai'i? And after the poor Hawaiian native proves a thirty-year-old alibi and comes close to an acquittal. What do you think?"

CHAPTER THIRTY-EIGHT

THE HAWAI'I POLICE kept Keahi in jail while the feds arranged to transfer him to a secure federal facility. Once there, Keahi would be in for months of investigation and debriefing to determine the incalculable damage he'd done to national security. Koa had only one opportunity to confront his former childhood friend. He had Keahi placed in an interrogation room, turned off the recording equipment, and made sure they were alone. Sitting opposite the former senator's aide, Koa asked the question that had kept him awake the previous two nights. "Growing up, we were friends. As close as brothers. When did that change, Keahi? What happened to our friendship?"

Keahi stared unflinchingly at Koa, remaining silent for a long time before saying, "You don't understand, do you?"

"Enlighten me," Koa responded.

"You were the glory boy. Straight-A grades. Rainbow Warriors football star. Babe magnet. Special Forces. Youngest detective on the Hilo force. Promoted to chief detective. Dating the hottest chick on the island. Hero catches Pōhakuloa killer. Hilo cop brings down a high-flying candidate. Police detective avenges the death of school kids. You've always had it all." Keahi fell silent, and Koa waited.

"What did I have? Mediocre grades. No athletic ability. Few prospects for college. Barely graduated from Kapiʻolani Community College. Whoever heard of KCC? It's not exactly the Harvard of the Pacific. Lucky to be an *unpaid* intern. A lousy assistant job, standing in the back row at news conferences. Fetching papers. Escorting visitors. Working for a pittance." Keahi raised his voice. "A fucking lowlife aide! As common as stray cats in DC. God, how I hate that 'aide' word."

Although stunned by his friend's bitterness, Koa kept his demeanor relaxed and his face impassive, waiting for Keahi to continue.

"A Chinese agent approached me while I was at KCC. It took a while, but he promised to make me rich. I did a few little jobs for him. He paid me, and one thing led to another. Then they had me work on one of the senator's early campaigns. The senator and I hit it off, he hired me, and I made the big time. I had the money to be *somebody*."

Keahi locked eyes with Koa before continuing. "When Wingate killed Baldwin, I knew you were going to make trouble. You're so damn tenacious. I'd long thought your golden boy image was too good to be true. The Koa I knew growing up threw a rock through a neighbor's window, smoked weed, and ran with the sovereignty brothers. And I always wondered about that missing week."

Koa felt his stomach muscles tighten but still maintained his calm.

"I knew you hadn't gone fishing like you said. I came looking for you, and your tackle was still in the shed out back of your house. I figured you'd shacked up with a girl. It wasn't until years later, long after Hazzard's death, that I wondered. Yeah, I knew your dad had words with Hazzard. I knew you were broken up about your father's death. I remembered seeing the bruises on your shoulder. I wondered, maybe even suspected. Yeah, I wondered if the golden boy hadn't done the deed." Keahi stared directly at Koa. "Was I right?"

Koa chose his words carefully. "That's crazy. You're out of your mind. Is that why you invented a phony grandson, got the senator to back his investigation, and lied to me about Anthony Hazzard being your father? Even tried to get me killed. All because you thought you could get me off your tail with your crazy, wild-eyed, jealousy-fueled suspicions?"

Keahi gasped and looked down at the table, unable to look Koa in the eye.

"You see," Koa continued, "after your man Kūʻula Kai took shots at me up in the Waimanu Valley, I got to wondering who knew I'd be there. You and Senator Chao were at the top of my list. Then you gave me the song and dance about Hazzard being your father. You had me for a while.

"After learning how you betrayed your country, I asked myself what other lies you'd told. I checked your birth certificate. Your mother named your father when you were born, and it wasn't Anthony Hazzard. I knew there had to be even more lies.

"You probably don't know that your man, pretending to be Bobby Hazzard, slipped up and said he 'didn't sign up . . . for dealing with wild pigs and getting shot at.' Seemed like an odd thing for him to say. So, I did some more checking. After learning that Anthony Hazzard's grandson Bobby is in the last year of his residency at the University of Virginia Medical School, I got your guy's fingerprints off the old Hazzard files and ran 'em through the bureau. He's a wannabe Broadway actor named Richard Tigue. But I gotta hand it to you, you prepped him well. He gave an Oscar-winning performance, even sobbing outside the old Hazzard cabin."

Koa paused. "Only by the time I put it all together, it was too late to save poor ʻAnalū Kāliʻi the trauma of a trial. Pretty ugly, you putting an innocent man on trial, but not, I suppose, for a man who has betrayed his country for decades." Koa rose from his chair, turned his back on Keahi, and walked to the door.

Behind him, Keahi said, "Watch your back, Koa. Your day will come."

For an instant, Koa considered turning back around to confront Keahi but realized that his enemy had nothing real and only wanted to taunt him. To hell with him. Koa stepped out of the room, closed the door, and called the guard to take the traitor back to his cell.

As he left police headquarters that evening, Koa thought about the ironies of his life. He was guilty of the most heinous act, the taking of another's life. That crime had driven him to spend his life pursuing others for similar evils. Some good, maybe even much good, resulted from his efforts, but redemption remained out of reach and always would. Try as he might, he could not erase the past. Worse, he was powerless to predict how lightning from his thirty-year-old tempest with Anthony Hazzard could strike at any time from any direction. He would never have guessed in his wildest dreams that his friend Kāwika Keahi would become his enemy. Even now, that enemy or another unexpected one might strike. Koa could never rid himself of the threat.

It was time to shut out all the world, save Nālani. He recalled her face, her smile, and her kisses, and the thought lifted his spirits. He needed to be with his *ipo* and hold her close. Being with Nālani, basking in the light of her love, would restore him. As much as anything could.

AUTHOR'S NOTE

Treachery Times Two explores two of my favorite themes. The first is about human flaws. Koa Kāne and Kāwika Keahi, who grew up together as close as brothers, are flawed human beings. Aren't we all? No leader, no artist, no doctor, no preacher, no corporate executive, no janitor, nor even a crime fiction writer is without some flaw. Yet, some people let their flaws define them while others strive to overcome theirs.

Keahi falls into the first category and Koa into the second. Keahi feeds upon and magnifies his treachery with arrogant disregard for the consequences and no self-reflection. Koa, on the other hand, recognizes his crime and struggles to make recompense for it. To Keahi, guilt is a stranger. To Koa, guilt and remorse are his constant companions. I sometimes wondered if these distinctions in how we reflect upon and react to our flaws aren't the defining characteristics of human beings.

I hope *Treachery Times Two* leads discerning readers to ask themselves where they stand on this spectrum. And please, no excuses on the grounds that nothing in your past even remotely resembles murder. In this time of COVID, it is not hard to find people who would deliberately or recklessly expose their neighbors, and even their families, to the risk of disease and the possibility of serious illness. Are they self-aware? Do they feel remorse? Does their bad act define them, or does their conscience lead them to attempt to act differently?

Self-awareness is not the same as a public acknowledgment, and the void between the two leads to my second theme—the human compulsion to hide our misdeeds. In my experience as an attorney representing clients, the urge to cover up our misdeeds is powerful. People routinely lie to hide their mistakes, large and small, frequently exposing themselves to even greater risks than would accompany full disclosure of their past actions. Thus, the common saying that the cover-up is always worse than the crime.

Here again, Koa and Keahi stand as two opposing bookends. Both are terrified of public disclosure, but Koa sets limits on the length he is willing to go while Keahi has no limits. Keahi would do anything to protect his crimes. Koa faces his dilemma and articulates the "red line" he will not cross. Still, one can debate the ethics of the line that Koa draws and wonder what he might do in the face of the ultimate test.

Reflective readers may find their parallels in their own lives.

PUBLISHER'S NOTE

We hope that you enjoyed *Treachery Times Two*, the fourth in the Koa Kāne Hawaiian Mystery Series.

While the other three novels stand on their own and can be read in any order, the publication sequence is as follows:

Death of a Messenger (Book 1)

A ritual, sadistic murder on the Army's live-fire training ground throws Hilo, Hawai'i's Detective Koa Kāne into the throes of the Big Island's cultural conflicts.

"This book's vivid, thrilling conclusion is both unique and atmospheric in a whodunit featuring a resilient sleuth successfully defending his native tropical paradise." —*Kirkus Reviews*

Off the Grid (Book 2)

A scrap of cloth fluttering in the wind leads Hilo Police Chief Detective Koa Kāne to the tortured remains of an unfortunate soul left to burn in the path of an advancing lava flow.

"Readers who crave watching a smart cop work in a crackerjack police procedural will find a beauty here. Want a good espionage adventure? It's here, too, with intrigue, betrayal, assassination."

—*Booklist* (Starred Review)

Fire and Vengeance (Book 3)

Never has Koa's motivation been greater than when he learns that an elementary school was placed atop a volcanic vent, which has now exploded.

"Moves with volcanic force to a heartfelt, gripping conclusion."　　　　　—Rick Mofina, *USA Today* best-selling author

We hope that you will read the entire Koa Kāne Hawaiian Mystery Series and will look forward to more to come.

For more information, please visit the author's website: robertbmccaw.com.

Happy Reading,
Oceanview Publishing